DARK OF THE EARTH

IVAN OBOLENSKY

SPECIAL EDITION

SMITH-OBOLENSKY
MEDIA™

Awards for *Eye of the Moon*

BEST FIRST BOOK "Fiction": 2018 IndieReader

GOLD MEDALIST "Fiction: Intrigue": 2018 Readers' Favorite

SILVER, 2ND "Mystery/Thriller/Suspense/Horror":
2019 Feathered Quill

GRAND PRIZE SHORT-LIST: 2023 Eric Hoffer

FINALIST "Legacy Fiction": 2023 American Book Fest

Praise for *Shadow of the Son*

"Containing surreal experiences with the occult, *Shadow of the Son* by Ivan Obolensky is an extraordinary paranormal novel that incites the imagination and chills the blood. Brilliantly written, the poetic lexis and rhythmic flow of the story create a timeless work of art. It captures the essence of an era long past, enchanting and transporting the reader to a world of gentility and urbanity. Brimming with mystery and intrigue, supernatural elements eerily whisper throughout the plot, creating an underlying gothic sense of horror and suspense." -5 stars, Susan Sewell for *Readers' Favorite*

Praise for *Dark of the Earth*

"Quill says: *Dark of the Earth* is the third in this series that just keeps getting better and better. While there are many second and third books in a series that just do not live up to their beginnings, this series is not at all like that: every new book is better than the previous one." *-Feathered Quill* review

The *Eye of the Moon* Series by Ivan Obolensky

———— ❖ ————

Eye of the Moon
Book One

Available in ebook, paperback, and audiobook.
Latin American Spanish adaptation of *Eye of the Moon*:
El ojo de la luna

Shadow of the Son
Book Two

Available in ebook and paperback.
Latin American Spanish adaptation of *Shadow of the Son*:
A la sombra del hijo

Dark of the Earth
Book Three

Available in ebook and paperback.

For his other writings, visit his website at
www.ivanobolensky.com

DARK OF THE EARTH

BOOK 3

A novel

Ivan Obolensky

Smith-Obolensky Media, DBA of Dynamic Doingness, Inc.

www.smithobolenskymedia.com
www.ivanobolensky.com

ISBN-13: 978-1-947780-37-8

Library of Congress Control Number: 2024909306

Special Edition: July 4, 2024

To Alice Astor Leydell-Bouverie, my grandmother, for the house she built, the life she led, and the stories that inspired me, and to Mary Jo for always being my first reader.

Character Map

Dodge family
Maw is the matriarch.
Robert the Bruce is her dog.
Her children are **John Dodge, Sr.** and **Bonnie Leland**.

Alice was John Sr.'s half-sister. Her husbands included **Lord Bromley** and **Arthur Blaine**.

John Sr. married **Anne** and **Johnny** is their son.

Von Hofmanstal family
Hugo (the baron) married **Elsa** (the baroness). Their daughter, **Bruni**, is engaged to **Percy**. Their younger son lives in Europe.

Percy's family
Percy grew up in the Dodge household as Johnny's best friend.
His mother, **Mary**, married **Thomas** and lives in Florence.
Lord Bromley was Percy's father.

Rhinebeck household staff
Stanley (the butler) is married to **Dagmar** (the cook), and their helpers are **Simon** and **Jane**. **Raymond** is Mr. Dodge's chauffeur.

Other guests at Rhinebeck
Malcolm Ault is a longtime friend of the family.
Dr. Angus Maxwell-Hughes (Cobb) is a family friend.

Jim and **Peggy Cushman** are the parents of **James Cushman III**, who is married to **Casey Duke**.

Prologue

For those who have read *Eye of the Moon* and *Shadow of the Son*, I have provided a brief synopsis of both the previous volumes below, but before I begin, I have a few words about the setting of the novels and the property called Rhinebeck:

My grandmother, Alice Astor, named it *Marienruh*. It was built in 1926 on a large tract of land adjacent to the Astor estate of *Ferncliff*. It was a wedding gift from Vincent Astor to my grandmother and her new husband, Prince Serge Obolensky. At one time, there was a miniature train that one could sit in, connecting the two estates. Champagne in ice buckets would be sent between the two houses, along with invitations to dinner. The people who came to visit were the living legends of that time. I recall with great clarity the children's area at the top of the house. It is all there in the novels.

Rhinebeck has always been a place in my heart as much as it was a place I lived in. There was a butler named Stanley, who was married to Marjorie, the cook. Both are buried in the Astor family plot not far from my grandmother. My Aunt Sylvia is buried there. My Aunt Emily is close by—my father, too, but I won't be buried in that place.

There is always rivalry, competition, and tension in a family filled with strong personalities, particularly one that stretches back to 862 AD and the very dawn of Russian history. There are generals, monarchs, princes, and even a saint back there. I know. I've read about them in Tolstoy and Pushkin. Russian history is filled with their goings-on. Their stories are not this story, but then again, I'm not altogether sure. Each of our ancestors has their say, even if only indirectly. They speak from inside us. History may not repeat, but I find it odd how the same themes and circumstances thread themselves in and out of our lives as if by some unknown and mysterious force. That, too, is in these novels.

Of course, they are works of fiction, but what is fiction really other than nonfiction by another name and maybe in a different time?

Synopsis of *Eye of the Moon*

Lady Alice, a legendary socialite, died reading a copy of *The Egyptian Book of the Dead* at her Rhinebeck estate in upstate New York. Johnny Dodge, her nephew, and his friend, Percy, who was brought up with Johnny in the Dodges' Fifth Avenue apartment, had been told for years that she had simply died. Nonetheless, questions continued to surface, and the press never quite let the story go.

Early one morning and years later, in 1977, Johnny shows up at Percy's room at the St. Regis and invites him to attend his parents' special anniversary celebration at Rhinebeck. Percy accepts despite an estrangement between the two friends that began when their trading partnership imploded several years earlier.

Attending the five-day house party are Hugo, the Baron von Hofmanstal; Elsa, the baroness; and Bruni, their daughter. Also invited are Johnny's grandmother, Mary Leland, known in the family as Maw, with her daughter, Bonnie, the half-sister to Johnny's father, John Dodge. A fierce competition has existed between the two siblings over who will inherit their mother's extraordinary fortune. Malcolm Ault, a very tall man and friend of the family, is also expected.

Arriving before the other guests, Johnny and Percy decide to do some research about Alice and discover a small statue holding an uncut emerald and a letter written by Alice that was returned to sender, unable to forward. The contents mention the statue and a disturbing incident in the jungles of Ecuador that makes them question everything they've been told. Johnny and Percy turn to Stanley, Alice's former butler, to find out more. Stanley agrees, but only if they promise to do whatever he asks at some point in the future. They promise, and Stanley tells them that not long after her marriage to Lord Bromley, his lordship locked Alice in a trunk to force her to do whatever he wanted. When he tried to make her sell Rhinebeck, Alice, with Stanley's help, drugged Lord Bromley and sent him to his club in New York in the same trunk. His lordship barely survived. Once recovered, Stanley informed him that Alice was divorcing him and would bankrupt him should he not agree. Lord Bromley acquiesced but swore he would have his revenge.

Stanley then mentions that Alice had a recurring nightmare about ancient Egypt. In it, she was cursed and compelled to remain halfway between life and death forever. Her experiences in the trunk convinced her that the curse was not only real but active in the present. After getting rid of his lordship, she decided to do all in her power to lift it. She studied the occult, shamanic practices, and archeology, while collecting ancient artifacts. At the end of his tale, Stanley shows them the secret repository behind a wall in Alice's apartment that holds the treasures and books she accumulated.

The next day, Johnny wants to know more about the occult and borrows a volume on demon summoning from the repository. He uses the little statue and a tincture that Alice used to aid in the summoning. He slips some of the tincture to Percy. The experiment is inconclusive, but Percy acquires a new intuition after taking it.

Percy falls in love with Bruni, but her father, the baron, takes an instant dislike to him, putting his potential relationship with her in doubt from the start.

Percy and Johnny eventually discover that the anniversary celebration is not the reason the guests have been invited. The estate needs money to survive, and a silent auction for Alice's treasures is being held in secret to raise the necessary funds.

Now that Percy is over twenty-five, Stanley delivers a letter to him from Alice in which she reveals that his real father is Lord Bromley. Further, his father's behavior turned abusive only after he was knocked unconscious in a riding accident. To honor the happiness of the love she shared with Percy's father and because Percy is the personification of the child they never had, Alice informs him that he is now the owner of Rhinebeck and all its treasures, provided they are not removed from the estate. Percy reveals this information at the anniversary white-tie dinner and informs the guests that the estate's treasures are not for sale, putting him in conflict with all the buyers and with Mr. Dodge, who has arranged the auction.

The next day, in a meeting with Mr. Dodge, the current trustee of the estate, Percy learns that the insolvency and the need to raise money through the auction are the result of a series of financial missteps by Mr. Dodge. Percy forgives him, and a solution to the estate's insolvency is worked out. The baron and Lord Bromley, through his agent, Malcolm Ault, agree to buy the treasures by splitting the cost while allowing the treasures to remain at Rhinebeck with one proviso: Bruni and Percy agree to marry. Percy proposes, and Bruni accepts. The novel ends with the financial crisis resolved and Rhinebeck with a more hopeful future.

Synopsis of *Shadow of the Son*

Shadow of the Son begins not long after the end of *Eye of the Moon*. Percy and Johnny decide to renew their business partnership, but Johnny needs his father's permission to leave the family firm and must travel to Rhinebeck to obtain it. As they discuss this, Percy receives a call from Bruni's former husband, warning him that the Von Hofmanstals are not to be trusted—particularly Percy's fiancée.

While driving up to Rhinebeck, Percy confides to Johnny that the intuition Percy received from the demon summoning has disappeared, and the friends decide to discuss both issues with Stanley.

Stanley tells Percy that he has done some checking on the Von Hofmanstals and has learned that two of Bruni's governesses died under suspicious circumstances at the family castle in Austria and that Bruni was implicated. Stanley suggests Percy discuss this with his fiancée to determine the truth and that he speak to Dagmar about his absent intuition.

Mr. and Mrs. Dodge arrive and add to Percy's troubles by informing him that the money from his father, Lord Bromley, has not been received and that his father wants to see the treasures with his own eyes before he puts in any money. To make matters worse, he is on his way to Rhinebeck to do that. In addition, the baron won't contribute his funds until Lord Bromley contributes his.

Percy, at Mr. Dodge's suggestion, decides to hold a weekend house party to resolve the financial impasse. Invited for the weekend are Maw, Bonnie, Malcolm Ault, Bruni, and her parents. Percy tells Bruni about this latest development, and Bruni decides to come up to Rhinebeck the next day. Percy meets with Dagmar about his missing intuitive gift. Dagmar, having worked with Alice to explore various pharmaceutical compounds, gives Percy a tincture that might restore his intuition. Instead, Percy has a vision that shows Rhinebeck in ruins. Percy decides to stay at Rhinebeck to prepare for the weekend and sends Johnny in his place to attend a previously scheduled dinner with the baron at the 21 Club in New York.

Bruni arrives, and the two have their first fight, which is resolved when Bruni agrees to tell Percy about the incidents with the nannies. They hike to a special rock near the river and drink some whiskey from one of Johnny's flasks, which happens to hold the tincture that was used during the prior demon summoning.

Sitting on the rock, Bruni reveals that she was responsible for both of the governesses' deaths but acted in self-defense. Percy is convinced and has another vision. This time, he travels to a hut where the person inside orders him to leave. He is chased by a monster but manages to get back at the rock before it can catch him.

The next day, Johnny arrives back at Rhinebeck and tells Percy that at the dinner, he met Lord Bromley and a man who looks like a prizefighter by the name of Cobb. Further, Percy's father will be arriving at Rhinebeck with the baron before lunch.

Lord Bromley and Cobb arrive at Rhinebeck with Bruni's parents. While taking a walk after lunch, his father gives Percy a choice of listening to the real story of him and Alice or simply receiving the funds he promised, which he has in check form in his pocket. Percy says he'll do both but doesn't bother to open the envelope his father gives him. His father becomes enraged because Percy fails to look inside the envelope to confirm the check's existence and the correctness of the amount. He says he would have given Percy another envelope as well but now won't. Lord Bromley opens the front door, sees a figure that looks like Alice, and collapses in shock. Percy picks up the other envelope. Cobb, whose real name is Dr. Angus Maxwell-Hughes, is Lord Bromley's personal physician and quickly takes his patient upstairs. He informs Percy that his father will recover, but not until the next day.

With Stanley's help, the envelope his father let fall is steamed open, copied, resealed, and returned to the doctor. In it, Percy learns that many of the treasures in the repository, particularly the little statue with the jewel, belong to his father and that his father has legal proof of that claim. His father states that either he leaves with the treasures or Percy allows him to remain with them at Rhinebeck indefinitely.

To add to his concerns, at that night's dinner, Elsa informs Percy that she can tell that Bruni is pregnant.

The next morning, Bruni explains that Lord Bromley has a hold over her father in the form of shares that Lord Bromley has refused to hand over because the baron failed to deliver to him the little statue with the jewel as agreed. Percy informs Bruni about her possible pregnancy, and Bruni realizes her mother is correct. Both are thrilled.

After Lord Bromley recovers, he and Percy sit down for a talk. His father gives Percy the check, and Percy now has half the money the estate needs. Percy also learns that his father wants to use the little statue to help contact Alice even though she is dead and that he is at Rhinebeck to beg her forgiveness and for her to beg his.

After lunch, Percy has another talk with his father and gives him the statue—only it's in pieces, having broken during the demon summoning mentioned in *Eye of the Moon*. Lord Bromley explodes in frustration and hurls the remains into the fire. Percy has finally had enough of his father's outbursts, and he tells him he is to be a grandfather and that Percy might have a way to help him contact Alice, provided he behaves.

That night at a white-tie dinner, the baron and Lord Bromley finally resolve their feud only to have Stanley deliver to his lordship a letter from his former wife that she had written to him years ago in anticipation of this moment. Lord Bromley reads the letter and expires immediately after. In it, Alice says that she has seen the moment in a vision and that she knows he deliberately withheld certain parts of a particular *Egyptian Book of the Dead* she was using to lift the curse. She warns him that if she isn't able to lift it due to what he did, he will suffer the same curse.

The novel ends with the financial matters of the estate finally resolved, Bruni pregnant, a wedding arranged, and Mr. Dodge turning over Dodge Capital to Johnny and Percy.

Of course, there are a vast number of details that have been left out of these brief overviews, but you will, at the least, be reoriented sufficiently to enjoy what follows.

I should also add once again that this is a work of fiction. The characters in this novel are not real, although some of the names are of people who lived. Most of them have passed away. None of them said or did the things I have written. I also set the time of the action in the 1970s before cell phones and computers.

One last point: *Dark of the Earth* contains some darker moments that readers of the prior books may not expect. By way of explanation, the underlying thematic structure of this series of novels, of which there will be four, is that they expand outward both in scope and subject matter, starting with the individual. In *Eye of the Moon*, Percy confronts who he really is, the son of Lord Bromley, and must accept the good and the bad that exists within himself. *Shadow of the Son*, on the other hand, deals with the handling of cunning individuals, particularly his father. Percy discovers it is possible to succeed by being intelligent and creative. In *Dark of the Earth*, the material world and those who place no constraints on their actions to achieve their goals become the focus. Evil, too, exists, and so do desperate people. What does one do when they come knocking at the door? That is the question, and to answer it, I suppose we had best turn the page and find out.

1

B runi and I were at the Connaught Hotel in London when the phone rang by my side of the bed and woke me.

"Hello."

"Percy? Is that you?"

The female voice sounded tinny and distant.

"Yes."

"It's Anne—Anne Dodge. There's been an accident."

"What? Who?"

"It's Johnny. His limousine crashed on the East River Drive. The driver was killed, and Johnny's in a coma at New York Hospital. The doctors say he may not pull through. Get here soon, Percy."

"I'm so sorry, Anne. We'll be there as quick as we can—tomorrow if possible."

"Sooner would be better," Anne said and hung up.

Bruni was awake. "What's happened?"

"That was Anne. Johnny was in a car accident and is in a coma. From what she said, it doesn't sound good. We need to get to New York."

"I'll start packing."

B runi and I arrived at the hospital the next day. The journey was marked by frantic motion followed by nervous waiting. In the hospital, it was the same. The doctors operated, and then again, but after each, their prognosis was guarded. They said at last that other than a lack of conscious activity, his body was recovering, but when he would regain consciousness was a question none could answer.

After several weeks, my hopes for a quick recovery faded, and darkness replaced the light he had shone upon my world. I felt his absence most keenly, and others did too. His parents were beside themselves, as were all who knew him. Bruni and I had decided to postpone our wedding until Johnny at least showed signs of recovery. Her parents weren't pleased with this decision, but they understood it well enough. I spoke with her father, the Baron von Hofmanstal.

"You're cutting things mighty fine, Percy. Elsa and I will extend the date by two months, but that's the limit. Our grandchild won't be born out of wedlock, and we're adamant about that. Get those doctors moving or ask your resident sorceress to make him something special. Whatever it takes. Time waits for no man … or woman—least of all, a pregnant one. I'll be calling my daughter and telling her the same. Two months, Percy, or I'm coming to see you with a dueling saber." There was a click as he hung up.

Not that I needed any more pressure. With Johnny's absence, I was now in charge of Dodge Capital. I showed up at the office every day, sat at my desk, signed what needed to be signed, and generally looked like I knew what I was doing. I would visit Johnny for an hour in the late afternoon. Always it was the same. He lay there sleeping, or so it seemed. *Did he dream in that condition? Did he notice the passage of time? Did he feel anything? Anything at all? Where had he gone to? When would he return?*

It was Dr. Angus Maxwell-Hughes who interrupted my thoughts. Bruni and I had been looking forward to visiting him in London, but that had been put on hold. I had written him a hasty explanation for our sudden departure and left it with the concierge. I hadn't expected to see him anytime soon, and at first, I didn't recognize him at all. He was in surgical scrubs, and a brimless cap covered his bald head. He looked like an ex-prize fighter masquerading as a surgeon.

Angus had simply walked into Johnny's private room, picked up the chart, looked at it, and went over to the side of the bed. He poked and prodded Johnny. He brought out a penlight, raised Johnny's eyelids, and examined his pupils, nodding as he did so.

"Angus?"

"Percy." Angus glanced at me for a moment and then at the chart.

"I thought you were in London. I sent a message."

Angus nodded and wrote something down before looking at me again. "I got it. It's why I'm here. The head of surgery at this hospital is a colleague. We spoke, and after our conversation, I decided to look at this case directly."

He replaced the chart and asked, "May I sit down?"

"Please." I moved a chair next to me.

The doctor sat and said, "I've spoken with Doctors Anderson, Duval, and Sistie. I've reviewed all their notes, surgical records, X-rays, blood tests—the whole lot. There is little that can be done for Johnny other than what's been done already. His body is mending, and that is good news. His doctors are some of the finest in the world, and they are likely correct in their optimistic prognosis for his body's full recovery. His brain is another matter. I won't mince words. Right now, Johnny's in a persistent vegetative state and has lost his higher brain functions. He appears to be sleeping and can't respond. How long he will remain in that condition is unknown.

"Most comas don't last more than two to four weeks. Any longer and recovery rates drop off. Typically, the return is gradual, with the patient awakening momentarily and then for longer and longer periods. In some rare cases, it's as if someone turned on a switch, and there they are back again, but such happy occurrences are the exception, not the rule. More often, the patient will require extensive physical therapy to restore them to their prior health. Sometimes, only a partial recovery is achieved.

"I don't know which it will be with him, but for now, his body is making progress, and that is reason for hope. Regardless, he will still need an extraordinary amount of care. Secondary infections are the primary concern at this point. In summary, be prepared for his convalescence taking much longer than you might wish."

"I see. What do you, personally, think will happen?"

Angus sighed. "It's hard to say. After twelve months, he'll transition to a permanent vegetative state. Recovery from there is remote. Our task, and his too, I might add, is to see that he awakens as soon as possible, and before that amount of time has elapsed."

"Can that be done?"

"It's possible, but I will get to that. Human bodies are peculiar things. We can see what is happening on the outside but not always what's happening on the inside. The body has many parts, which interact in extraordinarily complex ways that we understand at only a superficial level. Consciousness falls in that category. We may know it when we see it, but what consciousness is exactly, we really can't answer. Comas and the like tend to underscore that ignorance. The good news is that we have information from those who've recovered, which leads me to a suggestion that you might consider."

"And what's that?"

"Start telling him stories about your past growing up together. Try to connect him to his long-term memories. There is anecdotal evidence that doing so can sometimes lead to a more rapid recovery. My suggestion also solves your problem."

"My problem?"

"Feeling useless."

"Yes, so much so that I want to scream. On top of that, the baron has given Bruni and me two months before we must report to his castle to be wed, or he'll come calling with a saber."

"Yes, I know. He phoned me as well. His call was another reason for my being here. Just the same, take heart. Come back tomorrow with a story. Read it to him or recount it—whichever you prefer. He may not look like he's hearing you, but there are indications from those who recovered that they did and that hearing an accustomed voice speaking about familiar things triggered a response that helped them to awaken. At worst, it will do him no harm. It's up to you of course, but that is what I recommend for now."

"Then I will do that."

"Please. I am at a conference in Boston for the next several days, but I'll swing by to check on Johnny's condition before I return to London. We'll speak then. Now I must be off."

The doctor got up and was almost to the door.

"Angus?"

He stopped and turned. "Yes?"

"Thank you very much."

He nodded and left.

3

T he next afternoon, I sat down in a chair by the bed and stared at my friend. His face looked relaxed, and his breathing was regular. I could detect no changes from the previous day. I noted down in a small notebook his heart rate, respiration, and appearance. These would be my baseline measurements, I decided. Any excursion from those parameters I would interpret as a response of some sort. In keeping with Angus's suggestion, I decided to speak to him as if he were awake and listening. I started in.

"Johnny, I'm going to assume you can hear me, so feel free to interrupt at any time. You also have my permission to disagree or protest my versions of events in any way you wish—the more vehemently, the better. Frankly, even blinking would be sufficient to make my day, but before I begin, I want to emphasize that your recovery is not just up to me or your doctors. It's up to you. In fact, it may be mostly up to you. You must take charge somehow and wake up. I wish I could tell you how, but I don't know that answer. Once again, we've sailed into uncharted waters. I may even have to ask Dagmar to make you one of her little treats. I've placed that in the last resort category.

"For now, listen to my words, and if something sounds familiar, grasp onto it. Doing so will probably require a great deal of effort on your part, likely as much as you can muster. Please try, even if it's hard. I have my reasons for urging you. The longer you remain in your condition, the less likely it is that you'll recover, so your task is vitally important. Besides, I'm the one who must run Dodge

Capital in your absence. That was not my choice. I've had to make several changes as a result, like taking over your corner office and adjusting your chair."

I looked him over carefully.

"I'm sorry to be the one to tell you, I really am, but the backrest thing broke off. It hung down at an odd angle after your chair fell over—don't ask me how—so I removed it. Your secretary has the piece somewhere, although I fear it may have been thrown out."

I watched the monitors as I spoke, but they continued their monotonous beeping. Johnny, it seemed, was far beyond my reach. He was obsessed with that stupid chair. It had cost him a fortune and had dozens of levers and knobs to adjust every conceivable aspect of its position, tension, and comfort. After consulting the seventy-page instruction booklet, whenever he thought his position wasn't quite right, he would stop by my office to complain that it had gone out of true again and that it would take some time—his valuable time, mind you—to adjust it. I would offer my sympathies. Always suspicious as to the cause, he had gone so far as to inform the nighttime cleaning crew in writing *never* to touch it, let alone clean it. He most definitely had a thing about that chair, and now that I'd lobbed that bombshell in his direction with absolutely no effect, I realized that my task of awakening him would be much more difficult than I'd anticipated.

"Well, with that confession out of the way ... "

I looked at him again and sighed. "Forget I said that. Your chair's fine. I'd never sit in it anyway. It's too uncomfortable. Still, I would have expected at least a twitch from you. I will obviously have to get much more personal to reach you. By the way, Angus came to see you. Perhaps you are aware of that. He said that I should recount stories of our growing up together to help you reconnect with your long-term memories. I've thought about that, and I agree. I'm going to tell you a story every day. If you don't wake up, I'll get them published. Then where will you be? I suggest you gird your loins, my friend. I'm spilling the beans and naming names starting tomorrow. Count on it."

The monitors beat their steady cadence. Nothing.

4

The following day, I sat in the chair next to the bed. Johnny looked the same. His heart rate remained unchanged, and his breathing steady.

I looked at my friend and said, "Sitting by your side for an hour each day, every day, for weeks has done little, so today, I'm going to start telling you stories about our growing up together to help reawaken your long-term memories. Frankly, I don't know what else to do. Hugo has given me two months to heal you before he begins looking for me with malice aforethought. That means Bruni and I are on the clock, and so are you. Do recall that you're my best man and saddled with the task of getting me to the church and all that. Right now, we seem to have those roles reversed. I'll be conferring with Dagmar and Stanley this weekend to see what they might suggest, and given that, it is quite likely that more desperate remedies will be attempted. If I were you, I'd be more inclined to have the story idea work out, so pay attention and make this work for both of us.

"I'm going to start with that golden summer when you and I waited tables at Mario's—that small, expensive Italian restaurant on South Main Street in Southampton.

"In case you don't remember, your parents have several residences. This story takes place at the Southampton house, which we would visit during late summer. You changed history, but in case it slipped your mind, I'll tell you how."

I pulled out several typewritten sheets of paper from my briefcase and began.

"One lazy July morning while vacationing from university, we were informed by Georgia, the maid, that Mr. Dodge wanted to see us in his study right away. I knew from the 'right away' part that you and I were in trouble once again, only this time, I had no clue as to why. My heart beat faster as I followed you into the library. There, we found a severe-looking Mr. Dodge standing behind his desk, reading a report. He didn't acknowledge our presence. This was not a good sign, and my nervousness increased. That we were in trouble was confirmed when you and I started to sit. Your father didn't look up as he said, 'Don't sit down. No, not at all. We have a serious matter to discuss, and both of you will remain standing.' He looked up after a long minute and asked, 'Do you know what I have in my hand?'

"We said that we did not.

" 'I have here the June statement from the Bathing Corporation of Southampton. It is in the amount of two thousand, three hundred and forty-five dollars and eleven cents, and *that* is just the bar expenses. I am both shocked and dumbfounded at the amount. I want an explanation.'

"I had none, and neither did you. The magnitude of the bill was truly astonishing. You and I were speechless.

"You recovered first and said in a careful voice, 'Surely, there's been some mistake. How could we possibly have consumed that much? It's not possible. I think an accounting of some sort is in order.'

"Your father stared at you for some time before he said, 'Oh, I quite agree.'

"He picked up a fat manila envelope and flicked it in your direction. It skidded across the desk, teetered, and dropped onto the carpet. I picked it up and handed it to you. You peeked inside before pulling out the contents and laying them on the desk. The largest was a packet of bar bills with our signatures clipped to an adding machine tape. These had been inspected personally by the accountant, and by whose signature he, Mr. Charles A. Dunn, founder of the firm of Dunn and Co., auditors of several Fortune 500 Companies, attested to the correctness of the extraordinary total.

"You passed it to me. I looked at it, stunned, and put it down. There was no mistake. The sum was correct.

"The second item was a letter from Mr. Lord at Morgan Guaranty Trust Co., where the Dodge bills were sent for payment.

"In it, Mr. Lord alerted Mr. Dodge to the inordinate size of the June bar tab, and given that Mr. and Mrs. Dodge had been vacationing in Europe the entire month, he felt it necessary to question the bills' veracity. To him, it looked as if a great number of unknown persons had been signing for drinks in large quantities in their absence.

"In all fairness, we did have signing privileges at the club, but whether lunch included the bar had never been spelled out specifically. Having survived another year of university, we had felt the need for some relaxation. The bar signing privileges, we thought, although not explicitly granted, were nonetheless implied and should be exercised. This was a fine point, to be sure, and worthy of close argument; however, when measured against the astronomical size of the tab, our justification seemed rather feeble.

"You said at last, 'Well, there can be no doubt. That is the figure. In our defense, I would like to say that Arthur, the bartender, makes the most extraordinary Gin South Sides. He uses only the freshest mint, and with the addition of a Myers's rum float, has created a true nectar of the gods. It really is no wonder we consumed more than a few. I highly recommend them.'

"Mr. Dodge scoffed at that. 'Well, I'll tell you what I think. I think you both have sunk to a low level—a level normally reserved for degenerates and bums, of which this bar bill is more than adequate proof. But that indictment is high praise compared to a further matter that these receipts bring to light. Do you know to what I'm referring?'

"Once again, we said that we did not.

" 'Allow me to enlighten you. Not only have you both consumed such vast quantities of drink that it stretches all credulity, but you idiots overlooked the fact that each bill is time-stamped. It seems that in our absence, you started each day at 10:30 in the morning with an alcoholic beverage consisting of rum and gin!'

"Your father went on at some length regarding that point and at high volume. He concluded in his closing summation that we had both sunk to depths of depravity and moral turpitude few could say they had achieved at so early an age.

"Given the overwhelming evidence against us, I was forced to admit, when asked, that he was not incorrect, a point whose double negative seemed to incense him further. Actually, I think it was you who said that, but please feel free to voice your version of events."

I paused in my narrative and looked at Johnny for a response, but there was none. I continued.

"Your father frowned as he held the envelope in his hand and looked at us. After a moment's pause, he said with some severity, 'I've made my decision. Both of you will pay me back the entire sum of two thousand, three hundred and forty-five dollars and eleven cents in cash, to be earned through honest toil. Your privileges at the club are suspended until said amount is paid in full. I will inform Mr. Wheeler at the front desk to bar your entry until I tell him otherwise.'

"I felt distinctly lightheaded as your father stated that he had more to say. He added that we would be earning that sum, not at a job of our choosing, but his. He knew Mario of Mario's Italian Restaurant quite well. All it required was a phone call, which he made on the spot, and before we knew it, we were gainfully employed in the kitchen from 10:30 a.m. to 7:00 p.m., six days a week, starting immediately. Your father would have made it every day; only Mario's was closed on Mondays. Having rendered his sentence, he said, 'Now get out of my sight.' We did just that.

"You and I knew when we were beaten, and that rapid compliance was the only remedy until sufficient time had passed to lessen his outrage. We slunk back to our room to contemplate our future and recover from what had been a solid trouncing.

"After taking some minutes to reflect on what had just occurred, we both agreed that we had started drinking too early in the day, but the far more serious issue lay in our failure to notice the time stamps on the bills that each of us had signed. Such extraordinary and consequential oversights were inexcusable. Based on that damning analysis, you and I chose to accept our sentence without further comment and vowed to pay much more attention to such minutia in the future. In the meanwhile, we would labor in reparation for our shortcomings.

"When we arrived that afternoon, Mario took one look at us and determined that we were better suited to waiting tables. He had us grooved into the ins and outs of food service, having decided then and there to institute a lunch menu. After all, he had extra hands who worked for next to nothing other than tips.

"The news that Mario's was open for lunch slowly filtered through the community. Customers were mostly nonexistent until after the noon hour when the pace picked up and business turned surprisingly brisk. Mario was pleased with this new arrangement, and you and I were happy with the tips but not so thrilled with the level of effort and attention required to obtain them.

"By August, when Jimmy Buckley walked in one particular Friday at eleven in the morning, we considered ourselves seasoned veterans. I was fiddling with the menus when I noticed that you had ducked into the kitchen. I turned, and there he was. I gawked for a second before I seated him and delivered a menu in my most professional manner.

"Johnny, I'm sure you remember Jimmy Buckley, yes?"

Johnny made no answer.

"Picture in your mind a black-haired, blue-eyed Irishman of medium height but stocky with an enormous chest. I noted that he must have had a rough night. He was unshaven, bleary-eyed, and looked like he needed a serious pick-me-up. I hoped that in his less-than-functional state, he might not recognize me. He was a leading male soloist at the Metropolitan Opera and known as the 'Irish Tenor.' In his prior existence, he had been the handyman, occasional pugilist, and opera buff employed by the condominium that ran the building on Fifth Avenue in which you and I grew up.

"I waited a minute before returning to his table to take his order.

" 'Can I get you something, Mr. Buckley?'

"Calling him by name was not uncommon as he was well known, but in hindsight, may have been a mistake. He looked up, did a double take, and said in his Irish lilt, 'Jesus, Mary, and Joseph! Truly, God and all the Saints must be having a laugh. Here you are, Bucko, waiting on the likes of me, and I'm ordering from the likes of you. Oh, how the mighty have fallen, eh?'

"He'd recognized me.

"He turned and looked out the window. He said more to himself than to me, 'The Lord is indeed mysterious.' As I stood there with my pencil poised, he turned back and grabbed my arm. He was immensely strong, and I was powerless in his grip.

"He said in a loud, ringing voice, 'Vengeance will be mine, and you'll see it with your own eyes!'

"He let go, reached into his pants pocket, and took out a bulging wallet from which he plucked three one-hundred-dollar bills. He laid them on the table and growled, 'Bring me a large plate of the spaghetti Bolognese, a bottle of Barolo, and keep my glass filled until I want something else. These are for you, but only if I like your service, and not until I'm done. Now move it.'

"I wrote down the order as I backed away and scrambled to the kitchen.

"I put up the order slip and quickly grabbed a fine Barolo. I took it out to Jimmy's table. There, I opened it with suitable flare, poured a small amount for him to taste while giving just the right twist to the pour, and waited. Jimmy simply took the bottle from my hand and filled himself a proper measure. He didn't say a word. I backed away and went looking for you.

"I found you out back, smoking. You looked worried and said, 'Christ on a crutch! That's Jimmy Buckley! What's he doing here?'

" 'I have no idea,' I answered. 'He looks in bad shape. He asked for the spaghetti Bolognese, ordered some wine, and said something about vengeance. He seems a bit out of sorts, maybe even mental. He grabbed my arm, and I can assure you he's as strong as ever. He poured himself some wine and looks to have settled down.'

"You took a long drag of your smoke, looked at me, and said, 'My God, Percy, he knows!'

" 'You mean about the spaghetti?'

" 'Of course, about the spaghetti.'

" 'It could be a coincidence?'

" 'Not a chance. He comes to the place we work, orders spaghetti, and then goes on about vengeance. He knows for sure.'

"You flicked your cigarette down the alley for emphasis and said, 'Whatever happens, he can't see me. It'll send him over the edge. You're going to have to wait on him while I hide out here.'

"I saw that Fate was toying with us again, me in particular, and your distress was not without justification, considering what you had done to him several years earlier.

"In spite of having been ten years old at the time, you and I had managed to commit our share of offenses, but in this case, the blame was not solely yours. It was partly mine for being there and failing to prevent it, but it would be fair to say that the larger portion ought to fall on Kate, the Fifth Avenue apartment cook. Surely, you remember her. She was a spirited little Irish woman, who served fare worthy of a Michelin chef when it came to the parents' food, and slop that would make a hobo think twice when it came to ours.

15

"In those days, you and I were served supper at six in a small alcove off the kitchen. The room's single window overlooked a dark alley fourteen stories below and gave a bleak view of the back of the neighboring building. Your folks entertained guests for formal dinners at nine in the large dining room that overlooked Central Park. On one particularly busy week of back-to-back dinner parties, Kate served us Franco-American Spaghetti out of the can for three suppers in a row. On the Fthird evening, you looked at the now familiar mound of warm, unappetizing spaghetti on soggy white toast and decided that you'd had enough.

"You waited for Kate to go back to the kitchen before you got up, threw open the window, and scraped the entire mass off the plate with your fork and into the alley below. The spaghetti fell for three and a fraction seconds before making a most satisfying splat. You smiled at the sound, but that was cut short by a scream of such character and volume that it could only have come from what *The New York Times* would later describe as 'one of the truly great voices of our age.' The agonized cry rose and then faded away, but the words that followed remained imprinted on my memory forever. The speaker started in a low register, resonant and impassioned, before his voice took wing with such abandon and power that the roosting pigeons in the alley's nooks and crannies panicked in sudden swirls of gray feathers. Something great and terrible had awakened. 'I'm coming for you!' the voice cried out. 'By all the Saints, whoever you are, I'm coming for you! Look out! LOOK OUT!'

"You and I stared at each other and then quaked in terror. There could only be one such voice. 'Jimmy Buckley!' we cried in unison.

"Jimmy had charmed us, even when we were midgets. To our minds, he was a giant. He had arms that bulged with muscles. He could lift either of us over his head with just one hand. His voice was rich and filled with laughter except when he was angry. We

16

had seen him enraged only once, and that had been enough. Jimmy and the Dodges' chauffeur had squared off over a fundamental difference in opinion regarding Jimmy's mother. Jimmy struck so fast and hard that Mr. Dodge needed a new chauffeur in as little time as it took to break a pencil. Raymond was hired shortly after.

"We quickly dumped our plates in the kitchen sink and sprinted to our room, you to consider what had happened and me into the bathroom to throw up what little I had eaten.

"We were in trouble again.

"Punishment in the Dodge household was at least democratic. You and I were blamed equally for everything, demonstrating that justice knew no favorites.

"I remember opening the bathroom door, having resolved to meet my fate on an empty stomach. You were sitting on your bed, staring into space.

" 'Johnny,' I said. 'I think we need to come up with a story, like how you tripped or something, and the spaghetti just flew out the window. Barring that as a solution, I advise that we consider going off to boarding school earlier than planned.'

"You turned to me and said, 'No, Percy. It's about time we took a stand about the food. It's disgusting.'

" 'That may be, but … '

"I was interrupted by the strident ring of the service bell. If you recall, your parents' apartment can be accessed by the front elevator, used by family and guests, and the service elevator for deliveries. The service elevator opens onto a small foyer with a door leading to the service hallway and the kitchen. Each bell has a distinctive ring.

"The service bell brayed a second time. We crept out of our room into the main hallway and cracked open the service hall door. We could see Kate with her back to us, wearing her white and black uniform. It was she who had answered the back door, which was flung wide open. Beyond that was Carl, the head doorman, and in the corner of the service elevator, wearing an orange-tinted towel around his neck, was Jimmy Buckley. He was held by the arms between two burly maintenance crew members. Jimmy's face was red. He was shaking with either rage or some other strong emotion. It was no wonder he was accompanied by two powerful men. He had taken a direct hit.

"Carl did the talking.

" 'Kate, I hate to trouble you, but what are you having for dinner tonight?'

" 'You got me out of the kitchen to ask me what we're having for dinner tonight when I have work to do?'

" 'Now, now, Kate … '

" 'Don't you be 'now, now'ing me,' Carl. I don't have the time … and don't you be staring at me, Jimmy Buckley—you, who looks like something the cat dragged in.'

"I think Kate was a little sweet on Jimmy.

"Jimmy started to say something, but Carl shushed him and said, 'Kate, please, I'm asking all the tenants. It's important.'

"Vexed and having reached the limit of her patience, she answered loudly in her best Irish, 'Steeeaaaak! We be havin' steak. Now be off with you!'

"She slammed the door in their faces and mumbled something about time-wasters burning in the lower pits of hell.

"You and I bolted to our room and collapsed on the floor. We had dodged a bullet, and not just any bullet. We had dodged a .577 Nitro Express bullet, the type used to hunt Cape Buffalo. We thanked God, the saints, and any entity that looked after small boys that what we ate was of such little importance that the only answer to the question of what was for dinner was steak, the meal eaten by your parents and guests. We were of absolutely no consequence.

"That incident made an impression on us. There was never an objection to whatever we were served after that. We even said grace a time or two, which, if I remember, precipitated odd looks from Kate.

"It was soon after this incident that Jimmy Buckley disappeared. Later, we learned that he had become an understudy and then the lead in the role of Count Almaviva in Rossini's *Barber of Seville* when the current *divo* had come down with a severe case of flu. Jimmy's subsequent performances so captivated critics and all who heard him that he soon became a Metropolitan favorite.

"Now, he was consuming a mighty plate of spaghetti right in front of me.

"He was almost finished when his voice rang out, 'Bucko! Bring me another plate of spaghetti, another bottle of Barolo, and make it snappy!'

"I leaped to obey. I put up the order and opened another bottle of Barolo. I brought him a fresh glass and poured the wine. After picking up the used one, I went back to the kitchen to await his second plate of spaghetti Bolognese. As I returned to his table, I stumbled and almost dropped it in his lap.

" 'Easy now, young buck. What you playin' at?' He gave me a hard look that turned my insides to jelly.

" 'Nothing, Mr. Buckley. I tripped. Can I refill your glass?'

"He grunted his assent and said, 'Bring me a beer. In fact, make it two—cold ones!'

"I nodded and scooted back to the kitchen to find you.

" 'The man's calling for two beers,' I said. 'He's drunk one bottle of wine so far, asked for another, eaten one gigantic plate of spaghetti, and is now working on a second. On top of that, he's asking for beer. I think he's coming unglued. By the way, I almost dropped the plate in his lap.'

"You shuddered and said, 'Oh, you don't want to be doing that. I can still remember his face when he came up in the service elevator. The image still haunts me. Get him the beers. Go on! Quickly!'

"I stepped out of the kitchen, filled two large glasses of beer from the tap, and went out to his table. He took one of the glasses and drained it in one go before reaching for the other and doing the same.

"He gave a long burp and asked, 'What time's it?'

" 'Almost noon, Mr. Buckley.'

" 'Bring me a tall glass of milk.'

"Jimmy started to shovel the rest of the spaghetti into his mouth with gusto. I went back to the kitchen and told you that he wanted a tall glass of milk on top of all he had eaten and drunk.

"You were as surprised as I was and said, 'I hope he waits until he's outside before he unloads. Better get him what he wants and present him with the check as soon as possible.'

"I quickly totaled his bill, grabbed a tall glass of milk, and went out to take another look at Jimmy, who looked decidedly unwell.

" 'You got my milk? Good. Here's another hundred to cover the lunch. Keep the change.'

"I picked up the money as he looked out the window at a brand-new dove-gray Rolls-Royce Silver Shadow that had pulled up outside. The driver was a woman wearing sunglasses and a Pucci scarf. Jimmy nodded to himself, grabbed the glass of milk, and drained it in one long series of swallows. He got up, wobbled slightly, and then lurched to the door. He opened it without my help and made for the Rolls.

" 'Johnny!' I yelled over my shoulder, but you were already beside me as we watched Jimmy Buckley stagger around to the passenger side and get in. We heard the woman begin yelling at him as soon as he opened the door. It closed with a soft clunk, after which we heard nothing. We watched her head turn toward him as her arms flailed about in silent emphasis. After a minute, she faced forward, still talking, and put the car in gear. As she reversed into South Main traffic, the driver's window turned red as if someone had thrown a bucket of paint onto it from the inside.

"You and I made it through Mario's front door as more buckets of paint seemed to be splashing all over the inside of the car. The engine roared, and the Rolls leaped backward, smashing into the front of a Cadillac cruising down South Main. Rapidly changing direction, the Rolls jumped the curb and collided with a bench on the sidewalk with the sound of crunching metal and tinkling glass, followed by a long hiss. Iridescent green radiator fluid pooled beneath the Silver Shadow as steam rose from the engine compartment. We watched open-mouthed as Jimmy got out of the passenger side and looked at us over the top of the car. He was grinning from ear to ear. He staggered to the other side of the street and kept on moving down the block. The woman got out to chase after him but was prevented by the driver of the Cadillac she'd crashed into. The elderly man spread his arms wide to stop her from escaping.

"The woman hesitated. She was drenched from head to toe in what looked like reddish paint and began screaming at him in a foreign language. We heard the hoot of a police siren.

"We went back into the restaurant because the stench had just reached us. Without a doubt, Jimmy had unloaded his gigantic meal and then some, all over the inside of the car and the driver.

"We watched a policeman approach the Rolls. The woman started yelling at him, but the officer held back, not wanting to get near her. As he moved closer, she reached into the car, scooped up some of Jimmy's lunch, and began flinging it in his direction, yelling all the time. Eventually, he took the plunge and grabbed her. He cuffed her and put her in a squad car.

"It was not until the end of that summer that we saw Jimmy again. It was eleven in the morning by the kitchen clock, and Mario's had been open for half an hour. There were no customers. You and I were polishing glasses with our backs to the entrance when he slipped through the door. We turned, and there he was.

"He looked like a star. He wore a dark gray silk suit, a white shirt, and a dark blue tie. He looked tanned, fit, and rich. His blue eyes sparkled merrily.

" 'You young bucks busy?'

"We were so shocked that nothing came out of our mouths in reply.

21

" 'Come on, bring me a Coke and sit with me.'

"You grabbed a Coke. I filled a tall glass with ice and placed it on Jimmy's table. You poured. We stood nearby, unsure of what to do.

" 'Sit.'

"We sat.

" 'So what's with you lads workin' here?'

"We told him how an unexpectedly large bar bill from the beach club, as well as an early start to the day, had landed us in a culinary career, compliments of Mr. Dodge.

"Jimmy stopped smiling and looked serious. 'Don't you be taking to a life of drink. It's the devil's work, and that's the truth. You both are young yet. Don't let it get you like it got me. I'll tell you a story.'

"He hunched forward to tell the tale.

" 'I was a handyman in that building on Fifth Avenue. I loved the opera. I wanted to sing my whole life, but I couldn't. It was the drink, you see. I loved the whiskey. I couldn't keep away from the stuff. Then, one day, the Lord clobbered me. I was coming out the door into the alley when I got hit on the head by some hot spaghetti somebody had thrown from a great height. It knocked me down. There I was on the ground, drunk and angry. I swore vengeance on whoever had done it. I was covered in filth, but the truth was I was drunk and didn't see it coming. It was the Lord who reached down and laid me low. I swear I heard him tell me to either knock off the sauce and sing or be a murderous bum. Which man I would become was up to me.'

"You and I listened, not knowing where this was going.

" 'Now, I'm not stupid,' he said. 'It wasn't the Lord who did that, but some little shits who tossed some crap out the window that they didn't want to eat, and had I found out who'd done it at the time, I would have killed 'em. But I never found out, and my life changed. I swore that if I ever found the culprits, I might want to thank them personally. So, word to the wise, don't go down the road to drink.'

"He looked at you and then at me.

" 'You got me?' he said.

"We looked at him with our mouths open. *Did he know?*

"Jimmy Buckley reached over, grabbed both of us by the fronts of our shirts, and pulled us over the table, spilling his Coke, and shook us like a couple of rats. He yelled in a voice so loud my ears rang.

" '*YOU GOT ME?*'

"We nodded our heads up and down as if our lives depended on it. He tossed us back over the table and into our chairs, which tipped over backward and landed us in a heap. He stood up fast as lightning and reached out as if to tear our limbs off. We groveled and whimpered. Then he stopped, stood back with his hands on his hips, and roared with laughter.

"He laughed and laughed.

"We blubbered and blubbered.

" 'You should take a good look at yourselves. Jesus, Mary, Joseph, and all the saints, but I've waited a long time to do that. I feel better.'

"He stopped laughing.

" 'Well, serious now. I've had my fun, and you boys look like you could use a change of drawers.' He chuckled. 'I hold no grudge, and that's God's truth. You did me a good turn. Get up, go clean yourselves, and then grab three empty glasses. I'll be here.'

"You and I got up and went to the restroom.

"You said, 'Holy crap! I've never been so scared in my life.'

" 'Me, too,' I said. "I think he's finished with us, thank God. At least I hope so.'

"After a few minutes, we came out, still a little nervous. You grabbed three glasses as I cleaned up the spill and laid on a fresh tablecloth. Jimmy righted the chairs, and we all sat down again.

" 'Okay,' said Jimmy. 'Let's start over.'

"He pulled out a flask and poured a couple of fingers of whiskey in each of the glasses before handing them around.

" 'Drink up!' he said.

"I was so shaken that I gulped mine down. It settled me and loosened my tongue.

" 'Mr. Buckley, I thought you wanted us to stop drinking, and here we are, sharing a splash before noon.'

" 'Well, all things in moderation, eh? There's truth in what I said. I was hitting the whiskey and feeling sorry for myself for not having the opportunity to sing when you lot hit me with that horrible stuff. I got really pissed at you, but more at myself for not believing that I could sing with the best. I quit the next day, sobered up, and have been reasonably sober until you saw me last. I had you both going just now, didn't I? Trust an Irishman to tell you such a tale. It's what we Irish do.'

" 'So what about the chick and the Rolls?' you asked.

" 'That's temper. When you add drink to that, there's no telling what will happen—that and a whore of a woman to begin with, but I paid her back and then some.'

"Jimmy leaned forward. 'Here's how it was: that woman threw me over for another man—a rich man, richer than me, but that wasn't enough. When she left me, she said I owed her money. She wanted to see me and get what was owed. I put her off and put her off until I told her to meet me in front of Mario's at noon that day. I said I'd pay her in full. Well, she got paid in full. You should have seen her face. It was worth it. On top of that, she was driving that rich man's car. He'd given it to her as a gift, you see.'

" 'Mr. Buckley,' you said. 'I hope I never give you cause to seek revenge on me. I'm not in your league.'

" 'You're not, but I'll tell you a secret, Bucko. All that's great comes about by paying attention to the details. Life's all about managing the details, believe you me.' "

———— ✦ ————

5

I missed my visit the next day but saw Johnny the following
afternoon. I sat down and looked him over. Other than his heart
rate being slightly higher than two days ago, his vitals were
unchanged. I had no idea if that was significant.

I started in. "Johnny, I'm sorry I missed yesterday's visit, but
there are things happening at the office that required my attention.
Do you remember Casey Duke?"

I watched the machines—not a twitch.

"She called and wanted to know how her account was doing."

I paused and looked at Johnny again before continuing.

"Casey told me that you'd opened one for her a few days before
your accident, only I couldn't find a record of it anywhere. She also
mentioned that she'd given you a check for fifty grand, but it hadn't
cleared her bank. I couldn't find a record of that either. I told her
that I would look into the matter and get back to her. It was
extremely awkward. After her call, I had your secretary tear the
place apart, but it's a mystery as to where that paperwork went. If
you have something to add, anything at all, now would be a really
good time to mention it."

There was no reaction.

"In truth, Johnny, that's not the half of it. Do you know anything
about a pending gold trade? We got a last-day delivery notice from
the exchange this morning. I think I almost fainted. I handled it, but
good Heavens, Johnny! Have you opened positions I don't know
about? Really, you must wake up. I'm freaking out!"

Not a peep came forth.

I sighed and looked down at the brownish-gray linoleum on the floor. I stared at the tiles for a long time.

Finally, I said, "I have another story for you, but I'm not in the mood to tell it. All I want to do is kick you. I imagine others have used that technique, but I've never heard of anyone recovering by applying it. I'll restrain myself for now and return tomorrow in a hopefully more optimistic and less tormented state of mind. Please consider what I've mentioned and formulate a suitable explanation. I'm in desperate need of your help. I really am. A single word would make me more hopeful. There's so much I don't know about Dodge Capital's operations. In truth, I might have to ask your dad for help. There, I've said it. Things at the office are that desperate."

I brooded some more.

"Anyway … I can't bring myself to talk to you right now." I stood. "I'll be back tomorrow. Simply checking out of this world and leaving me hanging in the wind won't rid yourself of me. Die, and I'll hunt you down, and then … and then, I'll kill you myself. I really will."

I turned and stomped out the door.

———◆———

6

I returned the following day and sat down in the chair next to the bed. I noted the readings on the machines.

I looked at Johnny and said, "I apologize for yesterday's outburst. Talking to Casey after so many years and then not finding her account embarrassed me. I fell in love with her years ago, and it was because of you that I managed to speak to her at all. I'll tell you why, but maybe you remember?"

I waited for an answer, but Johnny kept his peace.

I sighed. "Perhaps this story is more for me than for you, but you'll hear it anyway. You haven't a choice right now. You're unconscious. Likely, you'll be amused, but maybe not. Please tell me when I'm done.

"Once again, I've written up some notes to help me along."

I pulled out several typewritten pages, unfolded them, and began. "You and I were seventeen that year and spending August at the Southampton house. That night, you were out on a date, which allowed me to get to bed early for once. I heard the phone ring by my bed, picked up, and glanced at my alarm clock. It was two in the morning.

"I heard the words, 'Collect call to anyone from Johnny Dodge. Will you accept charges?'

" 'Yes, operator, I'll accept.'

"Wasting no time, you said, 'Percy, grab two sets of clothes and the spare car keys. Bring them to the phone booth behind Michael's. Do it now, and for God's sake, hurry!'

"I heard a female voice screaming in the background.

"Before I could respond, I was interrupted by your father from the master bedroom extension. 'Who's this?' he rasped in my ear.

"There was a click as you hung up, and with no one else on the line, it was up to me to explain why his sleep had been disturbed. Several explanations tumbled through my mind or didn't, as was the case at that time of night. Other than your urgent need for two pairs of clothes, the extra set of car keys, and maybe some help in dealing with a distraught female, I had no ready answer.

"I frantically tried to think of a reply. I'd been dreaming of Casey Duke before you woke me, and thoughts of her still floated above my bed.

"I managed to croak, 'It was Mrs. Duke, asking about her daughter.'

" 'That was Helen? Why on Earth would she be calling about her daughter at this time of night?'

"I, too, wondered about that.

"Your father answered for me. 'Was she out with Johnny?'

" 'Yes … and she missed her curfew.'

" 'Typical. I'll have words with him in the morning, and you can tell him that.' There was a click and then a thankful silence.

"I hung up and sighed with relief. It was the best I could do, given the circumstances, only I wasn't sure whom you were seeing that night. I'd lost track of the many objects of your passions long ago. My panic from speaking with your father gradually subsided, but as I thought about fulfilling your demands, I grew uneasy. The Southampton house had three cars: your father's Bentley, your mother's Mercedes, and our rented Plymouth Valiant. You had the Valiant, which meant I'd have to steal either the Bentley or the Mercedes. Doing so was easy. The keys for both rested in a large bowl on the front table, but starting up and driving either down the gravel drive without waking your parents was impossible. That I'd even considered stealing one of their cars was itself alarming. I decided that I was hopelessly depraved, but you were in trouble, and therefore, so was I.

"I decided my Raleigh three-speed would have to do. I got dressed, grabbed two pairs of pants and two polo shirts, stuffed them into a laundry bag, put the spare Valiant keys in my pocket, and crept down the backstairs to the garage. I wheeled my bike out the side door, slung the laundry bag over my shoulder, and pedaled along the grass verge that flanked the driveway.

"Once I hit Dune Road, I got up to speed. Michael's was at the base of Lake Agawam on Jobs Lane. It was closed this time of night, but there was a phone booth behind it in the alley. I was there in twenty minutes, but when I arrived, I saw nobody.

" 'Johnny?' I asked of the darkness beyond the glow of the single streetlight that lit the alleyway.

"There was a moment's pause, followed by your voice. 'Over here by the bushes, but don't get any closer. Throw me both sets of clothes.'

"I did as you asked and tossed you the laundry bag. I heard snatches of angry whispers before you stepped out from your hiding place. Your hair was wet, your bare feet were muddy, and you'd put my shirt on inside out. I handed you the keys to the Valiant.

" 'Didn't you bring any shoes?' was all you said by way of explanation.

" 'Shoes? You didn't ask for shoes.'

"You sighed. 'I need some shoes. Give me yours.'

" 'Why?'

" 'Why? Because pedaling your bicycle at night in bare feet is nearly impossible without injury.'

" 'Oh,' I said.

" 'Oh, is all you have to say. Why don't you do something useful, like talk to Casey until I'm back with the car? She's in the bushes behind me.' You sounded impatient with my lack of understanding of the situation.

" 'Casey? Casey Duke? Me?'

" 'For God's sake, Percy. Enough! It's a long story, and I don't have time to tell you. I must get her home before she goes completely mental. Now, give me your shoes!'

"I gave up my sneakers. You put them on, mounted my bike, and said, 'What a night. I'll be back in a bit. Talk to her. Maybe you can calm her down.'

"On that note, you rode up the alley toward South Main, and I picked my way carefully around bits of broken glass to the bushes. I heard whimpering.

"I called out softly, 'Casey? It's Percy. Are you okay?'

" 'Oh, Percy. It was horrible.'

"Casey Duke, dressed in my dark blue polo shirt and my yellow chino pants, stepped into the alleyway and flew into my arms. She held onto me for dear life before bursting into tears. I gave her what comfort I could as she sobbed into my shoulder, and her breasts flattened against my chest. I realized that she wore nothing under my shirt. My awareness of that was exquisite. In a fraction of a second, I was in another world."

Wait! Did I just see Johnny twitch? I watched him like a hawk. After a minute, I decided I'd imagined it.

I continued, "Since you'll likely not remember a thing I've said, I might as well admit that I found love as a teenager difficult. You were always so popular, while I was barely given a second thought. That disparity puzzled me for years. I was so jealous of you back then. With hindsight, perhaps I should have been more grateful. You showed me firsthand that love creates as many difficulties as it mends.

"I, too, had my problems in that department, but far different from yours. I would meet a girl I liked and think of nothing else. I would become dronelike and clingy. Even speaking would become difficult. Words would disappear, and I would spill things or drop them. Such behavior baffled me and likely others as well. Whether because of my awkwardness or other factors, I was merely tolerated. Had I not been your friend, I think I would have been avoided.

"That night, everything changed. It was two-thirty in the morning, and I was experiencing unimaginable intimacy with a girl, who in any age, would have caused a sensation. She was a goddess at seventeen. I remember feeling the softness of her chest pressing against my own, and there was nothing I could do.

"Johnny, you may not have had problems in that area, but I did. I spent hours in the ocean up to my neck. Not because I wanted to but because of the embarrassing and unassailable distance between the waves and my towel. The curves of a tanned female body in a bikini would sometimes send me into a hormonal state that required a great deal of cold ocean to control, and at that moment, I was far from any ocean."

I looked at Johnny, but he kept silent. I concluded that his twitch was likely my imagination playing tricks. I continued.

"Casey's sobs gradually subsided until she finally put me at arm's length, looked down, and said, 'Jesus, Percy.'

" 'I'm sorry,' I said. 'I didn't mean to—it just happens.'

" 'I see. Why don't we sit on the stoop over there while we wait?' I remember cringing in embarrassment. Casey let go of me and made her way gingerly to the steps at the back of Michael's, brushed the stoop with her hand, and sat down at one end.

"Once she was seated comfortably, she looked at me again and asked, 'You don't happen to have any cigarettes, do you?'

" 'I do.'

"I reached into my pants pocket, discreetly rearranged myself, and fished out a pack of Marlboros with a lighter. I walked over to the stoop just as carefully and sat next to her, but not too close. I lit one and gave it to her before lighting up my own. We sat and smoked.

"Casey broke the silence. 'Does that happen to you often?'

"Her dark eyes sparkled in the night. I didn't know what to say. I'd never talked about this to anyone, not even you.

"I blurted out, 'More times than I wish. It's embarrassing. I spend a great deal of time in the ocean.'

"She laughed. 'I suppose we all have our problems. What a night! I feel lightheaded now that it's mostly over.' Casey cleared her throat. 'Thank you for bringing me some dry clothes. I read somewhere that sailors swear that they make all the difference. It's true. They even fit for the most part. Are they yours?'

" 'Yes,' I said.

" 'I'll return them washed and good as new.'

" 'Thank you,' I answered.

"I almost blurted out that I'd cherish them forever but managed to resist the temptation. I hurried on. 'What happened to you, if you don't mind my asking?'

"She took a drag and blew the smoke out into the alley, where it swirled under the light.

" 'That ... I'm not going to tell you. We would have to know each other a great deal better before I could.' She looked at me and said, 'It was traumatic. That's all I'm going to say. On another matter and more relevant, thank you for your help. I mean that. I'm glad Johnny has a friend he can call on day or night. I don't. I wish I did.'

" 'You don't?' That was a surprise to me.

" 'Nope. I have brothers, sisters, and plenty of friends, but it's not the same—too much rivalry and competition. Looking beautiful has its drawbacks.'

" 'I would think it would be quite the opposite.'

" 'There are moments when beauty is an advantage. First impressions are easy, but few, if any, choose to look below the surface. I have plenty of friends, but none whom I'm close to. You're luckier than I am. You have Johnny. Oh, what I'd give for a friendship like that.'

"I paused and said, 'Living with him is not as easy as you might imagine. He's difficult—not all the time, but often enough. You think I'm lucky? He's the lucky one. Things naturally go well for him.'

" 'He can think on his feet, but don't tell him I said that. We're not speaking at the moment. Does he make you jealous?'

"I considered her question. 'Sometimes. Often, I guess. He's handsome and really smart. What bugs me about him is that he's always getting me into trouble. I hate being in trouble. Tonight, I even thought of stealing Mr. Dodge's Bentley. I can't believe I considered it. Johnny can be a bad influence.'

" 'Yes, and tonight's a case in point.'

"We both sat, thinking about you."

I looked up at Johnny as he lay in the hospital bed and said, "I forget what it was I thought at that exact moment. I should think it was that you really were difficult to live with, but to be fair, I was likely just as troublesome. I was introverted and twitchy, yet somehow, you always managed to distract me with all your goings-on. I suppose I should thank you. I certainly was never bored. What I can hardly believe is that you're still doing it. My attention is once again fixated on you and the troubles you create, only now it's worse. You're in a coma. Now, what am I supposed to do? Some things never seem to change, Johnny."

I sighed.

"Anyway, back to my story. I remember telling Casey, 'I don't mean to give the impression that Johnny's a bad person. He's not. Trouble is his way of amusing himself. It's like a drug that stimulates his brilliance. I wish I was as smart as him. I simply follow in his footsteps.'

"Casey replied, 'He's lucky to have you then. It's wonderful to have an audience.'

" 'An audience?'

" 'Oh, yes. It's why he and I aren't going to work. We'd steal each other's spotlight for a start. Life with him would be too much competition and vying for attention.'

" 'That's too bad.'

" 'Not really. Better to learn now than later.'

" 'I suppose.'

"Casey sighed. 'I had high hopes, but it was fated not to work out. It's as if … Who knows why? I certainly don't. Changing the subject, where are you going to college?'

" 'Don't know yet. That's coming up.'

" 'It is. I think I hear a car.'

"It was you in the Valiant driving down the alley with my bike sticking out of the trunk. Casey stood and brushed herself off. I stood as well, reluctant to have our conversation end. She seemed eager to get home, but before she opened the door to the front seat, she turned and said, 'I enjoyed talking with you, Percy. Thank you once again for all your help. I'll see you tomorrow.' She got in. I closed the door for her and got in the back. You didn't so much as look at her.

"We dropped Casey at the stone pillars that marked the entrance to the Duke estate. Not a word had been spoken. She didn't say goodbye as she grabbed her purse, got out, and made her way carefully in bare feet up the gravel drive. You kept to yourself as I climbed over the seat and into the front.

"As we drove home, you squirmed a few times before saying, 'I hate wearing pants with no underwear.'

" 'Sorry,' I said. 'You didn't say you wanted a *full* set of clothes.'

" 'Sorry isn't good enough. A set of clothes implies underwear. And shoes!'

" 'I'll remember that in the future.'

" 'With socks. There must be socks.'

" 'Socks? We don't wear socks in the summer.'

"You were getting nitpicky, which meant that you were in a bad mood. You replied, 'That may be, but it's the thought that counts. Of course, the likelihood of you having to bring me another set of clothes on an emergency basis will hopefully be rather minuscule going forward, but then again, you never know.'

" 'I hope so. On another topic, I'm guessing things didn't go so well with you and Casey.'

I was feeling provocative. My outlook had brightened significantly with the thought that I might be seeing more of her.

"Reading my mind, you said, 'I wouldn't get your hopes up.'

"I snorted and looked away.

"You kept on driving and said, 'I hate to break it to you, Percy, but she's not for either of us. After tonight, she'll likely end up with someone rather plain and unremarkable.'

" 'I can be plain and unremarkable.'

"You glanced at me and scoffed. " 'Hardly. You're also connected to me, remember? That automatically disqualifies you. You'll see I'm right.'

"And you were right, as is normally the case."

I stopped as a nurse peeked her head in and said, "There's a phone call for you at the nurse's station."

I thanked her and turned to Johnny. "The story does continue, of course. You told me what happened that night, but can you remember what you said? I'll be back in a bit."

I went to the nurse's station and picked up the phone that was lying off the hook.

"Hello," I said. "This is Percy."

"John Dodge, here. How is he today?"

"The same."

"I thought as much. I apologize for interrupting your hour with him. I called because I think it's time we have a talk."

"That's probably a good idea. It's been difficult for me."

"I'm sure it has."

"I take it there are matters of which I'm unaware."

"There are."

"I look forward to our conversation then. Bruni and I will be up this weekend."

"Sooner is better. I want you to come see me tonight. Bring Bruni, of course, but this conversation will be between ourselves. Anne would love to see her while we talk. She, too, needs a friend. She is not entirely herself."

"I'm sorry to hear that. This must be particularly hard for her."

"It is, and I can only do so much. I've instructed Raymond to attend to you. He'll meet you at the hospital entrance in thirty minutes. He can drive you wherever you need to go and then up to Rhinebeck. You'll come see me tonight?"

"Most certainly. I'll bring Bruni if I can and look for Raymond out front."

"Good. We'll talk soon. Goodbye."

I said goodbye and called Bruni from the nurse's station. I told her that John Senior wanted to see me tonight.

"Interesting," she said. "I'm coming with you."

"Excellent. Likely, I'll need your advice."

"I'm sure you will. I could also use a break. This baby business is no picnic. How is Johnny today?"

"The same. I thought I saw him twitch, but I may have imagined it."

"Well, that's different. Come pick me up soon."

"I will. Be downstairs in an hour."

"I'll be in the lobby."

I hung up and handed the phone to the nurse who was waiting for me to finish.

7

I returned to Johnny's bedside and settled in my chair.

"That was your father. He wants to see me. I get the feeling there is more going on than I know. Perhaps you could fill me in before I see him?"

I waited for an answer.

"Not saying? Well, no surprise there. I still have some visiting time left. I'll tell you the rest of the story, only this time, imagine speaking the words. Perhaps that will help stir a memory or two."

I looked down at my notes and continued.

"We'd dropped off Casey and were driving along Dune Road when you said, 'I'm sorry I'm in such a foul mood. Thank you for your help tonight. I should have said that at the beginning, but it's been one of those evenings. You definitely saved my bacon.'

"I grunted, and you decided to lay it on a little thicker.

" 'No, really! You biked all that way. I would have taken the Bentley. Actually, no—that would have been a disaster. You were correct. I may even be in your debt. Now, will you *please* listen to my story?'

" 'Okay, you can tell me,' I said.

"You pulled over to the side of the road, and we got out. Mist swirled along the top of the asphalt. We stood leaning back against the front of the car, where it was warmer.

"You lit up a smoke and said, 'I couldn't possibly drive and tell you. Frankly, it's all quite baffling. I can't believe it ended so badly after such a splendid start. I picked Casey up at seven from her

37

house and took her to a nightclub in East Hampton. After that, we drove back and decided to go to the beach to see the ocean. I parked near the beach club in the section closest to Lake Agawam, to be less conspicuous. There were a couple of cars in the lot, but at that time of night, it was almost empty. I pulled my trusty flask of vodka from the glove compartment and a blanket from the trunk. We went over the dunes to the beach by way of Dune Church. There was only the slightest breeze. I laid out the blanket on the sand. I lit a small fire. We fooled around. We drank. One thing led to another, and then Casey wanted to go skinny dipping.

" 'The water looked inviting, and the night was fine. I was a little blasted and agreed. With that, Casey stood up without any clothes and looked out to sea. Her beauty at that moment took my breath away. I thought that if I died right then, my life would have been worth it. I really did.

" 'Unfortunately, my time in that ethereal realm was rather short-lived. We ran toward the ocean hand in hand and plunged into the waves without pausing. The water was cold, but the surf was low. We swam out a hundred feet or so to get warm, where we floated and treaded water. We drifted closer in and held each other. It was bliss. I was looking at the shore when I saw the beams of several flashlights approaching along the beach. I became concerned and pointed the lights out to Casey. They were coming mighty fast, and if we didn't do something quickly, we would be trapped naked in the ocean. We decided to swim for it, but we were too late. The lights converged on our blanket before we could get to shore. Rather than reveal ourselves, we decided to abandon our clothes and whatever else we had brought with us. We watched from the waves, and when the lights were all pointed down at the blanket and our little fire, we made a break for the dunes and the car.' "

I looked up at Johnny from my reading. He might have been interested, but I couldn't tell.

I sighed and continued.

"You smoked some more and said, 'We sprinted along the side of the church and across Dune Road. There were two police cars in front of the club, which explained the lights on the beach. We made it to the Valiant, but when we got there, I realized that I'd locked it, and that the keys were in my pants pocket. The good news was that I'd left my wallet in the glove compartment, and Casey had put her purse under the seat. All the police had was our clothes, a blanket, a flask, a lighter, cigarettes, and a key ring. I was working on breaking into the Valiant when another patrol car drove up in front of the club. It must have been a slow night. Shortly after, I saw bobbing lights come over the dunes and move toward the parking lot. We scurried around to the front of the Valiant and hid, but our situation was growing more precarious by the second. Casey began to freak out. Frankly, I wasn't doing much better. I wondered if the police attention was because I'd lit a fire. All I knew for sure was that the cops would eventually search the cars in the lot and that we had only one option: we would have to slip into the murky waters of Lake Agawam.'

" 'Good God!' I said. 'No wonder she was so weirded out. I wouldn't be caught dead in that lake. It's full of snapping turtles and catfish with venomous dorsal spines. Some grow quite large, you know.'

" 'Yes, and a horrid image of a snapping turtle biting through a broom handle was never far from my mind, but it gets worse—much worse. I can barely get my wits around the ordeal that followed. It was like we had been transported naked to a desert island and forced to survive any way we could. I couldn't allow either of us to succumb, but rescuing us from the situation cost me any possible future with Casey. All our social veneer vanished, and there we were: man and woman, naked, cold, desperate, and alone. We were pretty awful to each other.'

" 'Really?'

" 'It's no joke. The police started closing in, and Casey and I got into quite the argument. She blurted out that she'd decided to give up and surrender. I considered her suggestion for exactly one-tenth of a second. There was no way I was going to give myself up, stark naked, to a bunch of cops. I'd rather die, and that didn't take into account what I was doing with an equally naked teenage girl. It was well beyond anything I could imagine. Death was a better option. I asked her what her parents would think if we were arrested, and that did it.

" 'She began to moan in a weird way. Her teeth began to chatter, and words poured out of her mouth in shivered whimpers. She wouldn't be able to get into college. She'd be branded a criminal. Her name would be in the papers. She'd have a police record. Her life was ruined. She glared at me and snarled, 'This is all your fault—all of it.' And then she hit me. She hissed like a rabid cat and whacked me again, hard. I did the only thing I could. I took hold of her shoulders and shook her so hard and fast that her teeth clicked together.

" 'I hissed at her, rather too loudly, it turns out, to snap out of it. She could either give up, and all she feared would come to pass, or she could follow me. Flashlight beams pointed in our direction. The cops had heard something. I acted without thinking. I grabbed her by the waist and dumped her over the wooden siding that bordered the lake and into the water. I followed. It was colder and deeper than I expected, and the freezing water must have shocked her because she stopped carrying on. I motioned for her to be quiet and wait. Our heads were just above the surface. I held her hand to reassure her as I felt mud and God-knows-what-else oozing between my toes. It was a horrible sensation in the dark, and those damn snapping turtles were never far from my mind.

" 'That visceral sensation was heightened when I heard a splash. Beams of light played in that direction, and the cops moved toward the water's edge. We were now literally at their feet. I motioned to

Casey to sink below the surface. She nodded. We each took a deep breath. As we descended, the murk lit up with brownish-green beams of light that pierced the gloom around us. For once, I thanked God that the water was so filthy. The flashlight beams played about and then went dark. We waited hand in hand until Casey let go. I surfaced beside her and saw her frantically trying to clamber over the siding. I lifted myself up and saw the cops packing up and getting in their cars with our clothes and blanket. I hauled her back down. Casey fought and then screamed as she rocketed out of the water again. Luckily, the cops didn't hear her. Once I'd followed her up and over, she whimpered that something in the water had brushed her leg. She settled down as we hunkered down together behind the front of the Valiant, cold and wet, but relieved to have escaped so far.

" 'That peaceful interlude didn't last. After a few minutes of my unsuccessfully trying to break into the car, she started in on me again. She snarled that I'd gotten her into this mess and that it was up to me to get her out of it. Now!

" 'I had no idea what to do. I was just as cold and miserable, but she didn't seem to notice or care. She kept repeating that this was all my fault, and then I stupidly said that the skinny-dipping idea was hers, not mine. Well, that set her off completely. Finally, I couldn't take any more. Every man has a limit. I shouted at her to shut the fuck up. I couldn't think with all her carrying on.

" 'She shut up, and I told her that we had two choices: we could wake up one of the sleeping residents of the stately homes that dotted the shoreline, stand there dripping and completely naked, and ask to use their phone, or we could make our way to the phone booth next to Michael's on Jobs Lane. There, I could make a collect call without needing a dime and have you come rescue us. I said we could either swim or walk—her choice. She sniffed, stood up, held her head high, and began walking in the direction of town just like Lady Godiva but without the horse. It was a sight.'

41

"You took a drag as I asked, 'You walked stark naked all the way to Michael's?'

" 'That we did,' you said, 'but it was more like intermittent sprints from one form of cover to the next. We dodged approaching cars, snuck through people's yards, and then that Silcox dog nearly got us. It came out of nowhere and scared us both half to death. We ran for our lives. After our escape from the jaws of that beast, Casey turned into a zombie. I had to lead her everywhere and tell her what to do. Every now and again, she'd start whimpering. Eventually, we made it to the phone booth, where I dialed the operator and called you collect. As we waited, I told her that I was very sorry for what had happened and that help would arrive shortly. She came back to life and started in on me again. We fought. We said some pretty nasty things to each other. We acted like complete savages. Then, you finally showed up.'

"After a few moments' reflection, I said, 'Well, it's a miracle you both aren't in jail. No wonder she wouldn't talk to you. Just the same; you did the right thing. Getting busted with her would have been disastrous. She should realize that eventually. One thing you're also right about: I have zero chance with her. She'll see me and be reminded of you.'

" 'You are correct. What a travesty. It's like some deity looked down, saw us together, and decreed that such a union was forbidden. To ensure we understood, he or she showed us who we really were beneath the surface: brutish, fierce, intolerant, and rude. That image was too much for either of us to accept, and so our love ended before it had really begun.'

"We both thought about that.

"I broke the silence. 'Maybe that's true. Maybe it isn't. What I do know is that you and women aren't destined for long-term relationships anytime soon, so get used to it. I would also avoid skinny dipping in the future.'

" 'I think I've had a lifetime of it. Now, the night is still young, and I feel like a celebration.'

" 'Well, I wouldn't go too far in that direction. Your father picked up as you rang off. He asked who'd called, and I said rather coincidentally that it was Casey's mother looking for her. He wondered if Casey had missed her curfew.'

" 'Really?'

" 'Really.'

" 'See what I mean? How is that possible?'

" 'Be that as it may, he'll probably call Helen Duke in the morning, and that might prove rather awkward for all of us.'

" 'Likely he will, but let the chips fall where they may. Nothing anyone can do to me can be worse than tonight. I say we go home, celebrate, and watch the sunrise. It's almost a new day, and life has a wonderful zest right now. I survived against overwhelming odds, and you helped me do it. There is something supremely noble in that.' "

I put away my notes.

"We did celebrate if you'll recall, and I'd like to do so again, but not before you wake up. I thought I saw you twitch for a moment, but I wonder if I really did. Maybe next time, you could be a bit more obvious."

I stood and said, "If I were you, I'd also have a word with whatever deity was looking down on you and Casey that night and come to some sort of understanding—an amnesty or a reprieve would be best. Perhaps it will help. While you do that, I'll be talking with your dad and getting with Stanley and Dagmar. Perhaps they'll have a suggestion or two. Call me at Rhinebeck if you need me—just ring for the nurse."

8

I walked down the hospital corridor to the elevator. As I waited, I thought about John Senior lending me Raymond. I didn't know what to make of that. He was more than Mr. Dodge's personal chauffeur. It was rumored among the staff that when civilized discussion proved impossible, Raymond was called in—his was conversation by other means.

All Johnny and I knew about him was that his last name was Figueroa and that he was born in Puerto Rico. He also had a fiery Latin temperament and was fiercely loyal to Mr. Dodge for reasons that were never made clear.

When asked, Raymond would say, "You don't need to know that."

At night, he took the subway back to his wife in Brooklyn. Every weekday morning, he arrived in Manhattan to drive Johnny and me to school at 7:30 a.m. His schedule included picking us up at 3:10 p.m., but there were days when he never showed. Where he went during those times and why, he never explained, and we never asked. It was not our place to question what he did. In truth, we didn't dare.

Physically, he was short, cleanshaven in the morning but darkly shadowed by the afternoon. He had immense physical strength and looked like a pirate, an image he enhanced by wearing a small, yellow-gold hoop in his right ear and swearing at every opportunity—except when in the company of Johnny's parents. His suits were hand-tailored to accommodate massively developed forearms and shoulders.

He once told us, "I used to fight in Puerto Rico. Not your usual boxing, which I did, but the street kind—knives, baseball bats, whatever was handy. I once used a guy's arm. I kid you not."

I saw him in action one afternoon on Fifth Avenue near the Plaza Hotel when I was ten. Raymond was escorting me to a dental appointment in the Squibb building while Johnny was having lunch with his grandmother at Trader Vic's. A long black limousine cut the corner where we were standing. The rear tire jumped the curb and ran over Raymond's foot. Raymond didn't flinch. Instead, he cursed and gave the right rear panel of the errant car a tremendous blow with his fist. The metal dented and yelped like it had been struck with a sledgehammer. The wounded vehicle screeched to a halt, and a large, enraged chauffeur threw open the door and made his way around the car as a wrinkled old lady in the back wearing dark glasses buzzed down the rear side window and began screaming at Raymond.

Raymond glared at her and yelled, "Shut the fuck up!"

She stopped mid-word and raised the window as fast as she could. Raymond allowed the driver to come close before he decked him with a savage uppercut to the chin. The giant man rose onto his tiptoes before he crumpled to the ground.

My mouth hung open as I stared at his fluttering eyelids.

Raymond grabbed my arm as the light turned green and steered me across the street. He didn't look back, but I did. The man lay sprawled beside the car, the driver door open and his chauffeur hat on the curb. Cars and taxis began to honk like a pack of hounds that had cornered a fox.

A block later, Raymond stopped and took off his scuffed shoe. He looked at it critically and said, "That fucking guy ruined my shine. Check this out."

He showed me his black lace-up and tapped the front.

"Steel tips. You kick some guy in the crotch with one of these, you break his balls."

He chuckled as he put the shoe back on and then escorted me to my appointment.

To Johnny and me, Raymond lived in a violent and terrifying world that was brutal and barbaric compared to our own. We idolized and feared him. He was like a tiger—not the cute, fuzzy kind, but the real thing: visceral, deadly, and unpredictable.

If Raymond appeared crude and oafish in his manners and speech, he made up for it in the finesse with which he drove. His dexterity and skill were unsurpassed and nothing short of breathtaking.

Driving to school with him was exhilarating. Johnny and I would sit together in the front seat to get the full effect. He never wore a seatbelt, and neither did we. On side streets between the avenues, the Lincoln would float along at speeds of fifty miles per hour or more when we were late. Double-parked cars and trucks would barely slow the Lincoln as Raymond, with the precision of a surgeon, would thread his way between them with barely an inch on a side. At stoplights, Raymond would decelerate hard while stretching out his right arm to prevent us from being launched through the windshield, but always with such smoothness that it seemed like magic.

His driving skill was also legendary on the street. We'd heard tales of Mr. Dodge and his cronies betting immense sums on whether Raymond could get down to Wall Street within a set period of time. Raymond won more often than not. Such antics gained Mr. Dodge tremendous prestige among his rivals, who would try to lure Raymond away with promises of huge signing bonuses and outrageous salaries. Raymond declined them all.

My maunderings were interrupted by the elevator opening at the lobby. I couldn't recall getting into it.

I spotted Raymond waiting beside the long black Lincoln. He walked up to me.

"How ya doin'?" he asked. His dark eyes portrayed nothing.

"Fine," I replied.

He didn't move but stood looking at me.

"How's Johnny?"

"The same."

Raymond nodded and stared at me some more. He said at last, "Okay, to business. Here's how we're going to do this. When I pick you up, I open the door. That's my job. You *never* open it. I do that. If you don't see me standing out front when I pick you up, you don't get near the car. When we arrive at a location, I always get out first and let you out. You never do that. Got it?"

"Got it. By the way, we have to pick up Bruni on the way to Rhinebeck."

"We'll stop there first. As I said, if I don't open your door, you stay put. Clear?"

"Clear."

"Good. You follow my instructions, and we'll get along fine. I will call you 'sir.' You will call me 'Raymond.' If there's anything else you need to do or know, I'll tell you. That's it."

Raymond opened the door of the limo, and I got in the back. He went round to the driver's seat, put his chauffeur's hat squarely on his head, looked at me in the mirror for a second, and started up the Lincoln. He'd never worn a hat before when it was just me in the car.

———◆———

9

Wₑ swung by Bruni's office. Raymond didn't open my door, and I sat in the back with the engine running while he went into the building. He came out with Bruni. Once she was inside, Bruni gave me a kiss and settled beside me. Raymond got in, buzzed up the dividing window, and swung the car into traffic, all in one fluid motion.

Bruni whispered, "Raymond really does look like a pirate."

"He does, but I wouldn't tell him that."

"Oh, I most definitely will. I like pirates. Ours is named Gustav. Papa uses him whenever there's a problem."

"I see. Does he use him often?"

"Often enough. He's like a pocketknife. The time you need one is when it's not with you. I always carry mine in my purse for that reason. I suppose Papa does the same with Gustav."

"I'll keep that in mind."

"I would, but for now, I'm too exhausted to think. I'm going to sleep on your shoulder. Will that bother you?"

"Not at all. You go right ahead."

Bruni sighed, snuggled next to me, and promptly dropped off. I tried to do the same but was unsuccessful. I felt out of sorts. Raymond's presence and Bruni's comment about Gustav only added to my disquiet. I thought about work.

With Johnny in the hospital, I had the opportunity to examine Dodge Capital's books more thoroughly. What I found surprised me. The firm was in much better shape than its balance sheet might suggest or indicate—far better than I had been led to believe—as if the company was being made to appear vulnerable and in worse financial condition than it really was. Everything at Dodge Capital appeared normal on the surface, but my deeper analysis, Casey's missing paperwork, and the delivery notice from the Exchange said more was going on, but what that was exactly, I didn't know. Such anomalies were troubling but paled when compared to the accident itself.

I'd made inquiries into Johnny's mishap on my own. I'd told no one other than my secretary about the confidential reports I'd received from several investigative sources. Being able to gather such intelligence was one of the perks of working in the corner office at Dodge Capital. I'd read each report with care. All of them pointed to the excessive speed, the reduced visibility due to rain, and the slickness of the road surface as contributory but were unanimous in their findings. They placed the blame squarely on the driver, referencing the driver's blood-alcohol concentration percentage from the autopsy. His BAC was 0.18. That figure seemed excessive.

As to the details of the accident, each stated that the driver had lost control of the limousine while attempting to exit the East River Drive to the left at the Triborough Bridge on-ramp. The car had struck the exit barrier, or gore as it was called, head-on, but to the left of the vehicle's centerline, causing the vehicle to rotate in a rapid counterclockwise direction. The driver had died on impact.

Johnny had been sitting in the rear seat on the right side when the collision occurred. He should have died as well, but the rotation of the car, the vehicle's length, the tensile strength of the dividing window, and the compression of the dashboard had dissipated much of the force experienced by the rear occupant. The reports spelled this out in graphic detail and included plenty of diagrams and photographs. They were hard to look at.

There was also the odd coincidence of its location.

Johnny and I were familiar with that exit. Years earlier, and just before Christmas, Raymond had been instructed by Mr. Dodge to drive us to LaGuardia. We had been late leaving the apartment, and it looked like we couldn't possibly make our flight. Raymond had simply told us to get in.

Once the door shut, he floored the accelerator and began weaving through traffic. We had made it to the East River Drive without mishap and had been heading north when I noticed a dark Ford following us at high speed. I saw Raymond observe the car in his mirror. As it got closer, the Ford began honking. Raymond slowed to see who it was and allowed the car to pull up alongside on the right. The Ford's driver held a gold police badge to his window and motioned for us to pull over.

Raymond told us to hang on.

He let the Ford keep pace while he edged the Lincoln closer and closer to the detective's door. The Ford gave ground as our exit came in sight on the left. At the last possible moment, Raymond sheered away and up the exit ramp to the left. The tires shrieked as the gray knifelike gore came within inches of impaling the Lincoln. Johnny and I were flung sideways from the force of the turn, and as my face pressed against the window, I watched the detective hurl his badge at the dashboard in disgust as he was forced to continue straight. It had been a superb piece of driving, and Raymond had a smile on his face for the rest of the trip. Johnny and I had even made the flight. I knew the location was coincidental, but the oddity underscored my desire that nothing be overlooked.

In their summations, the reports concluded that the driver was at fault but noted that the exit had been built in the 1930s and hadn't been significantly upgraded since. Further, the turn was decidedly abrupt, and that a possible lawsuit against the city and the Metropolitan Transportation Authority was advised.

I thanked the agencies and their agents for their efforts but pointed out that more was required of them. There were several points that needed clarification, and it was my opinion that what I had received was, at best, only a preliminary account.

The first oddity omitted was that the limousine service Dodge Capital used was strict, bordering on obsessive, when it came to alcohol and drug consumption on the part of its employees. Drivers were subject to civil, if not criminal, actions in the event of discovery on the job. It was part of the service contract and strictly enforced. Why was their driver drunk?

There was another point I couldn't ignore. Johnny and I had a morbid fascination with accidents, mishaps, and disasters of all kinds. We would often speculate at great length as to the causes and possible preventive measures that should have been taken. Checking out a driver and their competency was high on the list. I also knew Johnny. He would speak to a driver he hadn't used to get a sense of him and always with those whom he knew. He told me that such conversations would set his mind at ease and allowed him to put his attention exclusively on absorbing the content of reports, which he liked to read while being chauffeured about town. There was simply no way that Johnny would have gotten into a limo driven by a chauffeur who was drunk, and of that, I was quite certain—unless he was drunk himself.

I asked for Johnny's blood tests to be followed by copies of his medical records. Perhaps I was being paranoid again, but given the nature of the accident, I didn't care.

Lastly, there was the context. Where was he going at that time, and why? LaGuardia or JFK airports were possible destinations but unlikely. Johnny didn't take commercial flights, and the company jet flew out of Teterboro in New Jersey. I wanted an hour-by-hour tracing of Johnny's movements, starting two weeks before the accident.

Since this was all being charged to Dodge Capital, I told the investigators that the added information I required was needed yesterday. I also mentioned the possibility of a bonus for their efforts, provided they delivered their results quickly and accurately.

———◆———

I must have dozed off because the car was turning down the slope to Rhinebeck's squared roundabout as Bruni awoke beside me. Stanley was at the top of the steps.

Bruni said, "How does he do that?"

"I've no idea," I said. "He just knows."

"It's remarkable, but I'm always happy to see him standing there."

"Me, too."

Raymond stopped the car at the bottom of the drive and opened the door for us.

Stanley came down the steps and greeted me. "Welcome home. We were expecting you on Friday, but sooner is better. At your convenience, I would very much like to hear all about Johnny's condition. Dagmar would as well. We've heard little and are most concerned, but first things first. Mr. and Mrs. Dodge are awaiting you in the drawing room, and refreshments will be served there shortly."

He turned to Bruni and said, "A warm welcome to you."

"Thank you, Stanley. It's always a pleasure."

"And mine, too. Please, follow me."

I paused out front to thank Raymond, who said, "I'll put the car away, but I'll be around whenever you need me. Just sing out."

Bruni and Stanley were already at the drawing room door, and as they passed through, I was alone in the foyer. I shut the front door and noted that the house seemed chilly, almost cold, and that the grandfather clock to my left, with its swaying ships of the line, clacked out a more somber, dirge-like cadence. I continued to the drawing room and felt the dead eyes of the marble statue of Alexander the Great follow me as I passed. I shivered.

John Senior and Anne were greeting Bruni as I entered. Anne saw me and came forward.

"How is he, Percy? Has there been any change?"

Her eyes filled with eager anticipation.

I said, "His condition was the same this afternoon, although I thought I saw him twitch today. It happened so fast; I couldn't be sure."

Her face lit up, and she took my hand. "Really? Oh, Percy, I feel so much better. I've felt so low—so busted up inside. Thank you for telling me. I know a twitch is a tiny thing, but I've had nothing to give me hope. Nothing at all. So, thank you for that, Percy. Thank you."

I looked at Anne carefully. Her reaction and her speech seemed exaggerated.

Anne let go of my hand and looked about, beaming. Bruni came up and hugged her, rocking her in her arms. Anne's face contorted, and she burst into tears. She collapsed onto Bruni like a child. Bruni staggered but held her up before slowly guiding Anne to the foyer door. Anne gasped for air that wouldn't come. Bruni signaled me with her hand to stay clear. She opened the door herself and closed it, taking Anne away.

Stanley entered from the dining room with champagne on a silver salver. I turned and saw John's face. He showed no emotion. Stanley offered each of us a flute of Cristal, which we accepted. He took those for Anne and Bruni with him as he silently left the way he'd come. I looked down at the bubbles in my glass and wondered if drinking champagne was appropriate, given the circumstances. It seemed horribly insensitive, but I drank anyway. Johnny would have insisted, and he would have been right.

"She's not well, Percy," said John softly, interrupting my thoughts. "And I suppose I'm not either. She grieves, and I comfort her as best I can. In her mind, she's already lost her son, and my words are no remedy for that. Whatever I say means nothing."

He looked down before continuing.

"Just the same, I'm happy to hear there's been a change, even if momentary. We've visited Johnny only twice since the accident. I know we ought to see him more, but I can't bring myself to do that, and because I can't, she won't. Perhaps it is the other way around. I don't know."

He looked at me. "I barely recognized him at the hospital. My son isn't dead, and I should be grateful for that, but he might as well be. He breathes, and they feed him somehow. I sense his essence has passed to somewhere else. He's just a thing now, and I don't know what to do to lessen that impression. I've turned away from visiting him because … because I'm unable to really look at him, not without breaking down completely, and then what?"

John sipped his champagne to cover his emotions.

He sighed and continued. "And that's not the worst of it. *My* Anne lies there beside him, and the giddy hysteria you saw is all that's been returned to me—that and someone else. That one begged me to fix him, and when I said I couldn't, she screamed that I was useless, that I had no feelings for my son, and that she hates me for what I cannot do. Anne, in all our years, has never said such things. Now, there is no peace between us, and I can't seem to find my footing."

He looked down at his glass again and continued.

"In a way, she's right. I should feel for Johnny more than just the hole his absence has created, but I can't seem to. Anne's feelings and mine are not the same in this, and yet I hurt. I can barely get out of bed each morning, knowing that by the time I fall asleep, the woman whom I've loved for over half my life will make my heart bleed as much as hers. She feels Johnny's loss every day, and she'll ensure I do as well, only it won't be his absence that I'll miss, but hers."

John looked away and then turned back.

"I do apologize, Percy. You see him daily. I can't imagine what that's like."

"John, I had no idea things were so bad between you and Anne. I would have come much sooner."

"I know, and I thank you for the thought, but there're other matters we must discuss. Why don't we move to the library? There, we can smoke cigars and have a proper drink. Stanley can find us and call us to dinner—that is, if there is a dinner tonight."

"By all means."

I'd never heard John talk that way. His pain was obvious and distressed me. If one of the most stable relationships I had ever known could founder so quickly and decidedly, I wondered how stable was anyone's, let alone my own.

———•———

11

As we passed down the hall to the library, I felt Johnny's absence with every step. He and I had walked this hall a thousand times. I glimpsed him off and on, like the glimmers I'd seen among the spreading shadows of almost evenings in this very place. More than his parents' marriage hinged on Johnny's reawakening; my sense of *being home* did too.

John went directly to the bar.

"Whiskey over ice? I'm having one."

"Please," I said.

John handed me my whiskey and reached for a cigar. Once we were seated comfortably, John started in.

"First, thank you for coming to see me. To be perfectly frank, I feel out of sorts, and it's a family trait to speak to others about what is perplexing us to see more clearly."

I nodded. "I'm familiar with that idiosyncrasy. Johnny will often lecture me for that reason."

"We are similar in that regard. This afternoon, I found myself talking to myself for lack of a listener. It made me doubt my sanity. That disturbed me more than I can say. It's why I asked to speak with you tonight."

"I would feel the same. What would you like to discuss?"

"I have questions, not only about the accident but about my son. What has he been up to? I'm sure you've wondered whether the accident was a random event or something more?"

"I have. I started an investigation to find out, but so far, nothing conclusive has turned up other than confirming that the driver was drunk."

"I know about your investigation. I was going to order one myself, but your secretary, whom I've known for many years, told me that you had that well in hand. She faxed me all their reports and correspondence. I apologize for not asking you directly, but you were unavailable at the time."

"You needn't apologize. It's your company, and Johnny is your son. I probably should have informed you before I started since it will likely prove expensive. In the future, I'll keep you informed."

"Please do, and for now, I wouldn't worry about the expense. It's urgently needed, even if it merely calms our suspicions. On another matter, I have a somewhat delicate question to ask you."

"Ask it."

"Was Johnny seeing anyone?"

"By 'seeing anyone', do you mean romantically seeing someone?"

"Yes."

"I don't know for sure. Normally, he doesn't talk about that part of his life unless it's in crisis, then I hear all about it, but usually after the fact."

John nodded. "The reason I ask is that shortly before the accident, an old acquaintance of mine, Jim Cushman, called me. He has a son about your age."

"James Cushman, the third?"

"That would be the one. He married one of the Duke girls. Casey, I believe. Do you know if Johnny was seeing her?"

"Again, I'm not sure. Coincidentally, she called the office the other day."

I told John about Casey's call, the missing paperwork, and that I'd even gone through Johnny's briefcase, which he'd uncharacteristically left at the office.

"Is that significant?"

"He always takes it with him when he's being chauffeured to catch up on reports."

John looked thoughtful. "Perhaps his travels that night weren't business-related."

"That was my conclusion."

"And likely correct. I asked about my son's love life because Jim Cushman told me that James and Casey were having difficulties and that Johnny had been pursuing Casey, and he was hoping that I might counsel Johnny to leave well enough alone while Casey and his son tried to work things out. I told him that I'd mention it, but the accident intervened."

"I had no idea that Casey was even married, but then again, I've been away so long I've no idea who is married to whom."

"Are you familiar with James?"

"I know who he is. He and Johnny had several clashes. We referred to him somewhat derogatorily as 'the third' since he always added that suffix to his name. I never liked him, but perhaps he's changed. For his sake and for Casey's, I hope so. He had a nasty streak."

"Not unlike his father. My only thought after he hung up was that he must be extremely concerned about his son's marriage to have called me about it. Perhaps it was a warning, and the accident was the consequence?"

"If it was a warning, it wasn't explicit. Just the same, it was while recounting a story about Casey that Johnny twitched. Again, it happened so fast, I can't be sure it really happened."

"That gives a bit more credence to the warning theory. You were telling Johnny a story?"

"I was. Angus suggested it."

"I thought he was in London."

"He swung by the hospital on his way to a conference in Boston. He suggested I tell Johnny stories about our growing up together. He said they might help him recover faster."

"So that's what you do every day when you see him? I had no idea. Perhaps you could tell me a story about him as well? I could surely use one."

"I'm not so sure that's a good idea. Johnny and I have had many adventures, not all of them flattering, and many included you."

John smiled. "That may be, but don't think for a second that I don't have a few of my own. Parenting you two was ... I doubt there's a word in any language that could begin to describe what that was like."

I laughed. "I believe it. I never really thought about parenting until Bruni's pregnancy. It made me wonder how you and Anne managed it. I have no idea what that must have been like. I guess I'm going to find out."

"You will. All I know for certain is that luck had something to do with it ... that and copious amounts of gin."

"I do remember your martinis over ice."

John chuckled. "I drank more than a few because of you two, but life was different back then. Anne and I always tried to walk that fine line between allowing you both too much freedom or too little. In the end, children must find their own way."

John puffed his cigar and continued. "To me, parenting is very much like standing behind a player at a chess match as a grandmaster. One is always tempted to whisper the best move. The child wins, but in the end, where does it lead? They become incapable of thinking for themselves, or they rebel against the constant interference. Children lack experience, and so parents override them as they often must. What is too much, and what is too little? Parenting, like most things, is a learning process on both sides, and one always forgets how smart children can be ... and how stupid. Just the same, I'd like to hear more about my son. I miss him."

"I miss him, too. Those stories I tell him keep him alive in my mind. It's like he's right there with me, and so I miss him less."

"I'd like to hear one then if you don't mind. I really would."

"Very well, I'll think of one over dinner and tell it to you after."

At that moment, Stanley entered and announced that the ladies were waiting for us in the drawing room and that dinner would be served once we joined them.

As we walked out of the library, John said, "Perhaps you could tell that story to Anne as well. I'm sure she'd love to hear it."

"Of course. How could I not?"

12

B runi and Anne were sitting together on the couch, holding hands, when John and I entered. They rose, and Anne said, "Percy, I do apologize for my earlier outburst. Bruni is delightful, and I'm so glad she's here. I feel much better."

"No need to apologize. Please allow me to escort you into dinner."

Stanley stood by the door as we made our way into the dining room. The leaves that extended the dining table had been removed, and what remained was the more intimate setting for four. I seated Anne and then Bruni opposite myself.

The first course was an endive salad with pears, gorgonzola cheese, and walnuts drizzled with a tangy dressing. Stanley poured a cold Sancerre for each of us. This was followed by roast lamb with mint sauce, roasted potatoes, and a puree of peas. Stanley had decanted a Pétrus, which he served with the lamb. The conversation was sporadic and sparse, mostly because our attention was on what we were eating.

After a dessert of Dagmar's signature pound cake and homemade vanilla ice cream, John asked, "Anne, did you know that Percy tells Johnny stories of their growing up together when he visits him? Angus recommended that he do so when he stopped by on his way to Boston."

Anne looked up, surprised. "Angus has seen Johnny? Is that right, Percy?"

"That's correct. He wanted to review Johnny's case. Besides, my future father-in-law was most insistent."

I looked across at Bruni.

Bruni smiled and said, "Papa is quite concerned about the wedding, which he reminded me has a time limit, and frankly, I'd rather not have the baby in the middle of the ceremony either. He prodded Angus to have a look at Johnny in person to see if his recovery could be speeded up."

Anne played with her spoon and asked, "So what did Angus say are the chances of that happening?"

I gave up searching my plate for more dessert and said, "Angus told me that all that could be done medically was being done and that I should tell Johnny stories about our growing up together to help him connect to his long-term memories. Apparently, this has helped others in his situation, and in keeping with that, I tell Johnny a story most visits. We've had many adventures together, so it isn't too hard to come up with one. I suppose it's been more of a help to me at this point. I find I miss him less since he's almost always on my mind throughout the day. I mentioned this to John and promised to tell him one. He thought you might like to hear it, too. Would you like that?"

"I would, but then I might turn into a puddle again—something I've been doing far too much of lately. Let me think on it."

"Of course, I also thought that I might tell it in the library while we have an after-dinner drink."

Bruni said, "That's a great idea. I love ancient brandy and a good tale. Come on, Anne, we get to sally into male territory for once. It'll do us both a world of good."

"Well, I suppose, but it can't be a sad story."

"Johnny and I don't do sad stories. Excruciating, embarrassing, and somewhat humorous? Yes, absolutely. Sad? Not possible."

"I'm halfway convinced, but tell me, does thinking about him all the time really help? I do it too, and look where it's got me."

"It has helped me, I think. I miss him, of course. Johnny is Johnny, but I know what he would say if he were there beside me, and his words, even if imaginary, help me through each day.

Johnny's always frowned on my dark thoughts. He thinks I'm being overly self-indulgent when I go there. I hear him tell me to knock it off, and the odd thing is … I listen to him, and because I do, I manage to quit that dark place. It's how I live. I can't get him out of my head, and believe me, I've tried."

"He talks to you?"

"He does, indeed."

"Well then, I'd like to hear a story about him, if only to hear what it is he said, but if I cry in the middle, you'll have to ignore me."

Bruni piped in, "Not to worry. I have hankies enough for both of us."

——◆——

13

W e gathered in the library. John got himself a whiskey while I poured the ladies and myself a brandy.

After I handed them each a snifter, Bruni said, "Come, Anne. Let's grab these armchairs and have a smoke."

They seated themselves, lit cigarettes, sipped their brandy, and relaxed. Bruni leaned over and whispered to Anne, "Now we know why the men always head to the library after dinner."

Anne took another sip of her brandy and said, "I see what you mean. We may have to make some adjustments. I'm sure that between the two of us we can manage it."

John and I smiled; at least, I hoped it was a smile.

John said, "Well, Percy? It seems our secret's out. You'd better hurry with that story."

"Most definitely, but before I begin, I'd like to ask each of you what kind of story you would like to hear. That may sound strange, but it's difficult to choose from among so many. Anne? How about I start with you?"

"Well, Percy, gathering the four of us in the library has lifted my spirits considerably, and since you're taking requests, I wouldn't mind finding out what happened to Mrs. Spence. You do remember her, yes?"

"Mrs. Spence, the nanny?"

"That would be her. I thought she had such potential when she was hired, and then she just up and left without a word. It was such a mystery to me at the time, and I still don't know what happened. Perhaps you can start with her."

"I will. John? How about you?"

"You mentioned earlier that you and Johnny knew James Cushman. I'd like to hear about him."

Anne looked surprised. "James Cushman? Peggy's son?"

"The very same," said John.

"Odd that you mention him. I had a call from Peggy a few weeks back, but then the accident happened, and I forgot all about it. She said that her son's marriage was a wreck because of what Johnny was doing with his wife, Casey. She gave me quite an earful, but I told her that the situation was only half as monstrous and traumatizing as she made it out to be. Helen was always 'seeing' someone else, and Casey is obviously following in her mother's footsteps. The good news is that in the end, Helen and Ambrose worked it out, and since it seems to run in the family, James and Casey will likely do the same."

"What?" exclaimed John. "You must be joking."

Anne laughed. "Not at all. We all have our stories, even me, and given that, I think we ought to do this kind of thing more often. That way, we both get the scoop about what's really going on a great deal sooner."

John nodded and smiled at Anne. "I think we should. I had no idea about Helen. I hardly know what to say."

"Well, there's more to tell if you're interested, but maybe not now. I must admit, I do love a good gossip, and by the way, Percy, this brandy is excellent. Maybe not as good as the one we drank the night your father exited this world, but really good. I'm sorry if we're straying too far afield. You were about to ask Bruni what she might like to hear."

"I was. Bruni?"

"I want to know more about Alice. I'd love a story about her."

"I'm afraid there's not much to tell from my end other than that I idolized her. I was far too young, but John might have a tale or two since they were siblings. John?"

"More than one or two, but going back to what you were saying, Anne, I had a call from Jim Cushman as well. He went on in the same vein."

Anne looked thoughtful. "The Cushmans really are displeased. Likely, there's more to it then. Each of us seems to know part of the story but not the complete picture. We must pool our knowledge. You and I will talk about this later tonight, but for now, let's move on. Percy, you have the floor starting with Mrs. Spence."

14

"Very well. I'll begin by saying it was Johnny's idea, not mine. I want to make that clear from the start."

"This should be good," said Bruni.

I looked at her for a long moment, and she said no more.

"We were eleven," I continued, "Alice had died the year before, and we were getting familiar with a new governess: Mrs. Spence. She was one of those women who went by Mrs. but arrived without a husband. She was middle-aged and of moderate build. I noted at once that her scrupulous politeness carried a steely edge, likely honed from long practice looking after juvenile delinquents. She also had a mustache whose overt display stunned both Johnny and me into open-mouthed wonder when we were introduced. We could only nod as we shook her hand and tried not to stare. The soft, dark fuzz on her upper lip wiggled like a caterpillar whenever she spoke. I couldn't take my eyes off it."

Bruni giggled. John looked amused, and Anne said, "I forgot about that. I remember hoping that you both wouldn't notice, but then you couldn't really miss it, could you?"

"Not really," I said.

"Even before we arrived at Rhinebeck for that spring vacation, Johnny and I had concluded that Mrs. Spence was unusual. In only a week, she'd managed to curtail our freedoms sufficiently to allow no time for mischief. Instead, we found ourselves playing board games, doing homework, or reading. We had tried to resist, but she always managed to gain the upper hand. It was an extraordinary achievement. By the end of the second week and our third game of

Monopoly, Johnny and I decided that enough was enough. It was time we took up the tattered flag of freedom if only to recover our self-respect."

I sipped my brandy and looked at John, Bruni, and Anne. Each of them had settled in to listen.

I took a puff of my cigar and went on. "To do that, we needed a plan, and not just any plan would do. She was that good. Johnny speculated that Mrs. Spence must have stepped down from a position of some authority—a reduction in status that she often regretted and whose loss precipitated her tendency to dominate those in her charge. He suggested we make her feel more at home to ease her aggression while we probed for possible weaknesses.

"I agreed. Johnny was always my superior in the subtle art of manipulating and persuading those who held sway over our lives. Nonetheless, I was still a keen student of the game. I watched every thrust and parry between Mrs. Spence and Johnny. Even Johnny had found her a worthy adversary and said so. I concluded that Mrs. Spence was better than good, almost superhuman, and certainly the best the adult contingent had fielded so far."

Anne interrupted. "Wait a minute. The adult contingent? Are you referring to John and myself?"

"Most certainly. To Johnny and me, there were two teams: *us* and *them*. Everyone who was taller or older than us was *them* and referred to as the adult contingent. You and John were 'the parents' and the captains. This configuration gave structure to our world. Your function was to constrain us, while ours was to test the suppleness of those constraints. Invariably, Johnny and I found that it was at the edges of what was permitted that we experienced the most adventure and the greatest amount of intellectual stimulation. Now, interrupt me if you wish, but realize that I've barely started the story."

"Well, I suppose I'll have to keep my peace, but really, Percy, we were always on your side."

"Of course you were, but you were also taller, bigger, and older. You had us at a disadvantage. We, on the other hand, were small and quick, like field mice living among cats. We loved you, but that didn't make the circumstances any different. Besides, the idea of 'us against them' cemented our friendship like nothing else."

"The enemy of my enemy is my friend," said Bruni.

"Precisely," I said.

John laughed. His eyes sparkled as he said, "I find this fascinating. Who knew? Please, continue."

Anne harrumphed and said, "This isn't quite what I expected, but do go on. I'll try to keep quiet."

"If you would. To continue, by the time we arrived at Rhinebeck, the war of wills had escalated to a feverish pitch. Johnny had finally admitted that other than Alice, Mrs. Spence had no equal. He even went so far as to suggest that Mrs. Spence's skill at controlling us was unnatural, bordering on the clairvoyant. To him, it smacked of dark and mysterious forces. If we were to have even the slimmest hope of victory, then new tactics and more potent methods were needed."

I relit my cigar as I collected my thoughts.

"The possibility that Mrs. Spence practiced the dark arts was discussed from the first week of her tenure. It started as a mutual feeling, grew into shared suspicions, and matured into a baffling certainty. To us, it was the only explanation. Johnny grew more and more irate. He said that such questionable tactics were contrary to the rules of fair play, and given that and his outrage, he felt justified in introducing equally mysterious weaponry in the form of a Ouija board."

Anne interrupted. "I'm sorry, Percy. You used a Ouija board? Here? At Rhinebeck?"

"I'll get to that, but to answer your question, yes, we did."

"Well, the house is still standing, so I'll let you finish, but Good Heavens, Percy! What were you both thinking? All I can say is we should have kept a much closer eye on you."

"I believe that's why you hired Mrs. Spence."

Anne shifted in her chair. "Well, be that as it may … go on."

"As we weighed its pros and cons, I remember Johnny saying, 'You know, Percy, the grounds of Rhinebeck might offer a tactical advantage. We should unleash it there over spring vacation. Besides, the spirits that inhabit the place might hear us and come to our aid.'

"I concurred wholeheartedly for once, exclaiming that fire must be fought with fire. I'd been devouring too much Tolkien at the time, reading being one of Mrs. Spence's permitted activities, and that may have explained my overly enthusiastic agreement. Under other circumstances, I might have argued against such a plan, but the rings of elven kings held sway over my mind, and I felt in my heart that what couldn't be overcome in reality might yield to something more transcendental and arcane if given a chance. In the end, I thought it worth a shot.

"In spite of its potential for unlocking her secrets, Johnny and I thought that simply using a Ouija board held no guarantee of success. What we needed was a multi-tiered approach.

"If Mrs. Spence used dark methods, then she must have come by them in some way. Both of us had studied Sun Tzu and felt that the oriental scholar, although not in the same league as Alexander, Napoleon, Suvorov, or Patton, had at least grasped the essentials of warfare and that his emphasis on actionable intelligence was compelling. We tried to find out more about her by first asking you, Anne."

"Yes, I do recall that conversation."

"You answered that Mrs. Spence was utterly marvelous and that she came highly recommended, having guided the Johnson twins successfully off to Andover, where they were happy and doing very well. Johnny and I didn't doubt their happiness. Of course they were happy. They were finally rid of her. We also asked you, John, but you told us to speak to Anne. That left Mrs. Spence herself as the only available source of information.

"I thought to start by asking her about her childhood, but my queries were met with skillful parries.

" 'When I was a child,' she'd say and then hesitate. 'Well, children each develop differently, but in the end, they become adults, the summation of their genetic makeup and the quality of their upbringing. Which do you think is ultimately more important?'

"She turned our questions into her questions and frustrated my efforts time and again.

"The day before we traveled to Rhinebeck, Johnny and I held a hasty conference while Mrs. Spence was occupied in the bathroom. I proposed that we investigate what she packed with her since it might point to what was important and necessary to her well-being. Johnny distilled this down to its essentials.

" 'In other words,' he said, 'we toss her stuff. Now, that's more like it. You distract her, and I'll reconnoiter.' "

"Really, Percy," said Anne. "Johnny didn't actually say that, did he?"

"He did. I'd floated the idea as a mere intellectual exercise, but I, too, felt stymied in my sincere attempts to understand her. She was reticent about herself to such a degree that I felt she must be hiding something. I even questioned whether she was, in fact, a woman. A speculation that brought all our activity to a standstill when I voiced it."

Anne interrupted. "How could you possibly have thought that?"

"She had a strong masculine side. Besides, she sported a mustache. What else was I to think?"

"You have a point. Go on."

"Johnny was in awe of the possibility and asked, 'Do you really think so?'

" 'I don't know,' I said, 'but there's only one way to find out.'

"Johnny exclaimed, 'Good God, Percy! What's gotten into you? Do you want us to open the door when she's in the bathroom?' Johnny was shocked.

" 'Absolutely not,' I answered quickly. 'Just keep the possibility in mind as you go through her stuff. To answer your other question, I have no idea what's come over me, but I'm convinced that we really need to check her out.'

"With this new turn, the war of wills had escalated well beyond anything we had experienced before. We were about to break the most sacrosanct rule of the game. Going through her personal belongings was not only immoral and underhanded but carried potential penalties and consequences too horrible to imagine.

"The morning of our arrival at Rhinebeck, I whispered to Johnny, 'Just be careful and *do not* underestimate her. She may use all sorts of tricks to know if anything's been rifled.'

" 'Percy, I'll be damned careful. I'll even check for hairs on the closet door.' Johnny was keen on Ian Fleming. 'But it's absolutely vital that I don't get caught in the act. You must do whatever it takes to keep her occupied.'

"We made a sworn agreement. I would hold her attention while Johnny did the deed.

"Terrain is always a factor in the subtle art of maneuver, and Rhinebeck was perfect. The squeaking stairs on the way up to our common room were a failsafe should Mrs. Spence come upon Johnny unexpectedly. He would have just enough time to hide.

"We were also on familiar ground, which gave us a temporary but significant advantage. The plan was for me to show Mrs. Spence my favorite book in the library as soon as possible, the one that contained hand-painted pictures on velum of the peculiar plants of South America. It was a rare single edition, and the drawings were originals. I thought it might hold her for a while.

"Mrs. Spence had been a little wide-eyed and distracted at the sumptuousness of the Rhinebeck estate. This we'd anticipated, and that morning, I asked Mrs. Spence if I could show her my favorite book in all the world, and she agreed. As we started down the stairs from the common room, Johnny said he had to go to the bathroom and would meet us in the library. Mrs. Spence balked at this, but I countered that I had been dying to show her the book for weeks. Such enthusiasm and her prior agreement to do so couldn't be denied. All went smoothly for the first ten minutes. I had Mrs. Spence beside me in the library with the book open on the desk. I showed her the pictures and asked her help in deciphering the captions laboriously penned in copperplate minuscules.

"I don't know what alerted her, but she suddenly became agitated and said that she had to go upstairs. She knew. I don't know how, but she did. The thought of her bursting in on Johnny ramped up my desperation in a heartbeat. I acted on the first thing that popped into my head. I confessed to Mrs. Spence that I loved her."

"What!"

All my listeners said the word simultaneously. I managed to shush them.

"If I'm completely candid, this wasn't a complete fabrication. I was fascinated by her, but others before me must have tried that ploy because Mrs. Spence looked down at me and said coldly, 'I don't believe you.'

"As she turned to leave, I threw myself on the carpet and grabbed onto her right leg as if to kiss it. She kicked out, but I held on like an oversized mollusk. 'Stop it! Stop it!' she screamed.

"Our struggle was interrupted by Stanley.

"He spoke softly but with as cold an edge as I'd ever heard him speak, 'What exactly are you doing with that child?'

"I still had hold of her leg.

" 'Don't just stand there, you idiot! Get him off me!' screamed Mrs. Spence.

"Stanley didn't move but asked in the same chilling voice, 'How exactly did he get there?'

"Johnny entered at that moment and called out, 'Mrs. Spence! What are you doing to Percy?'

"She gave a heave to her leg just as I let go, and she almost fell over. She was breathing heavily.

" 'You haven't heard the last of this!' she yelled as she stormed out the door.

"None of us were sure what she meant by that remark, including Stanley.

" 'She seems a bit of a hard case,' was his only comment. He turned to leave, stopped, and turned back. Looking at me, he said, 'I'm surprised you found that book. Leave it on the desk when you're finished. I'll put it away for safekeeping.'

"After Stanley closed the door, Johnny asked, 'Whatever were you doing with Mrs. Spence?'

" 'Long story,' I said. 'I just hope I bought you enough time.'

" 'You did, and you were correct. She's hiding something all right. I'll tell you about it in a minute. Let's find a quiet place away from here.'

"Johnny opened one of the French doors of the library and slipped onto the south lawn. I followed. He made for the hidden cathedral inside the Cyprus trees at the lawn's eastern edge. We couldn't be seen from the house, and if Mrs. Spence came looking for us, we had an escape route of sorts.

" 'What did you find out?' I asked as we hunkered down inside the trees.

" 'You were right. She booby-trapped the place. For a start, she left her door closed but only partially latched. The latch bolt is spring-loaded and normally clicks into place, but she had the bolt just resting on the plate. Touch the door, and the bolt would seat completely. I noted the setup but didn't think much of it until I made my discovery. On my way out, I configured the door exactly the way she'd left it. I was getting panicky by then, and it took me several attempts to get it right.'

" 'Did you find out if she's a man?' I asked.

" 'I didn't have time for that, but you're definitely right about one thing. She's up to something. Now let me finish.'

75

" 'Okay,' I said, 'But hurry up.' I knew Mrs. Spence would be on the warpath and searching for us in no time. We were once again on dangerous ground.

"Johnny continued, 'Okay. Once I was in her room, I stood in the center and looked about. Everything was ultra-neat and put away as you'd expect. I figured if she'd hidden anything, it would be in an unusual place—maybe between the mattress and the box spring—but I rejected that as too obvious. She's tall, and we aren't, so I figured it must be up high. There's an armoire to the right of the door, and I thought that the top looked promising, only there was no way to get to it without stepping on her bed and wrinkling it. I was sure that was deliberate. I took the desk chair from your room and stood on it. With it, I could just reach the top, but I couldn't see what I was reaching for. I almost went ahead, but something told me not to. Instead, I brought the desk chair from my room and put it on top of yours to take a better look. I'm lucky I did.'

" 'What did you find?' I asked.

" 'Two rat traps, and not your little mousey versions either. These were meant for cats or very large rats. Triggered, either one would have removed several of my fingers. I was so shocked that I almost fell off my tower. I had just managed to steady myself when I noticed a folder underneath. I carefully shifted the traps and peeked inside. It was filled with newspaper and magazine clippings, photographs, and handwritten notes about Aunt Alice! I wanted to read more, but by then, I was shaking. I put the folder back exactly the way I'd found it and put our chairs back the way they were. I rechecked her room to make sure I'd left no traces. I have no idea what she's up to, but those traps tell me she doesn't want anybody reading that folder, not without her knowing. I'm telling you, Percy, the gloves come off. She's bad news.'

"I said, 'I'm scared, Johnny. We should tell someone.'

" 'And who will believe us? Let's leave that for now. Tell me what happened to you.'

"I gave Johnny a blow-by-blow, including the bad part. Johnny stared at me.

" 'Percy, I don't know what to say. You actually said you loved her?'

" 'I know. I know, but she was on to us. She *knew* what you were doing. I don't know how, but I'm telling you she knew. I spat out the first thing I could think of and attached myself firmly to her leg, which I was determined to hold on to until I saw you walk through that door.'

" 'Well, it worked, I'll say that much.' Johnny paused and then asked carefully, 'You don't *really* love her, do you? She has a mustache, for heaven's sake!'

" 'No,' I said. 'Absolutely not! Although I think she's very clever. There's something about her I really like, but the traps have changed my mind. I just hope you left no physical evidence to make her think we planned the whole thing. Her sixth sense is pretty developed, but I can't believe she relies on it exclusively. As for my performance, she might dismiss it as nothing more than childish infatuation—at least, I hope so.'

" 'You did fine. A half-truth that expresses a vulnerability can be a most effective diversion. Well done, Percy. But even if I left no traces, she probably suspects I was up to something and will move that folder.'

" 'Which means it's pointless to tell anyone because there'll be no evidence where we said it would be.'

" 'Exactly.'

" 'What are we going to do?' I asked.

" 'Well, first thing on the agenda is to settle her down, or this vacation will be shot if it hasn't been deep-sixed already.'

"I said, 'I agree, and we should use that Ouija board. It's time to break out the heavy weapons.'

"Johnny considered that and said, 'You're right, of course. We must. The parents will never believe us, and Stanley … well,

Stanley is difficult to approach. He may believe us, but he has no authority over her.'

" 'Do you know how to use one?'

"Johnny nodded and said, 'I read the directions carefully. We rest it on our knees and place our fingers lightly on the planchette, a weird little table thing with a small window. It will move about and spell out words or answer yes or no questions. I think I should do the asking while you take notes. Other than keeping the board clean and free from dust, that's pretty much all it says. I mean, how hard could it be?'

"I thought about that. 'Not that hard, I suppose. Do you think it'll work?'

" 'I hope so. I aim to find out about her past and use that to get rid of her.'

" 'But what if something bad happens?' I asked.

" 'What do you mean?'

" 'You know what I mean. This house is pretty creepy.'

" 'That it may be, but what else are we going to do? We have no choice.'

" 'You're right. I can't think of another solution, but I'm leery.'

" 'Me, too. Do we use it, Percy, or not?'

"That we even considered using a Ouija board at Rhinebeck, of all places, was a measure of our desperation, which was underscored further by Johnny asking me seriously if we should.

"I mulled our predicament over and said at last, 'I'm not sure using a Ouija board is wise. In fact, I'm quite certain it isn't, but I sense in her something evil, and we must take the necessary steps to guard ourselves. Finding out more about her is one. I may not have been certain about using it before, but we have no alternative. So, yes, let's do it.'

" 'Then we're in agreement,' said Johnny. 'We use the board tonight, but we must simmer her down first.'

"We decided to pretend as if nothing unusual had happened and that I act painfully embarrassed as I apologized, a role that I felt was not beyond my capabilities. We went back to the house in search of her. We found Mrs. Spence coming down the main staircase. Before she could say a word, I burst into tears and said I was sorry. I was wound up enough as it was, so the tears flowed easily. Just the same, I had to resist the urge to clasp her legs in supplication.

" 'Stop your crying!' she said to me sternly. 'We'll talk about your behavior later.' And to both of us, 'Let's go back downstairs.'

" 'So far so good,' I thought. Johnny gave me a wink."

15

I looked over my listeners. John was smiling, Anne was frowning, and Bruni was amused. I sipped my drink and relit my cigar.

"And then what happened, Percy? Tell us," said Anne. "I can't believe I'm asking you for more, but then I did ask you to tell the story. Listening to it from a parent's point of view … well, I hardly know whether to laugh or cry."

"Laughter is much preferred, but I'll continue. To use the Ouija, we had to be alone for an hour without Mrs. Spence becoming aware of what we were doing. Our initial thought was to occupy her in some way while we went into Johnny's room and closed the door, but that proved impossible. Mrs. Spence preferred to have the doors open when Johnny and I were together. That way, she could do what she wanted while being able to monitor us. Johnny half-heartedly floated the idea that we all play hide and seek, but Mrs. Spence would have none of it. That left the middle of the night when she was asleep to do the deed. Again, this was harder than it appeared.

"Mrs. Spence slept with her door open. The squeaking stairs, which had been our salvation as an early warning system, now effectively trapped us. Given that, Johnny decided we would have to do it in his room and communicate by either writing notes or using sign language.

"I told him we were already doing that, but he put a hand on my shoulder and said in a normal voice, 'Not for long.'

"Mrs. Spence must have had the auditory acuteness of a Doberman because she asked Johnny from the next room what he meant by his remark. Johnny brazened it out by saying, 'I was talking about our teacher, Mr. Long. It was a joke.'

" 'I see … ' was all she said, but I knew she wasn't fooled. We found ourselves studying next term's lessons shortly thereafter.

"That evening, Johnny slipped me a note as we sat down to dinner. I dropped my napkin and read it: '2 a.m.' I'd grown so jumpy and paranoid by then that I scrunched it up and ate it with dessert."

Bruni and Anne laughed. Bruni asked, "What did it taste like?"

"I can't remember. Dagmar's cooking was always the high point of our days at Rhinebeck, but I have no recollection of what we were served that evening. All I recall was wondering whether the ink had marked my tongue and that Mrs. Spence might see it and interrogate me.

"That night, I'm not sure if I slept at all. I lay in bed watching the small, luminous hands crawl around the face of my alarm clock. At exactly two, I crept out of my bed. I'd left my door unlatched to not make a sound. I slipped past the dark opening of Mrs. Spence's room by sliding my feet along the floor in slow but random movements—my progress lit by moonlight shining through the frosted glass above me.

"Johnny had thoughtfully unlatched his door and was awake. As I started to close it, he motioned for me to stop. He wrote on a piece of paper: *I oiled the hinges and the latch, but we should wait.* He crept to the doorway, listened for a full minute, and then closed it silently.

"We sat cross-legged across from each other on the floor and paused again before Johnny reached under the bed and brought out a candle and the Ouija. He lit the candle, placed it beside us, and set the board on our knees. He placed the planchette in the middle of its smooth surface. We reached out and carefully laid our fingers on it and waited. Johnny had written down several questions in preparation. The list was beside him next to the candle. He looked down and whispered the first question.

" 'Where did Mrs. Spence come from?'

"The planchette didn't budge. He asked again but with the same response. He moved to the next question.

" 'Is Mrs. Spence a criminal?'

"No movement once again. Johnny took a deep breath, closed his eyes, and asked the board, 'What does Mrs. Spence fear most?'

"With that question, I noted a subtle change in the air, like a breath of wind from somewhere behind me. The planchette began to mysteriously move around the board, stopping first above the letter A before moving to the letter L, then I, then C, and finally E. The board had spelled out the word *ALICE*.

"Johnny and I were open-mouthed.

" 'Why does Mrs. Spence fear Alice?' Johnny asked, his voice rising in excitement.

"The candle sizzled. I felt something behind me to the left. I had goosebumps up and down my arms. We looked at each other wide-eyed as the door beside us opened slowly to the darkness beyond. Out of the black appeared Mrs. Spence, wearing a pink bathrobe. She stood silent and unmoving, staring at us for I don't know how long. Time telescoped to an impossible length before she said, 'Both of you back to bed. Lighting candles in the middle of the night is bad enough, but this ... ' She prodded the board with her toe. 'This is monstrous ... I will inform your parents.' She reached down and lifted the board up by a corner like it was a dead rat, holding it away from her. She tried the light switch with her other hand. She threw the switch several times. Nothing. She stooped once again and picked up the candle only to notice the list of questions Johnny had written out. She put down the candle and slipped Johnny's notes and the planchette into her pocket before picking up the candle again.

" 'Out!' she said to me. I scurried across the common room, slammed my door, and jumped under the covers, not daring to look behind me. I lay there trembling, wondering what was going to happen. I was quite sure that my worst fears were now justified. Johnny would be sent to boarding school, and I would be delivered to an orphanage. Both our lives were in ruins. We were in so much trouble."

"Surely you didn't think we'd send you to an orphanage. How could you possibly think that we would?" interrupted Anne.

"The world of a child is underscored by odd and irrational moments, Anne. Fear ruled my life. At least, that's the way it was for me. I had no compass and no direction. Johnny was those things for me. Without him, I would have been lost."

"I'm so sorry, Percy. We never knew."

"Of course you didn't. I never said, so how could you? Besides, I couldn't have told you anyway. To have voiced what I felt would have opened too big a door. I can talk about it now because the period we're speaking about happened long ago. At the time, there was nothing you, or anyone, could have done. Johnny never asked about the terrors that I felt. He simply made me look on the bright side. He always did that, and that's what saved me."

"Well, I suppose I feel better, but still, I'm shocked." Anne took a sip of brandy and said, "And then what happened?"

"The night grew stranger still. The world seemed frozen as if waiting. For what? I couldn't say, but in the midst of that, I fell asleep. I awoke to my alarm clock ringing by my ear. Johnny and I met in the bathroom. Mrs. Spence's door was shut. By the time we were dressed and ready to go down to breakfast, she still hadn't made an appearance. Johnny muttered that it was best to let sleeping dogs lie. I heartily agreed. I was jumpy and out of sorts as we made our way to the dining room. Thoughts of our pending doom slithered through my mind. You and John were due to arrive that afternoon, and with your arrival, our fates would be decided and sealed.

"At breakfast, I asked Johnny what happened after I was sent to my room. He told me that Mrs. Spence pulled the door shut with her foot as she left with the Ouija in one hand and the candle in the other, and that was all. Then he waited, but for what he couldn't say. He was expecting something to happen, but like me, he'd fallen asleep.

"As we ate our oatmeal, Dagmar came out of the kitchen. Seeing only the two of us, she asked, 'Where's the new governess?'

" 'Upstairs.' Johnny said.

"She looked at us more closely and said, 'Come. Come. It's a beautiful day. Why so glum?'

"Before we could answer, we heard the dining room door open. Johnny and I turned, and Mrs. Spence wandered in wearing nothing but her pink robe—open at the front. It hung about her shoulders like a cape with the belt dangling from a single loop as it dragged behind her like a tail. She looked dazed like she didn't know where she was.

" 'My, my … ' was Dagmar's only comment as she went up to Mrs. Spence, put Mrs. Spence's arms through the appropriate holes, closed the front of the robe, did her belt up after threading it through the loops, and led Mrs. Spence away. The dining room door clicked shut behind them.

"Johnny and I just gaped until Johnny said, 'Well, Percy? One thing is certain. Mrs. Spence is definitely not a man.'

"I nodded in agreement. We continued eating our oatmeal. We had no idea what to do, but breakfast at Rhinebeck has always held a charm, and the oatmeal was beyond description. We were almost finished when Stanley came in through the dining room door and stood looking at us. We put down our spoons. He had our attention.

" 'Dagmar is looking after Mrs. Spence. That woman won't be with us much longer. Perhaps an hour at most. Harry will put her on the train. If you thought there was something wrong with your governess, you should have told someone. Anyone. Secondly, it is not my place to instruct you, but I must ask, whatever were you both thinking? Do *not* use such methods here. You both know what I'm talking about. Do we understand each other?'

"We said we did.

" 'Very well. It's a beautiful day. Boys belong outside. Lunch is at noon. Now, off you go. I don't want to see either of you until then.'

"After giving us a no-nonsense look, Stanley ghosted back to the kitchen, and off we went.

"Later that morning, sitting among the Cyprus trees, we speculated endlessly as to what happened to Mrs. Spence. Johnny mentioned that the light switch worked fine in the morning. We didn't know what to make of that. Our only conclusion was that we must have fallen asleep during the good part. On the bright side, no governess ever survived more than a single visit to Rhinebeck. Our solution, therefore, was simple. If we didn't like our governess, we'd bring her here. Rhinebeck would do the rest.

"And that's the story of Mrs. Spence."

"So, Mrs. Spence went off by train," said Anne.

"That's what Stanley told us. By the time you and John arrived, she was thankfully gone."

Anne nodded. "I do recall Stanley telling me that she'd left and that he'd paid her what was owed out of the cash box. I asked him what happened, and he simply replied that she wasn't suitable. Since I was already a little sensitive about my previous choices of nannies, I let the matter drop. At least I know more now than I did, so thank you for the story. It's still disturbing, which is likely why Stanley kept the details to the absolute minimum. Perhaps a lighter one next time. This one left me a little uneasy."

"Okay, the next one will be lighter. Any questions?"

Bruni asked, "What do you think happened to her that night?"

"It's a mystery. Johnny and I hypothesized that after she sent us to bed, she used the Ouija herself. What happened exactly and how, I can't say."

Bruni nodded and said, "I see, and speaking of nannies, we're going to need one fairly soon. What'll we do then?"

Anne leaned forward and patted Bruni on the knee. "Not to worry, I'm an expert on the subject. I'll help, as will we all. Now, I want another story and a little more to drink, but not too much."

John got up to refill Anne's glass and said to Bruni, "And that help includes Percy, myself, Stanley, Dagmar, and your parents. You'll have all the help you need—probably too much. You'll have to beat us off with a club. Now, how about James Cushman, Percy?"

I smiled. "To portray how the rivalry between Johnny and James started and developed will require more than one story. Tomorrow is Thursday, and I must be at the office at the crack of dawn. I propose we have dinner early and that I tell the stories after. Bruni, you should sleep in rather than accompany me, work permitting."

Bruni considered my suggestion and said, "I'll do that, but it's not too late. Perhaps, John, you could tell one about Alice before we retire? That way, we get another story and leave the others until tomorrow. What does everyone think?"

John said, "I can tell you one. Anne, how about you? Would you like that?"

"You haven't told me a bedtime story in a long time. I quite agree, and if I get scared, you'll just have to hug me all night long."

"I can do that, too," said John, smiling.

J ohn puffed his cigar to collect his thoughts before he said, "To begin, growing up with Alice as an older sister was not easy. We were very different, for a start. Our mothers were diametric opposites. Maw is hardheaded, practical, independent, and a force to be reckoned with. Eleanor, Alice's mother, was none of these. She was extraordinarily impractical, frivolous, and in need of constant social interactions to make her feel alive. My father allowed her free rein in this. He found it impossible to say no to her. She, too, had a power but very different from my mother's. She had a mystical side that was as alluring as it was persuasive. This facet of her personality, I'm quite sure, passed to Alice.

"One night, not long before he died, my father invited me to have a talk. He and Maw had been divorced for some time, and we were alone together. Normally, when he and I sat down, we would discuss prevailing business conditions and the potential opportunities they presented. We rarely discussed personal matters, but not this time. He wanted to talk about Alice.

"My father knew that Alice and I could get very angry with each other and that we would do so often. This upset him for two reasons. The first was that we were family regardless of having separate mothers, and the second was that Alice was special—and to have a care."

John sipped his drink before he continued.

"My father told me that Eleanor had cast a spell on him and that mother and daughter were alike in this. He thought I might take that into consideration the next time I decided to incense my sister.

"I asked him how he knew this, and he replied, 'Eleanor told me.'

" 'And you believed her?'

"My father nodded and said, 'If Alice said she'd put a spell on you, would you believe her?'

"I didn't believe in any of that, at least not then, but if there was a person who could, Alice was that person. She had a way about her, and so I understood him.

"My father continued and told me that at the beginning of Eleanor's and his relationship, they had attended a white-tie New Year's Eve party, and as they danced in each other's arms, Eleanor related a dream she had when she was a child. My father commented that a New Year's Eve party was hardly the venue for such a revelation, but he let her continue.

"My father thought for a moment and then said to me, 'We were mid a waltz—Straus, I think. In her dream, Eleanor said that she'd seen a book, and in that book, at the bottom of the page, was written her name and another's underneath. As the music ended, Eleanor whispered that we would have a daughter and that her name would be Alice.' My father said that he laughed.

"He looked at me for a moment and remarked, 'I thought it was a joke, you see? After all, we had only been recently introduced. I thought to play along and told her, "But I need a son, for heaven's sake!" Eleanor smiled in that special way of hers, and at the first stroke of midnight, she spoke in a voice so low I could barely catch it: "You will—but not with me." My reaction was hidden by falling balloons and confetti. I remember reeling as if someone had walked over my grave, and I stumbled. Eleanor caught me, and as she held me, she kissed me. She kissed me in a way I'd never been kissed before, and I knew then that I was hers. We married and had our time together, but some years later, Eleanor grew ill and wished to live alone. She divorced me, and shortly after, she died. I've often wondered whether the divorce was intended to make her death easier for me to bear. I believe that was her intention. She was wise in many things, but her passing still affected me deeply. I would remember that kiss. The moment never ended for me, and perhaps it never will. Over time, I recovered, fell in love again, married your mother, and you were born. I had a son, just like she said, and now you know why I believed her when she said she'd laid a spell on me.'

"There was little I could say to that. After our talk, my attitude toward Alice changed. I became more wary of her, less contentious, and more observant of the things she did. It was not that she scared me. She was my sister, but I now sensed within her a power that was desperate to get out and that she held it back lest it become unleashed and roam about unchecked."

John relit his cigar.

"My father never told me what spell Eleanor had cast on him. Perhaps it was merely that he would fall in love with her, but all women have that skill, and some men, too. That she told him what would happen must have impressed him after it did.

"Foreknowledge has always intrigued me. Those of us in finance would pay almost anything for such an ability, provided it was true. Some doubt it exists at all, but I think it does. Those who possess it can never seem to profit personally from it. I don't know why that is, but I saw it in my sister. She never profited from her gift, and I think that's true of all who really have it.

"After our father's death, I told Alice what I've just told you. She said she knew what her mother had spoken about. The gift had passed to her and was difficult to manage. It wearied her. We made a new beginning after that. I agreed to help oversee her investments, and she agreed to help connect me with those she knew. It worked for both of us.

"One evening, shortly before her death, Alice and I met for dinner in London at the Connaught. We talked about our lives together. Over coffee, she said that at beginnings, we look forward, and at endings, we look back. I think she knew her time was short. As she put her cup down, she said, 'Strip away the face in the mirror, the body that we know, our sensations, our feelings and beliefs, our stories, our opinions, our obligations, our thoughts, all we love, all we hate, all we think we know, and what is left? Those who are truly holy are comfortable in that place. They glow with the light of their own being, ready for anything. I'm not comfortable there. I never seem to have enough time to do all that I must, but that's the way it is, not just for me but for most of us.'

"I asked if she was ill. She nodded slowly and said she was, but not to be concerned. 'The Wise promise that death is not the end, and I agree, but please note, they never say *how* it is we'll live again. I've seen a few of the other universes superimposed on this one. Alternatives exist, and not all of them are happy. What do you say we keep in touch after I'm gone?'

"I agreed.

"I took it as a bit of humor, but she was serious … I think. And now we come to the story I wish to tell you."

18

"Sometime after Alice's death, there was a series of incidents that took place in front of the New York apartment building on Fifth Avenue and not at Rhinebeck at all.

"In those days, I kept a strict routine. I would arrive home from Dodge Capital every weekday evening at 6:00 p.m. Raymond would pick me up and drop me off. On one such occasion, there was a large black cat sitting on its haunches to the left of the entrance. It sat immobile as a sphinx and followed my movements with pale yellow eyes as I entered the building. I stared at it as I passed and noted its unusual size, its piercing eyes, and the shiny blackness of its coat. I expected Carl, the doorman, to make a comment, but he greeted me normally. He mustn't have seen it. After all, one rarely sees loose cats on the streets of New York— least of all on Fifth Avenue.

"The next morning, on the way to the office, I asked Raymond about it. He looked back at me in the rearview mirror and scowled. He said it was the biggest damn cat he'd ever seen. The city was obviously going to the dogs. He laughed at his joke, and I knew the cat was not my imagination.

"That evening, and for the next several, the cat was there to greet me.

"Eventually, I asked Carl if he knew whose cat it was that was always there when I arrived. He said that he wasn't aware of any cat hanging about. He added that if there was one, he'd have shooed it off. Loose cats, dogs, rats, or kangaroos, it didn't matter; they weren't allowed near the building, least of all at the entrance. They made messes, and he was the one who had to see that they were cleaned up.

"The regular appearance of the cat puzzled me. I wondered if it showed up only at a fixed time of the day or solely when I arrived. I varied my routine to find out, but no matter the time, the cat would peer out from the bushes that lined the edge of the building and watch me. I even went so far as to return one morning at eleven, but the cat was there. It followed my movements with its yellow, almond eyes and yawned, amused perhaps by my antics.

"After that, I tried to point out the cat to Carl, but the creature would invariably make a fool of me by slinking off before it could be seen.

"Of course, my thoughts turned to Alice and her little joke about keeping in touch, and that disturbed me. If the cat was a message from my sister, then I'd certainly received it, and given that, how much longer would this little game of hers continue? I wondered what I would do if the cat became aggressive. I know that seems unlikely, but if you'd seen the size of it and experienced the unworldliness of the situation, you'd have had similar thoughts. It shouldn't have been doing what it was doing—waiting and watching me. I grew apprehensive and even a little fearful.

"Raymond and I fell into a routine. Raymond would stop in front of the building, get out to open the car door, and report whether the cat was there. Invariably, it was, and that began to irk him.

"Raymond has a belligerent and aggressive nature. He takes security seriously and is always suspicious of anything unusual. Any threat to me, even a passive one, he feels obliged to handle, and the situation with the cat was becoming most peculiar. Each day, Raymond asked that he be allowed to get rid of it, and each time, I told him no.

"The appearance of the cat was troubling, but it gave me comfort. It spoke to me of wonderful things, magical things, things beyond my understanding. I've always wanted to believe in miracles. I didn't need the actuality, only the possibility, and with it, the hope that life was more than just existence. The cat was like an invitation to another world, and I found myself tempted to accept. On the other hand, if I allowed Raymond free rein, the peculiar connection with my sister would disappear along with the invitation. I didn't want that, but then again, I did. My world, the world in which I lived, had become unstable. I'd grown indecisive and uncertain in my business. I didn't know what to do anymore, and everything I'd built began to sway. In the end, I couldn't allow my world to topple over. Too many others depended on me. After one particularly horrible, annoying, and difficult day, I told Raymond to deal with the creature in any way he wished.

"That next evening, as we drove home, Raymond assured me that the cat problem had been dealt with. When we arrived, he whipped open the door and croaked that the cat was still there. He asked me what I wanted him to do. I told him to ignore it, and I stepped out to see for myself. Sure enough, the cat was there, only this time, it hissed and bared its fangs. It gave out a sound halfway between a growl and a cry before it slunk off into the bushes. It had never done that.

"The morning after, Raymond asked whether I had any enemies he didn't know about because somebody was working something with that cat. He grumbled that the situation was getting spooky and promised that next time, he'd use a silver bullet dipped in holy water to make sure there were no future resurrections.

"That evening, to our surprise, no cat appeared. Nor was it there the next. For the following month, I would arrive at the building filled with apprehension, and each time, I'd breathe a sigh of relief when I didn't see it. Raymond felt the same. After many more months, we no longer looked for it, and Raymond told me that it was all an odd coincidence.

"Since then, I've asked myself many times if it was just a cat or something more. Raymond is sure that's all it was, although he can't explain how it showed up that one last time. When I asked him about it the other day, he told me not to be concerned. He always carries that silver bullet with him … just in case.

"So far, the cat has never returned, and that's the end of my story."

"Thank you for telling us," said Bruni. "It's a most unusual tale. Do you think it really was a message from Alice?"

"I don't know. As with all things concerning Alice, anything is possible. Each of us has witnessed the unusual when it comes to her, not the least being Bromley's death in front of us all. Given that, I wouldn't put it past her."

"Did Raymond kill it?" Bruni asked.

"I'm quite sure he did, although I don't know how. I never ask for details. It's how we work together."

Bruni said, "Papa told me that he does the same with Gustav."

"Hugo has told me that as well."

Bruni sat forward and said, "One last question: If the cat was sent by Alice, what was the message?"

"If it really was a message, then I think she tried to convey to me the idea that death is not the end. That may or may not be the truth, but that interpretation is at least hopeful and what I've come to believe, given all I've seen. At my age, I get to choose. It's one of the little perks that life bestows on those who manage to live long enough. I might also add that Alice loved to poke fun at my stuffiness and conservatism. Both were addressed like an inside joke, so it's possible Alice had a hand. I suppose I'll have to ask her at some point. Who knows if she'll answer, but I wouldn't put it past her. Frankly, I shudder to think in what manner she might do that."

We all laughed. Anne finished her drink and said, "I quite agree, and for a person who's gone, she's certainly about. If I ever get the chance, I must thank her. She always gives me hope. Johnny, on the other hand, seems to be doing quite the opposite. He's about but gone for now. Is that not correct, John?"

"It is, I think."

"I may sound terribly naive, but I now feel in my heart as if Alice is aware of what's happened and that she wants me to stop my worrying. Johnny's not in any immediate danger but in a kind of limbo. It may not be true, but I feel better believing that, and as you said, John, we *can* choose what we wish to believe. Somehow, that thought has allowed me to find my way back. I was in a very dark place—but no longer."

Anne stood and said, "Now, unless there are more questions, I think it's time for bed. Thank you, John, and thank you, Percy, for the stories. It amazes me that after all our years together, there are still things we don't know about each other. I can hardly believe it. On another matter, I must apologize to everyone here, and to you, John, most of all, for what I was only a few hours ago. I'm better now, and because I am, I know that Johnny can recover. I have no idea how, but I'm certain that he will. So, thank you all for this time together."

We stood and hugged her. I was thrilled that Anne was her old self once again.

After John and Anne went upstairs, Bruni and I strolled down the hall toward our bedroom with our arms around each other's waists.

Bruni murmured, "You and Johnny were so close growing up. Do you think we'll ever be that close?"

"In many ways, we already are. There is both love and great trust between us."

"There is, and I know how truly rare that is. To love and not to trust is a most horrible dilemma. I think that's what Alice must have experienced with your father."

"Yes, I quite agree." I sensed that Bruni had experienced that as well and asked, "Did that happen to you?"

As we reached our door, Bruni said, "It did with Bernard. Now, you must help me out of my things and speak with Dagmar and Stanley while I sleep. Like you said, we need a plan, and not just any plan will do."

19

I put Bruni to bed and made my way to the kitchen. I wondered what Dagmar and Stanley might suggest. I was desperate for a solution, but I doubted I had the nerve to spoon a drop of some concoction between Johnny's lips and stand back to see what happened. Extraordinary solutions, I'd found, created as many problems as they solved and in this instance, might even kill him. What then? The impact of such a mishap would be far-reaching and cataclysmic. I wasn't so rash, but I could feel my desperation rising. As day followed day, and days turned into weeks, the impulse to try every possible remedy would only grow until that last untried remedy remained, and then what? I didn't know and prayed it wouldn't come to that.

I found both of them waiting at Dagmar's table.

I said, "I apologize if I've kept you both up."

They stood, and Stanley said, "It's no matter. Without hearing about Johnny, we couldn't have slept anyway. Some tea?"

I nodded. Dagmar set out a service for the three of us, and we sat down.

Dagmar looked at me steadily and said, "Thank you for taking the time to speak to us. Please tell us in detail what happened with Johnny and where things stand as of this moment. Omit as little as possible since what may seem of little consequence may be vitally important when seen from another's point of view."

I went over all that had happened since that phone call in the middle of the night, including Angus's suggestion, the stories I'd shared, the twitch, the investigation, Anne's recovery, my hesitation at administering an untried remedy, and my fear that in the end, it would become necessary. I told them all I could.

As I spoke, they sipped their tea and listened with attention. Only rarely had I felt Dagmar's familiar warmth replaced by the icy coldness of her intellect. As I spoke, I noted how well she kept that part of herself hidden and that she and Stanley were eerily similar.

When I finished, Dagmar held me in her gaze and said, "Thank you for telling us all you have. I have some questions and some comments. I'm sure Stan has a few as well. For a start, the brain is not the only part of you that thinks. Other organs do as well. Right now, I'd like you to sip your tea and relax for a moment. When you're calm and at ease, simply summarize what you feel is happening with Johnny with as little conscious thought as possible."

It was an unusual request, but I did as she asked. When I felt settled and relaxed, I said, "Johnny's lost and can't find his way back to us."

Dagmar considered my answer and said, "That would make some sense, but more importantly, with your observation comes a solution. You must find him. That may seem impossible to do, but those who are lost must be found, either by themselves or by another. I suggest you sit with that, and tomorrow when you return, we'll discuss what must be done more fully. While you're away, there are references I must look over. I'm also concerned about your fiancée. You say she's tired. Is she always tired?"

"I don't know."

"You should ask her. For now, she should remain here."

"That she has decided to do. I'll be leaving for the office long before she wakes. I'll leave her a note and have her come see you in the morning."

"Please do, and thank you for telling us what has happened in such detail. I have no more to say. Stan, do you have anything to add before I clear the table?"

"One point, you said the car struck the gore to the left of the centerline. Is that correct?"

"That's what the reports said."

"Perhaps we should discuss why that may be important in my office and allow Dagmar to clear the table?"

———◦———

S tanley handed me a small whiskey and poured one for himself as we settled ourselves.

"You have thoughts about the accident, Stan?" I asked.

"I do. If the driver was drunk, then his reactions would be slower than normal but not completely absent; else, I don't see how he made it onto the East River Drive in the first place. He should have completed most of the turn, and so I would've expected the impact to have occurred to the right of the center line, not the left. It's a small thing, but it might indicate that the driver intended the car to continue up the East River Drive, only he was forced to deviate from that course. Crashing into the gore to the left of the center line would be consistent with that. It might be nothing, but then again, it might be something."

"I see your point. I'm not sure what to make of it."

"I'm not sure myself at this juncture. We need more information. Along those lines, I'm happy you're investigating both Johnny's movements prior to the accident and the intoxication of the driver. I would like to see the reports that you've accumulated. Sometimes, a fresh pair of eyes is helpful."

"I agree. Mr. Dodge received copies. I'm sure he'd be happy to pass them along."

"It might be best if you let him know that I'd like to read them."

"I'll be leaving at five so I'll write him a note, which reminds me: I'll have to let Raymond know."

"Allow me to take care of that. Raymond and the car will be out front by five, and I'll see that you're woken at 4:30."

"That would be wonderful. If you pass me some stationery and a pen, I'll write a note to John."

When I'd finished, I gave the note to Stanley to deliver. He took it and began tapping it on the desk.

"Is there something else?" I asked.

"Yes. You might consider inviting the Cushmans here for the weekend along with their spouses. It's short notice, but there is time to arrange it. If they were involved in what happened in any way, it might be best if we collect them all in one place."

"You wish me to add that to the note?"

"Please—and let Mr. and Mrs. Dodge know they will need to deliver the necessary invitations. They might have to lure them with a sumptuous dinner or two, which can be easily provided."

"You have a devious mind, Stan."

"I do."

"I suppose I have one also. I like your suggestion. I think I'll invite Malcolm Ault as well."

"Most certainly, and the von Hofmanstals. In fact, a dinner in their honor would be best. He is a baron, after all, and the Cushmans love that kind of thing. That is if it's the same Cushmans I have in mind."

"You know them?"

"I know of them. The Senior is rumored to be vindictive, intolerant of mistakes, and domineering, but nonetheless successful."

"Sounds like the same ones, and, in that case, speak to Mrs. Dodge. She's back in form and will probably be able to arrange the visit rather easily."

"Excellent. I'll do that. As for tomorrow morning, I'll see that you're awoken with some coffee, and if I don't see you before you leave, we'll confer again when you return. Early would be best."

"I agree."

Stanley handed me back my note so I could make the necessary additions. I did and passed it back.

We stood. "Good night, Stan, and please give Dagmar my thanks. It looks like we have another interesting weekend ahead of us."

"Oh, yes. I'm quite looking forward to it. Good night, Percy."

As I walked back to my bedroom, I thought about Stanley's last comment. He did have a gleam in his eyes, and I doubted that the dinners were the reason.

21

Raymond was standing by the car at five. We started for the city, and once we were on our way, I asked him, "Raymond, what are your thoughts about Johnny's accident?"

"You think it was more than an accident, right?" He looked at me in the mirror.

"I don't know for sure. It's being investigated. What do you think?"

"From what I've heard, the driver was blotto, and that makes no sense. Professionals don't do that. Too bad the guy's dead. An hour with him, and he would have told me everything. Johnny was seeing someone if that's news."

"How do you know?"

"Johnny's pretty obvious. I drove him and his dad. I watched Johnny in the rearview mirror. He'd smile to himself a lot. He couldn't hide what he was thinking, at least not from me."

"Did Johnny mention anything?"

"You know Johnny. He keeps his trap shut until it's over. You think there's a connection?"

"It's possible. One other question: Do you know anything about Jim Cushman and his son?"

"I've heard of them, of course. The son's that little shit from the Colony, right?"

"The same."

"I know 'em then. The father's a big wheel. I drove him and Mr. Dodge a time or two. The Cushmans have a place out in Locust Valley. Want me to check 'em out?"

"If you could. I'll be at the office until noon. After that, I'll pay Johnny a visit, and then we'll head back to Rhinebeck. You won't have a lot of time, but find out what you can, and let's keep it quiet. I don't want the Cushmans knowing someone's been asking questions."

"I may have to throw some money around."

"Do what you think is best. I'll cover your expenses."

"Sure thing. I'm going to like working for you."

"Likewise. I'm also going to need you at Rhinebeck over the weekend. The Cushmans will be there. It's being arranged."

Raymond smiled in the mirror.

"Better and better."

He dropped me at the office and peeled away from the curb like he had someplace to go. Where he was headed and what he would do there, I had no idea. He had connections that were very different from my own.

At ten, a preliminary report from one of the investigators came in via messenger. It outlined Johnny's activities during the two weeks prior to the accident. His days were spent at the office, but five of those nights were spent at Le Cirque on 65th Street and Shepheards Nightclub at the Drake Hotel, where he had booked a room on each occasion. He was seen in the company of the same woman, identified as Casey Cushman. I faxed a copy to John Senior as well as all the material I had gathered to Stanley's fax machine in case there was a delay getting the reports from Mr. Dodge.

Anne Dodge called at eleven.

"It's all arranged. The four Cushmans will be here for the weekend. Peggy's heard about Dagmar's cuisine and has wanted to sample it for ages. Elsa is delighted and will make sure Hugo attends. Malcolm accepted also. Oh, and Dagmar has Bruni in an apron. I've no idea what they're up to. Must run. There's so much to do."

I barely managed to say goodbye before she hung up.

By noon, I'd closed out several open positions in various markets so that I could concentrate on what was happening at Rhinebeck exclusively. I had run that by John Senior, who'd agreed. It's not that I couldn't decide for myself, but I thought involving him more might raise his spirits. I could well imagine Rhinebeck's quiet becoming a burden when compared to the market's gyrations and the lack of someone to talk to about them.

Raymond drove me to see Johnny. He had news, but I told him to hold off telling me until we were on our way to Rhinebeck. When I arrived at the hospital, the nurses at Johnny's station were excited. Johnny had stirred and thrashed about.

I sat down in the now familiar chair, looked over my friend, and said, "Twitchy, are we? I would be, too. Invitations to Rhinebeck for the weekend have been received by the Cushmans and accepted. Casey will be there. Too bad you won't be able to see her. Of course, if you wake up shortly, that might be able to be arranged. Dagmar has an idea, although I don't know what it is, and Stanley is looking over all the information I've received so far. Plans are in motion and will likely reach some kind of crescendo by the end of the weekend. I must get back to Rhinebeck, so I don't have time to tell you a story other than to mention that you always counseled caution regarding married women and, above all, to be discreet. You were neither, from what I've heard. Why is that? It's not my place to judge you. I can't, and I won't. You are my friend, and I'll always be in your corner. When you recover, which you will, we'll have some things to discuss, including reinvolving your father in the business. Like you, he thrives on action. Without it, he dims. Perhaps something similar happened to you? You couldn't stay away from her. At some point, you'll have to tell me all about it, but not now, Wonton."

Johnny and I loved palindromes.

"I must be off. One last thing. You might want to get in touch with your aunt wherever you are. Your mom thought that Alice might be aware of your predicament and be able to help. I know it's a stretch, but we've witnessed stranger things. Besides, we're seriously off the deep end anyway. See you on Monday. Everyone misses you, your parents especially, and me most of all."

I was at the elevator when a nurse from Johnny's wing told me I had a phone call at the nurse's station.

I returned, picked up the phone, and said, "Hello. This is Percy."

"How's your friend?"

It was my future father-in-law.

"Improving, I think."

"Good. Progress is progress. Elsa informed me that I'll be seeing you this weekend. Next time, speak to me directly. I also tracked down the doctor. He and Miss Leland will arrive in New York tomorrow. I invited them to Rhinebeck for this weekend on your behalf. They accepted."

"I see. I'll make the necessary arrangements to accommodate them."

"Do that. They'll accompany me and Elsa. How's my daughter?"

"In the kitchen with Dagmar, last I heard."

"Good. That may prove a benefit. See you tomorrow."

There was a click, and he was gone.

I got the impression that Hugo was miffed at my not personally delivering his invitation. Asking Bonnie and Angus was his way of evening the score—not that I wouldn't have invited them, but it did leave me uneasy. Thirteen at the dinner table proved unlucky for my father. Perhaps this time it would be unlucky for someone else.

———◦———

22

R aymond was waiting for me outside the hospital, and once we were on our way, I asked him about his news.

"Here's what I got. I stopped by the limo service and spoke to the dispatcher and two of the drivers hanging around the office. They know me. I asked about the driver who died, but they clammed up. The cops had been around asking questions, and that naturally put a damper on talking about him. They wanted six hundred with the understanding that what was said wouldn't come back and bite them. That's a lot of money in my book, but those guys were nervous.

"I offered two. We settled on three, a hundred each. They told me that nobody knew much about the driver who died. He'd been with them only a week. The interesting part was that the new guy wasn't supposed to drive Johnny at all. A more senior guy was supposed to do that, but he was called out on a job by someone who wanted that driver specifically and was willing to pay four times the going rate. That's huge, so Johnny got the new guy. According to the dispatcher who took the call, the client's name was Cushman. How's that for coincidence?"

"Quite a coincidence. I'll have to ask them about that. All four of the Cushmans will be at Rhinebeck this weekend. They confirmed."

"Good. You know, I can always stand by the door and look threatening when you pop the question."

"We'll see about that. Anything else?"

"None of the drivers like driving the Cushmans. They get in the car and immediately tell the driver, 'Take Madison.' He says, 'It's no good.' They say, 'Take it anyway.' Madison turns out to be a mess, and they arrive late, so they start yelling and blaming the guy. What ya gonna do? Nothin'. The drivers probably knew more, but I didn't have time to drag it out of them. I might swing by again and dig around. The guys were still jumpy when I left, which means that wasn't all of it."

"I think I'd be jumpy, too. They're likely caught between a rock and a hard place. Thank you for finding out what you did. How do you want to be reimbursed?"

"If you got it, I'll take it now. If not, next time we're in the city."

"I have it now."

I dug out my wallet, pulled out three hundred dollars, and handed over the money. I had raided the cash box at the office on my way out the door and had left a note to my secretary to replenish it. I had just enough.

Raymond reached back, took the money, and said, "That squares us."

We drove in silence for a few miles before he asked, "Getting those Cushman people to talk might be a problem."

"Yeah, I know."

"Want some advice?"

"Sure."

"You either make it safe for them to confess or you make it plain that there's a world of hurt comin' if they don't. Since the first case won't happen, you're stuck with the second. In a group, there's always a weakest party. Find out who that is and press hard."

I thought about that and nodded.

Raymond looked at me in the rearview mirror again and said, "Look. I know you're not gonna crush their fingers in a door or start bustin' their bones. You gotta play nice and polite with these guys. I got it. Go ahead and do that—but comes a time when nice don't work. How far you wanna go? Street fights have no rules, and sometimes, that's where you end up. It happens. When you find yourself there, you gotta commit to doing whatever it takes to win. Got a .45 Colt and a half-assed commitment? You won't pull the trigger. Committed? You pick up a chunky ashtray and do the same thing with a lot less noise. Winning and committing. They go together. So, promise me you'll do that. Do it, now."

I didn't expect to get into such a position any time soon, but what he said made sense.

"Okay, I promise to commit to doing whatever it takes."

"Good."

Raymond looked at me in the mirror some more and continued, "I know you think it's never gonna happen. Raymond's full of shit. I see it in your face. Maybe you're right, but if Johnny was targeted, then somebody was willing to kill him, and that somebody will be in your house. Do you know what to do? I'm serious. Tell me what you're gonna do."

"I don't know. I need to find out what happened, who was involved, and what they did. Once that's been determined, I'll decide what to do."

"Fair enough. That's a start, but the accident might be only the beginning."

"Why do you say that?"

"These are businesspeople. You don't bump somebody off because you feel like it. You do it to create an advantage."

"How so?"

"Think about it: The boss just retired, his heir's sidelined in the hospital, and an inexperienced new guy's in charge. To me, that's an opportunity."

"For what?"

"Pickin' up all the marbles."

"I hadn't considered that. What would you suggest I do?"

"Keep me close and in the loop. I think you're in a street fight but don't know it yet. You'll find out soon enough. For a start, think about your level of commitment. There's no second place if you're crippled or dead, and street fights do that. The good news is you're not alone in this. Keep your eyes open. My gut says the accident's just the start. I may be wrong, but I don't think I am. It's why I've been assigned to you."

"I see. What about Mr. Dodge? He's still the real owner, not me."

"Yeah, he is, but you don't worry about him. He can take care of himself. I know that. It's you I worry about."

"Thanks," I said.

"Don't mention it."

———◆———

23

B runi and Stanley met me out front on the steps, and we passed into the house. While Stanley went to open some champagne, Bruni and I paused in the foyer and held each other.

After a few moments, Bruni pulled back and said, "What's wrong?"

"Raymond thinks the accident's only the beginning."

"Tell me."

I repeated the conversation I had in the car. Bruni thought for a moment and said, "Once again, there's more going on of which we know nothing. I think you must speak with John."

"You think he knows more than he's saying?"

"Papa and John are the same in many ways, so yes. After all, he assigned Raymond to you, and he wouldn't do that unless there was good reason, would he?"

"You're quite correct."

"Which means this weekend will get much more complicated than either of us had anticipated. You'll also need to speak with Dagmar. She has something in mind for you."

"Did she happen to mention what that was?"

"Of course not. Dagmar is silent as the grave until she's ready. I did notice that she was doing a bit of research this morning— looking over notes and various volumes. God knows where she keeps them. She put them aside when I stopped by the kitchen and put me to work making sachets of herbs to make a tea that she wants me to drink."

"I think she's concerned about your tiredness."

"She is. She also wants me to remain here and rest, at least for the next few weeks."

"That's not a bad idea, but let's discuss that later. Shall we have some champagne?"

"Certainly, but only a little. Dagmar is restricting my alcohol intake. 'All things in moderation,' she said. Kiss me first, and then let's talk to Anne and John."

"By all means, but before I do, I think I need a moment to myself."

I kissed her. Bruni hugged me and said, "I understand. I'll say you're visiting the bathroom."

"That'll work. I won't be long."

Bruni entered the drawing room while I walked down the hallway to our apartment. The echoes of my footsteps underscored my doubts about being prepared for what lay ahead. Raymond had made it clear that I must commit to doing whatever it took to defeat the shadowy enemy that likely precipitated Johnny's accident. It was possible that they had further plans for me, but how was I to defend against them when, in my heart, I wasn't sure I could? Saying it was one thing; believing it, another.

When I thought about my situation, the predicament of the tethered goat came to mind, and, as much as I wished it otherwise, I was quite sure I was the goat. Long ago, hunters of tigers and lions tied a goat to a stake to lure them into the open, where they could be killed. This worked well for the hunter and, occasionally, the lion or the tiger but not so well for the goat. I wondered if Johnny, too, had been a goat. That question was troubling enough, but more so was the conclusion that no matter his brilliance, he'd been unable to avoid his fate. I was quite sure the same shadowy enemy had used Casey to get to him. Perhaps Casey was Johnny's goat? Could they do the same to me, using Bruni? It was easy to see looming threats in every direction.

I found myself at the door to our apartment. I entered the sitting room and sat behind the desk in Alice's chair. Long ago, she had written the letter gifting me Rhinebeck from this very spot. Here, she'd also written the letter to my father that he'd read the night he died. I wondered what she'd do if she was in my position.

She hadn't won the battle with my father, but she hadn't been defeated either. Perhaps that was the best anyone could expect. Defeats are never final, but neither are the victories. Alice had fought on, and because she did, I had to do the same.

As I let my mind wander, I recalled that goats weren't exactly helpless. They had horns and used them. Long ago, Johnny and I had been surprised to discover that goats killed people in far greater numbers than was generally believed. They also ate almost anything. They could have eaten their tethers and escaped but likely never knew their danger. The difference was I did. I considered what would happen if the tethered goat turned out not to be a goat at all. The devil was often depicted as a goat, and so was the creator of panic, the god Pan. That thought had me looking at my situation in a different way. I, too, had a dark side, only I kept it hidden and in check. It was a part of me I didn't want to know, and it reminded me of my father. I shuddered at the thought. Given the position I was in, perhaps it was time I explored it. Hugo had told me that greatness required all our gifts, including the darker ones. Perhaps I should do the same? Very well, I thought. I'll be the goat, but not the one expected.

The more I thought about it, the more I understood what Raymond had been telling me. I could be a sacrificial goat and go meekly to my slaughter, or I could be something more, a demonic goat, a different creature entirely—one who lured hunter and predator close before consuming both. Raymond had wanted my commitment. Well, I was now committed to be that other thing, and to my surprise, I felt a whole lot better.

———◆———

24

J ohn, Anne, and Bruni were sipping champagne when I entered the drawing room. I collected a flute from Simon and joined them.

Once I was made welcome, I said, "I have some news. According to Johnny's nurses, he thrashed about. Perhaps he's beginning to come around?"

Everyone was thrilled—Anne most of all.

She said, "Oh, that *is* good news, Percy. Really, it is. What do you think it means?"

"I'm not altogether sure, other than that it's a positive sign. Angus and Bonnie will be joining us this weekend, so you'll be able to ask the doctor yourself."

"Excellent, Percy. Excellent—but hold on. Doesn't that make thirteen at the dinner table?"

"It does."

"Well, I suppose somebody will be unlucky, but that someone will certainly not be me. On second thought, it might be best if we invite your mother, John. That will at least make fourteen."

John considered that. "I quite agree. With Bonnie coming, I think we must. Percy?"

"Yes, if the Cushmans had anything to do with the accident, Maw would want to be in at the finish."

Anne looked thoughtful. "Good point. She'd never forgive us if we left her out."

John smiled and said, "Allow me to take care of it."

"Good. I'm glad that's settled," said Anne. "And since I'm in charge of seating, I'll make sure Angus sits beside me so I can pump him for information."

I said, "Of course, and you might place Peggy on the other, so you can do the same to her. We do need to find out how the Cushmans are connected with Johnny's accident."

Anne said, "That we do. I must say, I really hope we're not barking up the wrong tree. That would be most embarrassing."

"It would be, but by gathering them all here, we have the opportunity to find out. John, would you agree?"

"I would, but to be effective, we need a plan. Percy, what do you say we take a walk and discuss it after we finish our champagne?"

———— ❖ ————

John and I stepped out the front door into afternoon sunlight and blustery winds. We strolled up the driveway toward the access road. Miles above, the brilliant sky held wispy clouds like blown feathers that sailed far out of reach from us below.

After we had walked some ways from the house, I said, "Raymond thinks the accident is just the start and that I might be next. He implied that was the reason you assigned him to me."

John walked and said after a time, "It's true. I meant to tell you yesterday, but the moment passed before I could. The news you brought about Angus having visited and how telling stories helped you cope shifted our talk onto a more positive plane that I didn't want to sully with darker matters. It helped Anne recover, and for that, I have no words to thank you. Anne and I healed the hurt between us after you and Bruni went off to bed. We barely slept, but both of us feel as if we did. So, thank you."

"You're very welcome. Would you care to elaborate on those darker matters now?"

"Not really, but I'll tell you. After I do, you'll understand my reluctance, but before I discuss that, I should tell you about Raymond."

J ohn looked down before he said almost to himself, "We all like to be in the right place at the right time, but occasionally, being in the wrong place at the wrong time is better.

"One hot summer night in New York, a man came out of an alley as I was walking past. I was looking in his direction when five hoods armed with switchblades and a machete attacked both of us. I remember thinking this is what a crime statistic feels like, but by the time the fight was over, four were down, and one was dead. Bruised and bloody but relatively unscathed compared to the muggers, I survived. The man from the alley did, too, but our troubles weren't over. A cop car happened to be cruising by, and a further melee ensued. Everyone who survived was arrested, including me. I was able to make a phone call. I suppose wearing a suit and holding a briefcase gave me some credibility when I protested that I was only a passing stranger and that the man from the alley and I had acted in self-defense. My attorney was prompt and bailed us out of jail. Over time, we were cleared of all charges. Bailing out the man from the alley was a logical decision. He'd done most of the work. I'd survived because of his lethal brutality and the heavy briefcase that I carried. It blocked several knife thrusts and was an effective bludgeon. I swung it about me with a desperate ferocity I'd rarely encountered in myself."

We walked in silence for a bit before John continued.

"Surviving almost certain death is its own exhilaration. Few of life's events can match it. To celebrate our survival, I invited the man for a drink. He agreed. I suppose he felt he owed me that in exchange for his bail. I doubt he would have accepted under other circumstances.

"We did look a little worse for wear, but there was a bar not far from the precinct that had probably served customers in worse shape. We went there.

"I drank whiskey. He drank shots of anisette and white rum. By the time the night had turned to morning, we had both switched to dark rum.

"The man told me his story in many bits and pieces. I told him mine in the same way—not all at once. We trusted each other in certain things, but not in all. To me, we were like dogs sniffing each other, trying to determine the other's measure. We weren't friends. That came later. Instead, we were *compañeros en la violencia*. I know some Spanish, and it is a fitting description of both of us. His was a brutal world—mine, the opposite, or so it is portrayed. Often, such disparate worlds collide with ugly consequences. Ours instead intersected, and out of that came a friendship that has lasted ever since. His name was Raymond Figueroa, and he'd come to New York City from Puerto Rico with nothing but his fighting and his wits."

We walked in silence again. I lit a cigarette and smoked.

John sighed and said, "It's odd, but all the true friendships of my life have come from violent beginnings. My lifelong bond with Hugo was formed after a not dissimilar episode in Spain. Anne came into my life as the result of a duel. Raymond from a mugging. I don't know why that is, only that it's true for me."

We walked some more before John said, "Raymond liked to keep up his skills by playing high-stakes poker. Whether he would win or lose, he'd flash enough money around to attract bandits, stick-up artists, and muggers. Most worked in groups, and Raymond preferred them that way. Strength in numbers gave such individuals confidence, and that, he told me, was their weakness. Besides, a gang gave him several opponents all at once, which was a more efficient form of practice than having to procure them one by one.

"When morning came upon us, he told me that the surprise attack was not a surprise at all. It had been the third time he'd walked out of that alley. With each, he'd feigned being more intoxicated. He apologized in his roundabout way for the inconvenience of roping me into a fight I had no wish to start. To him, our being picked up by the police was a sign. That brawl would be his last. Guns were now more common on the streets. He knew firearms but said they lacked artistry. A gun was no substitute for courage, merely an excuse. He was drunk by then, and so was I.

"I offered to take him wherever he wanted to go, but he refused. He told me that morning light drove bad men to their beds. None were about at this time. He thanked me for the drinks but said he'd make his own way home. Before we parted, he gave me a number to a hired car service and told me to reach him there should I ever need a driver. I kept that number and used him off and on. When my chauffeur ended up in the hospital, I hired Raymond on a permanent basis. Are you with me so far?"

"I am, indeed."

We walked some more.

John continued, "If given a choice, I prefer the violent world of which Raymond is a part. It is more overt, with fewer shades of gray. In our world, threats can be just as potent but are often subtle and carried out behind a veil of corporate deceit and financial maneuvering that makes it difficult to recognize even the threat until one finds oneself ruined.

"Dodge Capital has been under attack for some time. People who were eager to do business are no longer so eager. Even getting to speak with them has taken great effort. Friends I've known socially for years no longer proffer invitations. Lines of credit have mysteriously dried up, and when given at all, they are costly and laced with unfavorable terms. One could easily say that it's the business climate, but it isn't. It's as if someone is poisoning the well. One feels the result, but the source is elusive. This has been

119

the case for a while now, and I took steps to find out who is behind it. My plan was to follow Raymond's strategy: to appear weak and to portray Dodge Capital as an easy and accessible target."

I considered that and said, "I've examined all the Dodge Capital accounts quite thoroughly. The reality is altogether different. Dodge Capital is far stronger than it appears."

"It is, but feigning weakness can entice those who are hidden to come out into the open."

"That may be true, but even if they show themselves, they can't just take Dodge Capital away from you. You're privately owned."

"Even a moderate business can be coerced—large ones, too. In the American West, water was diverted, cattle rustled, and people disappeared or were outright killed. The owners who didn't comply were burned out and, if they escaped at all, moved on with only what they could carry. Some fought back. Many didn't. The corporate world acts much the same today but without the bloodshed. It uses legal sleights of hand and pressure, spelled out in contracts, credit terms, banking fees and costs, declined opportunities, refusals, and avoidance. The result is still the same. Those targeted are left scrambling for a pittance."

"Is that why you retired?"

"Not entirely. I had two reasons. The first was that you and Johnny were capable and competent enough to run the firm but lacked experience. By removing myself, you would gain some. The second is that whoever was behind the veil would try to take advantage of that defect and dare to venture forth and show themselves—certain you were no match for them."

"The tethered goat."

"The tethered goat."

"I realized that this afternoon. Johnny was your goat."

"He was."

"Does Anne know?"

"No."

"I see. Your ambush didn't go as planned. Will Anne forgive you, is my question."

John looked troubled and said, "If his accident was truly an accident, there is little to be said. If it wasn't, then I am to blame. Will Anne forgive me? She will try, but whether she can, I don't know. I will also have to forgive myself, and I doubt that will be any easier."

"Did Johnny know he was the goat?"

"He did, but he failed to take precautions when I offered them."

"Raymond."

"Correct."

"It was Casey, wasn't it?"

"I believe so. Wittingly or unwittingly."

"What are you going to do?"

"I'm not sure."

"You must tell Anne."

"Timing is everything in such things."

"And a reason to avoid telling her, only this won't keep. She might even know already. She's clever in that way. Of course, if Johnny should die, then that's another matter."

"I am more than conscious of that. It's why I haven't told her."

"I know, but do it anyway—tonight. If those behind all this are as clever as you believe, they'll exploit that omission. You can say that nobody's that smart, and that is true until you meet someone who is. Unfortunately for you and me, there's always someone smarter than ourselves, and then what?"

"Everything goes to hell."

"Exactly."

27

As John and I walked in silence along the access road, I thought about Johnny getting together with Casey again. Certain women, when paired with certain men, have leveled kingdoms. Johnny and Casey were likely such a pair. Johnny had been warned to leave well enough alone. Casey, too, but Johnny, being Johnny, had either ignored that caution or forgotten it. The question in my mind was whether Casey was toxic only when they were together or just plain toxic. She hadn't seemed that way to me, but I decided to tell Bruni their story. She, like her mother, was adept at reading people and situations.

As John and I walked, I sensed that he still had something on his mind. I asked him, "Is there anything more that I should know?"

John considered my question. "For now, no."

"Which means there's more."

"There's always more, but nothing concrete."

"Such as?"

"There's been no offer."

"Do you expect one?"

"Yes, if it's Dodge Capital that they're after, but that may not be the case. Perhaps someone wants me to suffer in some way. If the Cushmans are behind it, and I lean in that direction, this weekend should give them ample opportunity to reveal themselves. If it's only my business they want, then I'm on familiar ground. If it's personal, then I'm not. It's why I'm interested in your stories about James Cushman."

"To get a sense of him and the family?"

"Yes. Should there be no offer, no threats, no nothing this weekend, then I'm up against a truly formidable enemy—one who is a ghost. It's either that or an opponent who has the bravado and the discipline to waltz into their adversary's castle and waltz out again, taking pleasure in the pain they've caused while showing no outward satisfaction for having done so."

"Provided it's really them."

"Yes ... but so far, no other name has come up, only theirs, and the Cushmans certainly have the means."

"That name came up again today."

"Really? How?"

As we turned and started back toward the house, I told John what Raymond had found out.

When I'd finished, John said, "There's something there. What exactly? I don't know. Inviting them here was a stroke of genius on your part."

"Not mine. Stanley's."

"Yes, of course it was, but you were smart enough to act on it."

"How could I not? He's in his element. How much does Hugo know?"

"Everything—other than the reports you received today and Raymond's news."

"Has he offered any advice?"

" 'Wait' was all he said."

"Typical Hugo."

"Yes, but he's right, as is also typical of Hugo. For now, I must tell Anne about the whole business. I don't want to, but I must. You are correct in saying that I'm too vulnerable otherwise. I should have told her sooner, but what's done is done. We must discover how the Cushmans are involved and to what extent. We must draw them out."

"Lure them into the open, in other words."

"Yes, and then finish this."

"A tricky business."

"Extremely so, since by their doing nothing other than eating our food and smiling all the while, they will have achieved a by no means insignificant victory—particularly if it turns out to be them after all."

"It's like that staring game; whoever reacts first is the loser."

"Yes."

"I think I'll talk to Dagmar and Stanley."

"An excellent idea and better if it should come from you. We need to be prepared."

28

W hen we returned to the house, John went in search of Anne, and I went to look for Bruni. I found her in our sitting room. She was at the desk, reading a book on herbs and plants.

"There you are," she said, looking up. "How did it go with John?"

"Informative. Let's sit on the couch. I can hold you while you tell me all about your day, and then I can tell you about mine."

"Can I rest my legs on you?"

"Of course."

Bruni sat down at one end and swung her legs onto my lap.

Once she had made herself comfortable, she said, "That's better. I've actually been busy, but not in the usual sense. I filled sachets with herbs, fetched pots and pans, learned how to use a knife, and much more. Dagmar wants me to let my mind solve things on its own while I do something else. She said it's a necessary skill that improves with practice. So, I practiced. I found the whole idea strange but interesting. Dagmar is ... I don't quite know how to categorize her. The more I get to know her, the more I like her. She might even give me a run for my money in the smarts department, and I'm pretty smart. Strangely, we're most compatible."

"Like Stanley and me."

"Yes. I noted the parallel."

"Of course you did. That's excellent. Did you enjoy yourself?"

"I did, and that, too, was unexpected. So, what did John say?"

"Before I tell you, I'd like to reiterate everything that's happened so far from the day we heard about the accident till now in case I omitted vital bits. After that, I'd like your analysis of the situation and your advice."

"I love it when you let me help you. Tell me."

I told Bruni all that happened after Angus saw Johnny, including the Jimmy Buckley story and the one about Casey, up to and including my conversation with John. Bruni simply listened.

At the end, she asked, "Can you get me a cigarette?"

"I can't," I said. "You're sitting on me."

Bruni lifted her legs. "You mentioned the staring game. I called it the blinking game. Did you ever play it with Johnny?"

I got up and said, "On occasion. We preferred hide and seek since it was more like hunting."

I returned to the couch with cigarettes, a lighter, and an ashtray. Once we were settled again, Bruni asked, "When you played the blinking game, who'd win? You or Johnny?"

"We were well matched, I think. Johnny would disagree, but I won as often as I lost. How about you?"

"I always won."

"Which is why you're a good attorney."

"Yes. Stillness is its own skill—and patience, too."

"A formidable combination."

"And what is needed now. Did you love Casey back then?"

I considered the question. "I think I was infatuated. At that age, I tended to fantasize more than anything else. Besides, such feelings would well up, starting in my heart, spread out like waves of heat, and then consume me. It was as if I'd been struck by one of Cupid's arrows or by lightning. I had no control over how I felt once that started. The love I feel for you is different, but with certain similarities. Passion and love can coexist."

"They can, and I feel the same."

"Along those lines, Johnny had something special with Casey. Perhaps it was Casey's beauty and the shared perils they overcame. Johnny is often opaque about his romantic feelings, but I sense that he's yearned for her ever since. Was he infatuated? Yes, absolutely, but how long can an infatuation last before it's categorized as love?"

Bruni considered that. "It can be hard to know the difference. Without mutual trust, either can be perilous."

"Do you think Casey's poisonous when combined with Johnny, or just plain poisonous?"

"Either may be the case. Some women are simply toxic. Many think I am."

"Really?"

"It's quite true. I've been told that to my face many times. Such comments used to hurt, but I realized that others really do find me threatening. I never wished anyone harm, but I upended people's worlds with just my presence. I had that power. Many toxic creatures have specific markings that act as warnings to leave well enough alone. With humans, beauty can be such a mark—sexuality, too. It can be exuded like an odor, and those nearby go into a frenzy. Lethality is never easy to manage for those who possess it. There can be unintended consequences. One must learn when to reveal oneself and use it and when not to. Mama is a master of that art. I'm still learning."

Bruni stubbed out her cigarette in the ashtray.

She looked at me and said, "I was studying some plants just now. *Brugmansia* exudes a scent that can act to calm and give a sense of fulfillment. It's sometimes called the 'horn of plenty.' It lures those who might value it with its own unique song. Dagmar was telling me that plants sing. Deciphering their meanings and knowing whether their songs will harm or help requires great discernment and patience—like the blinking game. Plants don't lie, but they can certainly hide or camouflage their properties, sometimes with brilliant colors in the open, sometimes by means of scarcity and sporadic flowering. They play games just like us. They may appear as part of the landscape, but if observed over considerable lengths of time, they travel and communicate. Their sense of time is different from our own."

"You should definitely spend more time with Dagmar. You're beginning to sound like her."

"Really?" Bruni lit up.

"Really. So, what do we do?"

"Brief everyone as John suggested, and then don't blink. Whoever is behind this has great patience. We must listen carefully for their songs and then reach down to pull them out by the roots when they're finished."

"Okay, Bruni, maybe too much Dagmar."

Bruni laughed. "I wasn't exactly joking, but for now, Papa is correct. We must wait and see. There is some time before dinner. Would you care to look at some pictures in my plant book?"

"I don't think so."

Bruni giggled. "Me neither."

29

W e gathered in the drawing room. Anne and Bruni looked elegant in black cocktail dresses, while John and I wore dark suits.

Once we were supplied with champagne, Anne asked me, "So, Percy, now that I've been *fully* briefed," Anne glanced for a moment at John, who looked uncomfortable, and asked, "How exactly do we get the Cushmans to talk other than by jetting them to Austria and using Hugo's dungeon to persuade them?"

I was about to answer when Bruni said, "That could be arranged, but are we not presuming guilt?"

Anne looked at her, surprised. "You don't think they're guilty?"

"I see the likelihood but not the certainty."

"Well, Bruni," said John. "Since you're the attorney, what would you suggest?"

"To be certain, we must either ask them or let them tell us. Asking is easy, but by doing so, we telegraph our suspicions and our intentions. Likely, they'll expect that and be prepared. Our silence, on the other hand, will unbalance them. Guilty people see guilty people. They'll wonder what we're up to, how much we know, and what we intend to do. They'll ask questions to allay those fears, and doing so will bring about their downfall. We'll trap them with their curiosity, not their answers."

Anne looked at Bruni in wonder. "So we say nothing. By God, Bruni, but you're devious. I like you more and more!"

Bruni beamed. "I love to use my talents for a good purpose."

John nodded. "An interesting strategy, and if it doesn't work, we always have the direct approach to fall back on. Percy, what do you think?"

"The idea has merit, but what happens when they ask? How do we answer them?"

Bruni looked at me and said, "With evasion. We act as if we're hiding something. Doing so will arouse their suspicions. From what I've heard, secrecy and meticulous planning have been their strengths. By introducing the unexpected, we force them to improvise. Johnny's impending recovery might be a good place to start. They'll wonder what he knows and what he might be able to say. That will unsettle them. A rumor that Johnny's recovery is certain might create the desired response. They'll make mistakes, contradict each other, and then we'll have them. Percy, you must be our main coordinating point. What does everyone think?"

John raised his glass, "I like it. Let's toast to our guests trapping themselves. Percy?"

"I'll drink to that, but before we do, I must inject a word of caution. The Cushmans will be our guests, and lest we forget, that status has significance here."

Anne interrupted, "That's all very well and good, Percy, but what if they attack us in this house?"

I answered, "We always retain the right to defend ourselves, but attacking them without provocation is how I would interpret that constraint. None of us raised a hand against my father, and yet Justice was served in its own peculiar way. Perhaps it will be served again. For now, I propose a toast to Justice, should her help be needed, and that she be swift and sure."

I raised my glass, as did everyone else. "To Justice," I said.

"To Justice," everyone repeated.

After we lowered our glasses, Stanley said, "May all get what they deserve, but for now, dinner is ready. Please follow me."

How long he'd been standing there, I couldn't say.

30

We were seated around the smaller version of the dining room table, having consumed an appetizer of *Carpaccio di Manzo* with an unusual lemon, pine nuts, and caper sauce that, on its own, would have made the meal memorable. This was followed by red snapper with lemon, small, boiled potatoes in butter with herbs, and French beans with almonds. Raspberry sorbet came next for dessert. The wine was a rare, dry Chenin Blanc from the Loire region of France. I got the feeling that the dinner was oriented to a lighter diet because of Bruni's condition. Regardless, the meal was outstanding.

Over dessert, Anne asked Bruni, "So this weekend is to be a game of cat and mouse. What if one of the Cushmans blurts out that the car crash was deliberate? What then?"

Bruni answered, "I doubt they'll do that, but should that occur, then the admission opens the door to the possibility of restitution and redress."

Anne sipped her wine and asked, "What would that mean in this case?"

"That's hard to say right now," said Bruni. "We lack the necessary information to determine an amount. For a start, Johnny hasn't recovered. If the Cushmans are responsible, how much money would be sufficient to wash away the pain, the medical costs incurred, and the missing days of Johnny's life when he comes back to us?"

"A great deal," said Anne.

"Which is why I don't think they'll admit it."

"I see," said Anne. "From what you say, arriving at the truth is just the beginning."

"That is correct."

"What will come after?" asked Anne.

"Negotiations and a settlement, I should think."

"What if they don't want to negotiate or settle?" asked John.

"Then, depending on what's provable, the filing of criminal charges."

We all thought about that. Into the silence, I asked Bruni, "What if the evidence we gather is merely circumstantial?"

"From what I've seen, the threat of criminal action is often enough to start constructive negotiations, even if the evidence involved is flimsy. There's the adverse publicity to consider and the impact on one's reputation. From my experience, when someone deliberately and calculatingly acts to harm another, there are always legitimate reasons and justifications in the mind of the perpetrator for having done so. Some may be obvious and observable. Others may not be, like jealousy and the need for vengeance. Often, they stem from earlier beginnings—some much earlier."

John said, "Like a festering wound."

"Yes. When no resolution is wanted or even considered, that is often the case."

John turned to me and said, "On that note, Percy, I think it's time for your stories about James Cushman. Perhaps they can give us a clue."

We arose from our places at the table and settled in the library, the ladies with brandy—John and I with whiskey and cigars. I started in.

"John, you wanted to hear about the rivalry between Johnny and James Cushman. I have three stories in mind but with some caveats. First, there may be no connection between their rivalry and the accident other than our assumption of one. Second, I was out of the loop for many years. The marriage between James and Casey was one such significant event that I knew nothing about. Much else may have happened during that time between the three of them. Lastly, had Johnny been killed, even a superficial investigation would have uncovered the affair between Casey and Johnny, pointing toward James's possible involvement. James may be unsavory, but never was he stupid. Likely, he would use an intermediary. He schemes, and in this, he and Johnny are alike. Do you still wish me to continue?"

John said, "I will keep those points in mind, but I wish to hear your stories just the same. I never knew that Johnny had a rivalry until yesterday, and there seems to be a great deal that Anne and I don't know, not only about him but about you. We love you both and wish to hear more, particularly with Johnny's absence. Isn't that right, Anne?"

Anne said, "Absolutely. I may squirm, but I do love hearing stories about the both of you. It's embarrassing on occasion, but despite my astonishment, it's wonderfully necessary and grounding. Bruni? How about you?"

"I love stories in general, but stories about the people I love are the ones I like to hear most of all. Good company, a fine drink, a fire, and a good story? Is there really anything better?"

I looked at them all and said, "Very well. I'll begin at the beginning. The first time Johnny, James, and I met was at dancing class before we were teenagers. The rivalry between Johnny and James started there."

"You took dancing classes?" asked Bruni.

"Yes, we did. It was customary. Right, Anne?"

Anne smiled and said, "It was at the time and absolutely essential. How else were the boys to learn the dos and don'ts of interacting in social situations with the opposite sex?"

Bruni said, "I quite agree. I wish I'd had dancing classes when I was young. I love ballroom dancing."

I continued, "I do, too, but I only discovered its benefits years later."

"I'd like to hear about that," said Bruni with a mischievous smile.

"Perhaps you will."

"Then please continue."

I took a sip of my drink and said, "Very well. At the time, Johnny and I considered the classes more torture than pleasure. They took place on Thursday evenings from four to six during the school year in the ballroom of the Colony Club on Park Avenue. Mrs. de Rham was our instructor, assisted by her male companion, Buddy. There, the preadolescent cream of New York society was taught to Fox-trot, Waltz, Cha-Cha, Tango, Samba, and Bossa Nova. We even learned the Mexican Hat Dance and the Twist. The boys sported dark blue suits, white shirts, and ties. The girls, in equal numbers, wore blue, pink, or black party dresses, white socks, black patent leather shoes, and white gloves. I suppose we all looked like little angels, which, I assure you, we were not. The venue also supplied seating space in the form of little alcoves for parents, governesses, and guardians to watch the proceedings. They were always full and likely kept the classes orderly simply because we were performing before an audience. Music was supplied by recordings and, on special occasions, by a Lester Lanin orchestra.

"Our classes consisted of some forty boys and girls. There, the boys learned how to ask a girl to dance, how to perform the various steps, how to excuse themselves when they stepped on their partner's feet, and how to behave in polite society. The girls learned the same and were the more proficient. They were taller, more mature, and mostly tolerated their more immature partners, with the exception of one golden boy. All the girls would melt whenever he condescended to give them his attention. That boy was James Cushman, the third."

"No wonder Johnny didn't like him," said Bruni.

"No wonder at all. Mrs. de Rham would often ask James to demonstrate a dance step with his partner. The little girl would invariably blush bright red and almost faint with pleasure. He'd smile in a condescending way, lead his partner to the center of the ballroom, and give a typically flawless performance that ended with rapturous applause from all the girls and the adults observing.

"On one occasion, Mrs. de Rham called on Johnny to do the same; only he stepped on his partner's foot hard enough to have to call a halt. James yelled out, 'Nice one, Lead Foot!' Everyone laughed, including the adults. Johnny was mortified, and if he was ambivalent toward James before, he was no longer."

I relit my cigar and said, "James and Johnny, in spite of their competitive natures, were similar. Each was brilliant in his own way, handsome, and charismatic. Had they grown up together, just the two of them, I think that they would have become fast friends, but James was also very different.

"For a start, he always had a ready supply of cash and was the only boy who carried a sterling silver cigarette lighter, which he flaunted at every opportunity when the adults weren't looking. He would brag about how much he had to spend and put down others who didn't, particularly those who might be able to unseat him as the center of attention, like Johnny.

"James was also exceptional in another way. He could talk to girls and charm them. Attending dancing classes allowed him the opportunity to meet them. For Johnny and me, dancing classes threw us headlong into the delicate and perilous subject of the opposite sex of which we were unfamiliar and had little experience. That subject included Mrs. de Rham.

"Dancing with her was required. Inevitably, it would be my turn, and I would find my face pressed against her stomach just below her bosom. That was bad, but I dreaded how I'd feel should I suddenly grow several inches and find my face either squished between her breasts or looking directly at them as we moved about the dance floor."

Bruni giggled, John smiled, and Anne laughed. I continued.

"Mrs. de Rham was never indiscreet, but she never hid the fact that in this area, she had a lot to offer. I think this bothered Johnny more than me.

"He mentioned it after class one evening. He asked me, 'Why does she have to dance so close all the time? Do you suppose she gets a little jiggy? And where is Mr. de Rham in all this? Has anyone ever seen him?' "

Anne interrupted, "Jiggy, Percy? I haven't heard that word in years. I doubt Johnny said that."

"Oh, he said it, all right—that and a whole lot more. Johnny was going through a crisis at the time and was at that age when males demonstrated their affection by showing the opposite. In one class, we were all in line, two by two: boys on the right, girls on the left, waiting to march into the ballroom. James was in front of Johnny when Johnny made a comment about our instructor that I didn't catch. James told him to take it back. Johnny refused. They argued. Others began to turn in their direction to listen. Before it could get physical, Mrs. de Rham waved her arm to start the music, and we all marched in.

"It was shortly after this exchange that rumors about James being in love with Mrs. de Rham began to circulate. James would approach a cluster of girls. They would stop whispering, only to continue after he moved away. It didn't take him long to learn what was being said.

"Now, as far as I know, Johnny didn't start those rumors, although he may have, but whether he did or not, the damage was done. Whenever James finished dancing with Mrs. de Rham, the giggling would begin, and James would turn beet red. Soon, it became obvious that the comments had struck much closer to home than had been anticipated, and so they continued more overtly than ever. James was sure Johnny was behind these attacks and swore to take his revenge.

"Not long after this incident, the Soviet premier, Nikita Khrushchev, was scheduled to address the United Nations General Assembly. He stayed at the Russian Embassy, a few blocks up the street on the same side of Park Avenue as the Colony. New York's finest were very much in evidence during his visit, and in spite of the traffic snarls, class went on as usual.

"That evening, we were let out early, and Johnny and I waited for Raymond on the sidewalk outside along with the other boys and girls, including James. He sauntered over to us after a few minutes, smiled, and asked, 'Hey, Dodge, you ever seen a stick of Junior Dynamite?' "

Before I could continue, Anne interrupted, "Hold up, Percy. Junior Dynamite? John, have you ever heard of such a thing?"

John shrugged and said, "I've never heard of it."

Anne huffed and said, "It sounds dangerous."

I continued, "That is true, and we were all struck dumb. I doubt there was anything that James could have said that would have allowed Johnny to put aside whatever distrust he had for James other than that question. To us, Junior Dynamite was the stuff of legend. Many of the lads, including Johnny and me, had lit off firecrackers and the occasional cherry bomb. Johnny and I had even graduated to the upper end of the explosive scale in the form of an M-80, with its unmistakable silver cylinder and dark green fuse. But the absolute ne plus ultra, the tip of the top of explosive fireworks, was Junior Dynamite. Its existence was rumored but never confirmed. It had never been seen by any of us until now. The boys crowded around James and Johnny to have a look.

"James slowly pulled the legendary explosive from his overcoat pocket. We were hypnotized, Johnny most of all. It was nearly six inches long and exuded a latent power that was palpable.

"He asked Johnny, 'Do you want to hold it?'

"Johnny whispered, 'Could I?'

"James replied casually, 'Of course you can. Just be careful.'

"Johnny said softly in awe, 'I will,' and took it with trembling hands, raising his eyes to heaven to memorialize the moment.

"Whether James planned for that, I don't know. While Johnny was in his rapture, James moved quickly. He whipped out his sterling silver lighter and, quick as lightning, lit the four-inch fuse protruding from the end. The fuse glowed reluctantly for a moment before it burst into sizzling life, like an evil-sparking demon that had suddenly entered our world through a crack in the universe.

"There were gasps followed by panic. Starker and more tragic was the realization that dawned in Johnny's eyes and was equally reflected in my own. We had been horribly betrayed.

"James laughed hysterically as he ran to the open door held by the chauffeur, who stood beside it. He'd waited for his escape route to clear before lighting the fuse. He jumped into the back, screaming at the driver to step on it. As the man ran around the car to the driver's side, James rolled down his window and yelled at Johnny, 'I told you I'd pay you back!' Laughing like an insane little dwarf, I saw him roll up the window as he sped into the night.

"Johnny and I were frozen in space and time—the enormity of our situation, inconceivable and impossible to grasp. We were standing in front of the Colony Club at six o'clock in the evening on Park Avenue in New York City just down from the Russian Embassy, which was surrounded with floodlights and swarming with police, with a very lit and formidable explosive.

"Time stopped as it dawned on me that what had just been done could not be undone. As I looked at Johnny in horror, Johnny did the only thing he could. He gave the explosive to me."

"What? I don't believe it," said Anne. "How could he possibly have done that to you?"

"Well, he did, but before you feel outraged, you have to give Johnny some credit. He didn't run away and leave me. Instead, he looked around frantically. Later, he told me that he was searching for the least destructive place to put the damn thing, but he couldn't think of where that might be while he had hold of it. He passed it to me so he could gain a moment's quiet to solve the problem.

"Had our roles been reversed, I would have dropped it and bolted, but at that moment, I couldn't move. All I could do was stare at the smoking, sparking, hissing fuse that was disappearing at an alarming rate right before my eyes. In that small, quiet part of my mind that still remained, all else being in shock, I estimated that I had about 2.5 seconds until detonation and that it would be best if I wasn't holding it when that occurred.

"Johnny managed to croak, 'Behind you! Under the car!'

"I turned, still holding the smoking stick like a candle, and saw an empty limo parked in front. It was the work of a moment. I tossed it where Johnny directed and hoped for the best.

"An instant later, the Junior Dynamite detonated with a concussive blast. The car rose on its suspension and bobbed up and down while great quantities of smoke poured from underneath it. The sound was deafening. Raymond saw us, ran the light, and screeched the Lincoln to a halt as he leaned over and opened the front door.

"Raymond shouted, 'Grab anyone you know and get them the fuck in the car!'

"I heard him faintly through the roaring in my ears. Johnny leaped into the front and dived into the back to open the rear door. I yelled at my classmates, who were clustered together, to get in. They needed no urging, and in seconds, the Lincoln was packed with kids. I got in the front, slamming my door as Johnny closed the back, and the Lincoln gathered speed, heading south down Park. Raymond ran several lights, then whipped left around the island and traveled east until Lexington. He turned south onto the avenue and floored it. We sped at terrifying speed until Raymond whipped the car right onto a side street and pulled to the curb just before Park Avenue. Several police cars streaked along the avenue with sirens blaring and lights flashing.

"There was whimpering and real fear in the car until Raymond said in a voice that gained immediate and absolute compliance, 'Everybody, shut up!'

"More cop cars sped by. We waited for what seemed like a lifetime in total silence.

"After a few minutes, Raymond turned in his seat, looked at all of us, and said, 'Right now, you kids are safe. I do not know what happened back there, and I don't wanna know what happened back there. What I do want to know is where each of you lives so I can drive you home. I want no crying, no yelling, and no talking. I will ask the questions, and you will answer them.'

" 'You,' he said, looking at the little girl closest to the door. 'Where do you live?'

" 'Sutton Place,' she squeaked.

"Raymond wrote down all the addresses and then proceeded to drop each of the kids at their residences until only Johnny and I were left. He pulled over again and stopped.

"Turning to us, he said, 'Okay, I'm sure you're both scared shitless and maybe with good reason, maybe not. Lucky I was there.'

"Johnny and I mumbled our thanks and meant it. Without Raymond, we, and a lot of other innocents, would still be back there. We started to babble.

" 'Can it. Just shut the fuck up and listen.'

"He looked at both of us in turn, his pirate hoop glistening in the streetlight.

" 'There'll be an investigation. There'll be questions. There'll be cops. There'll be people trying to scare the shit out of you to get you to talk. They'll make you cry. It don't matter who's doing the asking. You say the same thing. You tell them, 'I don't remember.' That's all. Nothin' else, and I mean nothin' else. When they ask what happened? You say I don't remember. You say it over and over until they believe you. You act like a broken record. You remember nothin'. You understand? This is fuckin' important. Your future depends on it.'

"We nodded in agreement. He was a life buoy in a seething ocean.

" 'So, what you gonna to say?'

"We repeated in unison: 'I don't remember.'

" 'Say it again.'

" 'I don't remember.'

" 'What happened?'

" 'I don't remember.'

" 'Was Billy there?'

" 'I don't remember.'

" 'Good. You may get out of this yet. Now, I want a name. Who started this fuckin' mess?'

"We both said in unison: 'James Cushman, the third.'

"Raymond nodded and said, 'As far as I'm concerned, we never talked about any of this. Keep it that way.'

"We never spoke about what he'd said to anyone.

"Shortly after, when we were home, we thought it to our credit that Raymond knew we hadn't been the source of the incident.

Later, we wondered if he thought us too stupid or too tame. Whichever it was, we dared not ask.

"The fallout was bad but not catastrophic. The stories of all concerned were so confused, so contradictory, and involved so many big names of New York's high society, who each fielded a panoply of such extraordinary legal talent that a lid was put on the affair in short order. Johnny and I followed Raymond's advice to the letter.

"The story, reported in the press, was that someone had set a trashcan on fire near the Soviet Embassy to protest Khrushchev's visit and that it had been extinguished. That was all. Life returned to normal, or almost. Mrs. de Rham relocated to the River Club, and James Cushman never returned to the class."

A nne said, "That is all rather shocking, Percy. How come I've never heard about any of this until now? John?"

John shrugged and said, "It's news to me. To answer your question, I think we were in St. Barts with Bob and Beulah Phipps at the time. Come to think of it, Raymond may have mentioned something in passing, but I recall nothing specific."

"That would explain it. Just the same, all these stories are most disturbing, Percy. First, Mrs. Spence, and now this? Where have I been? It's like I've discovered another universe parallel to my own. All I can say is the younger Cushman better not try anything like that here. I'll bash him in the head myself. He obviously takes after his father."

"You know his father, Anne?" asked Bruni.

"I've known him for almost as long as I've known Peggy. I see her for lunch now and again. Peggy always complains about the trouble she has retaining staff because Jim is so high-handed and inconsiderate. They quit left and right. He tells her to find someone else, but that's not always possible with his reputation. It's irritated her for years."

"He sounds awful. Why does she stay with him?" asked Bruni.

"Why does anyone stay with anyone? The family really does have a lot of money, and Peggy's no spring chicken. Besides, Jim can be charming when he wishes. Perhaps he's also good in bed? Everyone has their reasons. A vexing normalcy can be far more appealing than the prospect of starting over."

"The devil you know is better than the one you don't?" said Bruni.

"Precisely. Financial security, social prominence, and the means to get whatever you want is no small thing. Many happily trade their souls for such an existence and find themselves belittled, berated, and abused in the bargain. Still, they choose to endure that life. They ossify, or petrify, I forget which one it is, and the energy needed to start over just isn't there anymore."

"Is that why she hasn't divorced him?"

"Perhaps, but Peggy's smarter and much tougher than she looks. There's also the old saying that the man may be the head, but the woman is the neck. Peggy makes sure that her husband focuses his attention in the direction that she wants. She knows how the game is played. Besides, why exchange a winning hand for a probable losing one? A woman must be practical above all else, and Peggy is practical."

Bruni considered that and said, "Interesting analysis, Anne. Thank you for that. My questions have caused us to digress. I apologize, Percy."

I smiled at Bruni. "It's just as well. Does anyone have any further questions?"

John said, "Only one: The young James acted callously and with no regard for anyone other than himself. Was he always like that?"

I considered the question and said, "Back then, he had a vicious streak. He saw only his superiority, and everyone else's inferiority, Johnny and I included. He could act against us without conscience because we were nothing. Whether such feelings and beliefs fade as we mature or whether they persist beneath a more sophisticated and calculated façade, I can't say. I suppose we'll discover the answer to that question this weekend."

John nodded and said, "I suppose we will. Did you see him often after that?"

"Not until we were teenagers, and then, more regularly. The Cushmans started spending Christmas and spring vacations in Palm Beach and in Southampton during the summer, just like us. When

James and Johnny met again, the opposite sex had become the center of their focus, and they were rivals once more. Now, should I continue, or should we take a break?"

Bruni wanted to go to the ladies' room. We chatted among ourselves until she returned, and I began my second story.

"During Christmas and spring vacations, all the prep schools would release their students around the same time, and traditionally, the Bath & Tennis Club in Palm Beach would hold a black-tie dinner dance early in the season for the younger set. It was a seated dinner for over one hundred and fifty with a live orchestra for ballroom dancing.

"The affair took place in a large, partly covered patio that opened toward a shallow reflecting pool, spanned by a small bridge that led to the tennis courts. The water blazed with turquoise luminescence from underwater lights. In the center of the patio was the dance floor surrounded by fifteen dinner tables set with pink tablecloths, around which five pairs of young people were seated, all in long, elegant evening dresses and black tuxedos. Place cards in front of each setting indicated where we would be sitting.

"That year, Johnny and I had turned seventeen, and we were excited. It was the first event of the spring season. I remember wearing a brand-new tuxedo from Brooks Brothers. I felt dashing and debonair. I'd even managed to avoid a haircut, so my hair was longer than usual. At the time, short hair was out. Long hair was in. I'd spent hours getting ready—Johnny, too. His golden locks shone with the burnished brilliance of a Breck Shampoo commercial. I tried to appear blasé, but underneath, I was looking forward to the dance. Together, we armed ourselves with new, refillable butane lighters and two packs of cigarettes each. We were as ready as we would ever be. As Johnny drove us to the club, we speculated as to which table we would be assigned to and who would be there.

"Johnny parked our rented Plymouth Valiant in the club's lower lot. We walked up the driveway, listening to the swishing palms and feeling the warm tropical air, enchanted by the promise of the evening. Normally, guests would give their keys to one of the many parking attendants, but since it was customary to tip them, and we had no money, we parked where the employees did and walked up to the entrance instead. At reception, Mr. Wheeler greeted us. He, too, migrated annually to Palm Beach like many of the club's members. His was a familiar face, and he indicated we were at table ten, closest to the pool. We thanked him and wandered up the stairs to the patio, following the strains of music.

"We found our table. The Merrill brothers were there along with four girls: the Perry sisters, Mimi Pulitzer, and Meg Patterson. There were four empty chairs. Mine was next to Mimi. Two empty seats, side by side, their backs to the pool, were to Johnny's left and Mimi's right. Johnny reached over and picked up the place cards. His eyebrows shot up, and he said to me across the table, 'You won't believe it, Percy, but there's a James Cushman and a Pamela Rickard assigned to this table. You don't suppose it's *that* James Cushman, do you?'

" 'It most certainly is,' said a voice behind him, and there he was. He smiled at everyone and took his seat next to Mimi. There was still one empty chair, the one between Johnny and James, assigned to Miss Rickard.

"James looked at Johnny and said, 'It's been some time, Dick. I see you still have Pepe hanging around.'

" 'Pepe? Who's Pepe?' I asked.

"Johnny scowled at James and said to me, 'He means you, Percy. Which means I'm Dick.' He turned to James. 'Hi there yourself, Jerkoff. It's certainly been a while. How's the explosive business? Booming?'

"The rest of the table perked up and leaned toward them. There was a whiff of aggression in the air. James lit a cigarette, chuckled, and said, 'I'm glad to see that some things never change.' To the table, he announced, 'I'm James Cushman, the third. My folks just bought a place next to the Kennedys on the ocean. It's a pleasure to meet you.' He gave a sparkling smile to Mimi, who was sitting next to me. 'Question for you all, does anybody know … ' James picked up the card in front of the empty place. '… Pamela Rickard?'

"There were murmurs that we didn't. James nodded, shot his cuffs, and tipped his chair back while placing his right arm possessively along the empty one next to him. I looked him over and was surprised by what I saw. Growing up had improved his appearance. He was fit and surprisingly good-looking. His tuxedo had been exquisitely tailored, and his black tie was perfect. Rather than wearing plain black studs on his starched, pleated, white shirt like Johnny and me, he wore diamond studs set in gold with even larger ones on his cuff links. His thick blond hair was only slightly shorter than Johnny's and seemed even more radiant. He already had a tan. The ladies at the table, I noticed, looked him over with interest.

" 'So, Pepe, how've you been?'

"I said, 'It's Percy, James, but I think you know that.'

" 'That's right. Maybe I do. Hey, I do apologize for leaving you and Josh in the lurch a while back. I don't know what I was thinking. I hope there's no hard feelings?'

"I shrugged. I didn't know what to say.

"James swung his gaze to Johnny and said, 'Wait a minute. It's Johnny, not Josh, isn't it? My mistake, and here we are, about to do some dancing. How about that?'

"Johnny remained silent.

"James continued speaking, unaffected. 'The Johnson twins told me to say hi. We're at Andover together. Too bad you two aren't there with us.'

"With everyone at the table looking at him, Johnny said, 'Maybe that's just as well.'

"At that moment, the band stopped playing. Dinner was about to be served. Coincidentally, every girl at the table started to frown. The Merrill boys stopped talking mid-sentence and stared at whatever was behind James. Puzzled, I turned in my chair and saw what could have been a vision stepping onto the bridge over the reflecting pool. She was tall and slender with shoulder-length golden hair that swept down, framing a face of classic beauty. Her eyes were large and blue-green, the color of the pool that radiated light about her. She wore a silver evening gown of thin material with a plunging neckline and no brassiere. The light beaming up from below left little to the imagination. The dress was a masterpiece, and the result, a pulse-quickening sensation. You could have heard a pin drop.

"Every eye stared at her as she looked about, noted the empty chair between Johnny and James, and glided in their direction as she held a gray fox fur stole in one hand and a Chanel clutch in the other. She moved with a sensual grace. To every young man present, she was the epitome of desire. To every young woman, she was a provocateur and an enemy. She hypnotized us all.

"She stopped in front of the chair to Johnny's left and James's right and waited. After a few moments, she breathed a delicate sigh.

"Both Johnny and James were transfixed until they realized that she was waiting to be seated.

"Both reacted immediately. Johnny sprang to his feet so quickly that he sent his chair skidding toward the reflecting pool. Both grabbed the back of her chair at the same time. An intense, silent, but nonetheless violent struggle ensued. The goddess gave them room. Their straining arms were shaking until Mimi pulled on James's jacket to get his attention. Immediately, he let go, and Johnny was caught dangerously off balance. He almost struck the fair lady in the face as he swung the chair upward in a high arc over his head before slamming it back down on the stone floor with a crack like a gunshot, missing the lady's delicate toes by inches.

Johnny's performance complete, he offered her the chair with a small bow and then tucked her smoothly to the table in a masterly fashion while James scowled and took his seat. Johnny paused a moment behind her, smiled at us, and looked down. He didn't move after that but stood there with his mouth open.

"Mimi and the Perry sisters started coughing. Meg joined in as Miss Rickard twisted around and looked up at Johnny. Johnny's face turned scarlet before he went off to collect his chair. He took his seat, his eyes wide and his breath ragged.

"James grimaced and grabbed a piece of bread. He gnawed on it viciously, like it might have been Johnny's arm. He glared at me and snarled, 'Don't look at me, Pepe!'

"He glanced to his right. Miss Rickard gazed straight ahead, looking at no one in particular. We waited for her to introduce herself, but she said nothing. Instead, she dropped her fur beside her chair and reached into her clutch. She carefully drew out a cigarette and fitted it into a black and gold cigarette holder. She put it to her lips and waited.

"Johnny was the first to react. He began to search frantically for his lighter, patting one pocket and then the other. James smoothly reached into a tiny inside pocket of his dinner jacket and brought out a solid gold Dunhill. He held it out, and she moved toward him. He flicked the roller once and then twice—nothing. Johnny searched more vigorously. I saw his face brighten as he reached into his right pants pocket but couldn't pull it free. James continued to flick his lighter faster and faster. The other males at the table, myself included, began to search for our lighters in an epidemic of convulsive groping.

"Miss Rickard simply waited while several events happened around her.

"James looked at his lighter with disgust and turned the flame up to the highest level. He brought it to his right ear to hear if the gas was escaping while he gave it one last flick.

"The Merrill brothers, lighters in hand, launched themselves across the fully set table, overweighting one of the table's legs. There was a sharp crack as it gave way in a slow-motion avalanche of plates, cutlery, ashtrays, and glasses that tinkled and clattered in the direction of Miss Rickard.

"Johnny freed his hand and lighter, ripping his pants.

"In amongst these sounds was a distinctive whoosh as James' lighter ignited like a Roman candle. A brilliant tongue of flame leaped toward the ceiling as the right side of his golden locks erupted in flames. He screamed like a burning heretic and grabbed for a glass of water that was sliding toward him, splashing it on his flaming head.

"My lighter was fully charged and gave a satisfactory flick as I stepped out of the way and lit her cigarette.

"Into this stillness, the lady said in a low southern voice, 'Thank you kindly. I'm blind as a bat. Can you collect my clutch and point me toward the can?'

" 'Beg your pardon?' I managed.

" 'The restroom?'

"I pointed toward the lobby. She handed me her stole. I picked up her clutch from the wreckage as teams of waiters appeared to clean up the broken plates and glasses. The Merrill brothers got off the floor and began to babble their apologies. All the party guests were on their feet, craning their necks to see what had happened. Johnny slunk off to the restroom to repair his pants. James was soaked and looked aghast in the mirror of Mimi Pulitzer's compact at what was left of his hair on the right side of his face. I think he was crying. He stank to high heaven.

"The band struck up immediately to shift the party's attention away from the wreck that had been table ten. I placed the lady's stole and clutch on a clean chair and stood to the side, waiting. When Miss Rickard returned, I asked if she might wish to dance. She grinned at me and said, 'You betcha, Pepe! Lead the way!' "

34

"Pepe? She called you Pepe?" asked Bruni.

I smiled and said, "She most certainly did. We made it my nickname. Pam and I went out for a year or two after that. We'd see each other on school vacations and on the occasional weekend in New York. Eventually, we stopped seeing each other."

"Why?" Bruni asked.

"She moved on to someone else, and I didn't have the strength to go after her. She was somewhat neurotic. She'd mention the possibility of suicide, which frightened me, at least until I realized it was an act. She could get me to do just about anything. I loved her, but more than that, I wanted to help her. In the end, I couldn't—nor could she fix me. She wanted me to be a man, only I wasn't ready to be one at the time."

"First love?" Bruni asked.

"That she was."

"I didn't mean to put you on the spot, but I do get curious," said Bruni.

"That's quite all right. John? Anne? Do you have any questions?"

Anne smiled at me and said, "More a comment than a question. You cleverly made off with the prize while everyone else wasn't looking. Was that deliberate?"

"I took advantage of the situation and was in the right place at the right time for once. Besides, I had a lighter that worked."

"You seem to be lucky in that way."

"I suppose. John?"

John thought for a moment and said, "There was the continued rivalry between Johnny and James, and perhaps with you as well. What interests me is the intensity. Did that escalate?"

"Their mutual animosity eventually boiled over, as you will hear."

John stood and said, "Well, let's continue, but only after I refresh our drinks."

35

W hen everyone was seated again with their drinks topped off, I asked my audience, "I have one more story to tell, but I'd rather not commit the error of going on too long."

Anne answered, "I would like to know how come their rivalry continued. John? What do you think?"

"I'd like to hear more. Bruni?"

"I'm for it. You grew up in such a different environment than my own. I'd like to hear another."

"Very well."

I took a sip of my drink and began. "Johnny and I were nineteen, and it was a warm and sunny Saturday in August. We were in Southampton at the Beach Club, looking out at the ocean.

"Johnny turned to me and said, 'Percy, I'm in need of funds. How much cash do you have?'

"I pulled out my wallet to be certain and said, 'None, I'm afraid.'

"Johnny said, 'That doesn't include your emergency stash. I know your tricks.'

" 'That's only for emergencies,' I answered.

" 'Well, I'm afraid the current situation qualifies. Give me whatever's in it, and I'll return it to you and then some tomorrow'.

" 'How are you going to do that?'

" 'I have a few ideas. Now hand it over.'

"I sighed. There was little I could do. I knew that Johnny would just keep pestering me until I gave in. I pulled my fifty-dollar emergency stash from my secret compartment and gave it to him.

" 'Thank you, Percy. Every little bit helps, and I can assure you that it's from such humble beginnings that fortunes are made. You'll see. I'll be back in a bit.'

"I sighed. Life was fiscally grim. I only hoped we had enough gas to drive to the Johnsons once Johnny returned. We'd been invited to Billy and his twin brother's house for an afternoon of hanging out at their pool. Johnny had designs on the tempting Miss Lorna Barre, who would also be there. He was intent on asking her out on a date that night.

"Johnny picked me up an hour later. We drove to the Johnsons and then up the long gravel driveway that led to an elegant three-story shingled house. The circle in front was filled with cars, but one stood out from all the rest. It was painted a dazzling lemon yellow with an orange racing stripe down the center. It looked fast and brand-spanking new.

"We parked and walked over to it. James Cushman III was leaning against the door, talking to someone in the driver's seat. He saw us and waved us over. 'Feast your eyes on my latest acquisition. This is a Dodge Challenger Six Pack with a custom transmission and a 425-horsepower, 426-cubic-inch engine. Is it beautiful, or what?'

"Johnny scowled but had to admit that it was beautiful. He grew even more perturbed when he glanced inside the dark red interior and saw Miss Lorna Barre gazing up in rapture at the owner. Lorna gave Johnny a nod and a smile; at least, I thought it was a nod and a smile. Whatever it was, it was very brief. She said to James, 'I have my learner's permit. Maybe you can give me a driving lesson?'

"James grinned and answered, 'Great idea! I'd *love* to give you a driving lesson. In fact, now is the perfect time.' He turned to Johnny and me without the grin and said, 'You boys will have to excuse us. I'm going to give this lady a lesson.' Beaming at Lorna once again, he announced, 'I'll take it down the drive, and then you can take over. How about that?'

"Lorna squealed, flung open the driver's door, and ran around the car to the passenger side.

" 'I'll be right back,' she said over the hood of the car, smiling at Johnny as she got in. James started the car with a roar, looked at Johnny coldly, and burbled off down the drive.

"The sight of James's new car, and a Dodge at that with James and Lorna in it, had darkened Johnny's mood considerably. He looked stormy.

"We walked round the house where some twenty or thirty guests were lounging about the pool deck, eating and drinking. Billy Johnson welcomed us while George, his twin brother, walked through the side gate, commenting that the 'love birds' had departed and likely wouldn't be back for a while.

"Johnny looked disgusted and stalked off. I went inside to shoot some pool. When Johnny was in one of his moods, it was best to leave him be. After losing several games, I came outside to the deck, where Johnny was surrounded by several of the familiar gang of teenagers we hung out with, arguing. I heard him exclaim, 'Oh, it's possible, all right!'

"The gang derided him loudly with, 'No way! You are so full of it! In your dreams!'

"Before Johnny could respond in kind, James and Lorna showed up holding hands. James asked what the fuss was all about.

"Billy Johnson called for silence and summed it up. 'Johnny here says he can drive from this house to Mitty's on a Saturday night in less than thirty minutes.'

"On the surface, Johnny's claim seemed entirely reasonable. The distance was no more than a few miles; however, this estimate didn't account for the traffic along the Montauk Highway, which consisted of two lanes separated by a continuous double yellow line. It was bad all the time, but on Saturday nights, traffic slowed to a mind-numbing, bumper-to-bumper crawl. It was the bane of Hampton existence.

"James heard the arguments for and against and stated that not even his car could make it in that time.

"Johnny scoffed. He stood up, looked James straight in the eye, and said, 'Your car, driven by someone who knows how to drive, could make it in twenty.'

"James said, 'No way.'

"They stared at each other. Johnny took a step closer and snarled, 'Five hundred says I can.'

"James glared at Johnny, and Johnny glared at James.

"Those of us watching waited for James to respond.

"To me, the bet looked like easy money for James, but I doubted he would accept. He wasn't one to take on excessive risks. I'd played backgammon with him on many occasions, and his play was conservative. Besides, James had nothing to gain by accepting. He had more than enough money. I looked at James again and realized that the clincher was the thrill of putting down Johnny in front of Lorna. Given that inducement, I decided that the wager would prove irresistible, and I was right.

" 'I'll take your money, but my car is not part of this,' James said.

"Johnny countered, 'Your car, or no bet.'

" 'You're not driving my car, and that's final!' yelled James.

"Johnny countered again, 'Two thousand says I am driving your car! You can ride shotgun if you want, but I'm the one driving— that's if you have the balls.'

"There were oohs and aahs and then silence. James looked at Lorna, who smiled back at him. Convinced, James said, 'Okay, Johnny Dodge. Let's see you put your money where your mouth is. Five thousand says you can't drive from here to Mitty's at nine tonight in under twenty minutes. You can drive my car, but you pay for any damage, and that's on top of what you'll owe me for losing. There it is—smartass—take it or leave it.'

"Johnny said, 'Done!' "

"Hold on, Percy," said Anne. "Five thousand dollars? That's a great deal of money even now."

"It's true, but both were caught up in the moment, Anne. The rivalry that had simmered and flared between them for years had at last burst forth into full public display. It was madness, and I said so, but neither listened to me. The oohs and aahs of those who sat at their feet made the decision irrevocable."

Anne considered that. "I see. It was like a runaway train."

"It was. To continue, the gathering disbanded, and all agreed to return at six to finalize the details.

"As we drove home, I asked Johnny how much he had in his checking.

"After a long pause, he said, 'I do believe I'm overdrawn, but not to worry. I've got this. You'll see.' Johnny turned to reassure me, smiling jauntily with a cigarette clenched in his teeth.

" 'What? Johnny! We're talking thousands here, and you're overdrawn? Are you out of your mind?'

"Johnny flicked his cigarette out the window and said, 'Settle down. In truth, I'm only on the hook for three. I put you down for two. James agreed readily enough, and I figured you wouldn't want to miss out.'

" 'You did whaaaat?! My God! When did that happen?' I started to tremble.

"Johnny said, 'Right before we left. It's only two thousand, for God's sake!'

" 'I don't *have* two thousand dollars. You can't do that! Stop the car! I'm going to be sick!'

"Johnny pulled over to the side of the road. I opened the door and got out, my stomach in an uproar.

" 'Come on, Percy,' Johnny said, walking over to me and patting my shoulder. 'You're acting like an old woman. I've seen what's in that checking account of yours. You've got at least four hundred, so get a grip. Besides, I have a secret weapon. Everything's going to be fine. Now, get back in the car. We have money to make.'

"I took my time as a matter of principle but got back in the car.

"As we drove, I asked Johnny, 'How do you know I've got four hundred in my checking account? *I* don't even know what's in my checking account.'

" 'That's because you never balance it. I did.'

" 'Really? That's good to know, but peeking at my balance and hustling me into a wager without my permission is really going too far.'

" 'Get over it, Percy. You want to crush that asshole as much as I do. Remember dancing class? It's time we paid him back. Besides, he walked right into it.'

" 'You planned the whole thing?'

" 'Indeed, I did.'

"The thought that I might not be overdrawn, Johnny's confidence, and his assertion that he'd planned this out beforehand had mollified my misgivings to some degree. Johnny was Johnny, after all.

"I harrumphed and said, 'I do feel a bit better—not that much, but a little. Now, what's this about a secret weapon?'

" 'Hah! I knew that would get your attention, but as the junior partner in this endeavor, you'll just have to wait and see. In any event, using James' car will make his losing all the more satisfying when I win, and by the way, your checkbook's in your top left-hand drawer by your bed.'

" 'Oh,' I said.

"We parked the car in front of the garage and met again downstairs. I'd put my check in my wallet.

"At quarter to six, we walked toward the Valiant. Johnny said, 'You drive,' and slid onto the passenger seat. I started the car.

"I glanced at Johnny. 'Where's the secret weapon?'

"Johnny smiled and said, 'In the trunk, but I'm not going to show it to you. The only way this is going to work is if you know absolutely nothing about it. Be your typical, nervous self, and let me do the talking.'

"I sighed. Life with Johnny was always like that. I said a small prayer.

"We arrived at the Johnsons, where James started in by asking Johnny in front of everyone how he would guarantee his side of the bet. Johnny countered with the same question to James. All was at an impasse until Billy Johnson mentioned that he and George happened to have five thousand dollars in currency on hand from a prior transaction that they wouldn't elaborate on and would be willing to guarantee the stakes for a twenty-five percent cut. Both James and Johnny thought this amount excessive, and twenty percent, or one thousand dollars, was finally agreed upon. To monitor and call the start, Billy and I would remain at the Johnsons while George, with a stopwatch in hand, would commandeer the pay phone at Mitty's to call the finish. The official clock would begin when Johnny had started the car moving and would run for exactly twenty minutes, by which time Johnny had either passed the gateposts or he had not. There would be no 'do-overs' or false starts.

"With the details worked out, we settled down to wait. Numerous side bets were made among the gang, and at 8:00 p.m., those who wanted to watch the finish, including George, James, and Lorna, made their way to Mitty's in a fleet of cars. They called in close to 8:45 p.m. It had taken forty minutes to make the trip. By 9:00 p.m., a continuous telephone connection was established, and an extension strung to the gate to call the start. A minute later, Johnny announced that it was time.

"Billy Johnson carried the phone to his position. He could see the Challenger and the driveway. He watched Johnny walk to the Valiant, take a cardboard box from the trunk, and carry it to the Challenger. Johnny got in and closed the door. Billy reported this into the phone to George in a loud voice like a radio announcer. 'Johnny's got a box. ... That's right, brother, tell James he's got what looks like a cardboard box. ... No, I don't know what's in the box. ... Wait a sec. ... Johnny's started the car. ... He's opened the driver's side window. ... Whoa! He's got a flashing red police light! ... That's right. ... He's stuck it on the roof. He's revving the engine. ... Start the clock! He's moving!'

"I watched the Challenger fishtail down the drive, then drift sideways as Johnny hit the road in a swirl of dust and gravel. The car screamed as Johnny floored it along the road leading to Southampton and the Montauk highway. He was gone in a moment, driving like a maniac.

"At the Johnson house, pandemonium broke loose. Those who had bet on James started screaming that Johnny's tactics invalidated the bet. Others roared their approval. An urgent discussion ensued between those at the finish line and those at the start.

"After much back and forth, those holding the stakes determined that the police light was obviously illegal but not contrary to the rules of the wager. The bet was still on.

"After ten minutes, everyone clustered around the pool phone to hear the latest from the finish line.

"A few minutes later, the phone crackled with the announcement: 'I see a flashing red light in the far distance. I think it's the cops.' After a few moments, 'Wait a sec, I think it's him. ... It's gonna be close! ... He might just make it!'

"At nineteen minutes ... 'It's definitely him. He's driving right down the center of the highway! Here he comes ... I don't believe it! He did it! Johnny won!'

"A howl of dismay split the air around me, along with several cheers. Similar sounds could be heard from the still-connected phone, followed by a click as the line went dead.

"All I could think of at the time was that I was saved. I didn't have to confess that I'd contracted gambling debts. I wasn't a spendthrift, destined to a life of fiscal oversight and conservatorship. Johnny had won! I repeated the words several times to myself and then out loud to be sure. Several of those who remained at the Johnsons looked at me with some animosity. Others crowded around and slapped me on the back in congratulations. Quite a few had won substantial sums of money while others had lost big. To the losers, it was a catastrophe. To the winners, it was vindication. To me, it was redemption. I started to laugh with wondrous joy. When a few of the losers began to look overtly hostile, I retired quickly to the Valiant and fled.

"By that time, I was so exhausted and relieved that I could barely drive, and since it would take me an hour to get to Mitty's, I went to bed.

"I awoke at 7:30 the next morning as Johnny walked in exclaiming, 'Man, what a night!'

"I peered at him and asked groggily, 'You just got in?'

" 'You guessed it. Where were you?'

" 'The whole thing wore me out, so I went to bed.'

" 'Well, that may have been for the best. The Challenger's in the shop, and I only just got a ride. I'm taking a shower, and then I'll tell you all about it.'

"After we had both showered and changed, Johnny said, 'I told you we'd win. Oh, by the way, here's your check.'

"Johnny handed me back my check for two thousand.

" 'What about the winnings?'

" 'Well, we need to talk about that. Here's four hundred. You might want to get that into your account rather quickly, as I may have exaggerated how much you have in your checking. You were a little overdrawn, but I didn't want to alarm you. Here you go.'

"He handed me four hundred-dollar bills and said, 'Oh, and here's your original investment back as well.' He handed me fifty dollars. 'You earned eight hundred percent—not bad.'

"I stared at him. 'Johnny, sometimes you're such a ... words escape me. Just the same; I thought you might have been exaggerating. This is all that's left?'

" 'Sad to say, but the thrill of victory led to a little overexuberance. I bought the house a round.'

" 'The entire house?'

" 'It was the least I could do. Many of the gang were feeling low, and we had definitely caused a stir amongst the locals, what with my doing a four-wheel drift through the entrance. One round turned into two, and by the time I decided enough was enough, I'd gone through most of it. James was so plastered by that time that I offered to drive him, Lorna, and George home in the Challenger. James was so drunk he didn't care. Lorna was in similar shape, and both went to sleep in the back.

" 'While we were cruising into Southampton, the transmission suddenly made a horrible grinding sound and refused to go into any gear, no matter what I did. I think I may have slipped the gearshift into reverse by mistake. Who knows? Luckily, Luke's Racing was nearby, although closed at the time. George and I managed to push the car to their garage and left it out front with James and Lorna still in the back, snoring like a couple of bears. I slipped some money into James's shirt pocket to help cover the repair along with the keys. I cracked the windows a tad and left them there. It was the least I could do. George and I hitched a ride to his place, and I walked the rest of the way. Setting your fifty aside, I had exactly eight hundred left, which I decided to split with you, and here we are.'

" 'Well, thank you for deciding that, but what about you and Lorna?' I asked. 'She was the point of the exercise, was she not?'

"Johnny sighed and told me that Lorna turned argumentative when she drank too much, and he couldn't possibly deal with a woman like that. He decided to give her a pass."

36

A nne said, "Now, let me get this straight. Johnny spent most of your winnings on rounds of drinks and car repairs. Wasn't that a bit unfair?"

"Not really. I gave Johnny my fifty and didn't expect to see that money again, but he gave me back eight times that amount. True, the risks for both of us were substantial, but the toast usually falls buttered side up when it comes to Johnny, and in the end, we both came out ahead."

John chuckled and said, "It also sounds like James would have had quite a hangover when he awoke the next morning."

"Yes, and a lot more besides, but what really sent him over the edge was Lorna's arrest."

Bruni interrupted, "Wait a second, Lorna was arrested?"

"That she was. James got the Challenger back from Luke just before the end of the summer but had to go into the city the next day. Lorna talked James into letting her hold the keys but failed to mention that she'd recently flunked her driving test again and still had only a learner's permit. Unbeknownst to any of us, a description of the vehicle had been passed around the local police departments. When Lorna took the car out for a little practice, the car was spotted. Lorna panicked, and a high-speed chase ensued. She was arrested after she crashed into a tree just outside Southampton Township. The car was totaled, but Lorna was unhurt. She was handcuffed and put in the back of a patrol car.

"There, she went a little crazy. She began to cry and scream hysterically. She couldn't or wouldn't stop. At the station, nobody could make out what she was saying—not the police, the medical people, no one. She had no identification with her and ended up in the psych unit of the county lockup in Riverhead. Meanwhile, her parents reported her missing, and a search ensued. Eventually, the two events were connected, and all got sorted out. Lorna was released into her parents' custody and, shortly after, told James that she never wanted to see him again since he'd stupidly given her the keys. After various legal wranglings, her parents sent her to a health clinic in Switzerland to recover. Lorna never returned to this country. I heard from Johnny that she later married a duke and became a duchess. All in all, I think she came out the best of all of us from that little escapade."

"Well," said Anne, "all this is news to me. What happened between James and Johnny after that?"

"James blamed Johnny for losing the bet, the car, and Lorna. He swore he'd get even, but the summer ended before he got his chance. The next summer, he traveled around Europe. From then on, I saw James only occasionally. Later, I left for California and lost track of everyone. During that time, James married Casey. How that came about and what happened between Johnny and James, I don't know. Johnny never brought it up. That's all I have, I'm afraid."

John said, "Well, thank you for telling us those stories. My question, Percy, is based on what you know of him: Do you think James arranged Johnny's accident?"

"It's possible but unlikely, in my opinion. That being said, there were always underlying issues between them. Johnny always had a thing for Casey Duke, and James ended up marrying her. Was that deliberate on James's part? Johnny then had an affair with her. Was that also deliberate? I doubt revenge was the overriding reason for either of their actions, but doing so must have given each of them some measure of satisfaction and likely intensified their dislike for the other. Certainly, James would want revenge on Johnny for sleeping with his wife, but was the accident his response? Maybe it was, but if it was me, I'd go with something more certain. Accidents are difficult to arrange, and the outcomes are often unpredictable."

John nodded and said, "I understand. From what you say, the accident wouldn't be his method of choice. What if the opportunity presented itself? Would he do it anyway?"

"Possibly. Bruni?"

Bruni said, "I have no opinion about James. I've never met him, but I do have a suggestion. I would upgrade Angus's announcement to one of Johnny making such a miraculous recovery that he might be able to walk through the door this Sunday. Hearing that, whoever is responsible is likely to panic. Then, we'll know for sure who did what. That being said, the more I hear about the Cushmans, the less I want anything to do with them."

John said, "I agree, but now that they've accepted, we're committed. Upgrading Johnny's recovery to imminent is an excellent idea. Angus might even go along with that. Percy?"

"I'll speak to him, of course."

Bruni stood and said, "On that note, I think it's time for me to go to bed."

We all rose. John and Anne thanked me for the stories and retired. As we made our way to our apartment, Bruni said, "Dagmar is expecting you and asked that I wait up until you return."

"Very well, I'll speak to her now. By the way, excellent idea at the end. I'll be back soon."

I gave Bruni a kiss and made my way to the kitchen.

37

D agmar and Stanley were sitting at the kitchen table, talking. They stood, and I thanked them for waiting up. As I sat down, Dagmar poured me a cup of tea.

After I'd made myself comfortable, Dagmar asked, "Has Johnny's condition changed since last we spoke?"

"He thrashed about, according to the nurses."

"That's good news. Perhaps he'll find his way back to us after all, and given that, do you still think he's lost?"

"Yes."

"Then let us continue with finding him. I once mentioned to you that certain individuals can travel to other worlds in their minds and that it's an ancient practice. Her ladyship had visions but different from yours. She and I worked together to discover more about them—she from the mystical side, me from the pharmacological. I've also said that you might have a great gift."

"You did, and that not all such gifts are happy."

"Not all of them are, particularly yours. We talked about shamanic studies. To the shaman, sickness and bad luck are spiritual matters, not physical ones. Her ladyship told me that a village can have many shamans. The best and most skilled are always the most expensive, not only because of their own unique powers but because of the many risks involved and the high degree of mastery required to navigate the different spirit worlds. Much, if not most, of that knowledge has been lost, but many believe that a particularly powerful and knowledgeable shaman can be called upon to help those equally gifted who come after. You met such a one, I think."

I thought about that. "The person in the hut?"

Dagmar nodded.

"I don't know if he or she will help me. I was called a demon and ordered to leave. After that, I was chased by something horrible and barely made it back alive. It was terrifying."

Dagmar replied, "I'm sure it was, but if you wish to find Johnny, then I think you must visit that hut again and convince the person there to help you find him. You'll likely need to give the shaman something in return at some point. What bargain you'll make is up to you, but I'd be careful what you promise."

"How am I to see that person again?"

"There are various methods, but the surest is through a tincture of certain plants. Given that, I've prepared a drink for you to take tonight. Stan can elaborate more fully on what needs to be done. I apologize, but I must wake up in a few hours, and there is much work that I must do to prepare for this weekend. Once again, I ask that you leave all the arrangements to us. Is that acceptable?"

"It is, and I thank you."

"Then, I will say good night. The drink is by your bed. Your fiancée wanted me to make another for herself, but I told her no. Drinking it might harm the child, and this task is yours, not hers."

"It is, but I'll have to decide whether to make that journey to begin with. I'm not sure I want to. That was one of the most frightening experiences of my life."

"I believe you, but fear is not the worst of emotions. It has the benefit of keeping us alive when rushing in would be fatal. I would let it guide you, not rule you. If it's any consolation, I'd feel the same. The question you must ask yourself is whether your friendship is worth the risks that you must assume to sustain it. After all, Johnny may come back to us in his own time, but in what condition? Will he be fully recovered or only partially? From my experience, the price we pay is commensurate with what we ask for. Nothing in this life is free, not even the air we breathe. Perhaps this task is your payment? Now, I must end our talk. Thank you for taking the time to listen and for your agreement. Good night."

With that, she rose and picked up the tea service. I thanked her and looked at Stanley.

"My office?" he asked.

I answered, "Of course."

38

Once we were seated again, I asked, "Stan, have you noticed that we tend to meet either late at night or early in the morning?"

Stanley chuckled. "I have. It seems we, too, pay for our friendship but with the hours of sleep that we deny ourselves."

I laughed. "It's the same with Johnny and me. By the way, what are your thoughts about what Dagmar said?"

"Dagmar has a mind filled with extraordinary knowledge. Few know what she knows. One must always listen to one such as her, and I would even go so far as to say, follow their advice. To not do so can have grave consequences, and believe me, you don't want to experience that."

"That's a story I'd like to hear."

"I might even tell it, but not now. We have your journey to discuss. As Dagmar mentioned, you should contact the shaman in the hut and ask for the knowledge necessary to locate Johnny and return him to us. One fact that might help is that this house was built on top of what used to be a circular depression. We called them dew ponds where I grew up."

"In other words, this house and the hut are connected in some way?"

"It would appear so."

"Well, that solves the issue of finding him or her. Just the same, such people certainly don't welcome those who come seeking answers."

"They may not. Their world is not our world, and their conception of it will be unlike our own. Their manners, customs, and courtesies will be different as well. In truth, we know so little about them and their beliefs. Her ladyship thought that there were many universes connected to this one and that ancient shamans knew this well enough to navigate and explore them. She said that being in our world exclusively was like being in a box. If all we're familiar with is the inside, what the box is doing in relation to everything else is difficult to know. How two universes interact is equally hard to imagine."

I nodded. "She was interested in many things and not just on a superficial level."

"She was. Such thoughts and ideas piqued her interest. On top of that, her ladyship was endlessly curious about indigenous people. She told me that many tribes believe we're influenced by spirits that we moderns cannot see. It is ironic that those tribes call us *ghosts*. They told her that only those who can perceive spirits and other worlds are considered genuine human beings. Such an unflattering point of view isn't hard to understand. We moderns only embrace what can be observed and ultimately measured, all else being relegated to delusion. Such an outlook has certainly made science successful. On the other hand, viruses couldn't be seen or imagined for years, and so we assigned their effects to other causes—ones we were familiar with at the time, like humors or the air. Mention bloodletting as a cure nowadays, and a doctor will look embarrassed before quickly adding that we know better now. Do we really? Science is like fashion; where it goes depends on what's in vogue and what research can be funded. My questions are: Who determines that, and why? To me, spirits may be like viruses before we were aware of their existence."

I thought about that and said, "Spirits are not a comfortable explanation. They're invisible and have no material substance."

"They certainly can't be measured, but her ladyship argued that people are routinely influenced by unseen, unmeasurable forces. Social niceties, familial obligations, political beliefs, and others'

171

opinions are immaterial and invisible, but when you consider their power to influence what we do and, in many cases, to fundamentally change and structure the world we live in, one must ask if spirits and ideas are so very different? One must also remember that anything remotely pagan or animistic was systematically exterminated and suppressed for well over a thousand years under the ministrations of Christianity, Catholicism in particular. Is it any wonder that we get nervous and uneasy when we talk about such things? Your journey to find Johnny is certainly contrary to the existing view."

"It is." I paused before I said, "To tell you truthfully, I'm hesitant."

Stanley nodded. "I understand your reluctance. On the other hand, what Dagmar proposes might work. Of course, it might not, but to me, the best approach is to be open to the possibility that it will."

I considered that. "What's invisible but nonetheless sensed seems to be a theme these days. Mr. Dodge is sure that he's under attack from an unseen enemy. Maybe he is. Maybe he isn't. Paranoia can be like that."

"Yes, it can be until it turns out to be true. Then, it wasn't paranoia at all but a brilliant intuition. If he's wrong, then a darker interpretation becomes more likely. For now, only time and what we can discover will reveal the truth. As to Mr. Dodge, he is rather savvy from what I've observed, but let's put that aside and end this discussion by saying that whether you decide to take the drink that Dagmar prepared or not, I support your decision. We'll speak after breakfast. Dare I say *good luck*?"

I smiled. "You most certainly can. Until tomorrow, then."

39

Bruni was in bed reading when I opened our bedroom door. She put aside her book. "There you are. The drink is by your side of the bed."

I came over to her and sat down. A small crystal glass of dark liquid sat on a white linen cocktail napkin by my bedside. I stared at the glass.

"I'm not sure what to do about that."

Bruni took my hand. "It can wait. Why don't you get ready for bed and then decide? I'd take it, but then, that's me. At least it won't harm Johnny."

"What about me?"

"Do you think it'll harm you?"

I got up and started to undress. "The past ones didn't, so it's likely this one won't either. The question I have is whether I should take it at all. My only justification is that I'll be doing something rather than nothing, but whether that's a sufficient reason, and more to the point, whether taking the drink will actually help Johnny, I really have no idea."

I finished getting ready for bed and got in on my side. Bruni said, "Come over here and let me hold you. I agree with what you said, but I'd be a bit more optimistic. Besides, I'll be here, and Dagmar told me that might make all the difference."

I kissed her. "Having you with me will always make a difference. It's my doubts that make me hesitate. Dagmar says I have a gift, maybe even a great one. I'm not so sure that's true."

"Everybody thinks that way at one time or another. Our gifts are part of who we are, but that doesn't mean we are fully aware of how significant or insignificant those gifts may be. To us, they are effortless and easy. To others, they are difficult, if not impossible. I think you have something special, Percy. I can't say I know what that is exactly, other than that you're attuned to something of which others are unaware. You create a bridge between that something and this place, like a conduit or at least a point of intersection. I can't express it any better, but you do that. I can't do that. It's a gift you have, and I think you must accept and learn to use it."

I thought about what Bruni said. "I hadn't considered what I do in quite that way. So, you think I should drink it?"

"It's up to you, but sometimes trying is all we have to justify doing anything when the outcome is uncertain and the possibility of success remote."

"I suppose I could try."

"If trying is the only option available, then I think you must. There's also the expression *use it or lose it* to consider."

"Yes, I suppose that's true as well."

I kissed her again and reached for the glass. I wasn't completely convinced, but I knew I had to try for Johnny's sake and maybe for my own. The concoction tasted as foul as I remembered. My world remained stable until the edges of the room began to move.

40

I opened my eyes and saw a million stars. They stared down with cool, indifferent brilliance as I lay on the cold ground looking up at them. There were so many. The bright band of the Milky Way angled across an inky universe from horizon to horizon. There was no moon. I sat up and looked about. As my eyes adjusted to the darkness of the Earth, I made out the lip of the circular indentation to my left. I was in the right place. A thin column of smoke was barely visible as it rose into the cool and still of the night.

I got up. I could barely see the ground. The grass was shorter than I expected. I wondered if someone had trimmed it. I took a step, stumbled, and fell flat on my face. My world exploded into bright, sharp-edged geometric shapes. They hung about me in exuberant patterns of yellow, purple, orange, and red that danced about before the scene transformed into crimson antlers that I could barely make out in the feeble glow of a few coals. I was hunched over and tied in a ball like a trussed chicken. I couldn't move my limbs. The antlers spoke.

"Ah, the demon who thinks he's not a demon. I told you not to wander in this place."

I recognized the voice.

I croaked, "I can see the red of the fire now."

"Well, good for you. Do you know why you're here?"

"I wish to save someone who's lost."

"Oh, really? When you can't even save yourself? I think not. You've come here to die."

"But why?"

"Why not? What cannot be outrun must be embraced."

I heard a howl. It started low and rose in pitch and volume before fading away.

"Hear that? Death is coming. Will you be brave and unflinching, or will you scramble on all fours to get away? Will it be messy or neat? Prolonged or quick? In the end, does it really matter? Do you know the answer?"

"I … I just want to find my friend."

"You haven't been listening. I will free you, and then you'll be outside. I think your death will be messy. You'll be ripped apart and eaten so fast you'll think you're still alive before you realize that you aren't."

A howl split the air again. It was much closer.

The voice in the antlers said, "You won't get away. Not this time."

The antlers and the hut dissolved into a kaleidoscope of colors before I was back at the edge of the indentation in the dark. The blue-white stars stared down from far above as I heard another howl. I thought I saw something hurtling up the grassy meadow toward me. I heard it grunting as it galloped on all fours. The hut was too far away now. I had nowhere to run, no place to hide, and this time, there was no base. I began to panic. I felt, rather than heard, the words, *What cannot be outrun must be embraced.*

Why not? I thought. I turned and spread my arms wide as I was struck with tremendous force and carried backward. Teeth, like jagged crystals, bit and tore into my body. I felt myself ripped to pieces. I watched what may have been my left arm disappear into the night. I hurt. Everything hurt. I hurt so much I couldn't think. I was a burning point of pain. I screamed and screamed until I realized that I didn't have a throat to scream with and stopped. For a time, I simply was.

41

I awoke with a gasp, reaching out to steady myself. Bruni was there beside me. I sat up, breathing heavily. Bruni sat up also. "Are you okay?"

I groaned, "I don't know. I'm here, and I'm alive."

"What happened?"

"I was eaten. Did I scream?"

"No, you writhed about and made strange sounds, but not very loud. You stopped breathing for the longest time. Dagmar warned me that might happen and instructed me to hold you. Had she not done so, I would have panicked. You're sweating a lot, too."

I noticed that. "I'm soaked and very cold. I should take a hot shower. Thank you for being here and taking care of me. What time is it?"

"Late, but not too late. I'll shower with you. Dagmar told me to make you feel and touch things."

"I do need to do that. I could also use a serious hug. I don't understand what happened."

"Hug first, shower second, and then you can tell me all about your journey in detail. Between us, we'll make some sense of it."

After a long shower, Bruni, in her kimono, and I, in my bathrobe, held each other on the couch in our sitting room. I had lit the fire, which popped and flickered in shimmering orange tongues. I looked at the little dancing flames and told her what had happened.

Bruni listened and, after I finished, said slowly, "I think you were being tested."

"If I was, I don't think I did very well."

"Maybe better than you think. You embraced what couldn't be outrun. There is something profound in that."

"Perhaps that's true, but I'm still no closer to finding Johnny."

"So you say. I'd look at it more positively. Do you feel changed?"

I considered the question. I did feel changed, but no words could possibly describe that transformation.

I told her, "Yes, but I don't know in which direction. I feel more puzzled than anything else. The ordeal didn't seem to make a difference. I'm still here. I'm still alive."

"You survived, and maybe that's the point. I, for one, am certainly glad you did."

"That makes two of us. You wouldn't believe the number of stars I was able to see when I was there."

"Did that other place seem different?"

"The sky was jet black, and because it was, I saw far more stars than I ever knew existed."

"That would make some sense—no city lights. For now, we should go back to bed and sleep. I won't ask you to carry me."

"I can if that is your wish."

"Really?"

"No. You're getting … "

Bruni put a finger to my lips, "Careful."

"I was about to say you're getting light as a feather."

"I doubt that."

"Maybe not. Come on, you know the drill. Put your arms around my neck. Thank God you left the door to the bedroom open."

42

I awoke feeling much better. Bruni was drying her hair with a towel.

She said, "Breakfast will be ready soon. We have a big day ahead."

"Yes, we do. The Cushmans."

"And my parents. Let's not forget them."

"I doubt that's possible. We must brief them."

"Yes, along with everyone else. Hurry, or we'll be late."

I noted that Bruni could be a lot like Johnny on occasion. I got up, showered, and quickly dressed in blue jeans and a light-blue, long-sleeved button-down shirt. Bruni wore a simple but elegant gray dress. I always appreciated that the dress code for breakfast was casual. Anne and John were already at the table reading their newspapers and drinking coffee. Stanley served us and discreetly asked that I stop by his office. I nodded and began the best meal of the day. The taste of the toast, the butter, and the marmalade seemed to transcend the ordinary. The bacon and eggs were as much a delight. Compared to last night, I was in heaven.

Once we finished, Bruni and I excused ourselves and made our way to the kitchen. Bruni put on an apron while I continued to Stanley's office.

He was at his desk, filling out a ledger. He put down his fountain pen and asked me how it went.

"Not well," I said as I sat down.

"Tell me."

I told Stanley what had happened in detail. When I finished, Stanley rocked back in his chair and said, "What occurred to you is surprising but not altogether unexpected. According to her ladyship, being torn apart and pierced by crystals was a form of shamanic initiation—a rite of passage."

"I didn't know that. Bruni thought it was a kind of test."

"Likely, she's correct. How do you feel?"

"Better than I've any right to expect."

"I could well imagine. My question to you is, will you continue?"

"I think I must. Johnny is still lost, and I must find him; only doing so has proved to be far more daunting than I'd imagined. The drink catapulted me into another existence that felt real, but then how could it be? I'm still alive."

"Therefore, it must be a dream or a hallucination?"

"Logically, yes, but I can't dismiss it so easily. Frankly, before this last experience, I thought that curing Johnny by finding and returning him to us was highly unlikely, but I was willing to try anything. Now, I think it might be possible. It was the stars in that other place that convinced me. Their clarity and overwhelming numbers blew my mind. I *knew* I was someplace else. It was no dream."

"I understand. Acknowledging that another world might exist is a stretch, particularly for those brought up in our culture. To give another perspective and perhaps some credence to what you said, I once overheard a conversation between a noted anthropologist and her ladyship. They were discussing genius and how rare it was to come across it, not only in this society but in the field. The anthropologist stated that hardly anyone believes that real geniuses exist outside our modern society, and certainly not among indigenous people. We look at them and see no reading or writing, only huts in the jungle, minimal tools, and abject poverty. He thought such condescension incorrect. The only real difference between us and them is infrastructure. Modern man sees and values only outward manifestations, not the minds within. He asserted that we're genetically no different from those of thirty thousand years ago and posited that should we sample indigenous populations, we would find a Newton or an Einstein among them. He argued that the distribution of intelligence and genius is the same across all human populations, regardless of where they were born or where they live. Granted, one might have to look carefully and across a great number of cultures, but they're there, even in a rainforest. The question that intrigued him was: What would such an indigenous genius think about?

"Her ladyship answered that she'd encountered such a person.

"The man became excited and asked her to tell him all about it.

"Her ladyship paused several moments before she answered. I recall her saying, 'I'm not altogether sure how to express it. His thoughts were extraordinarily complex—an abstraction quite beyond my ability to articulate even now. What I do know is that he saw worlds, not just this one—thousands of them, and how they intersected and interacted. His vision stunned me. It shook me to my core. For a moment, I glimpsed what it was he saw and understood. I don't know how, but I did, and then he smiled at me. He saw in my eyes that I'd seen the incredible vastness he held in his mind every day with no difficulty, and I knew then and there that I was the savage and he the giant.' "

Stanley paused a moment before he said, "Her ladyship's words stunned us both. That conversation forced me to admit that I did indeed equate the absence of outward sophistication with a lack of intelligence and knowledge. It is a personal defect, and such preconceptions make us all think that we're superior when perhaps we're not."

I thought about that and said, "I must admit I do that too. What I think about is certainly different from someone living in a jungle, but only in the subject matter, not in the number of specifics. In their domain, I would be inept and ignorant."

181

"And they in ours. Ignorance and intelligence are not the same. My previous employer once told me an amusing story about an English matron abroad. He said he was at a train station in Paris when he saw a large woman ordering a diminutive Frenchman to carry her bags. The man looked confused, but she was insistent. She took his hands, placed them on the handles of her luggage, and made a lifting motion. She repeated over and over in English, 'Lift. Lift. Come on, lift.' Her demands were impossible to refuse, no matter what language she spoke. Once she had him underway, she steered him outside to get a taxi and had him load her luggage. When all was packed away, she handed him five francs and departed. My employer had followed behind them and said to the Frenchman, 'Jacques, whatever are you doing?' The man shrugged and said, 'Helping a fellow ignoramus.' "

"My employer told me that Jacques had been at the station to meet him. Not only was he the scion of one of the wealthiest families in France, but he was also a brilliant polymath with a particular fascination for horticulture. The matron mistook him for a porter, but how she came to that conclusion is anybody's guess. Some people bulldoze their way through life. To the observer, they lack manners and act like brutes. My point is that we can all appear ignorant, but ignorance does not necessarily indicate a lack of intelligence. On the surface, they look much the same."

"That's true. I would have liked to have been a fly on the wall if they ever met again under different circumstances."

"Well, that's the thing. They did. The matron had traveled to Paris to judge an iris exhibition. She was the leading expert in England, and to their mutual surprise, Jacques was there as a fellow judge. They were introduced and, of course, recognized each other. The matron asked jokingly for her five francs back, which Jacques happily returned. Both were highly amused. Each thought the other a complete dimwit until they had a chance to interact professionally. They became friends and corresponded for many years. My employer swore it happened as he said, but to round out this discussion, few will believe what you say. Some never will, but that doesn't mean you're deluded or that they are blind or willful. We all see through the eyes of our respective cultures and judge accordingly. We moderns think in terms of science. Indigenous people think in terms of spirits. Perhaps both are right, and each path leads to the same place. To me, that would be sufficiently ironic. In any case, Percy, you have the chance to explore both. Who knows where that will lead?"

"An interesting observation. Thank you, Stan. Our talk has settled me. How are the preparations going for this weekend?"

"We are prepared. The extra staff will be here shortly, and our meal preparations are well advanced. It is just as well they are. I believe the first of our guests is about to arrive."

"What? So soon?"

"I'm afraid so. I would collect your fiancée and meet me out front."

I arose and asked, "However do you do that?"

Stanley chuckled. "I've had a lot of practice, Percy. Shall we?"

43

W e stood outside in a line as a battleship gray Jaguar E-type convertible burbled down the driveway toward the roundabout.

Bruni leaned toward me and said, "It must be one of the Cushmans. I can't believe they're this early. Still, whoever it is has exquisite taste in cars."

I agreed as the Jag stopped in front of us. The driver shut it down, and James Cushman III stepped out, grabbed a blue blazer from the back, and put it on. Stanley opened the door for Casey Cushman while Simon stood by to handle their bags.

James placed his hands on his hips, looked at all of us, and said, "Now that's what I call a reception. Percy? Which one are you? Ah, there you are. No hiding."

James walked toward me with his hand outstretched. He wore a white shirt with a paisley ascot, khaki pants, and brown tassel loafers. I disliked ascots and those who wore them. On top of that, I'd hoped to brief everyone before the Cushmans arrived, but that was no longer possible. Now, I had to entertain James and Casey when I wasn't prepared to do so. I considered sending them back the way they came and calling the whole thing off. Bruni must have sensed what was running through my mind because she whispered, "Smile, Percy. We have work to do."

I stepped forward and said, "Welcome to Rhinebeck, James. Allow me to introduce you to everyone."

"You forgot Casey."

Inwardly, I kicked myself. "Of course." I turned to her and said, "Casey, it's a pleasure to see you again," only my voice faded as I looked at her.

Casey took my outstretched hand, nodded, and released it. Her once-perfect features were tense and hard. The soft mouth I remembered was a thin straight line. I recognized her, but then I didn't. She wore cream-colored slacks with leather sandals and a white shirt. Her brown eyes seemed to glare at me beneath medium-length, slightly tousled brown hair. There was no warmth behind those eyes. None. I didn't know what to say.

Bruni rescued me. She stepped forward and said, "Casey, I'm Brunehilde von Hofmanstal, Percy's fiancée. So good to finally meet you."

Casey turned and gave her a brief smile. Bruni introduced her to Anne and John, while I did the same for James.

Once the greetings had been made, Stanley asked James if he would care for some champagne.

I heard him say, "Sure thing, Sport. Love your accent, by the way. Lead on."

We congregated in the drawing room as Cristal was passed around. I certainly needed something. It was times like these when I missed Johnny the most. I barely knew what to think of my guests or what to do. James was James. I was used to him, or at least I thought I was, but Casey? I stared at her as she sipped champagne and spoke to Anne. For a moment, she appeared to seethe like a basket of coiled snakes. I watched their mottled, silver, and black bodies slither beneath the surface of her skin, which heaved and stretched, barely able to prevent their bursting forth onto the carpet. I shuddered even in the warmth of the morning light that streamed through the French doors. I had to turn away.

James was sipping his champagne beside me, watching.

I turned to him, "Would you care for a walk after you've finished your champagne? I could show you the grounds."

"Maybe after a few more glasses of this stuff. You must be rolling in dough. By the way, you should mingle more and not stand in a corner. It's what good hosts do. Just some friendly advice." He smiled and walked off.

185

I'd forgotten how grating he could be. He wasn't wrong, but at least he seemed like a real person, more real to me than Casey. I turned to look out the window, and when I turned back, Casey was beside me.

"You didn't recognize me, did you?" By the time I turned to face her, she was moving toward James, who was speaking with John.

I took a deep breath. This wasn't going the way I'd expected. I seemed to be wrong at every turn. The world around me was in constant motion, and I couldn't catch up. It was as if I was standing beside a river, watching the water bubble over rocks and boulders that lay close to the surface. The current swirled and eddied in patterns that formed and reformed. I had rarely felt so detached, so lost, so separated from everything and everyone, so completely alone. All I wanted to do was cry, and I didn't know why.

Stanley cleared his throat and proffered me a cup of tea on a silver salver. I took it and drank. By the time I thought to thank him, he was gone. I realized after another sip that in some unimaginable way, it was Johnny's feelings that I felt. He wasn't far, maybe even close. The living room came into sharper focus, and I could breathe. Everyone was looking at me. I looked about, confused. I felt like an actor, stunned by the unexpected opening of the curtain, whose mind refused to remember his lines or even recall which play was being performed. I heard Johnny tell me to snap out of it and improvise.

I spoke, amazed that I could.

"First, James and Casey. Thank you for accepting. I'd like to welcome you both to Rhinebeck, not only on behalf of myself but on behalf of all of us here. We have certain traditions that you should be aware of. Some of them are ancient. Some are not. The first is that I am your host, and you are my guests. As your host, I offer you sanctuary and the chance to lay down whatever cares you carry. It is my duty to see to your needs and your safety. If there is anything you desire, I will do my best to provide it. Lunch will be served at one. The dress is semi-formal. Tonight, dinner is black tie and will start at nine with drinks at seven. Simon will show you to your room. Your bags are already there. It is early, and the day is splendid. Once you are freshened up, Bruni and I will happily give you a tour. Again, thank you for coming, and James, I look forward to meeting your parents. Casey, it's been many years. There's a lot of catching up to do. Once more, I thank you both. Please follow Simon."

I was relieved when they did as I requested, and the door closed behind them.

Bruni came up beside me and said, "Well, that was more than a little awkward, but good save at the end. I suppose we'll just have to put up with them for the next few days."

"Unfortunately, yes, but they're at least out of our hair for a few minutes. What do you think of them?"

Anne and John came up to us before Bruni could answer, and Anne said, "Well, please forgive me if I appear a little befuddled until they leave. Blame it on the wine and the brandy, which I intend to consume with abandon. At least we'll have other guests to lessen the load. I do hope a few more show up before lunch—nice car, though."

"Yes, and our plans need some rearrangements. We'll have to brief everyone separately."

Anne continued, "Too true. Would you like to hear my solution?"

I said, "By all means."

"Very well. John, why don't you take Hugo and your mother? I'll take the doctor—I need to speak to him anyway. Bruni, I think you should take your mother. Percy, Bonnie is in your hands, along with Malcolm. Does everyone agree?"

We all did.

"Well, good. Right now, I'm going upstairs. I need to recover. John?"

"I'll join you."

When they'd left, I asked Bruni again about her initial impressions.

Bruni paused and said, "I'll tell you, but first, what happened to you? You checked out for a few minutes."

"I did. It was Johnny. It's like I was seeing the world through his eyes. Casey was a bundle of snakes, and then I felt an extraordinary sadness and sense of separation from everything like I was a ghost. I almost started crying. Thank God Stanley brought me some tea. Without it, things could have gone far worse."

"It seemed that way to me. Who knows what the lesser Cushmans thought."

"As if I care, but James got in a couple of digs. I certainly felt them. In that, he hasn't changed. What do you think of them?"

"Casey's going to be tough. She's strung very tight. If she is to divulge anything at all, it must be to you. You knew her before she was a Cushman, and that might be enough. As for her husband, he's impervious. James thinks the world consists of James. He's arrogant and condescending but with a cunning that pinpoints others' weaknesses, errors, and vulnerabilities. I've seen that type before. He and my ex-husband would get along. Getting either James or Casey to reveal what they're up to won't be easy. I also think that Casey played Johnny deliberately but regrets it. Of course, these are just initial impressions. How about we take a walk outside? I could certainly use some air."

"And so could I."

I opened one of the French doors, and we stepped out onto the south lawn.

44

B runi and I wandered down toward the tree line at the south end. The morning dazzled under a dome of brilliant blue that stretched high above before fading into haze that girdled the horizon. The air was soft and still. Bruni asked for a cigarette. I lit one for her and another for myself.

Bruni smoked for a time before she said, "I think you need a strategy, Percy, something to guide you."

I sighed. "Likely, you are correct. Do you have any suggestions?"

Bruni took my arm as we walked. "I do. But first, let's review. The lesser Cushmans showed up early. That was deliberate, which means the senior Cushmans are taking this weekend seriously. The question is, Why?"

"Johnny's accident?"

"Perhaps, but just because that's our focus doesn't mean it's theirs."

"Raymond's conjecture?"

"It's possible. Whatever their motives, they want you unsettled first."

"Which I think they accomplished."

"If I'm right, this is just the beginning. In high-stakes negotiations, there's usually a B team, and their function is to get the lay of the land for the A team. The B team often makes outrageous demands or even threatens to walk out altogether. Their purpose is to gauge the willingness of the opposition to come to terms. When all is at a standstill, the A team steps in. They dismiss the B team's antics as overexuberance, inexperience, or just plain stupidity. They apologize profusely and beg forgiveness, having discovered exactly how flexible or adamant they need to be to achieve their ends. It's how the game is played."

"I see."

We walked together in silence for a time. Being with Bruni calmed me.

I said, "I suppose we'll have to endure whatever the B team comes up with. What else?"

Bruni stopped and looked at me.

"You're not just any host, Percy. You're the host of *Rhinebeck*, and Rhinebeck is far more than it appears. There are the darker and more sinister elements that reside here. They're locked into the foundation of this house, and as the owner of Rhinebeck, you hold all those aspects in your being."

I thought about that. "My darker side?"

"Yes. It's the part you must embrace."

"Strangely, I came to a similar conclusion." I told Bruni about my thoughts when I was sitting at Alice's desk.

Bruni said, "Good. Cultivating your demonic side is what's required now. It's why I've supported and encouraged you in your search for Johnny, in case you wondered."

"I did wonder."

Bruni took my arm again and said, "Keep working on that, and don't worry about what the Cushmans think of you. They'll try to get under all our skins to soften us up before they get around to saying what's really on their minds. Once that's out in the open, we'll be able to give them what they need."

"Which is?"

"A chance to start over."

"That doesn't exactly follow."

"It is illogical but nonetheless true. I, personally, don't wish them harm. I've noticed that people who do too many wrongs to others eventually turn on themselves. They sabotage their desires.

Take Casey, for example."

"She does seem bitter. If the Cushmans were involved, do you really think they deserve another chance?"

"Everyone does. It's how I'm able to function in the legal world. That, too, can be a dark place. I bring a light when and if I can. A good negotiation done well allows both parties to move forward—to start again, without the ground giving way beneath them. Their attention is on the future, not the past."

"Your father said something similar. What about pulling them out by the roots?"

Bruni chuckled. "That, too, is a form of starting over, only a little more severe."

I laughed. "I should think so. I'm glad we're talking. Looking back, I didn't want to deal with them. They're people from my past who knew me when I was immature, awkward, and unsure. I withdrew even more just now when I thought I got it wrong, no matter what I did. It was as if nothing had changed."

"I can understand that. The truth is you are who you are, past included, and to me, that's impressive enough, so relax and enjoy the game because that is what this is."

"It very well may be, but what if the Cushmans really are out to get me?"

Bruni squeezed my arm. "Embrace all who you are, and you'll have no trouble dealing with the Cushmans. Besides, they'll have me to go through first."

I smiled. "Yes, that, too."

I was looking toward the house when one of the French doors opened, and James Cushman stepped out. He saw us and started walking in our direction.

I said, "Thank you for our talk and just in time. I do believe that's James looking for me."

"Or for me," said Bruni.

"Perhaps for both of us. Let's find out."

W e continued our walk along the tree-lined border of the south lawn as James approached. Once he caught up, he said, "Percy, if it's not too much trouble, Casey wanted to chat with you. She's up at the house. That will allow Bruni and me to get to know each other. Don't worry, she'll be perfectly safe. Besides, from what I've heard, I'm the one who should be worried."

James chuckled at his joke as I said, "Very well. How are your accommodations?"

"Really nice, and I'm enchanted by the butler."

"Yes, Stanley is a treasure."

"Stanley. What a name. It fits. Where'd you find him anyway? I'd love to get one myself."

"I'm not sure that's possible. He came with the place."

"Well, too bad for me. Bruni, shall we continue to walk while Percy speaks with Casey?"

"Of course." Bruni kissed me and said, "Percy, I'll see you back at the house. Come, James. Let's head toward the tennis court while I tell you all about the thing that lives in the woods."

"Really? I don't scare easily."

"I'm sure you're a very brave man, which is why I'll tell you all about it."

I left them to it. I had no idea what Bruni was talking about, but I was quite sure she'd come up with something.

I found Casey in the drawing room. She had been watching me through the French doors as I approached.

"Casey."

Casey looked at me for a long moment before she said, "Percy."

"James said you wished to chat. Do you prefer to sit or walk?"

"Walk."

"How about toward the north? James and Bruni are to the south."

"That would be fine. This is quite a house. Is it really yours?"

"It is."

"I'd like to hear how you managed that."

"It was a gift."

She simply nodded. I took us through the foyer past the table on the left with the bust of Alexander and the tall gladioli in a vase. The casement clock to the right continued to count out the seconds as I opened the door, but the pitch was different. I paused to look at it. The ships tilted back and forth in a darkly swaying funerary march, slower now and more somber. Time stretched, and thoughts about Casey floated around me. I found myself in a memory, sitting next to her upon that stoop, smoking and discussing Johnny. I watched her. Casey had a special something in that moment, a glow that seemed to emanate from her center, but as I came back to the present, it was no longer there. I wondered whether she'd let it go or whether it had left her of its own accord. Perhaps she'd relinquished it for something else—something darker and more cunning.

Back in the present, I shivered. How long I'd kept her waiting, I couldn't say. I closed the door and walked down the steps. I apologized for my preoccupation.

Casey accepted my apology with a nod as we walked up the drive. After a few moments, she said, "You zoned out back there with the same blank look you had when we were served champagne. Are you on drugs?"

I smiled and replied, "No, I was merely thoughtful. Time moves strangely on occasion. I get impressions that dazzle me, like the blueness of the morning or the sound of the clock, and I get lost in it."

"Like a mystic."

I smiled. "Possibly."

"What were you thinking about?"

"Time … and you."

She sighed, "Percy, … sometimes, you can be so blind."

I nodded in agreement. "I've said that often enough about myself. Others have mentioned it as well. Perhaps you could tell me what I'm missing?"

"I don't know if I can."

"Try."

She looked at me carefully and said, "You really have no idea what's happening here, do you?"

"No, I don't."

Casey shook her head in exasperation. "Give me a smoke."

I passed her my pack and lighter. She fiddled with the pack, dropped it, stopped to pick it up, and finally lit her cigarette. She handed them back and very carefully took a drag.

I continued, "I was serious about what I said at the house."

"Said about what?"

"Sanctuary."

Casey scoffed. "Don't make me laugh. There is no sanctuary— not for me and not for you, although you might think so. Power, money, and influence are forces bigger than any of us. Those are what matter. They set each of our agendas. It's how it is."

"To you, maybe, but I think there's more to living than that."

"Cut the crap, Percy. You and Johnny floated through life—not like some of us. We had to scramble to get anywhere at all. You didn't. On top of that, you were gifted an estate. How many people can say that?"

"Not many, and given that, maybe what you say is true. Each life is different, but everyone pays for what they receive, one way or another. There are no exceptions. All I can think of is that you've somehow lost your magic, Casey. You had an inner glow that's no longer there. How could you let that happen?"

Casey stiffened. We stood facing each other at the top of the drive. There was stillness all about. She glared at me. "You can stop right there. I should never have come here. I'm going now."

She turned, flicked her cigarette away, and started back toward the house. I said in a voice I didn't recognize, "But you *did* come here!"

It was like an arrow traveling at impossible speed. It pierced her, and she returned. She stood directly in front of me and sighed. "So be it. I did come, Percy. I even tried to walk away just now, but you called me back." She paused and looked at me. "I guess we'll both find out the consequences of that. Do you know who the Keres were?"

"The Keres? No, I don't."

"You should. They are ancient Greek spirits who feed on violent deaths. Does that ring any bells?"

"Should it?"

"It should. One must be extremely careful around them. Your fiancée is one."

"What is that supposed to mean?"

"Nothing in particular. Johnny spoke to me about many things before his accident. He told me everything about you, this place, its secrets, the people who live here, the things they've done, what's hidden, and where. Everything. He told me all he could. I suppose he felt compelled. Love can be that way for some. I didn't stop him. I doubt I could have. There is also much he said that he hasn't told you."

"Such as?"

She chuckled. "Some things are better left unsaid. For now, I wish to interest you in a proposition, a proposal, if you will. Let's walk toward the river and the rock while we discuss it. You know the rock I mean. You fell off it, remember? As I said, he told me a great deal—too much, I'm sure."

Casey appeared calm, but I sensed her anticipation. She didn't look at me but took my arm as we walked. She said, "You and I have much to talk about. For a start, Johnny confessed that you were madly in love with me at one time. Is that true?"

I hesitated. "Perhaps that was true at one time."

"You never told me. You should have. Our lives would've been very different had you not been so afraid back then. Perhaps, deep down, you still love me but are too fearful of the consequences, should you wish to acknowledge it? Love has a mind of its own. It can submerge only to resurface years later. It's not uncommon. Alice grew hot and cold with your father, only to grow hot once more. Isn't that correct?"

"It is, but I'm not sure where this conversation is going."

"I have a purpose in saying what I have. You may not like it, but then you invited me. What did you think was going to happen? Now answer my question: Do you still love me?"

"What's the point?"

I was getting annoyed.

Casey squeezed my arm. "Don't be that way. Love can be hard to recognize. Besides, we're old friends. There is always love between old friends."

"That may be, but there's something more behind your words."

Casey stopped and looked at me. "You sense a threat but can't quite see it. That's what I mean about your being blind, so let me clarify it for you. I really am your friend and more. A spy in the enemy camp can make all the difference, so don't turn me into something else. That would be premature and decidedly unfriendly."

"What do you have in mind?"

"Let's walk, and I will tell you. The Cushmans want me to find out about Johnny—if he's said anything—but I won't even ask. I can't be bothered. I have something else in mind. Does this property extend to the river?"

I didn't like where this was going, but I decided to hear her out and answered, "Yes, it does, at least until the railroad tracks."

Casey smiled. "It's much larger than I thought. That's nice. Let's head back."

We turned and walked toward the house. A breeze sprang up, and the distant tops of rapidly expanding clouds were visible off and on through the trees. Leaves rustled above us in sibilant whispers I couldn't quite make out.

Casey continued. "Consider this discussion to be separate from anything the others have in mind. I won't tell you what they're after, so don't ask, at least not yet, but I can tell you one thing you don't know. Johnny asked me to marry him."

"Really?" I was surprised.

"Yes, but the accident happened before I could give him my answer."

"What were you going to say?"

"That I wanted to talk to you first."

"Me? Why would you want to do that?"

"Because I wanted to make you the same offer."

"What?" I stopped short.

She said, "Don't look so shocked. You aren't married yet, so it's not completely out of the question, and I know about the baby. That, too, hasn't happened, so all is up in the air. You're quite free to accept my proposal."

I stared at her, surprised. "So let me get this straight. You want me to marry you? Is that what you're saying?"

"Yes, that's exactly what I'm saying." Casey smiled and, for a moment, looked like the girl I remembered. She stepped closer and said, "Getting out of my marriage will be easy. The Cushmans hate me, but I'll still get a large settlement, so think of my offer as encompassing me and a dowry. I know your immediate reaction is to get all huffy and refuse, but think on it. Consider this, as well. My offer will also allow you to keep the child—or at least, one of you can, and that surely beats the alternative."

We were at the top of the driveway, and the house lay below us.

I couldn't believe what I was hearing. "The alternative? Is that a threat?"

"Easy, Percy. I haven't threatened anything. I'm simply making you an offer, but consider it a double-edged proposal if you wish. I know you love me, Percy, and now you'll have your chance to make that dream come true."

"There's no way I'm doing that. Not now. Not ever. You should leave! Immediately!" I was angry.

Looking at me in a provocative way, she raised the index finger of her right hand to her mouth and slowly rubbed her lips, removing her lipstick. She moved toward me as she raised her mouth for me to kiss. I pushed her away.

Casey stood back, angry, and then gave me a sly look. "I'm sorry you feel that way, but you should reconsider my offer. I'll give you a little time. I won't be dismissed so easily. Allow me to show you something. It might prove instructive."

She took a step back and ran her tongue over her lips, smiling all the while. A few seconds later, her face reddened and then turned purple. Her body gave a convulsive heave, and her head tilted back at an impossible angle, elongating and exposing the whiteness of her throat. Her mouth gaped at the sky. The veins and tendons in her neck pulsed and stood out like stretched steel cables. She took a gigantic breath and began to shriek. Her howl rose in pitch and volume to such a level of violence that I covered my ears. Her screaming was like a human siren that went on and on until it cut off abruptly. In the eerie silence that followed, her eyes rolled back into her head, and she collapsed to the ground, curling into a ball that quivered and shook on the hard surface of the road.

I was stunned. It was as if she'd become possessed by something violent and unrestrained. In that moment, she reminded me of the *maenads*, the female followers of Dionysius, that I'd seen depicted on Ancient Greek red-figure urns, their heads thrown back, singing at the sky. Was she feeling ecstasy or fury? As I looked around, I saw James sprinting around the side of the house. He was moving fast in our direction like an enraged bull. Casey was obviously one kind of trouble, but James was another and more immediate. I felt my rage take hold and moved to meet him. If blood was what was wanted, then so be it.

46

I had barely taken a step when the front door of the house flew open, and Raymond sprinted to intercept James. I had no idea Raymond could move so quickly. He was like a missile with a single point of focus. Twenty feet away from me, there was a hollow thud as Raymond connected with his target. James was big, but Raymond was doing what he'd honed to a fine art. In an instant, James was on the ground with his arm twisted behind his back. Raymond exerted pressure, and James screamed. He yelled, "She needs her medicine! She needs her medicine!"

Raymond got him up and brought him to me as Casey lay in a ball on the asphalt.

James repeated, "She needs her medicine! What did you do to her, Percy? What the fuck did you do?"

I was keyed up, but I said to James, "If Raymond releases you, will you be civil?"

"Look, I heard her scream, okay? I'm not going to hurt you. I wanted to get to her before this happened. If I find out you provoked her, then maybe we'll settle up, but right now, we need to get her inside."

"She's done this before?"

"Yes, yes. Let me pick her up. I'll carry her to the house. Please! There's no time to lose."

James was panting and looked anguished. I nodded to Raymond, who released him. By then, Bruni was rounding the house. Anne, John, Stanley, and Harry were outside on the steps. James picked up Casey and started carrying her down the drive toward the house at a brisk pace.

Raymond and I followed behind. I whispered to Raymond, "Thanks."

Raymond hissed, "*De nada*. What the fuck was that about?"

"Somebody's playing games. We'll talk in a bit."

"That we will. Something stinks, and it stinks bad."

"Don't I know it."

James took Casey inside and up the stairs. Stanley followed.

Anne and Bruni asked me, "What happened?"

I said, "Let's head to the library, and I'll explain. Raymond, why don't you join us?"

Once we were gathered, I stood and told them in detail about the conversation with Casey.

When I'd finished, Anne said, "They leave at once."

I looked around the room. Bruni was pale, and both Raymond and John appeared angry. Anne looked determined.

I raised my hand and said, "Let's discuss it before we make that decision. Bruni, I'm concerned about Casey's veiled threat to you and the baby. She also seems demented. Both of them should leave."

Bruni didn't answer right away but rose and went over to the French door. She looked out at the lawn for several seconds. When she turned to face us, only her professional demeanor showed.

"No, Percy. I will stay, and they will, too. Nobody can threaten me in my home without an answer. I will respond but in my own time. For now, I must put aside any emotional response, and I think that stricture applies to all of us. Rather, let's review what we know. Casey Cushman may be exaggerating about how much Johnny told her, but given the level of detail, we would be foolish to assume that she knows nothing. Likely, she's kept much to herself for her own use, but I doubt that's true of all of it. At the least, Casey has confirmed that the Cushmans have an agenda. She hinted she could be a spy. I think we should explore that. More importantly, she said that the Cushmans want to know if Johnny has said anything. They

201

must fear what he might reveal, and from that, we can infer that there are either aspects of Johnny's accident or information that he has that they would rather we didn't know. It is *not* confirmation that they are complicit, lest we be premature, but rather confirmation that they believe themselves to be vulnerable, and it follows that they must be. Why else would they be concerned?

"For myself, I think someone has gone to a great deal of trouble to arrange all that's happened now and before, including our inviting them. Perhaps that was to be arranged later, only we moved faster than they anticipated. Likely, they aren't as prepared as they would wish, and that is to our advantage. As for Casey, she is a threat but not *the* danger. The real one is that we have no concrete counter to what the Cushmans have in mind. That can only come about from knowing what they did and what they're up to. They *did* something. Of that, I'm certain. Knowing what and being able to prove it, if necessary, is their weakness and our best defense. We must focus on that. Everything else is a distraction. Does what I've said make sense?"

Anne spoke. "Since you have decided to stay, the Cushmans will now have both of us to deal with. I, too, have my methods. We'll find out what they did, and they will answer for it if need be. John?"

"What Casey said and did was shocking, but that was the point. You are correct, Bruni. We must keep our friends close and our enemies closer. They stay. Raymond?"

Raymond was standing by the door. He walked further into the room, looked at me, and then at everyone else. "The opening rounds are where you test your opponent's weaknesses and strengths. Sometimes, an opponent will go for a knockout right after the bell rings. Such tactics are nothin' new. Shake it off and work your plan. This fight's just beginning. For myself, I'd like to head back to the city and dig around some more. I'll return before things get outta hand. I know you probably want me here, but I can move in ways you all can't. Later this weekend, I won't have that freedom. It's best used now."

I considered that and said, "Do it, Raymond. The same arrangements as before."

Raymond looked happy. "Good, and don't worry about the guy upstairs. Hit him hard on the nose, and he's done. He'll bleed everywhere, so you're gonna need a towel. *Nos vemos*."

Raymond nodded to everyone and left. Once the door closed, I asked, "Comments?"

John said, "He's right, of course. If there's something there to find, he will find it, and we must use his flexibility while we can. Bruni, what do you expect to happen next?"

Bruni sat down in one of the chairs. "I mentioned to Percy about the A team and the B team. The lesser Cushmans are the B team. Their job is to undertake reconnaissance and to float suitably outrageous proposals to gauge our reactions. I doubt Casey's gambit was part of the overall scheme, but it might be. I suspect we'll hear some sort of excuse for her episode from James. Once that's been delivered, I'm fairly certain the senior Cushmans will arrive, and they'll follow through with something else before we get down to serious business. As Raymond said, this is only the beginning. I must say I do like that man, John."

John smiled. "Yes, I'm glad he's in my employ, but even happier that he's my friend. I'm relieved that he'll be here later this weekend. Anne?"

"Well, this morning has been full of surprises. There's now a bit of fear in the air, my own included, and that is bracing. We'll certainly not be bored this weekend. Whatever happens, Peggy and I will be sitting down for a much-needed and long-overdue talk. Knowing her the way I do, she must have something in mind for events to have gone this far, and I will find out what that is. I should add that if any of her family were involved in Johnny's accident, then I will ensure that she does what is necessary to see that justice is served—that I promise. Now, it's too early for anything more to drink. Why don't we ring for some coffee while we wait for James to give us his excuses?"

47

I rang for Stanley, and once he had arrived, I requested coffee for all of us.

As Stanley turned to leave, I asked him, "How did it go upstairs?"

Stanley paused. "Oddly, sir, if I may say. Once Mr. Cushman had placed his wife on the bed, I asked him if he needed any further assistance. He replied that he had everything he needed and added with a grin that he was deciding whether to medicate his wife using a suppository or a syringe since she couldn't take her medicine by mouth in her current state. He smiled again and assured me that whichever method he used, she would recover shortly. I informed him that a doctor was expected this afternoon, should one be required. He said that wouldn't be necessary and asked to use a telephone. I directed him to the library but suggested that if he wished some privacy, he could use the one in my office. His hosts were in the library now. Hearing that, he declined, and I left him to it."

After a moment to digest that news, I said, "I see. One point you should know. Casey's fit was deliberate."

"I thought as much. There are several games afoot. Simon commented that their luggage was unusually heavy. With your permission, I will know the reason for it once both are downstairs."

"Very good. Do take all necessary precautions."

Stanley smiled. "Rest assured, I will. Johnny isn't the only one to enjoy Ian Fleming, although I much prefer Len Deighton. Coffee will be served in a few minutes."

"Thank you, Stanley, and one last thing: Please see that the repository is fully locked and secured. I'll explain later."

"Very well, sir. I'll see to it at once."

Once Stanley left, there was a silence.

Into it, Anne asked, "What is the state of the Cushman finances these days, John? The lesser Cushmans seem obsessed with money."

John considered Anne's observation. "I noted that as well, but from what I know, the family is quite well off. I've heard no rumors to the contrary."

I was about to make a comment when Simon entered with coffee, followed by James Cushman close behind.

Once the service was laid out, I stood and asked James, "How is Casey?"

"Not well, thanks to you."

"Was it something I said?"

"Was it?"

I sighed, walked over, and stood directly in front of him. I looked him in the eyes before saying, "Casey was antagonistic from the moment she arrived while you flung barbed, sarcastic comments in my direction at every opportunity. If you dislike me so much, you should have declined my invitation, but instead, you accepted and arrived well before the time you were expected. I took that as another deliberate provocation to create the maximum confusion and disharmony. I'll tell you now that either you explain yourself or you will leave with Casey, your bags, and whatever upset you harbor, never to return. I will give you fifteen minutes. What do you wish to do?"

"Easy now, Bud."

"Bud? You call me Bud?" I started to lose my temper again. I stepped closer. "How dare you! My name is Percy, and you will call me by that name. Where are your manners? Your parents will be arriving this afternoon. Perhaps they can explain how they managed to raise someone like yourself. Now, I'm going to have some coffee as I listen to your story. I invite you to do the same. Do you wish it black or with cream and sugar?"

"Ah, black?"

"Black it is. Sit down. You have fourteen minutes. I suggest you start."

"I'm not sure I will."

"I see." I rang for Stanley again.

He arrived almost instantly. "Stanley," I said, "please bring me a towel?"

"Of course, sir." Stanley ghosted away.

"What do you want a towel for?" asked James.

"It's for you. I don't want you leaking blood on the furniture because I've had it with you."

I walked over to the desk, picked up a sharply pointed letter opener, and as James opened his mouth to say something, I stepped in very fast and pushed him hard against the door with my left hand. With my right, I thrust the point of the letter opener under his chin, just above his ascot. I watched the point prick deeply into his skin and held it there. James was bigger, but I had caught him completely off-guard. He tried to move, but the door prevented him.

His eyes were wide with surprise, and I felt dangerous and empowered.

"Are you finished with your rudeness?" I asked.

James nodded his head fractionally up and down—his eyes wild.

"Are you sure?"

He moved his head again.

"Good."

I took away the letter opener. James reached up to his neck as Stanley opened the door and pushed him out of the way. Had Stanley entered an instant earlier, I would have skewered James. It had been a near thing, and James turned pale. I took the towel from

Stanley, wiped the letter opener, put it back on the desk, and handed the towel back to Stanley.

The room came back into focus. My actions had taken only seconds, but by the end of it, I could see quite clearly how violence could become addictive.

I took a breath and told James, "Let's begin again but more civilly. I believe you said you liked your coffee black?"

48

James stood frozen, looking at me in disbelief.

I poured a cup and handed it to him. "Do sit down. It won't kill you."

He took it. James looked around at Stanley by the door and at John, Anne, and Bruni. Not knowing what else to do, he sat.

"Good choice," I said. "I'll reiterate what I said earlier. If I can help you, I will. Tell me what's going on with you two. I'm losing patience."

"Look," he said. "I don't feel comfortable talking about personal stuff in front of an audience." He looked around and said, "I'll tell you, Percy, but not everybody else."

I sat back and lit a cigarette.

"I understand, but I will be telling everyone in this room what you said, so I don't see how it will make a difference. Besides, everyone here has been affected in some way by your antics, so you have this one chance to explain yourself. What I said earlier still applies. If I feel you're being candid, I will let you stay. If not, you will be gone. I'm not sure how your parents will feel about that. Perhaps they'll decide to leave as well. It makes no difference to me. Those are my terms. Accept them or leave."

James thought about that. I noticed that mentioning his parents caused him to tap his fingers on his leg. Tentatively, I posited that he was here on their orders and that being tossed out on his ear would have consequences. The senior Cushmans had a plan, and James and Casey were part of it. He really had no choice, and he knew that.

"Okay, I accept." He sipped his coffee.

In the ensuing pause, I watched his mind go through its paces. Ever since I'd known him, James calculated what to say and how to act. The difference between us was that I'd grown up with Johnny. James had grown up with no one. His wits were all he ever had for company.

As he collected himself, I wondered whether delivering a story had been his intention all along or whether he was having to improvise. Whichever it was, he knew he had to be convincing. It didn't have to be true, but plausible enough to be believed. Of course, I wasn't going to send him packing no matter what he said, but he didn't know that—at least, I hoped he didn't. I simply wanted to put both of them on the defensive until reinforcements arrived.

He started in.

"You're right. I was completely out of line, and I apologize to everyone here. I arrived early to explain Casey's condition but hadn't gotten around to it. I was about to tell your fiancée, Percy, but Casey went ballistic before I could."

He paused again and looked at us. He shifted gears. "You don't believe me—fair enough. I'll tell you one thing that's true: I love my wife. I would do anything for her—only she's difficult to live with. It's how she is. I didn't make her that way. She was broken when I married her."

He hurried on. "In the beginning, I tried to appease her and do whatever she wanted to make her happy. My parents tried just as hard, but she was uncontrollable. She'd throw things—expensive things. She'd blow up and scream for no reason, and not just at home. She was an embarrassment. When she'd snap out of it, she'd spiral down into a depression that was so deep she'd become suicidal. I won't give you specifics because it would make you think less of her when she deserves more than just your pity."

James looked around to gauge our reactions. I watched him make adjustments as he noted our suspicions and our disbelief.

"She wasn't always the way she is now. I first met her at a party in Southampton. There was a tent. It had been raining off and on, and for an instant, the last of the light from the setting sun illuminated her as she arrived through the entrance in a long, dark gown. To me, she was an inspiration, and the timing couldn't have been better. My parents were putting pressure on me to settle down. I realized that before me was the perfect person. We spoke. We dated, and eventually, our relationship grew serious. After a time, Casey said she didn't want to continue. I was too full of myself, and she was still recovering from a prior relationship. She couldn't take any more emotional trauma. I persisted and told her that I wanted to marry her. She refused. I pointed out that she would have financial security and social standing. There'd be money for her to spend. She could keep going to the same clubs and locations she was used to. She didn't have to turn her world upside down by marrying me. I would give her what love I could, and perhaps she could do the same to me. Our match was far from ideal, but it could work to both our benefits, and that was the point. I demanded only one thing from her: that her world revolve around me and my family. I worked for my father. I still do."

James took a sip of coffee before he continued.

"There are social and business obligations that I must fulfill. She would have to fit in and contribute to those priorities, and as you know, they can be demanding.

"Casey understood. She'd grown up in that world, and deep down, she needed the security that I offered. Her life had been in constant economic and emotional turmoil, and I was a way to stifle her uncertainties and fears. We eventually came to an agreement. She didn't love me. She didn't think she could love anyone, but she could try. I told her it was the same for me, and so we became engaged. In time, we discovered that we didn't dislike each other after all, and something sparked between us. We married.

"I suppose all was as fine as it could be, and it was. That period marked a stretch of happiness for both of us. Then Johnny entered the picture, little by little. He and Casey didn't do anything at first. They'd sit down and talk at a party, that kind of thing, but even that bothered me. I took my jealousy and irritation out on her. Casey learned to avoid any gatherings where he might show up, but that wasn't always possible. Part of my job, and hers too, was to show the flag. We had to attend certain functions and act graciously no matter how we felt. Casey did all she could to keep Johnny at arm's length. I appreciated her efforts, and things settled down once again until I did a stupid thing."

Here, he paused and looked down.

"I'm not happy about what I did. I disappointed a lot of people, including Casey and my dad."

He looked up at us.

"Maybe it was the work. You've no idea how stressful it is having my father as a boss. He expects one hundred and ten percent from his employees and even more from me. My life was his. I was at the office morning, noon, and night. There was no end to it, and I needed some relief. I started seeing someone at work. We had an affair. It was just sex, but it was frequent and distracting. The woman was an analyst and dealmaker for the firm. A month later, a large transaction she was finalizing blew sky-high. It was an expensive mess and cost the firm a huge amount of money. It was bad. I mean, really bad. Dad went ape. A fortune had been lost, and he couldn't understand how such a disaster could have happened after all the planning, time, and personal attention he'd put into it. A thorough investigation was done, and everything came out.

"He called a meeting with the board and all the senior executives. It was standing room only in the conference room. My father called it to order by yelling at the top of his voice, 'You don't shit where you eat!' As that reverberated around the room, he yelled, 'Not in my house and not in this firm!'

211

"The woman was fired on the spot. I wasn't. Maybe you think that it helped that I was his son, but it didn't. My father isn't one to use that as a reason. Instead, he told the assembled staff exactly what I'd done and that firing me was too easy and too kind. Instead, he demoted me, and ordered my salary chopped by three quarters. Going forward, I'd be given only menial tasks, and that state of affairs would continue until he saw fit to change it.

"This, of course, got back to Casey. I'm not sure whether it was the affair or that the money dried up. My father is good at figuring out the maximum amount of pain that can be endured. He gave us just enough to live on, provided we were careful, but we weren't—more specifically, she wasn't. Well, I've learned one thing from that experience. If you ever marry a woman with the promise of financial security, and that security disappears, there'll be hell to pay, and believe me when I say that I've been paying. To answer your question, my dad ordered us to accept your invitation and to arrive as early as possible. I didn't want to do either of those things. Neither of us did, and we blamed you. Maybe my anger was misplaced. Maybe hers is, too. I apologize on behalf of both of us. The question I have is: Will you accept my apology and allow us to start over?"

I smoked and looked at James, saying nothing.

James shifted in his chair and murmured, "We'll behave. I'll behave."

Eventually, I nodded. "Thank you for telling us what you have. Before I make my decision, I have a question. Why is your luggage so heavy?"

James fidgeted in his chair and said at last, "It's food. Casey thinks she may be poisoned. She's heard your cook has poisoned guests in the past. Casey brought her own supplies to make sure that wasn't possible. She's a little paranoid—always has been."

He looked at me with uncertainty in his eyes. I looked back and said, "Thank you for telling me. Let us start again. Welcome to Rhinebeck."

49

J ames smiled tentatively and said, "Thank you for inviting me and my wife to this beautiful home. Now, if I may, I'd like to see how Casey is doing, and perhaps some tea could be sent up for her? I'll also make sure she gets the message and behaves herself."

"Please do, and tea will be provided shortly. Stanley?"

"I'll see to it at once, sir. Mister Cushman? After you."

Stanley held the door for James. Once it closed, I waited until I heard James's footsteps recede. Stanley rarely made a sound when he moved about.

I asked, "Okay, what does everyone think?"

Anne said immediately, "I doubt it could get any stranger, although I said that earlier this morning. Percy, could you reach into the desk drawer behind you and pass me the Hampton Blue Book? I'm calling Helen Duke. I have some questions about her daughter."

Anne got on the phone while the rest of us spoke among ourselves. After she'd hung up, she announced, "The maid said Helen and Ambrose are onboard the *Aires*, their sailboat, heading for Block Island and Nantucket. They won't be back before next week. I suppose that's convenient if you don't want to be checked up on. To be perfectly frank, Percy, I have the feeling we've invited the devil and his mistress for the weekend, only I'm not sure which is which. Casey should've taken up acting, and as for James, I don't trust anything he says. Anyway, that's my opinion. John?"

"Both are under a great deal of pressure. Right now, we must put them at their ease and continue with our plan. Bruni? What do you think?"

"I would keep a close eye on both of them and not let either of them or their parents wander about unaccompanied—not for a minute. Still, I'm a great admirer of the extemporaneous, and James certainly has a gift. Parts of his story were true. Much wasn't. Percy?"

I looked at all of them and said, "If James and Casey are the B team, then the A team will likely be worse. For now, we keep our eyes and ears open."

Before I could continue, Stanley entered and said that we should prepare to greet more guests.

50

A long black limousine eased to a stop in front of the steps. A chauffeur got out, ran around the back of the car, and quickly opened the rear door. I was hoping it would be my future in-laws, but no such luck. It was Jim and Peggy Cushman. They, too, were early. I'd never formally met them and noted that the senior Cushman looked like an older and more serious version of James. He, too, wore a blue blazer and white shirt, but with a blue and silver diagonally striped tie instead of an ascot. He was a large man in every way. His blond hair was brushed to the side to cover a patch of incipient baldness that must have been spreading for some time. James's mother, on the other hand, was also blonde and seemed much more vibrant. She wore dark gray slacks and a white turtleneck. She looked about her with a radiant smile, happy to have arrived.

As they stood before me, I greeted them, saying, "Mr. and Mrs. Cushman, welcome to Rhinebeck. I am Percy."

They nodded and seemed slightly puzzled by my introduction. Once we had shaken hands, I continued, "Won't you please come this way? Some refreshments will be served, and then you can unwind from your journey. Allow me to introduce you to my fiancée, Brunehilde von Hofmanstal. John and Anne, I believe you know."

Introductions and greetings were made, after which Stanley guided us inside. The ladies went first, and the men followed. As we passed through the foyer, Jim Cushman asked me, "Where are my son and daughter-in-law?"

"Upstairs, I believe. Casey had some kind of seizure this morning, but James told me that she should recover shortly. A doctor will be arriving this afternoon, should you have a concern."

"I see," was all he said.

I noted that the senior Cushman didn't look pleased, and his frown deepened when I asked him if this had happened before.

He said nothing until we were in the drawing room. "She has episodes, if you must know. Now, who are you, exactly?"

"I am your host."

Jim looked confused and turned to John. "I thought you and Anne invited us. This is your house, is it not?"

John said, "I'm sorry for any confusion. We did proffer the invitations, but I've never owned this property. It belonged to my half-sister. After her death, I held it in trust for Percy, who owns it now."

The senior Cushman looked surprised. "So, you've nothing to do with it?"

John spoke without emotion. "That is correct. The ownership change was a private matter, and since it occurred only recently, you wouldn't have known about it. That being said, your son and your daughter-in-law seem to be well-informed. I'm surprised they never told you."

The senior Cushman was silent.

John continued, "It's no matter. Our children always know the latest news and well before us older folk. The important thing is that you're here now and can enjoy all the delights of being a guest, irrespective of who owns what. Ah, here's Stanley with some champagne."

Jim snatched a glass from the tray and drank. I was standing off to one side, observing. The news that John Dodge wasn't the owner of Rhinebeck had certainly surprised him. I could only wish that his plans had a serious kink in them. I also hoped the lesser Cushmans would be thoroughly reprimanded and sent home. I doubted that would happen, but it was a happy thought.

216

Jim took another sip and exclaimed, "This is very good. Is it Cristal?"

"It is," I said. "I'm glad you recognized it."

The senior Cushman looked at me with a little more interest and said, "It's quite unexpected, but perhaps a little early in the day."

"It is, but Cristal is always served to guests when they arrive. For myself, I welcome any excuse to drink it. Simon is standing by the door and will show you to your room. Your bags are there, I'm sure. When you're settled, please join us. Lunch is at one. Now, if you'll excuse me, I have some other matters to attend to. John?"

John nodded to me and asked Jim, "How was your trip?"

I didn't hear the answer as I was already on my way to find Stanley.

51

I found Stanley in the pantry. "Stan, did you secure the vault?"

Stanley stopped what he was doing and said, "Let's discuss that in my office."

When we were seated, he said, "As per your instructions, I disabled the repository's unlocking mechanism. The vault cannot be opened by anyone for any reason for the next seventy-two hours. Her ladyship insisted on that security feature but never gave a reason for it. I can also confirm that nobody has been in the vault today. Although I dislike acting precipitously, sealing the vault is likely for the best, as it is one less thing to worry about."

"Thank you for doing that so quickly. I may have been a bit hasty, but what Casey Cushman said shocked me."

I told him what had happened with Casey in full and what was discussed while he was out of the library, including my agreement that Raymond return to the city to continue his investigation.

When I had finished, Stanley said, "Perhaps you weren't so hasty after all. Getting you to agree to her proposal of marriage was the intention. Since that failed, I expect she will try something else. What troubles me, of course, is that she cited Johnny as her source of information. I can't quite believe it, but who else could have told her all she knows? In addition, Johnny isn't here to defend himself, and we can't help but assume the worst. On the other hand, I would like to point out that Casey never said where the vault was located or how to open it. Granted, your falling off the rock is an unusually intimate specific, and conflating that degree of detail with her assertion that she knows all about the repository and its contents is not too difficult. She may have simply lied. Of course, we can't underestimate how much she knows, but overestimating that knowledge can be just as dangerous. Being fed bits and pieces by an enemy and scrambling this way and that in reaction is following the enemy's line rather than our own. If Johnny did say more than he should have, my only conclusion is that some form of coercion must have been used—likely through physical, emotional, or chemical means."

"I agree. Anything else makes no sense. I'm hoping she lied or that she exaggerated, but if not, those were my thoughts as well. Perhaps I overreacted."

"In time, we'll know the truth. One significant point is that James Cushman told you that his wife brought their own food to prevent them from being poisoned. From my experience, those who take such precautions tend to use the same methods. Perhaps she wishes to influence you the same way she did Johnny?"

"It's possible, but I don't see how. Johnny was in love with her. I'm not. If drugs were used, then I'm on unfamiliar ground. Just the same, I'd like to know if Casey and James really brought food or something else."

"I will personally verify what they brought with them and take every precaution to leave no traces. I'll do that when both are downstairs. Depending on what I find, I'll discuss the matter with Dagmar before recommending any action."

"Please do."

"Moving on. There is also the threat against your fiancée and the child. I assume your future spouse has decided to remain?"

"She has and was quite adamant about doing so."

Stanley smiled. "I'm glad to hear it. She is not one to retreat or hang back unless strategically warranted. Besides, her advice and counsel, not only to you but to Mrs. Dodge and the rest of the family, are vital. If this were a chess match, she is the queen, and because she has that status, we are obligated to take all necessary steps to keep her safe while not hampering her movements. For now, she is not to be left alone with any of the Cushmans, nor may she drink or eat anything unless I hand it to her personally. That injunction must be adhered to. I'm sure she will agree, given the circumstances. Thankfully, there will be several more guests to chaperone and watch over her. You will need to brief them thoroughly and discreetly."

"I will do that."

"Good. I suppose we knew that this weekend would be difficult on many levels and that we might have invited a potential killer, or killers, into our midst, but what's done is done. I will brief my staff to be extra vigilant and attentive. With Raymond in the city, Angus and I will be able to guard her. Lastly, what do you intend to do about Casey Cushman's offer to be a spy in the enemy camp?"

"Bruni feels we should explore that option."

"It is tempting, but then that was the point. If all of this was planned, then whoever is behind Casey Cushman would have set their trap accordingly. If Casey is acting independently, then she'll only divulge what she knows when you agree to marry her, and for that, she'll want proof of your intentions. Given that impossibility, I would delay a definitive answer until dinner tonight, where you should reveal to the table her marriage proposal to you and all she said in detail. Granted, that will cause a stir, but she won't expect it, and neither will anybody else. We may have to handle the fallout, but as a response, it's quite strong."

I considered his suggestion and said, "It's bold."

Stanley nodded. "It is, but I've often found that the best way to diminish the power of those who act clandestinely is to reveal what they're doing in as overt a manner as possible. Once revealed, their threat is significantly diminished. How she responds will also be of interest. I'll be nearby should my services be required. One piece of good news: Reinforcements are arriving."

52

Two limousines, one behind the other, swooped down the driveway in formation and stopped simultaneously. Both chauffeurs stepped out at the same time and ran around to open the doors. Bruni's parents disembarked from the first car while Dr. Angus Maxwell-Hughes and Bonnie Leland stepped out of the second. Out front to greet them were Bruni and myself, along with Stanley, Simon, and Harry. Anne and John remained with the Cushmans inside.

I was so relieved that I gave Hugo a hug, which surprised us both.

"*Mein Gott*, Percy. You actually look happy to see me."

"That I am. John will bring you up to speed. He and Anne are keeping the senior Cushmans occupied while we greet you. The younger Cushmans are upstairs."

"They arrived so early? They're obviously up to something. Elsa will be excited. She loves such provocations."

Before he could continue, Elsa slid up beside him. She looked stunning in a navy-blue Chanel ensemble, whose color matched Hugo's three-piece suit. While Elsa kissed me on both cheeks, Bruni did the same to her father and began speaking to him in rapid German. Elsa noted the exchange and said, "The plot is already thickening, judging from our reception."

"Which is why I'm more than delighted that you're here. I should think that this weekend will prove exciting enough even for you."

"I look forward to it then. I've also learned a few things. Have me on your right and Casey Cushman on your left at lunch. We might as well start early."

"I'll see to it. Now, how about some champagne and an introduction to the Cushmans?"

"Lead on. I haven't even set foot in this house, and I'm already aroused. My body is tingling all over."

I shook my head as she laughed. I handed her off to Stanley, who guided her inside. Bruni and her father went up the steps deep in conversation as I went over to greet Bonnie and Angus.

I called out, "Welcome to Rhinebeck. I'm so happy you both could come."

After we exchanged kisses and hugs, I said, "There are four guests whom you've never met: Jim Cushman and his wife Peggy, and the younger versions, James and Casey. Anne will brief you, Angus, while you and I, Bonnie, need to talk about your espionage skills."

Bonnie squealed. "This is about Johnny's accident, isn't it? Hugo gave us a heads up."

"That, and more."

"I knew it! Question: Is Mom coming?"

"Yes."

"Good. She'd never forgive you if you hadn't invited her. Mom lives to hunt whether astride a horse or in the drawing room. I once saw her ride a horse into a house, so I suppose she can do both. How's Johnny doing?"

"He thrashed about yesterday."

Angus looked pleased. "That's good news. Have you been telling him stories?"

"I have indeed. I'm not sure if they are responsible, but at least he's reacting positively. I'm hoping that you can stretch those indications sufficiently to announce that Johnny will be up and about with all his faculties intact very soon."

Angus looked amused. "I see where this is going. If it will flush out those responsible, I'm all for it. I'll talk to Anne, of course. I'm sure she'd like some reassurance."

I looked at Angus. He was never slow on the uptake. "You have that exactly right."

"Lead on, then. Bonnie, dear, after you."

Bonnie gave his arm a squeeze and said to me, "Angus is always the gentleman."

Angus winked at me and said, "Not always."

53

B oth the senior Cushmans were thrilled to meet the baron and baroness. I noted that Jim rubbed his fingers surreptitiously to ease the pain after he shook hands with Hugo. Elsa was charming to both. I introduced the doctor next. He looked at Jim Cushman and gave him a nod.

The senior Cushman withdrew his proffered hand and said, "Of course, you're English, my mistake." He then put a hand to his forehead and said, "Maxwell-Hughes ... Maxwell Hughes. I've heard that name before. Ah, yes," he said, looking pleased. "Do you happen to have a relative in the Foreign Office, by any chance?"

"It depends on the age," Angus said in his best Oxford, "If he was much older than myself, then it was my uncle. If it was around mine, then it was his son, my cousin."

"I see. It was the older one, I believe. How small the world is."

"Isn't it just?" replied Angus and stepped back.

I introduced Bonnie, and the senior Cushman grew enthusiastic. "It's a pleasure to meet you, Bonnie Leland. May I call you Bonnie?" Not waiting for a reply, he said, "Please forgive me, but I must ask. Are you related to Mary Leland—*the* Mary Leland?"

"She's my mother. Would you like to meet her?"

"Oh, I would very much."

"Well, today's your lucky day. She'll be here soon. She's looking forward to meeting you."

"Well, I'm more than flattered. The feeling is mutual."

"That's good to hear, but let me know how you feel by the end of this weekend."

"I will. I most certainly will."

After Bonnie moved away, the senior Cushman beamed and said to me, "I had no idea there would be so many guests, and one of the richest women in the world is arriving as well. That excites me. I must admit, I expected a much smaller gathering."

"I hope that's not an inconvenience. I made sure the house would be full in your honor. There were nine guests at first, but that made thirteen at dinner. The last time that happened somebody died, so I invited one more. Fourteen is a much luckier number. Of course, two might die this time, but I'm hoping not. There are no guarantees. Unexpected things happen in this house rather routinely, and not all of them have been good."

"What? Are you joking?"

I smiled. "Not at all."

"Who died, if I may be so bold?"

"Lord Bromley, my father, and right in the middle of dinner."

The senior Cushman looked shocked. "Good heavens! I'm not sure whether to offer my condolences or be offended."

"Well, let's not be offended. I just wanted to warn you. You and I are just getting to know each other, and I thought it prudent that I tell you. By the way, I've known your son for many years. He looks well."

"I'm happy to hear it. He's never mentioned you."

"I'm not surprised. We were never close. I saw James only occasionally. Johnny Dodge and I grew up together."

"Oh."

I watched him carefully. There was no reaction to Johnny's name, and my doubts took hold. I wondered whether the senior Cushmans were as heavily involved in Johnny's accident as I assumed. The senior Cushman seemed much less calculating than I'd imagined. It was either that, or he was very good at it.

At that moment, the lesser Cushmans made their appearance. Both were dressed for lunch. James had changed into dark gray flannel pants and wore a dark conservative tie rather than an ascot.

Casey looked elegant in four-inch dark blue stilettos that matched her sleek Pucci dress of blue and turquoise. Her eyes slid over me. She gave no indication of what had occurred between us. I introduced both of them to the new arrivals. She smiled a lot, chatted with Bonnie and Angus, and barely acknowledged my presence. Whatever her thoughts, they remained hidden behind a charming social exterior. Anne was right. She belonged on the stage.

Since lunch was in an hour, and some of us needed to change, the party started to break up. I went to collect Bruni, who was talking to her mother.

54

W e slipped out the door and down the hall. Alone in our sitting room, we hugged and kissed each other.

When we pulled away, Bruni said, "I needed that in so many ways. Now, let's sit. There's much to discuss."

Once we were seated on the couch, I repeated the talk I had with Jim Cushman and the one I had with Stanley.

Bruni looked thoughtful and said at last, "First things first, no food or drink unless Stanley serves it to me personally."

"That's correct."

"Then I will do that. Do you think Casey Cushman will go that far?"

"She might. For now, it's a necessary precaution. I don't want anything happening to you. Not now, not ever."

"Well, that makes two of us. Putting that aside, the situation here is like a puzzle."

"It is. Johnny and I would often hypothesize about situations to understand them better. We'd update, revise, or scrap them as we accumulated more information. You and I could do the same now."

Bruni smiled. "Good idea. I'll tell you mine when you finish yours."

"Okay, here's what I think. James mentioned a big deal blowing up and that it cost the Cushman firm a fortune. Maybe it did, and now the Cushmans have a financial crisis that can only be fixed by a large influx of capital. If true, then Dodge Capital would be an ideal target. It looks affordable on the surface and is privately owned, meaning minimal regulatory disclosures and a speedy transfer of ownership and assets. It's a possible fit, but I doubt John has any intention to sell. Perhaps the Cushmans are here to persuade him to do that, either with his agreement or without?"

"Then John's the real target, not me."

"I suspect that both of you are, but for different reasons. My guess is that Casey was part of the original scheme but is now hedging her position in case everything falls apart. Maybe she thought Johnny was her ticket out, discovered he wasn't, and came up with another solution?"

"You, because you own Rhinebeck."

"That's how I see it."

"Then what about the accident?"

"My guess is that the Cushmans wanted to find out if Dodge Capital was worth acquiring and how that could be done. Since James knew that Johnny was attracted to Casey, he told his father, and she was ordered to obtain that information. Likely, Johnny welcomed her attention at the beginning but grew suspicious. When he clammed up, he was drugged to make him talk. As to the accident, maybe Casey went way too far in her enticements, or Johnny found out something, and somebody decided to pull the plug before he could say anything. Whichever is true, it is highly probable that Johnny was drugged, dumped in a car with a drunk driver, and the accident followed, perhaps with a little help. Granted, that last part's sketchy, but it kind of works."

Bruni nodded. "It does, and the data fits what we know so far."

"It does. What's yours?"

"My conclusions fit nicely on top, but from a different perspective."

"I'm all ears."

"First, there's a history between John Senior and Jim Cushman. I watched them in conversation. Both tried to hide their dislike for the other, but contempt and loathing would flash across their faces when one of them looked away. The intensity of it shocked me and explained to me John's interest in Johnny's rivalry with James. I sensed from the beginning that he had more than just a passing interest. What bothers me is that John hasn't mentioned it."

"I know what you mean, and what you say makes sense."

"It does, but what confirmed that for me was the way Jim would smile and look at John. I'd seen that expression before but couldn't place it. Later, I remembered. I had a client who wanted to sue a colleague. I watched that man talk to his supposed friend just before the suit was filed. He had the same look of savoring the moment and almost gloating in anticipation. Jim Cushman may need John's business, as you said, but most of all, Jim wants to watch John suffer. If I were John, I'd be seriously worried."

I thought about that. "Then we must warn him. What you say aligns with what we know so far. Given that, Jim Cushman might want fewer guests present because delivering the blow would be more personal. As to John saying nothing of their rivalry, Johnny and his father are quite similar. They both withhold information deliberately. Given both our ideas, do you still think a resolution is possible?"

"Much has to happen before we get there, but eventually, a settlement must be negotiated. It's either that or the last act of *Hamlet*."

I chuckled. "Let's hope it doesn't go that far."

"Let's hope. My other concern is Casey Cushman. I have reservations about calling her out in front of everyone. For a start, we have no idea how she'll react, and we can do without another screaming fit."

"I understand. I, too, have some reservations. Why don't we hold off on that and float Johnny's imminent recovery for now? Should that revelation cause barely a ripple, we go with the bigger splash at dinner."

Bruni smiled. "I agree. One other point: We must find out what's feeding all this. Maybe it's whatever caused the rivalry in the first place—like a wrong that can never be put right. Another possibility is that there's somebody or something else behind the scenes—one who prefers to remain hidden but profits in some way or some unknown set of circumstances. Any agreement we might reach will fall apart unless we know who or what that is."

"What do you suggest we do?"

"You must speak with John. I'm going to start with Anne and Peggy. I want to know what might have caused their husbands to hate each other and who might want that to continue."

I smiled at Bruni. "What could be easier?"

She smiled back. "Finding a lost treasure?"

I laughed. "I should think. Question: Who should float the rumor about Johnny?"

"Anne said she'll see to it with Angus. By the way, Mama says she has some questions for Casey. She didn't have time to elaborate, but she can tell me before lunch."

"She asked me to sit her on my right with Casey on my left."

"I'll make sure that's arranged. Mama's onto something. Now, we best get ready for lunch. You know we do spend a great deal of time getting in and out of clothes. One would think we have nothing better to do."

"I've often thought the same, but such is life at Rhinebeck."

55

A crowd had formed in the drawing room by the time Bruni and I arrived. Meals, I realized, would be one large gathering after another. I preferred a much less social existence, but for now, I could only blame myself. I had invited them. As I looked over the room, I felt Johnny's absence once again and realized that ever since their arrival, the Cushmans had held the spotlight and my attention. It was time I changed that. As I considered what to do, I set my priorities: John would be first, then Bonnie, who still needed to be fully briefed, followed by Dagmar.

I saw John standing next to a small side table away from the crowd. He was pouring himself a drink from a decanter. I stepped quickly to his side and put my hand on his wrist as he raised his glass. He looked up, annoyed. Before he could say a word, I said softly, "Drink only from an unopened bottle and never from the decanter until the Cushmans leave."

John paused, still holding his glass. "Why do you say that?"

"Bruni isn't the primary target. You are, and nobody uses that decanter but you."

John put down his glass and looked at me. "What have you discovered?"

Since everyone else was on the other side of the room, I repeated my hypothesis in a low voice.

John nodded. "What you say makes sense. I'll be careful."

"Please. You're more than just a friend to me, so yes, be very careful. One other thing, what can you tell me about your rivalry with Jim?"

John looked at me coldly. "You think there is one?"

"Yes."

"Who told you?"

"Bruni. She watched you conversing with him and came to that conclusion."

John said, "She is perceptive; I'll give her that." He looked a little peeved. After a pause, he added, "It looks like I'll have to settle for champagne."

"Good. It's just while they're here, and John ... I don't know how to say this, but I have only your best interests at heart."

John looked at me for a long moment. "You do, but that doesn't make my telling you about Jim and me any easier. It's ... painful in so many ways, and above all, it's unflattering, but you're correct. The story has relevance, and you should know it. We'll talk after lunch."

He patted my arm and moved to the table where Cristal was being poured. I went in search of Bonnie. I found her talking to Angus. I steered both of them to the side table where I'd been talking to John. The Cushmans remained on the other side of the room, but I noted that their eyes flicked in our direction.

Turning my head away, I repeated what I'd said to John, Casey's conversation with me, and the possible use of drugs to make Johnny talk.

When I finished, both wanted to say something.

Angus said to Bonnie, "After you, dear."

"Thank you, Angus, and thanks, Percy, for the update. That senior Cushman's a piece of work. He's a brown-noser, for sure. I dislike the type, probably because I was one myself and now recognize the signs. They appear nice on the surface, but underneath, they're full of envy and hate."

"A brown-noser, Bonnie?" asked the doctor.

"An unctuous sycophant in your lingo, Angus."

The doctor chuckled. "Yes, of course."

Bonnie continued. "Now, this drug thing interests me." She turned to Angus. "Are there drugs that can make you do whatever you're told—like you're a zombie or a robot?"

Angus considered her question. "There are. What you're talking about is the holy grail of coercion, but like the grail, such quests are chimerical in the real world. The dosage and their toxicity are the problems. Too much, and death is the result. Too little, and it doesn't work. The right amount needed is a constantly moving target. Food ingested, alcohol consumed, mental disposition, absorption rates, as well as metabolic and expulsion rates are difficult to assess in the specific. Even weight and body type can affect the results. In addition, the delivery system can be problematic, particularly if clandestine, which usually is the case with such things. The Devil's Breath is one that comes to mind. Have either of you heard of it?"

"No," Bonnie and I said in unison. We moved closer to listen to the doctor.

Angus continued, "The Devil's Breath is endemic to Colombia, where the ingredients are plentiful. It's used by criminals to induce victims into emptying their bank accounts, opening their homes so that everything in it can be packed into a waiting van, or doing any number of things that the victim otherwise wouldn't. The drug is made from the seeds and leaves of certain plants, *Brugmansia* being one. They are ground into an ultra-fine powder, which is either inhaled or mixed with an oil to be absorbed through the skin. The preparation, dosage, and delivery all require great skill and constant practice.

"A friend of somewhat questionable repute looked into it extensively and told me about his findings. He said it was brilliant when it worked but equally disastrous when it didn't. Mistakes would happen. The target would drop dead. Other times, they began howling at the moon. He compared it to handling sweating dynamite or making homemade bombs from household items. A simple mistake and the operator becomes the victim. It happened to him. He almost died, which is how we met. Nonetheless, the hauls can be impressive. My friend gave it up in the end. The life expectancy of those who use such techniques is short and nasty. Death is often preferred to the madness that prolonged and acute exposure can generate. I could go on, but perhaps later."

"Whatever are you guys talking about?" said a voice behind me.

It was James Cushman III, with Casey at his side.

All three of us jumped a little. "We were talking about bombs," I said, turning to him.

"Bombs?" James looked at me with some incredulity.

"Yes, and their delivery methods. The doctor is an expert."

"Oh really? And how's that possible, Doctor, you being a medical man?"

Angus looked at James. His expression didn't change, but somehow, he seemed much more intimidating. He said softly in the manner of a chief of surgery speaking to an intern, "The concussive and shrapnel effects on the human body, blunt force traumas, and bullet wounds of all types and calibers are specialties of mine. I've had extensive experience in emergency medicine—car accidents being the primary cause of fatalities these days, although the effects of violent crimes now figure prominently."

James looked impressed. "Wow. Sounds like you're a good guy to have around."

"Not always. I like to pound people into oblivion on occasion. It's a bad habit that I've been trying to shake. It's been difficult for me, but I'm making progress. Lucky for me, and possibly for you, I now have other interests."

Angus smiled at Bonnie and patted her hand.

"Oh, Angus," said Bonnie, "you're so modest." Turning to James, she said, "He's world-class in everything he does, and I mean everything. Oh, I think that's Stanley signaling that lunch is about to be put on the table."

James continued to smile, only it seemed a little forced. Casey, I noticed, wasn't smiling at all.

234

———◆———

56

L unch for twelve is easily managed with five on a side and a host and hostess at either end. To my left was Casey Cushman. To my right was Elsa. She looked pleased to be sitting next to me and in front of Casey. Next to her was the doctor, followed by Anne and Peggy. Anne had seated Angus and Peggy to her left and right. She could pump either of them for information without shouting. Next to Peggy was her son, who was also to Bruni's left. To Bruni's right was Jim Cushman. I didn't envy her having to talk to either, but I doubted she'd be bored. Next to Jim was Bonnie. To her right was John, followed by Hugo. I noted that Anne often seated John and Hugo together. It was their preference. And finally, next to Hugo was Casey, completing the circle.

As Sancerre was being poured, I turned to my left to ask Casey if she had fully recovered after this morning. She looked a little frosty but said in an even voice, "I'm quite recovered, thank you."

Elsa smiled and said, "So, Casey, I understand you are given to fits or seizures. Do you have them often?"

Casey looked uncomfortable, but Elsa appeared caring and concerned.

"Now and again," said Casey.

"Are they epileptic in nature or more of the occult variety?"

Casey sipped her wine. "I'm not sure what you mean."

The word *occult* had caused her eyes to narrow.

Elsa went on and said, "By occult, I mean hidden from view. Epilepsy is the more easily diagnosed, while the causes of occult seizures are often opaque. Likely, they stem from unintended drug interactions, drug usage, physical exhaustion, high stress, or lack of sleep. In times past, they were associated with prophecy, clairvoyance, and divine callings. Do you ever speak in tongues?"

Casey looked uncomfortable. "No, I don't. I have no occult powers."

"Are your episodes contagious?"

"They're solely mine, I think, but thankfully they've been fewer."

"That is good news, but I must ask you … what happened at the Stantons'?"

Before Casey could respond, plates of *Carpaccio di Manzo* were served. It was the same dish as the other night, and I was delighted. I savored the first bite and was in heaven. I thought to myself that Elsa wasn't pulling any punches, but her tone and concern made it difficult for Casey to take immediate offense. On top of that, Elsa was not one to simply speak to hear herself talk. There was a point coming, and Casey must have sensed that too, for she had quickly consumed one glass of wine and was working on her second.

When the course was finished, Elsa started in again. "I heard that the Stanton family invested heavily in your in-laws' firm after one memorable dinner. Something about the man who was handling the Stanton money, going insane and tearing off his clothes in the middle of dessert. What puzzles me is that just before that, you fainted and collapsed into his arms. You say that your episodes aren't contagious. Are you sure? Have you seen a doctor?"

Casey looked like she wanted to leave the table, but once again, Elsa spoke with a softness that was completely devoid of any condemnation. Even I found myself nodding in agreement at the reasonableness of Elsa's words and tone.

Casey drank more wine and looked like a small rodent confronted with a cobra.

"Did you hear about that, Percy?" Elsa asked.

"No, I didn't."

Turning back to Casey, Elsa's countenance changed. Her eyes flashed as her voice barely rose.

"I know what you did to that man, Casey, but your secret's safe with me for now. Just the same, listen very carefully."

The cold, icy hardness of Elsa's voice rose in volume and carried throughout the room. Everyone at the table stopped talking and looked in her direction.

"Interfere in the pending marriage between Percy and my daughter again, or threaten my grandchild in her womb, and you will answer to the man who sits beside you. He has no foibles about skewering a woman, or anybody else for that matter. I, too, have no such compunctions. You sit at the high table, Casey. We don't play your kinds of games here. Do we understand each other?"

Casey turned very pale and nodded.

"Do you really, Casey?"

Casey nodded again and said, "Yes."

"That's better." Satisfied, Elsa looked down the table at the Cushman men and said, "Now you, sirs. Yes, you two."

Elsa paused until she was sure she had their attention before saying, "Gentlemen, you are free to act as you see fit. You know what I'm referring to. Your business is your business. My business is my family. Don't make my business your business! Not now! Not ever! My family includes my daughter and my future son-in-law. Do we understand each other, Mr. Cushman, senior, and Mr. Cushman, junior? Yes, I'm speaking to both of you!"

Jim Cushman looked at her and gave the slightest of nods. James looked at his father and gave a nod as well.

Elsa continued. "We have an agreement then, and I will hold you to it. Now, I apologize to everyone for my interruption, but that needed to be said. Now, let us enjoy this lunch. The meals here are pieces of heaven and should be eaten with all the attention and delight they deserve."

So much for making a small splash at lunch, I thought. I should have expected something like this. Elsa was Elsa, after all. Bruni smiled broadly at her mother in thanks. The Cushmans, not so much.

57

The second course of chilled jellied consommé with a dollop of sour cream followed immediately. I half expected the Cushmans to get up and leave, but the soup was that good, and they stayed put. I looked at Peggy Cushman. Peggy's countenance was like an Arctic wind blowing across the tundra in the middle of winter. She stared at Casey while her husband kept on eating, looking at his plate. James squirmed, glanced coldly at Casey, and picked up his wine glass. Casey watched him from our end for several moments. He stared back at her with obvious contempt until she put her attention back on her soup. I half expected another fit, but so far, all was quiet. The only sound was the clatter and clink of spoons.

Into this silence, Angus's voice rang out. "John, I don't mean to shout, but I have some news. I called the hospital just before lunch. They said that Johnny is making a splendid recovery and that his memory and faculties will likely come through intact after all!"

"Really?" said John. "Did you hear that, Anne? Let us raise our glasses to my son's unexpected recovery. Wonderful, Angus! Thank you!"

John rose from the table with glass in hand and asked that everyone do the same. The Cushmans paused as they digested this latest piece of information. Peggy Cushman stood and congratulated Anne on her good fortune. The rest of the Cushmans followed. Jim Cushman looked relieved. His son put on a plastic smile while Casey did the same. Angus had played his card at the right time, and all that could be done had been done. It was time to see what bubbled to the surface.

It didn't take long. Poised with her glass raised, Casey trembled as she stood beside me. Her hand shook, and her wine glass slipped from her fingers. It shattered on the edge of her bowl with a tinkling sound. The Cushmans turned in her direction as one and looked like they wanted to slap her silly.

At this, Casey whimpered and started to purse her lips. I reached over and hissed, "Don't you dare, Casey. It's over. We know everything." She looked at me in terror and promptly vomited into her soup.

Elsa whipped around behind me and was beside her in an instant. "Allow me, Percy."

Casey swayed as Elsa held her arm, wiped her mouth with a napkin, including her lips, and led her out of the dining room. Her husband ran around the table from the far end and followed. I was quite sure he didn't want a shaken Casey talking to Elsa while she recovered. Staff began the cleanup as Stanley announced that everyone should move to the drawing room while order was restored to the dining table and that lunch would recommence shortly thereafter.

58

I stood at the door as my guests filed past. Bonnie whispered to Angus, "Damn it! I really liked that soup."

Angus consoled her. "There, there. I'm sure arrangements can be made."

Peggy and Anne came next. Peggy asked Anne if there was a room where she and her family might have a private chat."

Anne replied, "The library is down the hall on the left, and it's virtually soundproof."

"That should do. Thank you, Anne."

She turned to her husband and said, "Get both of them and meet me in the library. Do it now."

Jim Cushman nodded and looked grim as he went to collect James and Casey, who were sitting on the couch in the drawing room next to Elsa.

Bruni was last after Hugo and John. She slid up beside me, and we made for a spot near the French doors and a little privacy. Bruni said, "That should nullify the threat against you and me. I spoke to Mama before lunch, and she told me what she'd found out. Casey used some kind of drug on that banker at the Stantons'. Had you not pushed Casey away when she tried to kiss you, that might have been you—either that or you would have been in her thrall."

"What? Are you sure?"

"Absolutely. Mama has a knack for finding out what others would rather not. She told Jim Cushman that whatever he has in mind for John is not her business. She won't interfere, provided no harm comes to you, me, or the baby. It was the best that could be arranged on short notice. I meant to give you a heads-up, but you were with Angus and Bonnie. I apologize."

I kissed her. "No need. You both did brilliantly."

Stanley slipped up beside us and said softly, "There's something you both should know. I listened at the library door. I expected a diatribe by Mrs. Cushman, but none followed. She actually sounded pleased, if not relieved, as did all of them."

I considered that. "That is difficult to explain."

Stanley continued, "It is. To add to that, I managed to inspect the younger Cushman's luggage while they were downstairs. They contained no food items. The excess weight was from a large metal briefcase packed inside Mr. Cushman's bag and a similarly constructed square one in Mrs. Cushman's. That one contains a number of bottles. I could hear clinking and liquid sloshing about when I shook it. I can't say what's in Mr. Cushman's. Both were secured by a robust five-digit combination lock. There was also a small piece of dark thread on the right side of each of the bags containing the cases. I put them back the way they were."

"Thank you, Stanley. Thoughts?"

"Two different cases for two different plans. Should they go missing after all our guests have arrived, the Cushmans might find themselves in a quandary."

"Heavens, Stanley. That's a bit bold, even for you."

"It's just a thought."

"Let's keep it that way for now. How long until lunch is back on the table?"

"About five minutes."

"I must speak with John right after. We'll talk when I'm done. Thank you, Stanley. You might want to collect the Cushmans."

"I'm headed that way."

With that, Stanley drifted off. I turned to Bruni. "What do you suppose is going on?"

"The Cushmans are regrouping and taking stock before they get down to business, which I suspect we'll hear about before too long, maybe this evening."

"Is there anything we should do in particular?"

"Nothing for now. Speak with John. What he says will be key. I also think stealing those cases might be an interesting gambit. It's been done before. In the meantime, I'm unusually hungry."

59

L unch was reconvened, despite the absence of Casey and James, who had retired upstairs. Their places at the table had been removed, and I found myself between my future-in-laws. I concentrated on the fresh bowl of jellied consommé with a dab of sour cream that was placed before me. The taste was heavenly. Others were equally enchanted, and conversation around the table was sparse.

As the next course was served, Hugo said, "Since your best man is making progress in his recovery, you can now set a date for the wedding. Tell me by the end of the weekend, yes?"

"Yes, of course," I said.

Hugo smiled. "Good. No more delays. Understood?"

I nodded. Hugo smiled broadly, amused at putting me in an awkward position from which only an affirmative response was possible.

I turned to Elsa and said softly, "Thank you for saying what you did."

Elsa smiled. "Sometimes it's best to put everything out on the table where it can be seen by one and all. That way, there can be no mistake, and everyone knows where they stand. With certain people, one must be clear from the outset lest they take advantage. By the way, I thought Johnny's pending recovery an interesting gambit. I take it my daughter had something to do with that?"

"She did."

"Let's hope you can deliver. What interests me is that the Cushmans seem more relaxed now that the news of Johnny's possible return has been delivered. That doesn't quite make sense unless the Cushmans wanted Johnny out of the way, but not completely. Do you know why that is?"

"I don't. It's what I wish to discover. Bruni told me this morning that everything that's gone on so far is preliminaries and that the Cushmans will be getting around to telling us what they want fairly soon."

"I'm sure they will, but have a care. They lie, and nothing constrains them. The driver was killed, yes?"

"He was."

"Consider that for a moment. If the Cushmans are responsible, then they've ignored the most fundamental rule of human conduct: to avoid taking another's life. It must follow that to them, life, like death, has little consequence or meaning. It's certainly true that sometimes one must take a life in order to survive, but I wonder at the long-term effects of having done so even then. A light has been extinguished. What that means, I don't know, only that it means something. Hugo? You have more experience with this than I do."

Hugo sipped his wine. "I do. I've seen death and caused it. I struggled with the mental effects of having done so until I decided to live what remained of my life to the fullest as myself—warts and all. It was either that or be consumed by doubts and reservations. One can atone if that makes one feel any better, but in the end, one must either embrace all one is or destroy that part which is responsible. With such an erasure, one must be less than who one was before, yes?

"I once told you, Percy, that greatness requires everything. Living with our best and worst is not easy but necessary if one is to be whole. Many are not comfortable living such a contradiction, but then I'm not like everybody else. Long ago, I asked myself, Why be someone other than who I am? To be anything else is to live a lie. Consider this. Lies require constant work and effort to sustain them when the truth is simpler, stands on its own, and needs nothing. Which would you prefer to be? Someone you are not, or who you really are? I don't need to think about who I am. I know, and that has made all the difference. But back to the Cushmans. Talk to John. He'll tell you about them, or he won't."

I nodded. "Thank you both for your words and observations. I'll be speaking to John shortly."

Crab cakes with a sharp sauce and a green salad were next, followed by lime sorbet. Lunch came to an end, and Bruni announced that coffee would be served in the drawing room for the ladies and in the library for the men. We rose from the table. I noted that all my guests were smiling and that lunch, in spite of the interruption, had been a culinary success.

As the men moved down the hallway toward the library, John and I slipped out the front door and up the drive. The morning's distant cumulus clouds had drifted closer and grown in size as their tops flared and extended into the upper atmosphere. Below, breezes blew one way and then the other as John and I walked among the shifting patterns of shadow and sunlight.

Halfway up the drive, I said, "You were going to tell me about you and Jim Cushman."

John stopped and looked back at the house for a moment. "Yes, and I thought about how to tell you over lunch—interrupted, of course, by Elsa. Frankly, I felt more than a little miffed that she left me out of her arrangement, but I realized my rancor was irrelevant. We all wish to avoid the consequences of our follies, but in the end, who but ourselves can ultimately resolve them?"

"Unfortunately, I think that's true."

"It is, and telling you about Jim Cushman isn't easy. I've acted badly. Of course, his behavior toward me has been equally deplorable, but with Johnny's accident, he and his family have crossed a line, although that has yet to be determined. Whether Jim played a part, I don't know. On the surface, we spoke of other things, but he had an air of satisfaction and a hint of joyful anticipation. It took great effort on my part not to punch him in the face. I'm sure he saw that, and my struggle likely pleased him. Really, I came within a hair's breadth of physically attacking him."

"Well, good that you didn't. Bruni said that she saw the tension between the both of you and was concerned. Have you ever tried to end it?"

"Once long ago, but he used that moment against me, and I never tried again. Right now, his plans are close to fruition. Peace is the furthest thing from his mind."

"I understand. Just the same, something must be done. Soon, it will get completely out of hand, and then what?"

"I don't know. Our conflict has been going on far too long to simply stop. Even now, I think to myself, if I can avoid the scheme he has in mind, all his planning will be for nothing, and that will drive him mad. To me, that's a delightful thought and underscores the essence of my side of the dispute. I relish creating his disappointment and distress far more than the pain and agony I might experience should he succeed against me. I think it is the same for him."

"That is unfortunate. What does Hugo say?"

"That this feud will be my ruin unless I end it."

"That makes some sense. Did he suggest how?"

"He counseled that I ruin him utterly, kill him, or make peace, but whichever course I choose, to do it quickly."

"Which is it to be?"

"Peace is better, but just because I want it doesn't mean I can achieve it. I can't seem to extricate myself without either doing more harm or receiving more of the same, and that is my dilemma."

"I see. Would you like my help?"

"I would welcome it, but I don't see how you can."

"In my opinion, resolving the matter must start with you. Jim won't listen. He already has his plan. As an illustration, here is what your conflict looks like."

I stuck out my elbows, pushed one palm against the other forcefully, and said, "This is what's happening now. You two are butting heads, locked together in combat like two mountain goats. Watch what happens when I take away one hand."

My left palm was left floundering with nothing to push against.

I said, "It takes at least two opposing forces to have a collision. With one removed, there can be no impact, so, in essence, there can be no conflict."

"You want me to remove my side and make it go away?"

"As impossible as that sounds, that is exactly what I want you to do, but even if you decide to do that, you may choose to put it all back when he hooks you once again, and we're back to where we started. Hugo is correct. You must end this conflict one way or the other, and once and for all. It makes no difference what Jim thinks or does in this, only what you decide and what you do."

"That may be true, but how am I to do that?"

I considered his question. "I think you must discover why you continue to create the conflict. Jim baits you in some way, and then he hooks you. Likely, you do the same to him. Understanding the nature of the bait may allow you to avoid the hook. You held nothing back when you told me what happened with the Maintenance Trust, and we were able to resolve the matter. Tell me the full story between you two. I promise to make no judgments. At the very least, by telling me, you will gain some distance and perspective."

We walked for a minute in silence.

John sighed. "I suppose it couldn't hurt. I meant to tell you anyway, but what's been holding me back is not just how and where to begin but what you'll think of me when I'm done. I've kept it hidden and made a thousand excuses for what I did. I was young. I was stupid. The list goes on and on, but in the end, none of them can absolve me."

247

"Unfortunately, absolution is not always possible, but at some point, we must move on, forgiven or not."

"I suppose. Jim certainly can't forgive me, and I can't seem to forgive myself—or him. Oddly, he should be thanking me. Without an enemy, or at least a worthwhile opponent, some men have no purpose—no passion. Jim is like that. Without me, he would be so much less."

After a moment, he said, "Perhaps, we are the same in this?" He chuckled. "I never considered that. Maybe I should be the one thanking him rather than the other way around."

We continued to walk while John was lost in thought. Like Johnny, his father needed to ease himself into what it was he had to say, and walking helped. The overly complex resolved to simplicity eventually. I waited.

After several minutes, John began. "Jim Cushman and I were at boarding school together. It was our senior year, and one of the rites of passage—one I wanted to be remembered—was to do a senior prank. The school had a large chapel with compulsory attendance every Sunday. I thought to liven things up by tying a horse to the altar railing the night before and leaving it there. The horse's presence would certainly create a stir on Sunday morning. The school was in a rural area, and there were horses nearby. It was just a question of haltering one and leading it into the chapel. I floated the idea to Jim, who thought it was a great idea."

"You were friends?"

"We were until I betrayed him. I'll tell you how. That Saturday night, we decided to do the deed. Unfortunately, two significant details escaped our attention. The first was that the floor of the chapel was made of polished stone. The second was that standing a horse for hours, tied to a railing, may be typical in Western movies but hardly applies to a highly strung thoroughbred in unfamiliar surroundings. Haltering the horse and then leading it from the pasture, along the road, and into the chapel at night proved extremely difficult to begin with. The horse was skittish, and I was barely able to hang onto its head when it would rear and attempt to run off. It was a constant battle, but I managed to lead the horse to the chapel and through the double doors with Jim urging it on from behind.

"I guided the horse up the aisle to the altar as it danced beside me. I tied the lead rope to the railing and hoped it might calm down. It didn't. When we moved away, it pulled back strongly against the rope. Its front legs braced against a step as it lowered its hindquarters almost to the floor to apply sufficient force. The railing gave way with a crash, and the horse fell over backward. On its back, it thrashed about, twisting from side to side to get its legs underneath itself. Right side up at last, it tried to stand, but the hooves were shod and couldn't get a purchase on the smooth surface. Sparks flew in sheets from its iron shoes as they struck and skidded on the stone. Its legs collided and scraped against each other, the pews, and the floor. We tried to help it up, but there was little room, and its legs were thrashing every which way. The horse grew more frantic and began to scream. It kicked out violently, and we had to stand back. The air stank of burnt hooves. With a massive effort, the horse was almost up when it fell into the pews with a terrific crash. One of its legs became entangled in a kneeler. It tried to free itself, but a leg was caught fast. It bucked and heaved. There was a snap. The horse screamed as the leg came free. It dangled at an impossible angle. The lower part flopping this way and that, attached only by skin and tissue. The horse gave a heart-sickening cry that reverberated off the walls and the high ceiling of the chapel.

"Its pain was like an electric current passing through me. I smelled the burnt hooves and felt the impossibility of the situation. There was no way to fix this—no way to make everything go back to the way it was. I knew then that my life, the one I'd known and loved, was over. My world had become unhinged from one moment to the next, and something inside me fractured. I felt my mind snap like a bone. *I have to get away. I have to get away right now.* I felt those words inside me like living things as I made unfamiliar little bleating sounds. The words roared through my head like a mad wind and commanded me. I obeyed, and they followed me into the night like a murder of crows, streaming behind me in the dark. I fled, filled with the horror of what I'd done, pursued by the terror of the consequences to follow. I ran blindly, frantically, and desperately until I couldn't run another step and collapsed.

"When I came to, I was alone. I didn't know where I was, other than that it was dark, and I was on a verge beside a country road. I'd forgotten completely about Jim. I got up and walked along it in what I thought was the opposite direction to my flight. My mind calculated that my head must have pointed away from the grim horror and my feet in the direction I had come from. The night was chilly, and I trembled from the cold and the fearful uncertainty of what would happen when I returned. I thought of fleeing altogether, but I had no money and only the clothes I was wearing. I walked until I came across a sign indicating that it was three miles to the town near the school. I was shocked that I'd run that far in my flight, and yet I couldn't recall a single step.

"As dawn broke, I walked along the stone paths between the school buildings, and all was silent. There was no screaming from the chapel. The stained-glass windows were dark, and two long wooden horses that hadn't been there before barricaded the doors. I returned to my dorm room and saw no one. My roommate was still asleep. I lay down and didn't wake up until noon."

John seemed to come out of a reverie and asked for a cigarette. I gave him one.

He lit it and continued, looking down. "I got dressed after I awoke and went to lunch. It was Sunday, and all the talk in the hall was about Jim, his expulsion, the screaming horse, the gunshot to end the torment of its existence, the corpse still in the chapel, the canceled service, and Jim's refusal to utter a single word to anyone, not teacher, student, policeman, or member of the clergy. He was last seen walking with a suitcase in the direction of the train station.

"To be frank, I was relieved that I'd not been connected to the crime. No one had seen me, but I couldn't bring myself to stay silent even though I wanted to. I knew I had to own up to what I did. I vacillated back and forth until I finally called my father and told him what had happened. He listened, asked a couple of questions, and hung up the phone. He arrived on Monday morning with a cadre of attorneys and accountants. There was a closed meeting with the headmaster and later with the school's Board of Trustees that had been urgently convened. A restoration of the chapel, a modern ice hockey rink, and a new science building were offered but refused. Unbeknownst to my father and myself, the horse had belonged to the daughter of a US senator from whose pasture the horse had been taken. Its death had caused an uproar. The senator said he would not be pressing charges because he was an alumnus and making the incident public might damage the school's reputation, but short of criminal charges, the maximum penalty should be levied upon those responsible.

"The headmaster had informed my father of this detail, and once the meetings ended, the headmaster ordered me to his study. As I stood before him, he said that my cruel and cowardly behavior reflected such a profound lack of character that he would not tolerate my presence on school grounds for one second longer than was absolutely necessary. I was to leave immediately and fervently hoped that he would never have another occasion to lay his eyes upon my odious presence again. After physically throwing me out of his office, he slammed the door. By this time, my father had left. Not knowing what else to do, I walked down the hill to the train station. Nobody said goodbye, and I never returned to that school."

John sighed, flicked the cigarette away, and walked in silence for a time before he said, "That, of course, was not the end of the affair, only the beginning. Such extraordinary happenings have their own lives, and their grim echoes never cease. I didn't graduate the next month as planned, and the prize I'd been awarded for academic excellence, of which I was so proud, was handed to someone else. Utterly embarrassed and humiliated, my father resigned from the Board of Trustees of the school and, perhaps to ease his shame, made an anonymous donation of a new science building. He never really forgave me for what I did or the mortification he endured, and I never graduated from high school or university. You may not know that, but it's true. Instead, I learned my trade in finance, starting at the very bottom, sorting mail. I apprenticed whenever possible to people who knew their business, and where more theoretical knowledge was required, I took undergraduate and graduate-level courses as supplements. I learned what I needed and discovered that degrees mean nothing in the long term. Only knowledge and the willingness to use it matter in the end.

"The repercussions continued. Maw disinherited me at once and wouldn't speak to me for years. I was only reinstated after Sarah's death, but that was for Bonnie's benefit, not my own. For that reason, I never coveted her money with sufficient enthusiasm. The inheritance was her means of control, but it was the horse's death that damned me. She never forgave me for that sin and still hasn't. She'll bring it up at odd moments to let me know she still remembers. Such reminders never cease, particularly when I feel a sense of pride. I imagine it's the same for Jim, but I don't really know."

John and I walked in silence for some minutes. This was a part of John I'd never known, not in all our years together. I felt his shame, his embarrassment, and the deep-down seething anger and resentment toward all who damned him and for all the pain that followed. The hurt was written on his face in lines that were familiar, but I had never recognized them for what they were until now.

I said, "I don't know what to say. How did you recover, John?"

John sighed. "Hugo did that—him and an old gentleman named Don Javier."

"Who is he? I've never heard him mentioned."

John smiled. "He's dead now. Don Javier was a Spanish aristocrat and friend of my father's. To me, he was a saint, mentor, and life raft all rolled into one. After the disaster at the school, my father didn't know what to do with me. He called Don Javier to find out. The conversation was not quite what he expected. Don Javier told me later that he laughed mightily at the story when he'd heard it and told my dad that it was only natural for sons to work at cross purposes to their fathers. How else were they to become men? He pointed out that Spanish blood runs hot, cruel, and reckless, obviously just like mine, and to send me to him at once. Having no other solution, my father agreed.

"I traveled to Spain and entered the old Don's household. He spoke English but insisted I learn Spanish. He told me that his family had hated the English tongue ever since the ghastly summer of 1588 but had condescended to pick it up again in 1807 through the direct intercession of Arthur Wellesley, the Iron Duke, whom his family greatly admired. Like those of his lineage who preceded him, Don Javier was a gentleman of the old school. He believed fervently in the power of almighty God, a man's honor, and the captivating beauty of Spanish ladies. He made each his life's work.

"After I arrived, he questioned me closely about my panic— what triggered it and what I remembered. Rather than condemn me, he said my experience was valuable. By knowing panic intimately, I could appreciate its extraordinary power and be able to recognize it, not just in myself but in others. Fear requires management, and courage is a skill. He said that I must hone the first and learn the second. He made me study fencing and dueling to bolster my courage. The Don believed that it was the nature of all young men of any worth to get themselves into more trouble than they could

253

possibly handle. For this, I had to prepare and be able to defend myself.

"I met Hugo at the fencing school Don Javier sent me to. It was an athletic club, mostly for younger men, that taught the use of foils, sabers, and epees at a high level of proficiency. Hugo was an advanced student there, and we became fierce adversaries. Late one night, we happened to be walking together in the direction of our homes when we were attacked by robbers. They wanted to kill us and take our money. We fought them off. Later, over a great deal of celebratory wine, I told Hugo about how I ended up in Spain. He said, 'Dismiss the incident from your mind. So what if you didn't graduate? You certainly graduated tonight. I'll even give you a certificate, but now we must flee. That body won't bury itself, and I can't be bothered. Unfortunately, a few of the wounded were locals and may expire. There'll be reprisals and the police. Running away isn't cowardice when it's prudent. Say your farewells to Don Javier. Tell him that you've grown into a man. Give him your thanks, receive his blessing, and then we're off to the Pyrenees *muy rápido.*' We argued the entire way as to who had done what, and by the time we had reached his castle in Austria, between us, we'd slain an army."

60

J ohn smiled at the memory. "It was a turning point for me. I hadn't run. I'd certainly been afraid, but I'd held my ground and fought back. I asked myself, Was I still a coward? To be sure, I talked this over with Hugo. He told me in that abrupt way of his that fear was an addiction, and I was an addict. I didn't understand that and asked him to explain. He said that fear is like a drug. It sharpens the senses and activates the mind. To be afraid is to be present wholly in the now, but like any drug, it can be abused. In moderate amounts, fear is what lets a gambler know he's alive. Indulged over too long a period, one becomes paranoid, like a spy operating behind enemy lines. Too much too quickly, and there is panic. Overdose and one dies of fright.

"I considered what he'd said. It made a kind of sense, and Hugo continued: 'Fear is an addiction like living is an addiction.' He asked me why people endure lives of only quiet desperation. I answered because they must. He said, 'No. They live that way because they are addicted to life in whatever form it takes, and like any addict, they will do anything and everything to keep their habit going. They are compelled.' I asked him, 'Then what's the answer?' Hugo said, 'To court death.' I must have looked surprised because he laughed and said, 'You want to conquer fear? Be willing to die. It really is that simple and no more complex than that. You're not a coward, John. You're an addict. Recognize that and be done with it. Free yourself.' "

John and I walked in silence for a time before he said, "Has my story surprised you?"

"You know it has. I knew none of this. Please continue."

"Very well. After vacationing in Austria for a few months with Hugo, I returned to New York and went to see my father. I asked for another chance. I said I'd changed, and my father saw those changes in me. Alice, too, helped smooth the way. She regarded me as only an older sister can. She saw me as a bit of a wild child, a loose cannon, but one who was at least well-made and would eventually turn out fine. She told my father this, and he believed her. I was given a second chance.

"That was a beginning, but in my heart, I was deeply afraid of seeing Jim Cushman again. I was terrified, and so, once I was settled, I sought him out. He had gravitated to finance and trading, just like me. I ran into him one afternoon near the exchange. He didn't want to speak to me, but I pleaded with him, and reluctantly, he agreed. We went for a drink, and after several meetings, he mellowed and told me that he'd come to a decision. He would put the past behind him, and we would start again. It was a moment of indescribable relief for me, and he knew that."

John walked in silence before saying, "We are all compelled to act in certain ways. How such compulsions implant themselves into our lives, I cannot say. Some we are aware of, and we take steps to prevent them from acting against our better interests. Others we can't see. They hijack our minds as we embrace them as our own best thoughts. It's these that do the most damage. For me, it was the belief that the past and all its unintended wrongs *could be* forgiven and forgotten. I desperately needed that to be true. I couldn't live with myself otherwise, and that compulsion blinded me. Others can see us far more clearly, and Jim did. He used my craving to ensnare me. I couldn't help myself.

"Not long after we had met again, Jim and I went partners in an investment scheme. He urged me to put in all I had, and I did. It was a disaster, but that had been his intention from the start. I had been skillfully set up. While I tried to grasp the extent of the wreckage that had been my life's savings up to that point, he told me that this was only a taste. He would never forgive me for what I did to him. I'd destroyed his life, and he swore I'd pay for that until one of us was dead. He spat in my face and walked away. The conflict between us truly started from that moment.

"I suppose I should be grateful to him for revealing his true intentions when he did. I had only a relative pittance at the time and none of my family's money. Had he waited, he could have done me irreparable damage. After his declaration and on reviewing the destruction of my savings, I realized that Jim had used my own need for absolution against me, but compulsion cuts both ways. I could use his need for retribution against him, and I did. All I had to do was leak that I was involved in a project, and he would come after me. It was so easy. I almost bankrupted him, but miraculously he survived. Oddly, I was still compelled, but this time in the opposite direction. I could and would forgive nothing. I used my outrage and my anger to spur myself to greater heights. Jim, too, realized his blindness. He became more subtle. Our war continued but at a slower pace, and I grew stronger. Strangely, he did too. It hasn't stopped.

"Destroying me is still his obsession. His destruction isn't mine. I can forgive him because he was not the one at fault. He can never forgive me because I was. Now I'm not so sure. The accident changed that. It's where we stand now."

John walked in silence, and I said, "Thank you for all you've told me. What do you think he has in mind for you?"

"Prison, I think. I suspect it's something to do with some information I received. I knew the source was questionable, but I bought heavily, and the investment has worked out far better than I expected. Trading on inside information is illegal. I'm sure he planted it and has the necessary proof. What he doesn't know is that I considered that possibility at the time and can document I acted without it. My independent analysis is sound, but regulatory bodies are notorious for being arbitrary, particularly if one has the ear of someone on the inside. I don't doubt Jim has such an ally. Should I be investigated by regulators, and the findings go against me, I will go to jail. I'm sure he'd like that."

"What can you do?"

"My initial reaction is to fight. He wants to gloat and tell the world he's won. He'll act prematurely. He always does. Some things about ourselves we can never change."

"What about putting an end to all of this?"

"I've considered what you and Hugo have said, and I must agree. It's time to end this. The exact how is still unknown, but I have the bones of it."

"Which is?"

"I'll forego prosecuting and taking his family to the cleaners for the attempted murder of my son. It's as Bruni said. We trade one for the other. The certainty of my destruction for the certainty of his. We call it even and move on."

61

W e had arrived back at the house. I told John that the idea was sound and thanked him for all he had told me. John said, "Our talk clarified what I must do. You mentioned the hook and the bait. I can see both more clearly. The hook is the rage he can instantly generate in me. I suppose that's rooted in my reaction to my cowardice. The bait is the chance to belittle him, to make him wrong, and vindicate myself. I also understand that our conflict has everything to do with how I view myself—whether I can see myself as worthy of my own admiration. Unfortunately, I can't seem to do that."

I looked at John and said, "I understand your feelings. Absolution is not always possible, particularly when we must forgive ourselves, but as I said, there comes a time when we must move on, forgiven or not. You are worthy, John. I believe that even if you don't. Perhaps you're simply compelled to think the way you do? Perhaps you should do as Hugo suggested: recognize your own addiction and be done with it. Free yourself."

John smiled. "I wish it were that simple. Maybe it is. The best I can do is promise to work on it. Thank you for insisting I tell you. I think I'll go and talk to Jim now that he's here. Perhaps I can ignore the bait after all, and that would certainly be a step in the right direction."

John made his way to the library as I went in search of Stanley. I found him in his office and brought him up to date.

Stanley rocked back in his chair and said, "What you've hypothesized makes sense. I'm also pleased that the baroness managed to check any moves against you and your fiancée. That is certainly a relief. Of course, Mr. Dodge is still in jeopardy, but he has the makings of a plan, and that is good. I would still like to get my hands on those cases once everyone has arrived. I know that may seem at odds with our usual mode of operation, but doing so will remove the temptation to use whatever they contain. Anything else?"

"I'm concerned about Johnny's recovery. The reality is that without his awakening and his testimony, we have nothing."

"That is true enough. Are you concerned about revisiting the shaman?"

"More than a little, and that is only the start."

"I understand. All of this is unknown territory, but I take it you're willing to try again."

"It's what I must do. Tonight, if possible."

"I will let Dagmar know. I doubt you would be able to get a word in as she is busy preparing dinner, so I'll take care of that. Anything else?"

"Yes, secure those cases. We can return them when they leave. Use your discretion as to when and how. One thing I'm quite certain about. I'd like another round of Hamish's brew when we manage to resolve all the issues before us."

"Most certainly, but there is much that must happen before then, and I imagine there will be more to deal with that is as yet unknown. It's only Friday."

"Yes, I was thinking much the same. Well, I must get back to the fray. Let's keep each other informed."

"Of course, and Mrs. Leland should be arriving shortly. In fact, I do believe that's her car coming down the drive. She'll want tea, of course."

62

W e were all outside standing in a line to greet her—Angus, myself, Bonnie, the Dodges, the von Hofmanstals, and all the Cushmans, including Casey. I was quite sure that Jim had ordered that all the Cushmans be there, given Maw's reputation. I wondered how she would greet them.

Her long black car stopped out front, and before the chauffeur could even open his door, Maw, in mink and jeans, stepped out and marched directly up to Jim and James Cushman, ignoring everyone else. Her white bull terrier, Robert the Bruce, trotted behind her.

"I take it you are the Cushmans?" she said to father and son. Before either could respond, she snarled, "I have but one thing to say to both of you. If either of you had anything to do with my grandson's accident, I will cut off your balls, place them upon a silver salver for my personal viewing, and then toss them into the fire. Be warned. Now, step aside."

With that, Maw elbowed her way through both men and marched up the steps, followed by Robert, who eyed them coldly as he followed. Halfway up the steps, Maw's voice rang out again, "Stanley! Tea! In the drawing room! Now!"

Stanley said, "Yes, ma'am," and was gone in an instant.

The Cushmans stood there with their mouths open, not knowing what to do. Jim Cushman looked about with an odd expression. Peggy looked furious while James rubbed his stomach where Maw had elbowed him.

On impulse, I said to Jim Cushman, "You might want to leave now while you still can."

Jim Cushman seemed to come back into himself, and rather than explode, he smiled broadly and said, "My God, what a woman! No wonder she's so rich!"

I stared at him. He looked like one of Maw's foxhounds that had been thoroughly scolded. Invariably, they would wag their tails, grinning like fools, happy to know their place. I shook my head in amazement.

Jim took my arm and whispered as we walked up the steps.

"I'm certainly not leaving. No, not at all. Do you think I can sit next to her at dinner? Would that be possible?"

I considered his request and thought there was no accounting for human behavior. I replied as we walked through the foyer, "I'll make the necessary arrangements. Lucky for you, Mrs. Leland was only irritated. You should see her when she's mad."

"Really? Have you experienced that?"

"Oh, yes."

"Well, that must have been something. Marvelous woman. Simply marvelous."

We made our way into the drawing room as Bruni slipped up beside me and whispered, "That was refreshing."

"It certainly was," I said. "And the more she pummels Jim, the more he seems to like it. He and the rest of the Cushmans will be on their best behavior, at least up until dinner. I promised he could sit next to her. I'll let Anne know."

"Good idea. How did it go with John?"

"You were correct. I'll tell you about it shortly."

"Please do. We'll talk after Mrs. Leland simmers down a little."

"She may not."

"Yes, and I'm not sure what to do about that."

"You and me, both."

Maw, I realized, would not be easy to placate or appease. She wanted blood, and *an eye for an eye* was her code. It was another complication that I hadn't anticipated.

63

S tanley served Maw her tea. She sipped and sat on the couch in the drawing room as we each made our obeisance in turn. Robert sat on his haunches to her left, eying each of us as we approached. John then formally introduced the Cushmans. Maw condescended to give Jim and Peggy Cushman a few words. James was next. She stared at James and finally gave him a nod, and shook his hand. James smiled in return. Casey Cushman came after, but before she could be introduced, Robert rose from his sitting position and blocked her approach. Casey tentatively moved forward, but Robert's lips curled back, and he gave a growl from deep in his throat. Robert's teeth seemed to grow out of his mouth. In an instant, he had transformed into something alien, menacing, and dangerous. Casey froze with a hand to her throat and then backed away.

Maw eyed Casey and said, "Robert, enough."

Robert stopped his growling, his teeth receded into his mouth, and he turned around. He went back to Maw and sat back down on his haunches in exactly the same position he had assumed originally. His black eyes showed nothing as he watched and waited.

Casey remained frozen. The hand at her throat trembled like a captured bird.

Maw said, "Approach me. I want to see you."

Casey took a hesitant step toward her as John said, "This is Casey Cushman. James Cushman's wife and the daughter of Helen and Ambrose Duke."

"Is she now?" She looked at Casey in a detached way. "Do you have anything to tell me, girl?"

Casey took another step toward her and tentatively reached out her hand. Maw shook it but didn't let go. "Well?" she asked.

Casey looked down at the gnarled claw that held hers and mumbled that it was an honor.

"So you say. Look at me when I talk to you. You *do* know that I'm offering you a chance?"

Casey raised her eyes. Maw stared at Casey for some moments and then released her. Casey stepped back, staring at the woman gazing back at her, and said, "I ... I don't know what you're talking about. Really, I don't."

"I think you do. I will take your answer as a second refusal. Now, it is necessary that I ask you a third and final time. Do you have anything to tell me?"

Casey looked at her husband and then at all of us. There was something happening here that she didn't understand. She shook her head.

"Your answer is only valid if you speak it."

Casey murmured something unintelligible.

"What? Speak up!"

"I have nothing to say."

Maw paused and stared at her. "Very well. I accept your answer. Events will play out as they will, and your future with it. Percy, perhaps you and Bruni could take Robert for a walk while I speak with Mr. and Mrs. Cushman in the library. Robert will obey you." Looking down, she patted Robert and said to him, "Be good," and to the Cushmans, "Shall we?"

64

M aw left with the senior Cushmans for the library, and I announced to the remaining throng that drinks would begin at seven, black tie, and that everyone was to amuse themselves until then. Robert stood to my left, looking up at me and Bruni, waiting for one of us to command him. I opened one of the French doors, and the three of us stepped out onto the lawn. I had to look about to get my bearings. Massive clouds like huge gray battleships sailed steadily in the direction of the sinking sun, their tops burnished in brilliant bronze. The lawn lay before us, cast in shadow as we walked.

Bruni and I wandered down to the edge of the south lawn. Robert streaked ahead to explore the undergrowth. He raised his head above its green surface and looked at us. Reassured, he disappeared beneath, moving in the direction of the tennis court and the truffle-like treasures buried there.

As we strolled, Bruni said, "That introduction was mysterious. What do you think Mrs. Leland is up to?"

I considered Bruni's question again and said, "Mrs. Leland has a side that's difficult to put into words. She's very much like the Cumaean Sybil, who bargained with the last king of Rome. In case you're unfamiliar with the story, the Sybil offered Tarquinius Superbus nine books of prophecy for an outrageous sum, but thinking the price too costly, the king refused. In response, the Sybil lit a fire, selected three, and burned them. As they turned to ashes, she demanded the same amount for the remaining six. Even more outraged, the king refused again. Three more went into the fire. The Sybil now offered the remaining books at the same price, but the king hesitated, and the sybil picked them up to consign them to the flames. Panicked, the king stopped her and agreed to her terms. The Sybil was paid, and the three volumes were considered so valuable that they were stored beneath the Capitoline Temple of Jupiter in a special vault to be consulted only under dire emergencies."

Bruni frowned. "I see what you mean. Mrs. Leland is much like Alice but oriented in a different but no less mystifying direction. She's also one the richest women in the world, which certainly confirms her ability to bargain like the Sybil. What do you think will happen to Casey?"

I thought about that. "Nothing good. She gave Casey three chances, which likely means that even Maw's a bit horrified by what the future holds for her. Nonetheless, Casey refused them all, and with that, her fate is sealed."

Bruni nodded in agreement. "I want to say, Poor, misguided fool. Wake up! But it's too late for that. There's no going back. I wonder if Mrs. Leland is explaining that to her in-laws?"

"Perhaps she is. On another topic, would you like to hear about my conversation with John?"

"Please."

I related the story that John had told me and my earlier conversation with Stanley.

When I finished, Bruni said, "This whole mess is going to be difficult to resolve, but I think it's possible. Stanley removing those cases will certainly create some upset when Casey and James find them missing. On the plus side, their threat will be significantly reduced. It's a fair trade. John will have to make a similar transaction. He must exchange the certainty of Jim's destruction for the assuredness of his own and hope the one will cancel out the other, but to really make that work, Johnny must recover and very soon. Only then will we know for sure who did what."

"Those are my thoughts as well. I intend to make another attempt to find him tonight."

Bruni gave me a hug as we walked. "I thought as much. I'll help you all I can."

"Being beside me will be enough."

Bruni gave my arm a squeeze. "Let's hope. Now, is there anything else that must be done before dinner?"

"Not that I know. Let's return Robert and then you can try on dresses for tonight."

"You just want to see me naked."

"I do, which is why I suggested it."

Bruni smiled at me in that way of hers and said, "And you can model some underwear. That will work for me."

Before I could respond, Bruni put two fingers to her lips and gave a piercing whistle. Seconds later, Robert appeared from the bushes at a run. He skidded up to us, holding a flaccid tennis ball in his mouth, which he began chewing. He stood looking up at Bruni with his black, beady little eyes while working his jaws with vigor.

Bruni put her hands on her hips, looked down at him, and said, "You know that's not going anywhere near the house. If you drop it and leave it there, nobody will touch it. Now spit."

Robert spat and stood over the soggy remains, looking wistful. He gazed up at her again and gave a whimper. Bruni said sternly, "Absolutely not."

Robert eyed what was left of the ball for a few seconds more and then followed Bruni. I thought: *If only Johnny could do that.*

65

Having changed for dinner, Bruni and I were passing through the foyer to mingle with our guests when Stanley whipped past us and opened the front door. In stepped the tall man, Malcolm Ault.

He waved at Bruni and me, thanked Stanley for opening the door, and said, "I see I'm just in time. I'll change and be down shortly. How is Johnny? Is he recovering? I've had no news."

"He is," I said. I went on to explain briefly what was happening here.

Malcolm nodded thoughtfully and said, "I'll be happy to help in any way I can. Be down in a flash. We'll talk more then. By the way, I have a message from your mother, but later. Must run!"

With that, he mounted the stairs three at a time, followed by Simon, who scrambled after him with his suitcase. Stanley watched them fly up the staircase and said, "Since all our guests have arrived, I'll take care of that other matter. I tried to find out what Mrs. Leland spoke to the Cushmans about but could hear nothing. At the very least, whatever was said was discussed calmly."

I nodded and looked at Bruni. "If it was significant, I'm sure we'll hear about it. Thank you, Stanley. Do you know what's for dinner?"

Stanley smiled. "Dagmar told me to tell you that the dinner will surprise you and that the drink will be by your bed by the time you retire. If it's not too late, Dagmar and I will be available should you wish to consult us."

"Thank you, Stanley. I'd like that."

Stanley nodded and ghosted toward the kitchen. Bruni and I entered the drawing room.

Other than Malcolm, we were the last to enter. I grabbed two glasses of Cristal and gave one to Bruni. I noted that John and Anne were talking to Jim and Peggy Cushman. Whatever friction that had been there seemed to have dissipated. John looked like himself, and even Jim looked happier. Maw was speaking with Bonnie and Angus. Robert was in his sphinx position close by—half under the couch. James and Casey were talking with Bruni's parents. The men wore black, their white shirts dazzling. The ladies were in dark blue, green, and black—the colors muted but with shimmers from silk and satin punctuated by the flashes of gems. As if by mutual agreement, the volume had been toned down a few notches. Frankly, it was a relief. Perhaps we all felt that way.

Bruni sipped her champagne and said, "The calm before the storm?"

"If it is, we should enjoy it. Since our guests are behaving, we have a few moments to observe and comment. Casey looks recovered. She may survive yet."

"She might. Survival is one of the hallmarks of all of us here. We're like tigers in a circus. We give the appearance of submission and compliance to those with the power to alter our lives on a whim, but underneath burns a flame that can never be extinguished."

"Tyger Tyger burning bright?"

"Yes, and Casey cultivates the appearance of a lamb, but that's a lie. I need to find out more about her."

"By all means. I'll wait here for Malcolm."

"Yes, and your mother has a message. Catch you after dinner. It's time I get to work."

With that, I watched Bruni move gracefully beside Casey and, in seconds, had her to herself. I quietly thanked the spirits that lived here for sending Bruni into my life. She took my breath away and held it wherever she went and in whatever she did.

I heard the voice of Malcolm beside me and from above, "She has the grace of her mother and her father's force of personality. Those things are part of her, like the blueness of her eyes and the color of her hair."

"Yes, and I feel blessed each time I look at her."

"I understand what you say. I am happy that there are those for whom you and I would do anything. They brighten up our world. Alice did that for me—your mother, too. When she and I transported your father's body to England, we spent five days together looking at the ocean. The ship's bow would push up the swells before they passed under the hull, flinging their tops in brilliant sheets of spray before they continued on beneath us undeterred. It was mesmerizing, hypnotic, and restorative in a way I've never experienced. Your mother has a soothing influence. Often, by saying nothing, we said everything. At other times, she told me about her life and those she'd met along the way. I did the same. It was a magic time for both of us. At the end, we thanked each other with a gratitude that neither of us had felt before."

"That sounds delightful."

"It was. She and I spoke on the telephone before I traveled. She asked me to tell you to remember to be kind and merciful and that you would know what that meant when the time came. She said it was important. Do you know why she said that?"

"I can't say I do, but thank you for delivering her message. Perhaps she saw something. She, too, has her moments."

Malcolm looked about him. "There is a tension here. It's like being at school just before choosing sides in a game. I know the Cushmans, but who's the young woman speaking with Brunhilde? Do I know her?"

"That is Casey Cushman—Casey Duke before she married the son."

"Helen and Ambrose's daughter?"

"That's correct."

"Most interesting. Your mother spoke about her."

"I'd love to hear what she said."

"That is best discussed when we're alone and have a bit more time. I just hope that Johnny recovers soon. He's part of this place in my mind, and I sense his absence most keenly."

"Me too. He's why we're all here, and that too is odd, given that he isn't."

Before we could continue, Stanley entered the drawing room and asked that we make our way to the table. Dinner would commence once we were seated.

66

S tanley stood by the door as we made our way inside. The dining table had been extended to its maximum length to accommodate us all. The tablecloth was a dazzling Chinese white, and the plates with borders of deep cobalt blue imbued the table with a conservative elegance. There were no reds or golds to tempt the emotions. Two giant silver candelabras gave off the only available light. Beyond the expanse of the table was darkness and the shadowy forms of those who would serve us.

I found myself seated between Peggy and Jim Cushman. Jim was to my right. Next to him was Maw, with Angus beside her, followed by Anne and John, and then Elsa. Bruni sat at the end between her mother to her left and Malcolm to her right. Next to Malcolm was Casey, followed by Hugo, Bonnie, and then James Cushman. It looked like Anne decided I should know the Cushmans better, while Bruni had a lighter time with Malcolm and her mother. Inwardly, I grumbled, but the arrangement was fair. Bruni had put up with the Cushmans at lunch. Now, it was my turn. I thought to myself that I should be thankful that there were fourteen for dinner rather than that unlucky number.

I helped seat Peggy and sat down. A Grgich Hills chardonnay was being poured as the first course of duck spring rolls with a plum dipping sauce in small silver bowls arrived. The flaky, crispy rolls looked delicious sitting on the plate, and I hadn't even tasted them. I waited for my guests to begin. Peggy cut hers with her fork, speared a piece, and dipped it in the plum sauce. She put it in her mouth. Seconds later, she looked like she had passed into another world while Jim and James were grinning, having done the same. I followed.

Peggy said, "This spring roll is quite beyond anything I've ever tasted or imagined. Are all the meals here like this, Percy?"

"Pretty much. They range from the spectacular to the miraculous. With Dagmar's cooking, each day is memorable and enchanting."

Peggy nodded. "I heard that her culinary skills were unsurpassed, and now I know why. She has quite a reputation. I heard she is a witch."

"Then you heard correctly."

"Aren't you afraid that she'll use her witchcraft on you or that one of your guests might accuse her of such practices?"

"She's used her witchcraft, if that is what you call it, on me many times. Even now, she's working her magic. Consider what you're eating. As for anyone accusing her of illicit practices, the unfortunate soul will never taste such perfection again. Ironically, they would rue the absence of her witchcraft, not its presence."

"Has that ever happened?"

"Not recently, although I heard her previous employer gave up food pretty much altogether after she left. She rules here. I simply protect her, make sure she has everything she needs, and acquiesce to whatever she demands. It's a most workable arrangement. She needn't be concerned. She will always be treasured and revered."

"Then why is she working only in the kitchen?" asked Jim Cushman.

"Why are you working only in finance, Jim? May I call you Jim?"

"You may. I work only in finance because I like it, and I'm very good at it."

"And there you have your answer. You and she have that in common."

Jim nodded. "You don't order her about?"

"Hardly. With brilliant individuals, one must always allow them sufficient freedom to express themselves. Such efforts must be actively supported. Da Vinci was an employee, was he not?"

"I suppose that's true."

"It is. Leonardo died while working for Francis I. Who remembers Francis? Hardly anyone. Who remembers Leonardo? Everyone. With Dagmar, it's the same, only on a much smaller scale."

"I see, but I expect employees to behave like employees and do my bidding since I'm the one paying them."

"And I expect gentlemen to act like gentlemen, but that doesn't mean they will. Demands, orders, and strong-arm tactics have only limited effectiveness. Domination is what motivates those who use such methods. Stanley and Dagmar have worked here a long time and know far more than I ever will. Who am I to tell them what to do or how to do it? I've found that the appearance of power is not the same as wielding it. Most men desire the trappings, not the substance. They want deference and obeisance to reassure themselves that they're in control, while those who truly hold the reins are happy to let them feel that way. Isn't that correct, Peggy? May I call you Peggy?"

Peggy put her fork down and laughed. "Of course you can. What do you say to that, Jim?"

"Money talks power to power."

"That may be, but … " I added. "Words speak more clearly, although maybe with less force. How was your discussion with Mrs. Leland?"

Jim pursed his lips. "Sobering and informative."

"Then you should drink more wine. Peggy? What say you?"

Peggy finished her last bite and said, "Mrs. Leland takes familial interference personally, like the baroness, and has given us her views. We gave her our assurances that we would be able to construct an outcome that even if it didn't align with everything she might wish, it would nonetheless prove satisfactory to all."

"I see. How might you do that, do you think?"

Before any of the Cushmans could reply, a new course was served. The plum sauce rang in my ears and mouth like a bell. I looked up at Bruni, who was smiling. She noticed my glance and gave me a surreptitious wink. She knew it was heavier going at my end of the table. As I looked around, I noted that my guests were all enchanted. Hugo had his eyes closed as he savored the memory of his last bite.

The next course was *Sole Grenobloise* with small, boiled potatoes and baby asparagus with hollandaise sauce. The wine remained the same.

James, who was sitting beside his mother, sipped the wine and said, "I can't believe the food here. It's *fan-fuckin'-tastic!*"

Peggy whacked him on the arm. "Watch your language."

"Sorry, Mom, but it really is."

I didn't know whether it was the wine or the plum sauce, but I said, "Thanks, James; I'll let Dagmar know that she has another fan. Given the need for a satisfactory outcome, we might as well get started. Question for you and your father: How's the plan coming? You know, the one where you finally put John Dodge in the ground and win it all?"

Nothing was said in answer to my question for several moments.

James said at last, "Dad? Perhaps you would like to answer that."

Jim thought that over and said, "It's difficult to say at this point. Peggy dear, what do you think?"

"Oh, Jim! You haven't called me *Peggy dear* in ages. Did I ever tell you how randy you make me when you call me by that name?"

"No, you haven't, but I'll certainly remember that going forward … Peggy dear." He laughed uproariously, and Peggy did, too. James followed. I chuckled. It really was quite funny in an odd way. I looked up and caught Bruni looking at me in surprise. She made a face as if to say, *Whatever is going on at your end of the table?*

I shrugged in reply, but she was right. Something was going on. Since my end was acting unrestrained, I thought to ask, "So, James, what's the real story with you and Johnny?"

"Which one? There are several elephants in the room right now. If you mean the one about Johnny and Casey, he and I had a conversation or two about that. Johnny swore he would leave her alone, but he went ahead and had her anyway, figuring I wouldn't find out. Did he really think I was that blind? Look, he's your friend. I get that, but to me, when it comes to my wife, he's a treacherous little shit. I felt a touch of satisfaction when I heard about his accident. That may not be to your liking, but it's the truth."

"Are you telling me you didn't try to kill him?"

James wiped his mouth with a napkin. "Absolutely not. If I'd wanted him dead, he would be dead. He's not dead, *ergo* I didn't try. Besides, I'd be a prime suspect. Jesus, Percy, I wasn't dropped as a child. I was Phi Beta Kappa at Princeton. Arranging for Johnny to die in a car accident would be risky and problematic to begin with, but those risks would become unmanageable if I were stupid enough to let him live, assuming I set out to kill him in the first place. That would make no sense. Granted, I was disappointed when, at lunch, the doctor said that he is likely to survive with little adverse effects. Again, I mean no offense. I didn't try to kill Johnny, and that's a fact. We're speaking plainly like we ought to for once, but let's stop all the accusations and dig in. This is really good!"

"Yes, it is, but that accident didn't happen on its own."

James stopped eating again while his parents continued, listening all the while. "Then it wouldn't have been an accident."

"I doubt it was."

James took another bite, put down his fork, and looked at me. "Maybe you're right. Someone arranged it. It's possible. On the other hand, maybe the crash was accidental, and it was Johnny's bad luck along with some divine retribution that caused it. I don't want to argue, but it's easy to blame someone or something other than those we care about. We instinctively blame someone else when something goes missing. I've done that often enough. Maybe it's the same here? Of course, I'm stepping onto dangerous ground, but have you considered that?"

I said, "I'm certainly aware of that possibility as much as I'm cognizant of Johnny's foibles. On top of that, I'm certainly biased in his favor and likely always will be. I suppose I'm equally biased against you, but I'm willing to change my mind. Are you?"

James said, "I'm not adverse. The truth is I don't dislike you, Percy. I just don't like you, and I'll tell you why. In all the years we've known each other, you've never once given me a reason to *want* to like you. Maybe I did the same to you, and that's why we are where we are. Between you and me, we ought to work on that. It might make a difference down the line."

Peggy said, "Yes, I've not made myself likable often enough, and I think we all should make more of an effort in that direction."

Jim said, "I quite agree."

Our end grew silent. I put what James had said aside for now. He wasn't wrong.

The next course was a steak Diane with *pommes frites* placed around a small bowl of aioli with an orange tint. Beside them was a side of creamed spinach. The wine was a 1973 Stag's Leap Cellar. James commented that Stanley must be aware of the Judgment of Paris in which the French took second place to California with this particular vintage. I agreed and took a sip. The wine was excellent. I sampled the steak. The mustard sauce was divine, and the meat could be cut with a fork. The mushrooms had a tangy taste unlike any I had tasted before and were slightly chewy but just enough to be interesting. The aioli was sharp, yet all together, the many subtle flavors blended into a sensation that reminded me of trumpets. Not the metallic taste of the mouthpiece but the brightness of the sound produced.

Silence had broken out at our end. I heard Maw comment to Angus, "You are very candid tonight, Doctor." I heard Angus reply,

"There comes a time when facts stripped of their embroidery speak with greater clarity."

As I looked around, I saw Bruni listening raptly to Malcolm. Elsa, too, was eagerly attentive. Hugo was listening to Bonnie, who was whispering in his ear. Casey looked like a fawn whose mother had left her. She sat unmoving, hoping she was invisible. She picked up her fork and ate. Perhaps she thought that by not eating, she might draw attention to herself. She looked about and saw me watching her. *If it wasn't James, was it you?* I thought. She might have read my mind because she shook her head and looked positively terrified. I wondered which fear that was, the fear of being unjustly accused with no defense or the terror of having been at last discovered?

The senior Cushman put down his fork and asked, "Percy, what do we do now?"

"About what?"

"About everything. What is unsaid at this table is only the tip of an iceberg that extends far below the surface. Its hidden bulk can only mean disaster—one that we are rapidly approaching—like those on the *Titanic*."

"Let's hope it's not that bad, although I'm aware of what you say. Perhaps we ought to speak frankly about what we know to be true and say what we really think for once rather than let it pass."

"But what about the cost of doing so?"

"Revealing what we'd rather not is always difficult. I would talk to Bruni. She is a master at working out what others can't seem to manage. It's what I recommend."

Peggy said slowly, "We'd rather talk to you."

"And why is that?"

"We have our reasons. You seem less biased."

"I doubt that very much, but I'm willing to listen if you're willing to say what's really on your mind."

Jim said, "Peggy dear, what do you think?"

Peggy grinned. "I know your tricks, Jim. You're going to keep throwing that sobriquet at me until I drag you upstairs, you wicked man. I agree, but let's not think too long, or the moment will be gone. James? Would you like to start?"

"Sure. Here's our situation in a nutshell. We have a big financial hole that needs to be filled. An exogenous credit event mushroomed and caught us by surprise. It wasn't supposed to happen, but it did. Right now, the balance sheet looks good on paper, but an audit will show the world we have no clothes. No lender will touch us once they put the pieces together, so normal credit channels are out. We need a temporary cash infusion to get us through. Forty will do it—eight months max, and then we're clear. Dodge Capital has enough liquidity in combination with our own to make the whole thing work without too big of a squeeze. I spoke to Johnny about all of this and used Casey as a go-between to start things off. That didn't go as planned, but Johnny and I did manage to sit down and crunch the numbers while I gritted my teeth, knowing what he was doing behind my back. We came up with a package that works for everyone. Dodge Capital stands to make a bundle, given time. The problem was getting Johnny's dad to sign off on the deal. Johnny thought he could manage it and was about to play Henry Kissinger when the accident intervened. You think we tried to kill him, but Johnny's death would hardly be to our benefit—quite the opposite, in fact. My money's on the baron sitting over there. I find his presence more than a little coincidental and disturbing. As I said before, there are a number of elephants in this room, and his being here is only one of a whole herd of pachyderms traipsing about."

I thought about what James had said. That Hugo may be involved surprised me, but if there was blood in the water, I'd expect a fin to break the surface eventually, and Hugo certainly had the power, the speed, and the teeth. He also had a nose for such things.

I thanked James and asked Jim Cushman, "What about the Stanton money?"

Jim sighed. "That was a desperate play. Casey pulled it off, and their money helped, but it wasn't near enough."

"Is your situation really that bad?"

Jim looked glum. "Eight months is an eternity. A shortfall of that size can't be hidden for even a fraction of that time. So, yes."

"I see. What about your plan to send John to prison?"

Jim smiled. "Sometimes, one must use a stick rather than honey."

"And you think force will do better in this instance?"

"If one is to be taken seriously, force is a requirement. So, yes, I thought to use the threat to work something out. It saves time."

"That might work, but force is often overused and leaves an aftertaste that can last far longer than one might wish. Do you have the figures?"

Jim looked at his son. "Did you bring the case?"

"It's upstairs."

I coughed and said, "Actually, it isn't. I had both of your cases removed at my order. The safety of my guests is my responsibility. Casey was being a little free with her drugs, and they constituted a danger, given that she threatened me and Bruni."

"What?" The Cushmans looked shocked.

Before they could react further, I said, "I'll have that case returned. The other will be handed back to you when you leave. Moving on, I'd like to see the numbers tomorrow. If they make sense, I'll see what I can do to intermediate with John. Will that work?"

The thunderstorm of their outrage subsided as quickly as it had sprung up.

Peggy took a breath and said, "That will work."

Silence reigned again at our end while all those other than Casey were laughing and smiling. Dessert was next, and flaming dishes of Bananas Foster Flambé were set before us. Against the darkness that surrounded the table, the blue flames of burning rum were like tiny offerings to unknown gods as we watched them flicker and disappear before we tasted.

The Cushmans were enchanted.

As I took a bite, I still felt I was missing something. I had one more question. When everyone had finished, I asked, "Who ordered the limousine the night Johnny had his accident?"

The Cushmans looked at each other.

"What limousine?" Peggy asked.

Both Jim and James looked puzzled.

I continued. "On the night of the accident, a client by the name of Cushman rang up and requested the driver who was scheduled for Johnny. The fee offered was tempting, and another less experienced driver was substituted. Do you know anything about that?"

Peggy looked thoughtful. "Is that why you invited us this weekend? To ask us that?"

"Specifically? No. That information came to light after the invitations had been sent. There were suspicions before that, and I thought it best to sit down with all of you and have a frank discussion to clear the air. A weekend visit seemed the best way to accomplish that. Would you agree?"

Peggy looked at Jim, who said, "You suspected that one of us arranged the accident."

"The data pointed in that direction."

James grimaced and said, "Mom? Dad? Did either of you make the call? Because I didn't."

They shook their heads.

James continued, "And what have you decided about us, Percy?"

I looked at each of them and said, "Based on what's been said, thinking you made the call may have been in error. I make no apologies other than to say that the question of whether the accident was an accident is still open in my mind. In that regard, I thank you for telling me what you have. As to inviting you, would you have thought and acted any differently, being in my position?"

Jim looked a little grim. "I cannot fault your logic, and your inviting us may actually turn out to have been a help, although not done with that intention. Peggy dear?"

Peggy smiled. "Please return that case, Percy, and James will give you the proposal. As for myself, I feel conflicted about you, but as my son said, I don't dislike you, Percy, but whether I end up liking you still remains to be seen. I believe you to be sincere, and that is something. Do you think the same of us?"

I thought about that. "I do. You wish to resolve matters, and that's a start. There is, of course, more to be said. Tomorrow should give us sufficient time to do that."

67

B runi stood and announced that the ladies should pass through to the drawing room while the men should make their way to the library. I rose and thanked each of the Cushmans for their company and their words. They thanked me in return. I stepped to the side as my guests filed past and spoke with Stanley. I asked that he return the larger case to James Cushman while retaining the smaller one until the Cushmans left. Stanley said that he would see to it. I made my way to the library.

Cigar smoke hung in foggy layers about the room while port, whiskey, and brandy were poured. Everyone was talking at once. I poured myself a port and lit a cigar. Angus was speaking with Malcolm. I joined them and asked how they liked the dinner.

Malcolm said, "Fantastic fare. Dagmar's meals seem to get better and better."

Angus was smiling in agreement. He looked like a tipsy friar as he said, "Yes, it was quite beyond my expectations. Rarely are mine met, but in this case, the experience was beyond what I thought possible. I doubt I'll forget that dinner anytime soon."

I smiled. "Well, I'm happy that you both enjoyed it and thank you, Angus, for your words at lunch. Now, if you'll excuse me, I must speak with the baron."

They smiled again and raised their glasses to me.

Hugo was standing by himself, facing the fireplace and holding a cigar. His drink was on the mantel.

"Did you enjoy the dinner?" I asked.

Hugo turned to me. "Very much. Such meals have a special place. Stealing that sorceress of yours is tempting."

"Don't you get any ideas."

The baron chuckled. "Oh, I've thought about it extensively. I just haven't come up with a suitable offer."

"Well, I hope that keeps you busy for a long time. And speaking of offers, what do you know about the Cushman proposal to John?"

"I haven't seen it, but I'm aware of the need."

"Care to fill me in?"

"You know the gist of it. The Cushmans don't chitchat about the weather, but whatever happens going forward, I will benefit. Should their proposal be rejected, I'll be able to pick and choose from the wreckage that will follow. If they should succeed, then perhaps John and Jim can lay aside their differences, and everyone, including me, will breathe a little easier."

"I see. The Cushmans are suspicious of you."

"And I would feel the same if I was in their position, but I'm not in their position. Perhaps all will turn out well for them. Perhaps it won't. Since all becomes perfection eventually, you needn't worry or be concerned. Maybe they shouldn't either?"

"I find myself involved nonetheless."

"That doesn't surprise me, Percy. You're drawn to puzzles and the mysterious. It's your compulsion. I was thinking about your friend, Johnny, just now. I miss him and Lord Bromley. Someday, I'll miss Elsa, Bruni, John, and even you. I, too, have a compulsion, but in a different direction. I'm compelled to celebrate my living and my life. You should, too. In the end, it's never the finery, the deals, or the wealth, but the feelings and memories of having experienced them that are priceless. You should marry Brunehilde soon. I would do that tomorrow."

"You keep saying that."

Hugo sighed. "I do because neither of you seems to understand that all advantages and opportunities are temporary. They can disappear in a breath of wind or a flash of lightning. One moment, the impossible is possible, and the next, it isn't. I've seen it happen.

Obviously, you have not. Both of you remain oblivious. I'll say no more on the subject—at least until tomorrow. Now, do you have some rare brandy we might consume? Find something suitable and then return. I'll be here … but not for long. Be quick."

I left him and managed to find the bottle of brandy Anne had raved about at the back of the lower shelf of the bar. I returned to the baron and handed him a snifter.

We clinked glasses. After he sipped, he said, "This is better. Do you have a plan for this weekend, Percy, or are you playing it by ear?"

"A bit of both. My aim is to find out what happened with the crash."

"And how's that going?"

"It could be better."

"I presume you're looking for justice?"

"Yes, if it's warranted."

"Then consider this: Justice is not only blind, but she's running around half-naked with a drawn sword. How can that possibly end well?"

68

The baron and I finished our brandy. I said good night, collected Bruni, and escorted her to our apartment. While she was getting ready for bed, I went to speak with Dagmar and Stanley. They were waiting for me at the kitchen table, drinking tea while several of the staff cleaned, dried, and stored plates, cutlery, and the many other implements of the dinner service in velvet-lined cases. Dagmar poured me a cup as I sat down.

I took a sip and, once I was settled, asked, "May we speak freely here?"

Stanley said, "You may. I doubt we'll be overheard, given the activity and noise around us."

"Well then, first things first. Thank you both for the dinner. It was superb. The guests were enchanted, and so was I. I noted that the conversations seemed less restrained, maybe even uninhibited."

Dagmar nodded and said, "People naturally speak around issues rather than address them. It was my intention that more be revealed than less, but I wouldn't mistake candor for the truth. They are not necessarily the same. I'm pleased your guests were delighted. That, too, was my intent, and I accept your compliment for having accomplished that. Now, to more immediate matters. Do you still wish to continue your search for Johnny?"

"I do, but that, too, is opaque and almost as confusing as discovering who did what regarding the accident. What I thought I knew, I may not. The Cushmans, other than Casey, implied they played no part. Either they spoke what they considered to be true or they are superb liars."

Dagmar nodded. "What they said was what they wanted you to hear. It need not be a lie. They spoke their minds—what they thought. That doesn't mean everything they said was the whole truth, although the dinner made that more likely. Remember that investigations and discoveries are primarily about discarding what is irrelevant and examining what remains—usually, those areas that don't make sense or are contradictory. With people who lie professionally, one can only identify them as such by examining their histories, listening carefully to what they say, and noting inconsistencies and falsifications. Unfortunately, by the time one is certain, it's often too late. The sad reality is that people lie in a thousand different ways and for a thousand different reasons. On top of that, the truth has as many faces as a lie. One must always be alert and on guard when the stakes are high—like now. Trust nothing but your own good sense, but let us set that aside for now. Stanley told me about your last visit to the Shaman. I would expect a different welcome this time."

"I hope so. Do you think my ordeal was a test or an initiation?"

"Whichever it was, you will have a chance to ask for guidance. Trust your instincts in this. They will support you, but only if you let them. The drink is by your bed. I will say good night now. Perhaps you could drop by tomorrow, and you and I could simply talk? I'd like that very much."

"I'd like that, too. I'm hoping that one day, I might have a little more time. I used to blame Johnny for my constant lack of it, but since I continue to have the same problem, I must have something to do with it. That being said, I'll make the effort."

Dagmar smiled. "I would enjoy it. I'll let others clean up here. Stan, do you have anything to add?"

Stanley said, "Nothing other than that I returned the larger case as requested but not the smaller one."

"Thank you, Stan. I have much to tell you, but I'd rather we speak tomorrow morning if that's all right?"

We all rose as Stanley said, "Tomorrow morning then, and best of luck."

"Thank you. I'm sure I'll need it. Once again, my thanks to both of you. Good night."

69

B runi was sitting up in bed, reading. The drink was on the side table, but I ignored it.

As I got undressed and made myself ready for bed, I asked, "How was your end of the table?"

Bruni put down her book. "Delightful. Mama and I have rarely had the chance to sit together and talk, so that was an unexpected pleasure. Malcolm was to my right and was quite the raconteur. He enchanted us with stories of the Caribbean and Scotland. He is a fascinating man. How did it go with you?"

"Perplexing."

I told her all I could remember and added, "The Cushmans, particularly James, have suspicions about your father. I spoke with Hugo after dinner. Since he wins no matter what happens, I doubt he had anything to do with the accident. He's circling patiently while the matter is resolved."

"That's what he does. Besides, Papa likes Johnny far too much to want anything bad to happen to him—or to you, for that matter."

"Really? He's never said so."

"If he's talking to you, he likes you. If he's not, he doesn't."

"Good to know. You are aware that he's planning to steal Dagmar?"

"Of course he is, but we won't let him. Now sit down next to me. We need to discuss your journey. Are you still reluctant?"

I sat down beside her and held her hand. "Reluctant is not quite the right word. A significant lack of confidence may be a more accurate description of how I feel."

"Then you need more faith. You do know that you trust others far more than you trust yourself?"

"I am aware of that."

"Then change your mind. Of course, if your name was Cushman, then I'd be a bit more circumspect."

"You still don't trust them?"

Bruni looked at me, and I fell into the blueness of her eyes. She kissed me and said, "I don't. They're desperate. Desperate people will say and do anything to ease their situation. No option is ever off the table with them. After all, they're drowning. One shouldn't get within arm's reach, but if you must, approach them from behind so they can't see you. Should you swim directly at them and offer your support, they'll climb all over you and push you under to take a breath—their breath, not yours. It's what they do. It's not personal. They're desperate, and so they are absolved. The only sin that you can commit in this situation is to expect something different."

"In other words, my attempt to assist them may be in error, and we really are in a street fight."

"We are, my love—but in a very nice location. Let's put all that aside. It's time to find Johnny if you can."

"It is. Let's hope he isn't so desperate."

"Rescues are never easy, from what I've seen. Likely, he too is desperate, but maybe not in the way you expect. Be prepared is all I ask."

———◆———

70

Having resolved to go ahead, I reached for the tincture and drank. It tasted foul, no matter how I tried to alter the taste in my mind. As I lay back on top of the covers with Bruni next to me, the ceiling began a slow pirouette. The brightness of the room grew dim and then faded altogether. I was adrift in an inky sea.

I opened my eyes, and a million sparkling points of light looked down. I shrank from their cold stares, but the ground held me in its grip. I smelled wood smoke and looked about.

A voice next to me broke the silence with its familiar grating dialect: "Is it someone dear to you whom you wish to find?"

I sat up and became aware of a dim gray figure sitting cross-legged beside me.

I answered, "Yes. Yes, it is."

The figure sighed and said, "That is most unfortunate. They are the worst. They will use many tricks and deceits to keep you with them. They'll even use your love for them against you. Trust nothing that they say, only what they do. To them, you will be like a rock speaking, a tree whispering, or a flower beckoning—you are hints of another time and place. You must be forceful in your intention but subtle in your ministrations. You must seduce them using their own desires to lure them into following you. They won't come willingly. They can't. I told you not to wander in this place, but you disobeyed, and now you find yourself beside me. Regardless of the reason, restoring life is as perilous as taking it. Poor fools are you and I but blessed and in strange ways. You must trick them into believing that you can fulfill their dreams—you must outwit them. They will certainly try and outwit you—to keep you where they are. You may die beside them hopelessly entangled. It has happened often enough. It is what they do and the risk we take. To them, we are like demons, powerful and mysterious, but not to be trusted or believed.

"I will ask the Goddess to help you, but her help isn't up to me. The gods follow a different call—one that is beyond our understanding. Your guide pants behind you. He is eager to be off. Follow him. He'll lead you there and back. Return with or without the one you seek. Returning here is your only true obligation. Fail it, and you're damned. You'll also be dead. You'll have little time to work your spell and set the hook—no more than a hundred breaths. More than that, and you'll be lost. Be vigilant and careful. Trust no one but your guide. To repeat, one hundred breaths is all you have—no more than that. Breathe slowly. Start counting now. I'll be waiting for your return. Now go!"

71

I rose to my feet and turned. Robert the Bruce stood in front of me. His beady little eyes crinkled in amusement. He spoke in my mind, "Surprised to see me? I think you'll look at me quite differently now. We must move to where he is. He sits by a pool, endlessly gazing at himself—so typical. Just decide to follow me, and we will get there like in a dream. You're on your third breath. I will help you count. Ninety-nine and a long hold is all you have. Be calm and relaxed. Now, let's bustle. We have little time. Follow me!"

We moved slowly and then faster and faster. The ground became a blur, the woods parted around us, and then we were over water moving upriver so quickly that I couldn't take it in. We stopped abruptly in a peaceful glade after traveling a great distance. There was a pool in the middle with a surface so still, I could see the heavens reflected in its waters. A weeping figure hunched over it.

Robert spoke in my mind again. "He's twitchy and weepy—has been for a while. Left alone, he'll turn into a willow. Don't get too close. I'll make the introduction. Breath count?"

"Seven."

"Good. At least you can count. Stand back."

Robert went up to Johnny and began poking him with his nose. The hunched figure stood up and looked around.

"Is someone there? Come out. Don't be shy. I can't see you, but I know you're around."

Johnny put his hands out in front of him as if he was searching for someone invisible.

"I can sense you. Say something."

I called out, "Johnny?"

"Who's there?"

"It's me, Percy."

"Who's that?"

Robert said, "He can't remember anything right now. He's too far gone. You're going to have to get him to follow us. Dazzle him a little. A tennis ball might work. Breath count?"

"Ten."

"Wrong. It's eleven. Focus. Use a mirror. Birds fall for that all the time. Imagine you're holding a mirror. Just make it up as you go along. Anything can happen here."

I held a mirror in my hand. I made it eight inches by twelve like a photograph and pointed it at Johnny.

"Hey, what you got there? I see something. Ohhhh, I like that. It looks like me."

Johnny took a step toward the mirror. I backed away. Johnny seemed almost childlike. At least he was walking toward me.

"Keep following me, Johnny. Would you like a cake? I have lots of cakes."

Johnny stopped. "Cake? I want a cake. I like cakes."

"Well, follow me, and you'll get one. Come on, let's run and get a cake."

"Okay, let me hold your hand while we run."

Robert hissed, "Don't ever let him touch you. You've got the right idea. Make him think of cakes, really good ones, like salmon cakes. I love salmon cakes with hard icing. Paint them in his mind. Make him taste them, feel them, smell them. Lure the little twerp but no touching. Never."

"Only when we're there, Johnny," I said.

"Where's there?"

"Not far."

"Okay."

I thought of all the cakes I'd eaten and imagined one of Dagmar's best.

"You can have one of Dagmar's finest, like this one."

"Dagmar? I know Dagmar. Her cakes are extraordinary."

Robert hissed, "Breath count?"

"Twenty?"

"Wrong. Twenty-four. Look, you have to focus. Screw this up, and you really are done. You'll be trapped. Get him moving faster. We don't have all night."

"Come on, Johnny. Let's chase Robert the Bruce. You'll get a Dagmar cake when you catch him."

"Oh, no. I hate that dog. I always have to chase him."

"Which is why you must chase him now. Quick! He's getting away. After him!'

Johnny lunged at me. I was just able to stay out of reach. He was very fast.

Johnny looked sly. "I almost gotcha, didn't I?"

"You almost did. Bet you can't run as fast as Robert and me. Try and catch us. Just try."

Johnny lunged again, and I was barely able to avoid him.

I yelled, "You call that running? This is running."

I began to move quickly, but Johnny was almost on top of me before I knew it. He was very fast. I began running for my life. Robert was loping ahead, and I was following him with Johnny behind me.

Robert said, "This way. And you don't have to breathe so quickly. You're at fifty-six. Keep just out of reach. Be prepared for him to … Crap! He got distracted. Johnny's got the attention span of a chipmunk."

"What do I do?"

"Think yourself behind him. Taunt him and then run. He's a sucker for that. I do it to him all the time. You're at sixty now."

Johnny was hiding behind a tree.

"Johnny, you're it. Can't catch me."

Johnny whirled. I made a flashing light and moved away. He roared and lunged for it. I ran. We began moving very fast. We were almost there when he stopped again and collapsed in a ball among the trees. He began to weep.

"Come on, Johnny. You're almost home. Get up."

"I can't, Percy. I can't. I did bad things—really bad things. I remember now. The closer I get to where I'm going, the more I remember."

"Casey will be there."

"She will? James will have a fit."

"Won't that be grand?"

"It will, but I betrayed you, Percy. I betrayed everyone. I told her everything, Percy. Everything, and I don't know why I did that. She, too, has secrets."

"It's no big deal. We'll work it out together. I'll even give you a yellow pad like this one." I showed it to him. "Just come home, Johnny. All will be forgiven and put right. You'll see."

"But what about me? I'll have to live with me. I don't want to live with me."

"But I do, Johnny. I do."

"Casey is evil, Percy. She's evil—and I love her."

"I know. We'll think of something. We always do. Now get your ass up and moving. We're running out of time."

"I can't."

"You can and you will. You need to fix the shit you've created, or so help me, God, I'll murder you myself. You grew it. You chew it. You once told me I was too self-absorbed. Look who's self-absorbed now. We'll make it right. You'll see. Come on. We have a thousand dreams to make come true. We can rule the world, and you can be emperor. I'll stage a triumph in your honor, but only if you follow me.

"Really?"

"Really."

"You promise?"

"I promise."

"I'll hold you to it, Percy. I'll hold you to it."

"I'm sure you will, but you'll have to catch me first."

He lunged, and I moved away just out of reach. I sped as fast as I could toward the dew pond and the hut. How many breaths? I had no idea. Johnny was right behind me. He was changing as he ran. His legs grew longer, and he began to gallop on all fours. His shoulders grew massive, and there were evil-looking fangs protruding from his mouth. He had transformed into a monstrous, darkly mottled creature with blazing red eyes chasing me. He wasn't Johnny at all. He was something awful and horrific. He was a beast consumed by greed, dishonesty, and lust. He wanted to lap the life out of me, to feed upon my soul so that he might live and breathe again.

I made it to the hut and collapsed.

I heard the voice say, "Now you know why finding and returning those we love is the worst. We see inside them and the darkness that lies within their hearts most of all. Why else would they be here? It is the price that must be paid. We see them for who and what they truly are deep within themselves, and we pay for their retrieval and recovery with the drops of blood that leak from the breaking of our hearts. Just remember we are blessed and in strange ways. That is the covenant."

72

I sat up next to Bruni in our bed. I could think of nothing but the horror that I'd seen and the immense sorrow that I felt at what lay within my friend. It broke my heart. I clung to Bruni and cried.

Bruni simply held me. After a time, I stopped, but I still held her.

I whispered, "Don't ever put me in the position where I have to rescue you like I did with Johnny. I couldn't bear it."

"That bad?"

"Worse than anything I could have imagined, but it's over. I don't know what will happen now. I found Johnny and returned him; at least, I think I did. This is all quite new to me. I have no idea what happens next, other than that I won't be visiting that place anytime soon. Not for love or money—and for love least of all. I feel ripped apart."

Bruni said, "A shower will do you good. You're here now. Let us savor that blessing, and then you can tell me what happened. I'll share your burden if I can. What's done is done. It's over."

"What you say is true, but I fear it's only the beginning. Just hold me a minute longer. I'll bounce back, but not very high right now."

We put the world on pause for a few more minutes. I showered and lit the fire, which merrily popped and danced, independent of anything else, I felt more grounded and less emotionally spent. I told Bruni everything. Afterward, we sat on the couch in the dark and held each other. I let the minutes flow by and watched them bubble past like water flowing over pebbles in a stream. As they sped along, I was able to distance myself from what I had experienced.

"How are you feeling now?" Bruni asked.

"Stirred but not shaken."

"Was that a joke?"

"A poor one, to be sure, but I think a sense of humor is vital with this kind of thing."

Bruni smiled. "It is. I'm glad you are recovering. I'm also glad Robert was your guide. I'll look at that dog quite differently now."

"And me too. He has a certain charm and a peculiar, sarcastic sense of humor. I wouldn't mind your thoughts at this point, but before I hear them, I want a smoke and a glass of water. How long was I gone?"

"Not more than ten minutes."

"It seemed a lot longer."

"A lot happened. I'll take a smoke as well. In the meantime, I'll consider what to say. It's quite a bit to take in and has several ramifications."

"I know, and not necessarily pleasant ones."

"No, not at all, but where there's life, there's hope."

"I quite agree."

I got up and collected ashtrays, cigarettes, and glasses of water. I poked the fire to liven up the flames before I sat back down.

When we were comfortable again, we smoked and drank. I said, "We do have interesting conversations in the middle of the night."

"We do, and you always end up carrying me to bed at the end of them."

"And I will again when we're finished."

"I'm so glad. I'll hold you to it. Now, to the matter at hand: Johnny obviously feels guilty and did things he regrets. He feels he betrayed everyone and everything. Maybe that's true. Maybe it isn't. Does that seem about right?"

"It does. He didn't want to return because of what he did. I had to trick him."

"Given his frame of mind, I doubt there was an alternative. Regardless, he is not just a beast. We all hold back what we dare not reveal or allow to escape. You saw what he keeps deeply hidden within himself. Such intentions drive him from inside, and few are those who don't harbor something similar. If we weren't self-centered and consumed with a lust for life and self-preservation, spurred on by greed, anger, or whatever, the world would eat us alive, and that world includes our siblings. The runt of the litter is spurned for its weakness, not its strength. The weak can ruin all our chances because they cannot pull their freight should we depend on them. In battle, I would much prefer a madman to a saint."

"Maybe long ago. Not so much now."

"The rules haven't changed, only the veneer. Civilization done well prevents the beasts within from running completely rampant. I've noted that those of questionable strength always prefer weakness around them. It's why they make it popular. To me, that may be expedient but ultimately foolish. Our intelligence may allow us to avoid a life-or-death situation, but when evil's breaking down the door, I want that beast within. I want to be able to pick up an axe or something similar and have at it. Casey said I was a *ker*, a demon. She isn't wrong. I am that, but not all the time. My capacity to keep that darker part of me in check while using it when I must is my redemption. I wouldn't be holding you in my arms without both my good and my bad. Is Johnny any different, or is he any worse? I doubt it. Wouldn't you agree?"

"I do. I love you for all you are. Johnny, too, has that status with me. He flickers between the good and the bad. He's always been like that, and if I'm honest, I wouldn't be beside you either without him being everything he is, both good and bad. I suppose what surprised me was the intensity, the depth, and the pervasiveness of the evil that I saw. It consumed him from the inside."

Bruni thought about that and said, "Unyielding strength comes from deep within us, and I doubt it has anything to do with politeness and our higher selves. You saw Johnny at his worst, but you've also seen him at his best. He was a light for you growing up.

He saved you. Given what's happened, I think he'll need the same from you, and maybe for some time. It will be your chance to lead him out of his darkness lest it consume him once again, and that task will be mine, too, given that we're together."

I leaned over and kissed her. "You are very wise and really lovely right now. Thank you. I feel much better. I didn't think I'd feel this way anytime soon. Johnny will need my help, and I will help him."

"I'm happy for that. Now I think it's time you carry me to bed. I want to see you flex your muscles."

"Oh really? Well, you shall. Put your arms around my neck, and I'll carry you."

"Both of us."

"Both of you."

73

B runi and I strolled into breakfast. We were a little early, but John, Anne, Hugo, and Elsa were already down and seated. The dining table was at its maximum length. Fourteen starched, embroidered placemats lay beneath unadorned bone China plates flanked by sparkling heavy silverware. The heft of the breakfast knives and forks at Rhinebeck was always reassuring first thing in the morning. With the current configuration, Bruni was far away, with Anne and John on either side of her.

Hugo sat to my right, hiding behind the *Financial Times* with Elsa on my left. She gazed past her husband into the morning light that streamed through the French door behind him. I looked at Bruni and then at her. Once again, I couldn't decide who was the most beautiful. Elsa paused in her reverie and looked at me. I think I blushed. She smiled knowingly and went back to doing whatever she had been doing, obviously pleased. I sipped some more coffee. Other than the six of us, no one else was down.

Their tardiness didn't bother me. The morning looked fine from where I sat, and I was in the mood for white toast, butter, and strawberry jam with crispy strips of bacon on top. Few considered this combination to be the culinary miracle it was. This morning, Dagmar sent me toast and bacon accompanied by two slices of scrapple, some apple butter, and a perfect fried egg. I almost clapped my hands in delight. Given that start, it was going to be a good day.

Johnny and I had often debated whether a good beginning guaranteed a good ending or whether it portended a disaster. Having experienced both, along with several other possible permutations, we would often ask each other what type of day it would be before discussing our predictions. Invariably, we would resort to Johnny's first rule of Prophecy and Prognostications: namely, that all omens are good. The rule, almost a law, had yet to be disproved and was therefore deemed valid. It served the important function of obviating our need to worry incessantly about the future, something we did anyway, but given our tendency to go to extremes, invoking the rule prevented us from giving up before we had even started. I said to myself, *It's going to be a good day. All omens are good.*

I was savoring the moment when Maw strolled in with Robert close behind. I eyed the not-so-miscreant Robert and immediately began to eat faster, lest some misfortune or quirk of fate prevent me from completing my breakfast in full. In this, I was not wrong.

Maw sat down beside Hugo while Robert sat on his haunches to my right, staring at me with those beady black eyes of his. I ignored him and ate faster. He yipped his disapproval. Maw noted the proceedings and said, "He wants a walk, and I think rather soon. He'll only get more insistent, Percy, so I would gracefully relent while you can. Consider the alternative."

I ate like a madman and swallowed the last bite. I swigged some coffee to wash it down before I said, "You're quite right. Besides, he and I have a few things to discuss."

"No doubt, and I want to see that proposal before you send it on. You know the one I mean. I'll be waiting for it and you when you return."

"Yes, ma'am."

With Maw, speedy acquiescence was always recommended first thing in the morning. Maw unhinged early in the day was an experience to be avoided at all costs. I waved goodbye to Bruni, who blew me a kiss. I opened the door for Robert. He bounded through, and I closed it behind me.

The morning spread before me was glorious. It was everything a morning in the country should be. The breeze was balmy and sweetened with the faint scent of grass. The sky was clear, blue, and untroubled. I hadn't seen as fine a morning in as long as I could remember. Robert looked at me, gave a snort, and bounded toward the tree line beyond the manicured lawn. I lit a cigarette and strolled after him, astonished by the beauty of the day. The blue morning light seemed to bathe the Earth with promise. What had gotten into me? Perhaps this is what it was like to be blessed, and in strange ways. If it was, I appreciated the gesture.

I followed Robert and watched him root among the trees before completing his business. On impulse, I called out, "Hey, Robert, what do you think is going to happen with Johnny?"

He didn't answer but continued to wander before he lunged for something and came to me with a grungy tennis ball in his mouth. He chewed it vigorously and spat it in my direction.

I picked it up gingerly, flicked it away, and wiped my hands on the grass. Robert bounded after it, caught it neatly on the bounce, and came back to me before spitting it out again.

"Not saying. Well, I don't have a clue either. I'll throw it five more times, and then we're heading back."

After the fifth throw, Robert went into the underbrush and came out without the ball. He looked at me for a long moment and headed for the tennis court. I followed not far behind but at a leisurely pace. Since the day was so perfect, I went along. The crows were there, strutting about inside the baseline. Robert went down the steps, entered the court, and assumed his sphinx position beside the net. The crows didn't move, but every now and again, one would chuckle and caw. Another would follow. I waited at the top until Robert rose up, turned, and trotted back up the steps. He was making for the front of the house. I followed and watched him sit down on his haunches at the top of the steps, looking up the driveway. He gave a bark, looked at me, and then banged his nose against the front door. I let him in.

James Cushman was coming down the stairs. He had a folder in his hand.

"Morning, Percy. Here's that proposal. Let me know what you think. Are you coming into breakfast?"

"Already had it, James, but I'll have some more coffee."

I opened the drawing room door, letting James and Robert pass through. The dining room sounded like a convention. Every seat was taken except mine and one for James. There really were a lot of people having breakfast, far more than I was used to, but having seconds wasn't a bad idea. I thought about Robert, but he was already underneath Maw's chair. He had told me something, but I had no idea what that was exactly.

74

I sat down in a chair at the table by the window in Maw's room. It was the same chair I had sat in when she had delivered her ultimatum to me not so long ago. She was reading through the Cushman proposal, page by page. It was extensive, with numerous footnotes. In essence, it transferred ownership in several entities to John as collateral for two rounds of cash to be delivered a month apart. Having read it, I thought that on the surface, it appeared acceptable, but I had been a party to enough transactions of this type to know that what appeared fine on the surface was often murky below. Maw flipped pages while I waited. I looked out the window and saw Casey and James walking together at the far edge of the lawn. They were arguing because I heard Casey's faint screeching and the deeper rumble of James in counterpoint. I watched James grab her arms and pull her close. They hung together for a moment before Casey shook her head and pulled away. Maw cleared her throat and drew my attention back inside. She put down the proposal and looked at me.

She asked, "What is your recommendation?"

"I want to run it by Bruni before I offer one."

Maw scowled and said, "Pfft! I want to hear what you think. If I wanted to hear what she thought, I would have asked her. I asked you, so tell me."

I sat back. "The proposal might work, but there are a lot of moving parts."

Maw sat back as well and looked at me for a long moment.

"Do you know the steps I go through when I look at a proposal?"

"I don't, but I'd certainly be interested in finding out."

Maw smiled. "You and many others, but it's really quite simple. The first question I ask myself is: What do they want? Is it clear? The second is what do I want and is that also clear? The third is whether by refusing or accepting do I get what I want? Lastly, I imagine how many ways I'm being screwed. More specifically, how do the terms and conditions of the proposal forward or prevent that from happening? Given that criteria, do you think I would accept this proposal if it was presented to me?"

"I think you would refuse it."

"Why?"

"It's too complex."

Maw looked pleased. "Precisely. There is too much hidden in the footnotes."

Maw passed the proposal back to me. "I'm glad I read it. Such documents yield glimpses into the mind of the proposer. Real life is complicated. Uncertainty, unknown risks, and random occurrences make it so, but that is more of a reason that a proposal be straightforward without being overly simplistic. Too much complexity means something is being obscured or that the thinking is muddy. Too little, and one is left wondering about the sophistication of the proposer. If I were you, I'd put it to John and advise him to tentatively agree while he insists that he be given sufficient time to look at it more closely. Having delayed his final answer for as long as possible, he should then refuse and walk away."

"I would agree, but why not refuse outright?"

Maw looked at me as if I was being deliberately dense. She said, "The answer, Percy, is to gain insight. People tend to be prepared to negotiate a refusal but not so prepared for an acceptance. By tentatively agreeing, the Cushmans will relax and give us the opportunity to see them with fewer defenses in place. From my experience, it's sometimes best to release the reins and give a horse its head to see what it really plans to do. Only then can one discover how far it can be trusted. One must, of course, be prepared for disappointment, but *knowing* the answer to that question is much preferred to merely guessing and then finding oneself broken on the ground, wondering how one got there. Each rider must decide this at some point, and maybe every horse as well. Have your lady look at this by all means, but that is what I would do. I'd also be interested in what she might advise."

"I'll do that then. Thank you for your thoughts."

Maw rose. "By the way, I haven't received a wedding invitation. Is that still in the works, or has it been indefinitely postponed?"

"Not at all. Johnny is my best man. Bruni and I delayed to give him time to heal and then participate."

"Many would agree with what you say. The difference between myself and others is that I see excuses for what they truly are: excuses. One can dress them up and call them reasons, but that is to confuse one with the other. Reasons support a decision; excuses come after. I suggest you marry her, Percy, and have done with it. We'll all feel better. You do remember Edmond Dantes?"

"From *The Count of Monte Cristo*?"

"Exactly. When opportunity and good fortune knock softly on your door, you can't throw it open fast enough. They rarely knock twice, and they will never ring the bell. They are subtle and discreet. If there is no answer, they will leave, and when they're gone, they're gone, never to return. Yes, there may be others that come along, but they are never the same, and there is never a guarantee that they will choose your door and not somebody else's. It is the hardest lesson to learn, so I will make it easy for you. I *want* my invitation, Percy, and I *will have it* by the end of next week. No excuses. Do we understand each other?"

"Yes, and you will get one, Mary. I promise. Have you been talking to the baron by any chance?"

"Of course, I've been talking to the baron, but not about that. If both of us have mentioned it, then I would do something about it rather quickly. What more of a hint do you need? A flash of light, a puff of smoke, and a disembodied voice? Really, Percy, you can be quite thick sometimes. Now, off you go. I'll see you at lunch."

75

I thought about our conversation as I walked down the hallway toward my apartment, holding the document in my hand. Maw was right about what I was holding and about the wedding. With the baron and Maw working together, Bruni and I would either have to take some initiative and have a proper wedding or risk being ambushed by a priest when least expected. I passed through the sitting room, went into the bedroom, and closed the door. I placed the Cushman proposal on Bruni's bedside table and sat on the bed. I took a sheet from a small notepad and wrote a message asking her to review the attached at her earliest convenience. I added in the postscript: *We need to get married very soon. I hear the sound of drums rising and falling on the wind. The natives are getting restless ...*

I opened the bedroom door to the sitting room and saw Casey working the dummy light switch that opened the repository. She whirled and saw me. I hadn't heard her enter the apartment. I stifled my surprise.

"The switch to turn on the lights doesn't work," she said as she held my gaze. "Is this where you live? I was never given a tour and wanted to see it."

"It's customary to knock."

"I did, but there was no answer."

I decided to act as if nothing unusual had occurred. "This used to be Alice's sitting room. The bedroom is behind me."

"Can I see it?"

"You can."

I was happy that the maids had been at it. Everything was neat, orderly, and put away. I held the door open as Casey looked in. She stood close to me.

She asked, "Do you still refuse my offer of marriage?"

I sighed. "I think the baroness made that clear, as did I."

"Both of you did, but you deserve another chance. What's it to be?"

"The answer is no."

"Very well then. Thank you for the tour."

She turned, then walked through the sitting room, and out the door, not bothering to look back at me.

A few seconds later, Bruni rushed in.

"Was Casey just in here?"

"She was."

"What did she want?"

"To ask if I'd reconsidered her marriage proposal, but that was just a cover. Her real purpose was to get into Alice's repository?"

"Wait a second! The repository is in this room?"

"It is. I'd love to show it to you, but I can't. Once the locking mechanism has been deactivated, the vault is sealed for seventy-two hours before it can be reopened. Alice insisted on that feature. After Casey said she knew everything, I asked Stanley to deactivate it."

"I do recall you telling him that. If the vault is in this room, where is it?"

"It's behind you and camouflaged to look like a blank wall. Toggling the light switch opens it."

I went over and flicked it on and off.

I turned back. "It doesn't work, as Casey discovered. Perhaps she'll question all that Johnny told her? I'm sure being unable to open the vault put a crimp in whatever she had in mind. I would also like to apologize for not telling you about its location sooner since it's in our apartment."

"Was that deliberate?"

I shrugged. "I suppose it was. Stanley thought it best that you be let in on the secret only after we were married, given that the matter with the two governesses hadn't been resolved in his mind. I agreed at the time, but that caution no longer applies. I trust you absolutely, and unfortunately, the time to show it to you never really presented itself until now."

Bruni nodded and looked a little sad. "The past ... my past at least ... never really goes away, does it?"

"Not really. I wish I'd managed to tell you sooner, but I didn't. I can't change that either. Can you forgive me?"

Bruni came close and said, "Yes, I can. I know all about secrets. They can make for awkward moments. Revealing what is necessary without holding back is the best way to avoid that sudden twinge of not saying or wondering who knows what. What hurts is the thought of you not trusting me. I am worthy of that trust, and I forgive you for your doubt. I think I would have done the same. When did you plan on telling me?"

"I had no special set of circumstances in mind. When it was appropriate seemed the best course—like now."

Bruni kissed me before saying, "Since we're sharing secrets, I have one as well."

"I'm listening."

Bruni hugged me and said into my shoulder, "James told me on our walk that Casey might try to lure you away from me. He said it's a game she plays and that she is very skilled and adept at doing that. Many have fallen before her. I didn't tell you because it is rare for someone to get to me. It was the only thing he said that scared me. I suppose I'm still scared."

I put Bruni at arm's length and looked at her. "That will never happen. Are you jealous?"

"Me? Jealous? Whatever gave you that idea?" She smiled. "Maybe a little, but I still think your secret was bigger than mine."

I smiled back. "Perhaps it was. Let's just call it even and be done with it."

We held each other, and when we let go, I said, "In spite of James implying that he is used to Casey's machinations, he is quite possessive when it comes to her. He was anticipating Casey doing exactly what she did and wanted you as an ally. He's really quite insecure in his marriage. I also saw both of them arguing from the window while Mary was reading the proposal."

"You're right. He saw a weakness and used it. He's cleverer than I thought."

"I think that's been the undoing of many, and speaking of which, Mary was interested in your thoughts on the Cushman proposal to John. It's there on your bedside table for your review."

"I'll read it, but before I do ... " Bruni walked over to the wall by the light switch and ran her hand over the surface. "I can't see anything that would indicate a door."

"It's very well concealed. Once locked, only a professional could open it, and even then, it would require some serious explosives or cutting tools. Perhaps Casey wanted to do a little pilfering?"

Bruni turned. "I wouldn't put it past her, or any of the Cushmans for that matter. Having pieces from that vault would be a good insurance policy against John saying no. I'll look at that proposal now. What are your plans? Have you heard from the hospital?"

"I'm going to speak with Stanley first and perhaps have Angus call the hospital."

"That will be exciting. Find me right after."

"I certainly will."

I found Stanley in his office.

He rose and asked, "Well? How did it go?"

"Better, I think, but first, let me bring you up to date. We have some catching up to do."

"I have some time right now. Can I offer you a splash, Percy?"

"A small one would be fine, Stan. I have to keep my wits about me since it's Saturday, and things usually start getting out of hand around this time."

Stanley chuckled as he poured two small whiskeys, gave me one, and we both sat down. I told him about the dinner conversation with the Cushmans in detail, what happened with my late-night adventure, my meeting with Maw, and Casey trying to get into the vault.

Stanley thought about what I had told him for some moments before saying, "Let us take each item separately, but to begin, it seems you were correct in securing the vault. The Cushmans are a slippery bunch, Casey Cushman in particular, but before we get started, I received a phone call from Raymond early this morning. He said he would be returning before lunch with news that he wished to tell you in person. Given that he was in the city, I took the liberty of asking him to pay Johnny a visit to gauge his condition firsthand. He said he was planning to do that anyway and would report his condition when he arrived. Now, I have a question about what was said at dinner. The Cushmans, other than Casey, asserted they had no knowledge of the phone call to the limousine service and denied having anything to do with the accident. Is that correct?"

"Not precisely. They said quite specifically that they had no intention of killing Johnny, but whether they were involved in the accident, they never confirmed or denied."

"I'm glad you made that clear. That is a subtle but significant distinction."

"It is, but before we discuss that, thank you for asking Raymond to look in on Johnny. To be frank, I've been more than a little leery about calling the hospital and finding out if his condition has improved. I want to know, of course, but then, I don't. I ask myself, 'What if it worked?' That would upend much of what I thought I knew, but more distressing and more of a reason not to make the call is: What if it didn't? With a negative response, any hope I have will vanish. I'll be left with nothing—back where I started—telling Johnny stories in the late afternoon as his recovery grows more remote with each passing day."

Stanley nodded. "I understand your hesitation. I would feel the same. Either outcome is significant, but we will deal with either as best we can—and in the best possible way. It's what we do. The good news is that you needn't do a thing. Now, shall we continue?"

"Yes, but thank you for saying that. We were talking about the Cushmans and their skirting the issue of their involvement. I noted they seemed puzzled by my question about the call to the limo service. I haven't asked Casey yet. Johnny told me last night that she is evil. Perhaps she is. Perhaps all of them are. It's a puzzle. They act like villains, but then they don't. On top of that, I like all of them a little—not a lot—just enough to feel conflicted. If Johnny were here, I'd feel surer of myself, but he isn't, and so I'm left endlessly wondering what to do and what to think."

Stanley considered that for a moment and said, "Right now, it appears you have a paucity of information. Given that, one either gathers more or there are facts that you've previously ignored or dismissed as irrelevant that are not. If I were to ask you to use as little thought as possible, what do you feel is really going on?"

I paused a moment. "I'm missing something important. I can also sense a threat but can't quite grasp it other than that there is one."

"I see. Sometimes, you just have to think about other things while your mind sorts it out on its own."

"Bruni was telling me about Dagmar teaching her to do something similar—to let her mind work while she did something else."

"Precisely. That technique takes disciplined patience. You have to will yourself to let the matter sit. Unfortunately, our time is up. My duties are beginning to press. After you deliver the proposal to Mr. Dodge with Mrs. Leland's recommendation, we will simply have to stand back and see what happens once again. In the meanwhile, there's Raymond's news, lunch, and the feast tonight to look forward to. Everything will work out, Percy. It really will. You'll see."

"Of course, it will. Your talk has settled me. I've decided to ask Angus to call the hospital now rather than wait for Raymond to arrive and tell me. How about a toast?"

"To what?"

"To all omens being good. Those were Johnny's words, and they have kept me on an even keel more often than I care to mention."

Stan chuckled. "All omens are good. I'll remember that. Does it work?"

"It seems to. I'm still alive."

We raised our glasses and spoke the words. I put down my glass and told Stanley that I'd keep him informed. I left in search of Angus.

316

77

I found Angus with Bonnie in the library. Bonnie was reading a book while Angus had his briefcase open and was looking through a medical file at the desk.

I said, "Good morning. I take it both of you slept well?"

Bonnie put down her reading. "Remarkably well. The dinner was fab."

"It was. And how about you, Angus?"

"I slept like a baby, having drunk far more than usual, but then the dinner demanded it. How about yourself?"

"I slept well, what sleep I had. I wanted to ask if you could check with the hospital to find out how Johnny's doing. That is if it's not too much trouble?"

"I can do that. Do you expect a change?"

"Perhaps. Johnny can surprise at times. Besides, it's Saturday, and that usually means the unexpected. I thought I'd give that element a chance."

Angus chuckled. "Why not? Is there a telephone? I'll do it now."

"Permit me." I took the telephone with its extension cord from its little table and placed it on top of the desk. Angus reached into his briefcase and pulled out a sheet of paper with names and telephone numbers.

I said, "Dial one, two, one, two, and then the number of the hospital."

Angus dialed as I sat down next to Bonnie. We waited.

"Nervous?" Bonnie asked.

"A little."

I heard Angus say, "Good morning. This is Doctor Maxwell-Hughes. Please put me through to the nurses' station on the seventh floor, East Wing, if you would be so kind. ... Yes, I'll wait. ... Good morning, Nurse, this is Doctor Maxwell-Hughes regarding Johnny Dodge in 706. What is the patient's status this morning? ... Really? ... When did that happen? Has Dr. Sistie been called? ... Please, I'll hold."

Angus put a hand over the mouthpiece and said simply, "He woke up."

And then, "Carlos, what's happened? ... How long ago? ... How are his vitals? ... Good Heavens, that is unexpected. ... What's the message? ... I'll relay it ... "

"Angus," I interrupted, "Raymond, the chauffeur, will be at the hospital shortly."

"One moment, Carlos, I have two conversations going at once. ... Percy, Raymond's already there. I'm back, Carlos. Please continue. ... I don't see why not. ... He'll be coming here and into my care. Send whatever you expect him to need. ... Yes, that would be fine. ... Yes, of course. ... How's his memory and mental acuity? ... Yes ... Yes, I'll extend my stay. Tuesday would be fine for his follow-up. ... At eleven. ... We'll be there. I'll bring him myself. ... Can you push through his release? ... Good, good. ... Excellent, Carlos. Congratulations, and I'll personally thank the staff on Tuesday. ... Wonderful, Carlos. ... What was that? ... I have no idea. ... I'll call you after I examine him. ... Well done, again. ... Quite right. This is what we live for. ... Yes, I'll keep you informed. I have your home number. Reach me through my service should you need me. They'll find me. Unfortunately, they always do. ... That was a joke, Carlos. ... Goodbye. ... Yes, of course, I will. ... Goodbye."

Angus put down the phone and looked at me.

"Hell's bells, Percy. Johnny's out of his coma and apparently in good mental condition. Physically, he'll need some time to recover his strength, and his diet will need some looking after, but both can be taken care of here. He's being released, and Raymond is with him. I expect both to arrive before this evening. Sooner than that, if getting him out of the hospital doesn't take all day. Carlos is looking after it, so I shouldn't expect too many delays. I must say, I'm damned surprised. Damned surprised. Your request that I phone the hospital seems more than a little coincidental. Is there something I should know, Percy? Tell me!"

Bonnie piped in, "What great news! I love being here. It's so nonstop. Both Angus and I are good at keeping secrets, so tell us, Percy. We're trustable. Aren't we, Angus?"

"Bonnie, my love, Percy looks to be in shock. I think something medicinal is needed first, but yes, whatever is said will go no further. Allow me."

Angus got up, put some whiskey in a glass, and said, "One other thing, when Johnny awoke he kept repeating, 'Don't sign. Don't sign.' Is that significant by any chance?"

Angus handed me the drink. He also pulled out a handkerchief and gave it to me. I needed both.

78

I sat there stunned. My anguish, suffering, and uncertainty over Johnny boiled out in tears of relief as I fell into a state of sublime emotional emptiness. I took some moments to gather myself. With Johnny's message, the landscape had changed again, and with it, any doubts I had about the Cushmans' intentions. Hostiles really were inside the castle walls, and it was time they were cast out. What I needed was a plan, but I couldn't think of one.

I dried my eyes, handed back the doctor's handkerchief, and drank my whiskey.

I said, "Thank you, Angus. I needed that. This is wonderful news. As to why I asked, I will tell you, but not now. I barely know what to think, and the explanation would take too long. Those who should be told the news must be informed as soon as possible. Anything less would be callous and insensitive. I will do that now, but first, a question: Is Johnny's memory intact and fully functional?"

Angus considered my question. "Carlos stated that Johnny's return was almost instantaneous. One moment he was in a coma, and the next, he was ringing for the nurse. He's been articulate ever since and has no slurs in his speech. He was understandably quite upset when he learned how long he'd been out. He also appears to be fully mobile. Given that, I'd have to say yes to both; however, I'll be examining him thoroughly when he arrives and will be able to give you a more accurate appraisal when that is complete. From what I've been told, he's in much better shape, given the length of time he was bedridden, than anyone might expect. All in all, I'd say the news is better than good."

"Thank you for that information. I'm concerned that Johnny might not be able to remember everything that happened to him. Do I have reason to worry about that?"

Angus thought for a moment. "Occasional lacunas or memory gaps are not uncommon after so traumatic an event, particularly regarding the moments directly leading up to it. I can tell you now that there were significant amounts of psychotropic drugs and alcohol in Johnny's system at the time of the accident. I didn't tell you at the hospital, Percy, because they were medically irrelevant in that they didn't cause his coma and wouldn't have helped you or him in any constructive way that I could imagine. Now that he's returned, that information has forensic implications, not only as to the clarity of his recall but to the reliability of his testimony should events proceed in that direction."

I nodded. "Thank you, Angus. That is something to consider. For now, we must pass along the news we have. I will be speaking to Anne shortly, and she will want to know firsthand what Dr. Sistie said. Bonnie, I think you should brief your mother. She might also want to hear from you directly, Angus. What will happen is anybody's guess, but I'd expect turbulence and a bumpy ride once Johnny arrives. Do either of you have any suggestions?"

Bonnie said, "Keep Johnny's return under wraps if you can. The shock of his arrival will certainly create some excitement in the Cushman camp. You might gain some insights."

Angus added, "I must also brief the kitchen as to what Johnny can and can't eat over the next several days. Could you arrange a short conference? That will give me a chance to speak with Dagmar, something I'm very much looking forward to doing. That's all I can think of for now."

I stood. "Very well. I'll be briefing Stanley and Dagmar next. Stanley will find you, Angus."

Turning to Bonnie, I said, "I think Johnny's return will surprise everyone, even if he's expected. Thank you both for sharing this moment with me. I doubt I'll forget it anytime soon."

Bonnie and Angus rose. I hugged each of them in turn. I left the library and went in search of Stanley.

79

S tanley was coming down the stairs, and I said, "I have news. Dagmar will also want to hear this."

We headed for Stanley's office and collected Dagmar on the way.

Once the door was closed, I said to both of them, "Angus called the hospital and was told that Johnny awoke and appeared to be in good condition. He is being released from the hospital as we speak, and Raymond will be driving him here into Angus's care once he is discharged. How long that will take, and when he will arrive exactly, is unknown. Likely, it will be after lunch. The doctor will also want to coordinate with you, Dagmar, as to what Johnny can and can't eat. We'll see what kind of shape he's in when he arrives. Anyway, that's the news, and as far as news goes, I can't think of any better than that."

Stanley and Dagmar had tears in their eyes as they hugged each other, almost jumping with joy. I heard Dagmar say, "I want a drop of the good stuff, Stan, and I don't mean maybe."

Stanley laughed and said, "I was planning on breaking it out when the Cushmans were sent packing, but now is better. The sun is certainly out, and the birds are singing, but not as brightly or as loudly as my heart. Percy, that really is the best of news. I can hardly contain myself. But first ... "

Stanley grabbed three cut-crystal glasses from the side table, opened the bottom desk drawer, and pulled out a three-quarters full bottle of Hamish's brew.

"I've kept this close by—more in hope than in anticipation. I'm glad I did."

He carefully poured a shot into each of the three glasses and handed them around.

Stanley continued, "First, a toast. To Hamish, to Johnny's return, and no less importantly, to you, Dagmar, to you, Percy, and to me. To each of us for helping make Johnny's recovery possible. Others may dismiss our claim. I say go right ahead. We know in our hearts the truth of it. Let's raise our glasses and repeat after me: 'To Hamish, to Johnny, and to each of us!' "

We repeated, "To Hamish, to Johnny, and to each of us."

I sniffed the extraordinary scent that wafted up from my glass. I closed my eyes to concentrate on the taste, which drifted one way and then another like the undulating movements of a symphony. I was about to take another sip when Dagmar interrupted.

"We each have a sip or two left, and I want to make a toast as well. To you, Percy. Stanley told me all about your travels. I'm so very proud of you. To Hamish and to Percy!"

"To Hamish and to Percy!" we said and drank.

There was one sip left. I said, "There are two others we should toast besides ourselves. Without Bruni, I would've been lost, and without Robert the Bruce, Johnny would never have been found."

I raised my glass and said, "To Hamish, to Bruni, and to Robert the Bruce!"

We repeated the words together and swallowed our last remaining sip. We put down our glasses, intoxicated by the moment, swept up in our happiness, and enchanted by the whiskey.

I said, looking at both of them, "Well, that was truly something. Moments don't come any finer than this. Of course, there is more to follow and likely some unpleasantness, but the thought of having spent this time together toasting Johnny's return is one I'll always cherish. Thank you both. By the way, Dagmar, what *is* for lunch? I never seem to know."

Dagmar smiled. "Unfortunately, I can't tell you right now. Lunch has providentially taken on a different theme, given the news, so you'll just have to wait and see. For now, I'd like to thank both of you for participating with me in this moment. It was priceless."

Stanley said, "Amen to that."

I left them to find Bruni.

80

B runi was at Alice's desk in the sitting room, looking over the Cushman proposal. She looked up as I came in. "You have news?"

"I do. Let's sit on the couch."

Bruni came over and sat down beside me.

I said simply, "Johnny woke up."

Bruni put her hands to her face and exclaimed, "He did? The rescue worked? Oh, thank God!"

Bruni started to cry and hugged me.

Once her tears stopped, she said, "This is huge."

"It is huge. I don't know if it was strictly the rescue or partly coincidental, given that Johnny was already showing signs of recovery, but I'd like to think that I had something to do with it. Regardless of the cause, Johnny is out of his coma and will be arriving sometime between lunch and dinner. Raymond is with him. I was with Angus when he called the hospital. He and Bonnie were overjoyed, and so were Dagmar and Stanley. Johnny also had a message. He repeated the words 'Don't sign' several times after he awoke."

Bruni hugged me again and said, "This is a good day."

I held her and said, "It certainly is, but coming back to Earth for a moment, what do you think of the proposal?"

Bruni sat back. "I'd much prefer a celebration, but to answer your question, there are several partnerships mentioned in the footnotes that have the potential to saddle John with a great deal of debt should he assume ownership. The proposal is, for all intents and purposes, a Trojan Horse, cleverly presented like the Greek original but amateurish in design. Professionally speaking, I'd have been far more subtle, but that's me. The end result of John's signing is a potential disaster. I recommend that John delay his answer until Johnny arrives. What he knows or doesn't will determine what happens going forward."

"Well, with that opinion, you're in good company. Mary Leland thought the same."

"Oh, I like that. But back to Johnny for a second. All I can say is, *Wow! Wow! Wow!* Regardless of how it came about, I'm thrilled. I'm pretty sure it was you, but I admit to my bias. The doctors will dismiss what you did, of course. They'll say that his recovery was unusual but not exceptional since others have done the same. Have you told Angus about your part?"

"I avoided the question. I should also mention that Johnny had indications of psychotropic drugs and alcohol in his system at the time of the accident. How much, the doctor didn't say, but he did mention that their presence may have forensic implications."

Bruni nodded. "Most certainly, but let's not get ahead of ourselves. You do know Angus won't give up until you answer his question."

"I know. Eventually, I'll have to tell him."

"I'd like to be there when you do."

"I'll make sure. Angus and Dagmar will also have to coordinate Johnny's diet. That, too, is a conversation I'd like to hear, but putting that aside, what concerns me right now is what happens when Johnny arrives and the Cushmans realize the jig is up."

"I think they'll be stunned initially, but I doubt they'll simply roll over. It's why I think Raymond is correct when he said to prepare yourself for a street fight."

"I'm inclined to agree, only I don't know what that means. How far the Cushmans will go is also unknown. Just the same, I'm glad Raymond will be around to keep things civil. I must give John and Anne the good news and deliver that proposal. Bonnie will speak to Maw, and you must brief your parents."

"I'll do that now. So, no rest, no celebrating, and no peace for the wicked right now."

"Absolutely none, I'm afraid."

We hugged and kissed, after which Bruni jumped up and down a few times before she went looking for her parents. I picked up the proposal and went to see John and Anne.

81

I knocked on the door to the master bedroom. John answered. "Can I help you, Percy?"

"I have some extraordinary news. May I come in?"

"Yes, please."

I had never really inspected the master suite at Rhinebeck. That area was off-limits to Johnny and me for most of our lives, and once the property passed to me, I considered it exclusively Anne's and John's domain, never to be imposed on. It was larger than I recalled, with a bedroom, bath, and its own sitting room.

I heard Anne call out from the bedroom, "Who's there, John?"

"It's Percy with news."

Anne stepped out. "Well, let's sit down and hear it."

There were two comfortable chairs and a couch. I sat down on one of the chairs while Anne and John sat on the couch.

"Has Angus spoken to either of you recently?" I asked.

"Not since breakfast," Anne replied.

"Then you haven't heard. I asked Angus to call the hospital this morning. Johnny has awoken from his coma in good condition! Raymond is with him, and Angus has arranged Johnny's release from the hospital and into his personal care. Johnny will be arriving here sometime after lunch."

From the word "awoken," Anne and John looked to be in shock.

"I had the same reaction," I said. "Angus gave me some whiskey. Do you have some here? Anne? John?"

They just sat there for a moment before both of them started to cry and collapsed into each other's arms. I let them have their moment and waited.

John was the first to respond. "Are you sure, Percy?"

"I was there when Angus made the call. It's not a fabrication. It's fact."

John said at last, "I don't know what to say. I always thought it *could* happen, but never that it would. Johnny's full recovery was always too much to hope for and so not to be believed. Oh, Anne, are we dreaming?"

Anne continued to cry.

I smiled, caught up in their joy, and was filled with heady anticipation that Johnny would be here soon. It was like the dawn of a brand new day, not just for me but for all who held him in their hearts.

I said, "This is not a dream, I can assure you. Angus and Bonnie know, as do Stanley and Dagmar. And, of course, I told Bruni. All have been overjoyed that the impossible has become fact."

John wiped his eyes with a handkerchief and passed it to Anne.

"Well, Percy," Anne said, "I doubt anything can surpass this moment. I will see my son again. How wonderful! ... But I must ask, Percy, how recovered is he?"

"As far as I know, he's fully himself. We'll know more when we see him. Given that, he should be able to tell us many details, but maybe not all at once, and maybe not everything."

Anne frowned. "Why do you say that?"

"Sometimes we aren't proud of what we've done in spite of the willingness of others to overlook and forgive our shortcomings. Recounting what happened may be painful for him, and there are the underlying issues that existed prior to his coma—his affair with another man's wife, what he did specifically for or against the Cushmans, and his disclosures to Casey, whether coerced or not. We see his miraculous return. He might see it as a reawakening to a daunting reality. Please forgive me. I don't wish to lessen your joy, but I've had time to consider what might happen going forward, and I have concerns."

Anne thought about that. "In other words, this isn't over."

"I don't believe it is."

John said, "I know what you mean, of course. We must temper our delight with the understanding that all might not be as spectacular or as final as we might wish."

"To my mind, it would be prudent to dampen our expectations. I could be wrong, as is often the case, but in this instance, I would be delighted if I am. On another matter, I have a proposal from the Cushmans with me, but with the caveat that the first thing Johnny said when he awoke was to repeat the words, 'Don't sign!' I believe this document is what he was referring to. James Cushman told me that Johnny was on his way to Rhinebeck to convince you to sign it, but the accident prevented that from happening. What puzzles me is that Johnny didn't have this document or his briefcase with him at the time."

John asked, "May I see it?"

I passed it over. "I've read it and had Bruni look it over, but before we continue, please allow me to brief you both on what happened at my end of the table last night."

I told them both in detail about the conversations I had with the Cushmans.

John said, "So they're in dire straits, and this proposal is their lifeline, so to speak."

"That is correct. There are also other points to consider."

"Such as?"

"Johnny may not be able to recall everything leading up to the crash. He may have blank spots in his memory. I suppose the Cushmans are in a similar position. They, too, have no idea how much or how little Johnny will be able to tell us."

John said, "That is certainly true. We'll just have to wait and see. What did you think of their proposal?"

"There are parts hidden in the footnotes that may prove disastrous if you were to agree. Bruni thought it was a Trojan horse, and so did your mother."

"I see. I will look at it just the same. Oddly, I would like to help them if I can. Our talk, Percy, has changed me once again, but that continued feeling depends on what Johnny can tell us. For now, I am so happy; it makes no difference what happens next. I must say I do feel like celebrating, but I will refrain until I see him. Anne?"

"I think I must follow your example. You are correct, Percy. We must take what joy we can but temper it, given the many issues that are ongoing. Do you have a plan that we can help along?"

"I can't say I do, other than to keep silent until Johnny's arrival. Maybe the Cushmans are prepared for Johnny's return, given that Angus announced the possibility at lunch yesterday, but I doubt it. After the initial greeting, I will need to sit down with Johnny and go over what happened. I don't know how he will stand up to that, either physically or mentally. He may be exhausted when he arrives, but we must have certain questions answered very soon. Much of our planning and what follows will depend on what he says. The other matter I'm concerned about is that the Cushmans may assume we know everything and do something desperate. I believe that Peggy will be key to either making that happen or preventing it. I'd like to know what she intends. I also don't know how you might find that out, Anne, but I would like you to try."

Anne said, "I will take a walk with her if I can, only I'll be so happy that she'll wonder why I'm dancing about and singing. Don't hold your breath, Percy. I may get nothing, but I will try. John?"

"Sounds good to me. Unfortunately, if she also sees me skipping down the stairs as well, she'll know that something's in the wind. We'll do what we can, and by the way, Percy, do you know what's for lunch?"

"Dagmar is adjusting the menu, so who knows? Perhaps she'll bake a cake?"

"In that case, I'm seriously looking forward to it."

"Me, too. I'll see you both downstairs for drinks before that. To me, no matter what happens, it's a good day. Johnny is coming home."

82

I left Anne and John and knocked on Malcolm's door. He opened it in his bathrobe.

I said, "I have some news to tell you. May I come in?"

"If it's urgent, of course. If it's only semi-urgent, it will take me only minutes to dress for lunch, which I must do anyway. We could meet in the foyer, take a stroll up the driveway, and you will have my complete attention. Would that suffice?"

"It would. See you downstairs shortly."

I made my way to the staircase and met James and Casey, stepping onto the landing.

James asked, "Any news on that proposal, Percy?"

"It's being looked at as we speak. I'm sure John will have some questions for your father. They will talk, and then we'll see."

"Fair enough. How is Johnny?"

I put on my innocent face and said, "I'm not altogether sure at this exact moment, but I'm certain to have an update before long. Thank you for asking. And how are you both this morning?"

James said, "Looking forward to lunch. The meals here are fabulous. Isn't that right, Casey?"

Casey looked to be on edge but answered smoothly, "The meals here are very good, so yes. I also understand that Alice collected many jewels and artifacts, some of them noteworthy. Do you ever take them out and show them to guests?"

"On occasion, but unfortunately not this weekend. Perhaps another time—provided you would want to return, and I invite you. Please don't take my refusal personally. I wouldn't be able to show them to anyone right now, even if I wished to. Do you have an interest in such things?"

James was looking at Casey with a glassy stare as Casey said, "Diamonds, emeralds, and rubies are always a girl's best friends."

"They certainly are, but don't forget the sapphire or the lowly topaz. Now, if you'll excuse me, Malcolm and I were about to take a walk."

At that moment, the tall man stepped out of his room dressed for lunch in his Old Etonian tie, dark-gray flannel pants, and blue blazer.

As Malcolm towered over them, he nodded to me and said, "Good morning to you both. It's always a pleasure to finally put a face to a name, Casey."

Casey's eyes squinted up at him. "I trust what was said was good."

"Good, bad—so much has changed over the years that few can tell the difference. What matters is that you have my admiration and respect, and that is still a good thing even today. Really, I'm delighted, Casey. Now, if you'll excuse us, shall we, Percy? That is if I'm not interrupting."

"No, not at all." I turned to James and Casey. "See you both at lunch."

The Cushmans nodded. As we left them, I heard James mumble something to Casey as they walked down the hall, but I couldn't make it out. Casey overtly mentioning the treasures right after I caught her trying to open the vault seemed brazen. As I walked down the stairs, I wondered if she had wanted to verify that they even existed. It was a puzzle. Whatever her reason, she had said it deliberately.

I opened the front door for Malcolm, and we stepped into the late morning sunshine. The sky had yet to hold a cloud. Above us, its sweeping blueness encompassed the world. We walked up the drive before Malcolm asked about my news.

"Johnny has recovered and will be here before dinner."

The tall man gave a low whistle. "That *is* extraordinary news. When did you hear?"

334

"Just after breakfast. His recovery was only a hope until this morning. I've been spreading the word to everyone other than the Cushmans. Hopefully, Johnny will be able to tell us more about the accident and what the Cushmans are up to."

"Is the accident why you invited them?"

"It was the initial inspiration, but it turns out there is more going on. With Johnny's recovery, we may get some answers, but much will depend on what he can remember."

"I see. There appear to be a great many crosscurrents going on between the families, but I'm a bit in the dark as to what they are specifically and what they might mean. Could you tell me?"

"Of course."

I gave Malcolm a summary as we walked up the drive and along the access road in the direction of the Hudson.

Malcolm considered what I told him for some moments before he said, "Would you like my help in deciphering all of this? I can sometimes see things others can't. I suppose being so tall is more an asset than a hindrance in such instances."

"I would like that very much."

"I'll try then. Your father used to tell me, 'Malcolm, people lie. They have thoughts and desires they'd rather hide. They put up smoke screens and dissemble. When all makes no sense, one has likely missed the truths hidden among the lies. To get to the heart of it, one must either reduce the noise or amplify the signal.' "

"What does that mean?"

"Shortwave and ham radio are passions of mine. Your father was just as interested. In the Bahamas, I have quite a rig. It's prudent to have one down there. Hurricanes come piling through, and all communication goes by the boards. I end up passing messages back and forth when the telephone lines are down. A radio signal can be difficult to detect if the source is far away. The signal you want can get stepped on by competing broadcasts. It can be obscured by static or even buried in the hiss created by the sets themselves. We call such interference *noise*. Sophisticated tuners, noise-reduction circuits, and boosted antennas help, but as a rule, to isolate a long-distance signal, one must either reduce the surrounding noise or amplify the signal. Your mother sent you a message. Have you thought about it?"

"Not really. She asked me to be kind and merciful and that I'd know what she meant when the time came. To whom and for what? I have no idea."

"That was the message, and I think it's an excellent starting point. In other words, she sent you a signal, and I think it's worth further amplification. The question I would ask is, Who needs your mercy and your kindness, and why would they need it? Can you tell me?"

"I can think of several people who might. John Senior, for one. Johnny, for another, and of course, the Cushmans themselves."

"Of those you mentioned, who has acted the worst and needs your mercy the most?"

"Johnny, for sure, and maybe Casey."

"From what you've told me, I would agree. As I mentioned last night, your mother spoke about Casey. Allow me to explain why mercy and some kindness may be needed in her instance."

Malcolm cleared his throat. "On our voyage, your mother and I had moments of profound quiet looking at the swells, but during meals, we spoke about many things. In one of those conversations, I mentioned how well I thought you'd turned out and wondered if growing up away from your real parents may have contributed to that outcome. I explained that in my world, it was fairly normal for boys to see their fathers and mothers only rarely. Boarding schools, the military, marital separations, and postings overseas, all of these were fairly routine at the time, and many who experienced those circumstances turned out well—myself included. Your mother countered that for everyone who did, there were likely a dozen who didn't. She said her one consolation was that she had had a son rather than a daughter. I asked her why she thought one was better than the other. We'd had a few cocktails, and that may have allowed her to express herself more freely.

"She told me that daughters are harder to keep safe from harm, particularly where love is concerned. In the heat of the moment, one thing often leads to another, and our culture discourages such passions by being particularly intolerant of unintended pregnancies in the young and unmarried. Should that happen, such unanticipated occurrences are quickly concealed, and for good reason. Our society will stigmatize, ostracize, and destroy the offenders. Finding oneself pregnant, the poor girl, or victim in this case, becomes paralyzed by fear of discovery and able to do nothing. She can't confide in her family or even in her friends for fear of the consequences. There is no place to go and no one to turn to. Such girls sometimes resort to desperate measures that can cost them their lives. I agreed with her assessment and told her that it was a grim reality that I could scarcely imagine. Having been in similar peril herself, your mother made it a point to offer help to those in such circumstances. She said she had such an opportunity and that the young girl's name was Casey Duke."

"What? Casey got pregnant?" I stopped in my tracks.

Malcolm halted as well and said, "She did, and it wasn't by her current husband since it happened well before they married."

"You're not serious."

"I'm quite serious. Your mother told me that Casey dared tell no one in her family about her condition and didn't know what to do. How the two connected, Mary never told me, only that they did. At your mother's suggestion, Casey traveled to Europe for a year, had the baby, and then returned to the United States."

"Her parents didn't find out?"

"No one did. Not the father, not her parents—nobody. Her parents still don't know."

"Who's the father then?"

"That is, of course, the question. I think I know, but I'll get to that in a moment."

"Fair enough. Can you tell me when all this happened?"

"Your mother wasn't specific as to the when, and likely that omission was intentional. The story she told me was that Casey announced to her family that she wanted to go to Europe for a year and explore it on her own. Her parents refused to give their permission since she was underage. Casey's insistence and their opposition grew so heated that her parents finally confiscated her passport to settle the matter, but Casey would not surrender. She broke into the family safe, stole her passport back, and took whatever money had been kept there for emergencies. The incident caused a deep rift with her parents, and they cut her off financially. Casey left for Florence, and eventually, the baby was born. I assume it was either sent for adoption or raised in secret. Which it was, or whether it was a boy or a girl, I don't know. Your mother wouldn't say. After a year, Casey returned home on bended knees to her parents and begged forgiveness. After a time, she was forgiven, but only partially. Her parents allowed her to live with them but refused to give her any financial support whatsoever. I'm sure this created a hardship since it's likely that the child required financial support. Casey got involved with James Cushman. After a time, they married."

"So, James is categorically not the father?"

"He is not. He was the solution."

"Then who was the problem?"

"Who did you say needed your mercy and kindness most of all, other than Casey?"

"Johnny."

"I'm sure he's in need of both since he's likely the father. The question I have is: When did he find out? I believe that the child's existence has driven much of what's happened between them and around us even today."

——— ❖ ———

83

We walked along the access road in silence. I lit a cigarette and thought. What Malcolm had revealed filled my head with a thousand questions. Did James Cushman somehow find out her secret? Did his parents know? If they did, I wondered how they might use that information as leverage to facilitate the Cushman bailout and whether it was connected to the threat I sensed but couldn't articulate. It certainly had the right order of magnitude. I also wondered what would happen between Johnny and James, Johnny and Casey, and between John Dodge and Jim Cushman when all of this was finally brought into the open. There were so many ramifications to consider.

One small positive was that Malcolm's story allowed me to see Casey more clearly. It explained the profound difference between the girl I knew growing up and the woman she became. No wonder she'd lost that glow. She'd been wrecked. If Johnny was the one responsible, what might she wish to do to him? For certain, she needed financial security. The question was, how far would she go to obtain it? From what I'd seen, she'd go very far indeed. I also wondered how James would react when he found out. What might he do? If he knew already, what had he already done? All of these questions and their possible answers clattered inside my skull like a pair of dice being shaken in a cup before they were thrown down in a game of backgammon.

After some moments, I said to Malcolm, "Other than learning the true identity of my father, I can't think of any other piece of information that has answered so many questions while managing to generate so many more. Malcolm, do you think it's really true?"

"Given what we see happening around us and knowing your mother, I would say it has to be true. Wouldn't you?"

"I think you're correct. It must be true. The question is, what will happen next?"

"I'm not altogether certain, but I think that dinner tonight is an event not to be missed. Whether that information will be revealed before, during, or after, and who will be the one to do so, is what I would like to know. That it will be disclosed one way or another before the night is done is almost certain. Given that, you'd best work out how to prepare. The revelation will come at the people gathered here like a bowling ball. Which pins will be left standing, if any, is the question. I suggest we head back. I'm sure you'll need to consult with Brunehilde, at the very least. She's as intelligent as she is beautiful, and brilliance is needed now."

"Yes. Thank you for telling me all you have. I always learn something when I talk to you."

"I'm glad to hear that. If there's any way I can assist, all you need do is ask. For now, you can see more clearly and from a greater height. What it all means in the end will simply have to be lived to be discovered. That may not be any great consolation, but as an observation, it encapsulates much that I've learned these many years. Namely, that life continues but not always in the ways we anticipate. Surprises lurk around every corner, and they can change the world when least expected in an instant. I know. I've experienced such shifts more often than I care to mention."

We had arrived back at the house, and Malcolm opened the front door.

84

In the foyer, we parted company. I needed to change for lunch. I walked down the hall in search of Bruni, who was in the bedroom slipping on a light beige crêpe dress while simultaneously putting on a pair of tan heels.

"Well," I said, looking at her, "all has changed once again."

"Oh, yes?" Bruni turned her back. "Tell me while you zip me up."

As I complied, I said, "Here's the latest bulletin. Before Casey married James, she had a child, and I'll give you two guesses who the father must be."

Bruni whirled. "What?! You must be joking."

"I'm afraid not. Malcolm told me."

Bruni sat down on the bed and stared into space while I began to change for lunch. After a few moments, she said, "I believe that's the piece we've been missing. Johnny is the father?"

"I don't know for certain, but I'd wager a small fortune that he is."

"That answers several questions but poses so many more."

"It did the same for me. What do we do?"

Bruni thought. "Nothing for now. Besides Casey and Malcolm, who do you think knows?"

"No one, I should think."

"Should it be revealed, John and Mary will likely be thrilled. The Cushmans maybe not, particularly James."

"He might go a little wild." I began to tie my tie.

Bruni stood up and looked at herself in the mirror. "I think he will. I'll want specifics on what Malcolm said, but later. What happens if Johnny arrives when we're at the table?"

"I have no idea. All I know is that I'll welcome him with open arms and be overjoyed. Besides, it's Saturday. At Rhinebeck, everything happens on Saturday."

Bruni said, "I've noticed that. Kiss me, and then let's venture forth to see what happens next. My mind is buzzing."

I kissed her. "Mine, too. We could both follow Dagmar's advice and let our thoughts take care of themselves for now while we do something else. Who knows? It might even work."

"An experiment then. I'm game."

"Me, too."

We walked down the hall hand-in-hand. I murmured, "The experiment doesn't appear to be working. The implications of all this keep surfacing and demanding attention."

"I know what you mean. Maybe champagne will help?"

"Let's hope."

I opened the door for her. Everyone was there. Everyone, other than the Cushmans, looked at us expectantly. Perhaps they thought we might be Johnny.

85

B runi and I went over to Simon, who offered us two flutes of Cristal. We sipped and smiled. Cristal is a happy brew, and it showed in our faces.

Bruni whispered, "I'm off to mingle. Casey is standing alone. You might want to speak with her."

Bruni moved toward her mother while I went over to Casey. She stood looking out at the lawn by one of the French doors, dressed in another Pucci ensemble, this time mostly dark green with matching high heels. She sipped her champagne.

I said, "If you have a moment, I wanted to ask you if you might like to take a walk with me after lunch?"

Casey turned. "Don't tell me you've changed your mind."

"Not exactly, but talking to an old friend and maybe starting over might be a good idea."

She looked at me for a long moment. "I'd enjoy that. A fresh start is always a chance for something new to develop—not that we are likely to go in that direction. You've made that clear, but I could use a real friend right now. Do you remember our late-night talk while we sat on the stoop at the back of Michael's in Southampton?"

"I do. It's the memory of it that makes me want to speak with you."

"Then I look forward to our walk."

"After lunch, then."

As I turned, James was there behind me. He seemed confrontational. I wondered if any male speaking to Casey, other than himself, sparked that reaction. He asked, "What's the word?"

I looked him over. "I haven't heard one way or the other. I'll let you know as soon as I do. I understand your concern."

James looked back at me steadily as Stanley opened the dining room doors and announced that lunch would be served as soon as everyone was seated.

My guests crowded into the dining room and began searching for their name cards.

I went around to Bruni, who asked in a whisper, "You'll be speaking with Casey?"

I answered softly as I seated her. "Yes, immediately after lunch."

"Good. See you after."

"Of course."

I went round to my end. I was seated between John and Jim. Anne had arranged to have the three of us together. John was on my right. Jim was to my left. Next to Jim was Bonnie, followed by Angus. I could tell this pleased them both. Next to Angus was Anne, followed by Malcolm. Maw sat beside Bruni. Elsa was on Bruni's left. I imagine that Elsa had managed to switch the place cards because Hugo sat next to her. Anne tended to separate husbands and wives. Hugo was followed by Casey, James, and Peggy. It was an interesting arrangement. I thought that dogs and horses would be talked about at one end while business was discussed at the other.

To begin, a cold Sancerre was poured, and chilled vichyssoise, one of my favorites, was served in iced silver bowls. I always wanted more than the small amount presented, but likely such a small serving was wise. Dagmar's vichyssoise had a special potency and tasted so good that I always wanted a tureen for myself. Of course, that would mean foregoing whatever came after, and that inevitably had me feeling better about the minuteness of the amount. One taste and I was transported.

After Jim finished his soup, all else being secondary, he got right to it and asked, "John, have you managed to read the proposal?"

John put down his spoon. "I have. It is complex, and I prefer something more straightforward. I wish to set aside the proposal you have given me and substitute another that is simpler. Perhaps you could let me know the exact amount you require on Monday morning—a telephone call will suffice. On Thursday morning, I'll see that a check is delivered to your office for that amount, along with a blank loan agreement. Fill it in as you see fit and return it to me. Will that not work better for you?"

Jim looked at John for some time. "Are you serious?"

"I am. There's been a great deal of trouble between us for which I've been responsible. It is my desire that we lay that trouble down and leave it there. Supplying you with what you need in as simple and efficacious a way as possible may not absolve me in your mind, but it does manage to relieve me of it in mine. I want to end our conflict once and for all. If you cannot, I understand, but know that in that case this transaction will be our last, and I will have nothing more to do with you. I simply won't respond to any overture you make. That decision and the loan offer have nothing to do with you or anything you did—it is strictly my choice. I know myself well enough to believe that any other decision on my part will find me back where we started, looking over our respective shoulders. I don't wish to live like that anymore. Do you?"

Jim looked surprised and slightly baffled. He looked at Peggy, who nodded.

"You really are serious?"

"I am. What do you wish to do?"

"I can't quite believe you."

"I understand your disbelief. I can hardly believe it myself, but what I've said is my final decision. I've discussed it with Anne. We will carry through with the loan regardless of your intentions. We've decided that this is what we must do to live in peace. It's really quite selfish—all things considered. It has everything to do with us and with myself in particular—not you. That may be difficult to believe, but there it is."

Jim looked perplexed. "You're taking away the game."

"I am. It's served its purpose. It made both of us powerful and rich. I was speaking to Percy about our conflict, and in doing so, I realized that I was incorrect in my resentment and anger toward you. I have much to thank you for. Without you, I would never have achieved what I've achieved. You may find yourself having similar thoughts. Of course, you might not, but I do thank you, nonetheless. The loan with terms of your choosing is an expression of both my gratitude and my past culpability. I'll leave it to you to work out the proportions."

"This is not a trick?"

"I've said it in front of witnesses." John looked at those at our end of the table. "Consider it a verbal contract."

Jim nodded. "Then I must accept."

"Good. We have an agreement then. And what about that other part—your intentions toward me going forward? Do you have an answer?"

"That part won't be easy for me to work out."

"It certainly wasn't easy for me either, but that is something you must decide on yourself. I can't do that. Just the same, I would appreciate a definitive answer before you leave on Sunday. The financial arrangements stand, irrespective of your decision, and exactly as I've stated."

Jim took a sip of wine. "I must think more about that, but for now, the financial matter is settled. You have my sincere thanks and my family's as well. We are saved. Now if you excuse me, I must sit quietly for a few minutes to collect myself. I really could use a whiskey, if you don't mind."

I nodded to Stanley, who returned with a whiskey on a silver salver. He served it to Jim as the soup course was whisked away and replaced by Maine lobster, melted butter, lemon, and a small green salad. I heard Bonnie give a small squeal of delight. Lobster was her absolute favorite. Silence reigned throughout the table. Lobster was another of my preferred dishes, and since I had taken charge of Rhinebeck, I noted that it was served more regularly at formal lunches. The lobster was absolutely perfect; its taste— exquisite. The table hummed in satisfaction.

The last course was homemade lady fingers and vanilla ice cream. I was hoping for a cake but realized that Dagmar would require more time to make one. The dessert, too, was superb.

As lunch came to an end, Jim Cushman remained subdued. He hadn't spoken a word. I had no idea what was running through his mind, but something had changed in him. He dabbed at his eyes once or twice. Peggy looked concerned while James drank wine with abandon, obviously very pleased. Casey looked thoughtful. The rest of my guests seemed oblivious to what had happened at my end of the table, and that was more than satisfactory. They were enjoying themselves.

I waited by the door as my guests passed by. Bruni and Elsa were arm in arm, talking in German with a rapidity I couldn't follow. Hugo patted John on the shoulder and looked pleased. Peggy guided her husband by the elbow while her son looked like he could dance a jig. Bonnie and Angus were talking quietly. Bonnie gave me a wink as she passed. Maw and Robert stopped beside me. She said simply, "Robert needs another walk."

I looked down at him, and he looked up at me—his expression opaque as usual. I said, "I was going to talk to Casey just now."

"Excellent! You can accomplish both—how efficient. Find me when you're finished."

"Yes, ma'am."

Maw smiled. "You know, Percy, you'd make a very good butler. Take that as a compliment." And off she went to the drawing room. Robert hadn't budged and stood in front of me, waiting. Casey came up beside me. She saw Robert and stepped back.

I told her, "You'll be fine. He needs a walk, and that's a good excuse to get outside and look about. Are you ready?"

Casey didn't move. "No, not really. I'm wearing heels, and walking outdoors in them is not recommended. Are you sure the dog won't object?"

"Change your shoes by all means. While you do that, I'll ask Robert what he thinks. Would that work?"

Robert sneezed before Casey could respond.

"There! You see? He'll be fine. Why don't you meet me at the front door in a couple of minutes?"

The three of us passed through the drawing room and into the foyer. Robert and I waited as Casey went upstairs. I stared at the clock. It sounded normal for once. I wasn't sure what that meant, but it seemed hopeful. Robert stared up at the ships as they tilted one way and then the other. His black eyes flicked back and forth as he watched them.

After a few minutes, Casey came down in white flats. I opened the front door. The haze had thickened, and the sky was now a milky blue. Fog would blanket the grounds before long. Robert bounded over to one of the urns and lifted his leg. He looked at me as if to say, *What are you looking at?*

I grinned. Casey asked, "What's so funny?"

"Robert watering the urn. He has a certain sense of humor and an unusual history. He used to belong to Johnny, but Johnny traded him to his grandmother for a fortune. He's a magical dog, I think."

"Johnny traded him for a fortune?"

"He did. Robert looks after Mrs. Leland now, or perhaps it is the other way around. It's difficult to know with dogs."

"That creature still scares me."

"He can be intimidating. Do you get scared very often?"

"I'm scared all the time these days."

I looked at her for a moment. "That would be extremely wearing."

"It is."

Robert headed for the tennis court. We followed at a leisurely pace.

"I remember you telling me long ago that you wished you had a friendship like mine with Johnny."

Casey looked down. "I did say that. You saved me back then. I thought I was going to lose my mind. One moment, all was wonderful. The next, I found myself naked and running for my life. I can hardly believe it happened, but it did. Still, there are worse predicaments."

"Not very many, I hope. That night has always remained in my memory. Unfortunately, you and I lost touch not long after. Since we're starting afresh, may we speak candidly?"

"I'd like that. I need a friend right now, someone who is at least a little bit on my side. Right now, there is nobody."

"What about James?"

"He's more an ally than a friend. He and I have similar goals. Occasionally, he's my tormentor, but overall, he's been a stable partner in the confusion that is my life."

"Not a lover or a friend?"

"Someone you have sex with and gives you money isn't necessarily a lover or a friend."

"I see."

"I doubt you do, but by the end of this conversation, you may have a better understanding."

We paused at the steps leading down to the tennis court. I invited her to sit while Robert went to the other side of the court and began searching for lost treasures.

I watched him as I said, "Well, I certainly won't be your lover. A friend, maybe. What do you have in mind?"

Casey thought and said slowly, "Someone who can save me would be nice."

I pulled out a pack of cigarettes and passed her one. After I had lit hers and one for myself, I said, "That may be difficult. A person once asked how I could possibly save another when I couldn't even save myself? It was a valid question. It still is. Rescuing another is, at best, a temporary solution. In the end, the only person who can save us is ourselves. Besides, those in need of saving rarely listen. They're too busy fighting to survive."

"You saved Johnny ... and me, once."

"So you say, but did I really? Given what little I know, the reverberations and repercussions of you and Johnny together that night have continued to this day. Johnny is brilliant—brilliant enough to save himself, I think, but to really succeed, he'd have to change how he views himself. I can't do that for him. I think the same might apply to you."

"It might, but I doubt I can. I'm more like a shuttlecock in a badminton tournament. I get swatted in one direction, float high in the air for a time before I fall, and find myself swatted in another."

"Sort of like Helen of Troy."

"Perhaps, but whether I ascend to Olympus or get hung from a tree by a gang of Rhodian women is still to be determined. If I could, I'd like to decide my own fate for once."

"How are you going to do that?"

Casey sighed. "I've thought about it often enough but have come to no conclusion."

I smoked for a few moments, stubbed out my cigarette, and said, "Well, you'll need to figure that out rather quickly. Johnny will be here soon. What will you do then?"

"Today?"

"This afternoon, in fact."

I looked at her. She was startled by my news. She noted my stare and looked down at her hands. Her body gave a slight tremor, and she flicked her cigarette away. She spoke in the direction of the tennis court. "That's a surprise. I didn't expect to see him any time soon, and with good reason. I don't wish to look at him or think about him. I may appear blind, but I'm not. I know he's bad for me. I know I'm a disaster for him, but there is little either of us can do. We always manage to find each other, and shortly after, trouble follows. I can't seem to keep away. He can't either. When I see him this time, I'd like my world to remain somewhat right side up, but I hold out little hope for that."

"If you're drawn to him so much, why didn't you agree to marry him when he asked? Instead, you asked me. On top of that, you're already married to James. Do you have an explanation?"

Casey didn't answer right away. After a time, she said, "I was wrong to marry James, but the truer and more honest answer is that

I'm greedy. I can never have enough of anything. I wanted most the financial security James promised. I wished to own all the jewels and riches Johnny described and hinted might be his. I covet all the estate and all the grounds you own. It's as simple as that."

"But why?"

She looked at me. "Are you asking why I'm greedy or why I keep asking people to marry me when I'm already married?"

"Both, I think."

Casey sighed. "I'm a puzzle even to myself, but that doesn't answer your question. I've become the woman I am through too many errors in judgment. I know what the wielding of real wealth and power is like. I was brought up in that world. Unfortunately, the Cushmans aren't in the same class as my family and never will be. What sent me over the edge into madness was the realization that, at one time, I could have had it all—everything, in fact—only I let my heart lead my head. I was misled. Even now, I wish I'd been more discerning—more circumspect. I should have thought it through, but I did not. Stupid, stupid me."

Casey paused again and asked, "Do you understand now?"

"I do in part, but not completely."

"Then let me be clearer. I love Johnny, I always have, but then I *hate* him just as much. I blame him for everything that's happened to me. Long ago, I had to decide whether to accept him as my partner. The conclusion I came to at the time is still valid. Alone, we are unsuitable for anyone. Together, we're like a wrecking ball. He's inherently untrustworthy, fickle, and dishonest—just like me. He can't keep promises. It's how he is, and yet I find him irresistible. My mind and my heart are in a constant state of war as to whether to run to him or flee, and those conflicting urges have ripped me to pieces. I'm broken and can't put myself back together. Yesterday, when we met again, you offered me sanctuary. You have no idea how cruel that was. You should have used a rusty razor or cheese grater. Either would have hurt me less. Sanctuary has always been my dream, but I can never find it. The last time I experienced such relief was a long time ago—the day before the night we talked on the steps."

We sat silent for several moments.

I said at last, "I suppose we all want sanctuary. The problem with finding it is that one never wants to leave. Then, little by little, one realizes one is going nowhere. What then?"

"We become restless and do things that jeopardize it. We take chances."

"Which usually leads to trouble. The heart risks. The mind weighs, but in the end, the heart always wins. It plays according to its own rules—ones we have no control over. Prevented, it will sour what the logical and more analytical self thinks it has achieved—and then what?"

"The magic leaves. The world grows drab, and you get me, or at least what's left."

"So it would appear. But what about your child?"

Casey's mouth hung open for a moment. She sprang to her feet and whirled to look down at me. Words like bullets followed. "How do you know about that? How dare you even ask me! Who told you? Who?"

I rose and said quietly, "My mother sent me a message via Malcolm. She asked that I be kind and merciful and that I would know it when the time came. That time, I believe, is now. I'll help you if you let me. You want a friend? Then you have one. I am here, and my mother is the reason. She is not against you, nor am I."

Casey trembled. Her hands clenched and unclenched like talons.

She looked about wildly before saying, "I can't believe this is happening. When James finds out … "

Casey moved her arms about her head as if swatting away flies and wailed, startling the crows, who rapidly took flight. She stopped and let her arms hang by her side. She sat down heavily. I sat down as well. She stared into the distance as she pulled out her hair one strand at a time. For a moment, I thought she'd lost her mind again, but she shook herself, cast aside what she'd collected, and calmed her features. She turned and looked at me steadily with the ghost of a smile. Her brown eyes were inordinately bright and wet.

She whispered, "He can't do it. He can't get rid of me, Percy. I know too much. It doesn't matter."

She smiled to herself and then laughed. She clasped her knees and rocked from side to side, humming softly. She stopped suddenly and looked at me again. "You see? Almost doesn't count."

She stared into my eyes to see if I understood. I felt the hairs at the back of my neck stand on end. I saw only madness. She was wandering in some other land.

She whispered, "Don't tell James. I never wanted to kill Johnny, Percy. I swore I did, and James believed me. Hurt him, certainly. Make him suffer, but not kill him. Love and war are not so very different. We've spoken, and you know more about me now—how my life has been. I must tell James the news. Johnny's not a vegetable anymore. He'll be so disappointed, but then he'll realize it's for the best. Johnny isn't dead. We're safe. The child won't matter. Even if he finds out, it won't matter. I'll make him understand. He'll do what I say. He always does what I say in the end."

Casey stood and brushed herself off. I stood as well, not knowing what else to do. Casey started to walk away when I asked, "Are you all right?"

"Perfectly all right."

I wasn't so sure. "Do you see that dog anywhere?"

Casey looked about for a few moments. "No, I don't, but you'd best find him. That crone will pluck out your eyes if you don't. Now, wouldn't that be something?"

She turned and continued back to the house. I stared at her back. She was scary mad, but to have carried on in spite of that heavy burden meant that she was far stronger than her appearance might suggest. Johnny would have to tell me about his accident. Was Casey the instigator? Perhaps she was. *He'll do what I say. He always does what I say in the end.* Maybe killing Johnny was never their intention, just some possibility. Maiming isn't killing, after all. There was the pain and suffering to savor, and with any luck, that might last a lifetime. They'd get to watch like voyeurs, but not anymore. That made some sense, given their dark thirsts. I shook myself to stop that line of thought—I had other priorities. First and foremost, I had to find that dog.

I walked down the steps and around the tennis court. I entered the woods and walked in the direction of the river. The air was cool, and a low mist had formed in patches over the hollows. The trees were silent. I called out for Robert. I whistled. No response. I returned along the path I'd traveled with still no sign of him. At the top of the steps leading to the tennis court, I saw a long black Lincoln turn down the drive. I knew where Robert was. He was waiting out front. I began to run.

87

I sprinted round the corner just as the Lincoln crunched to a halt. The tableaux before me, like some staged diorama, stopped me in my tracks. Everyone was there, even Dagmar in her apron. It was their expressions that transfixed me. Raymond was frozen as he moved around the back of the car to open the rear door. I noticed Anne next. She had raised her right hand to her throat, her face fearful but hopeful. John was beside her, his mouth open, staring at the door, perhaps wondering what might step out. Hugo stood beside John with a hand on his shoulder, his eyes slitted like some Oriental mystic. Maw stood beside the three with the severe expression of a Sybil. She watched and waited. Bruni stood next to Maw. She held Elsa's hand while her mother had an arm around her shoulder. The Cushmans stood beside them—Casey held firmly around the waist by James, her face the color of broken porcelain. Peggy and Jim Cushman stood beside them, their expressions halfway between fear and awe, wondering.

Stanley, to the side, held himself erect like an eagle. Dagmar held his arm, her cheeks wet with tears. Angus, with Bonnie beside him, was closest to the limousine. He leaned toward the car door, ready to receive his patient. At the back, on the top step, stood Malcolm. He towered over everyone, seeing everything, but the only one who noticed me as I stood at a distance on the verge was Robert. He lay sphinxlike on the gravel, panting. His head was turned toward me, and his black eyes looked into mine as if to say, *Look what we have done.* Time ceased to exist for a moment or a year. I saw in that frozen instant of forever the forces and intentions of each of them. Their potency was poised like the bow pulled to its maximum extension by the black-haired female figure standing beside me. The razorlike fins of the arrowhead glinted in the milky light of early afternoon. Was I dreaming again? I must have been. I absorbed everything all at once: the hopes, the fears, the rage, the joy, the terror, and the tears. I stood at the shoulder of the huntress and saw what she saw. I watched from the verge for what came next and sent them all, each and every one, my fondest hopes and the very best of all my wishes. It wouldn't be enough. I knew that, but what else could I do? I felt rather than heard the snap of the arrow's release and the thrum of the bow string. I turned, and only a hazy flicker marked where she had stood.

Had she even been there? Time restarted. The world unclenched, and Johnny stepped out of the car, helped by Raymond. I hadn't seen the arrow's flight or where it struck. I walked toward them all. Robert still looked at me, his ears pricked and alert. He had seen what I had seen. It was no wonder his eyes were always opaque. Mine would be, too.

88

Johnny looked a little pale and moved with an infirmity that was unfamiliar, slower, and more hesitant. Raymond held him by one arm, and Angus took the other. Johnny protested that he could walk and thanked them for their attention, but they didn't let him go. They guided him toward the house. Anne came up first and enveloped Johnny briefly in her arms. John came next and did the same. One by one, Bonnie, Bruni, Maw, Hugo, Elsa, and then Dagmar, followed by Stanley. Malcolm pushed forward and placed a hand on Johnny's shoulder. Johnny smiled at all of them and saw the Cushmans. He nodded in their direction. They stepped back and gave him room, their faces smiling to hide their disquiet.

Those who had crowded around the resurrected Lazarus must have acted the same. They must have wondered whether to embrace the man if that was what he was now—he who had kissed the lips of death and returned. Perhaps they thought to wait before fully committing to his actuality while trying to convince themselves that nothing had changed, when deep down, each must have known that everything was different now.

Perhaps that was why I held myself at the edge rather than swarming forward through the throng to greet him. I wanted to, but I felt uncertain about what our reactions might be, particularly my own. I used the crowd as an excuse to remain aloof. Besides, I was too emotional to do anything but watch.

As Johnny entered the house, he turned his head and looked back. Our eyes met, but before either of us could respond, he was inside. I followed, still unsure, acting like a fool.

I entered the foyer, and Stanley closed the door. He said as we walked toward the drawing room, "Forgive my intrusion, but not everything has changed between you two. I used to feel the same when Lady Alice would return. I'd wonder whether our relationship would alter, and I'd grow nervous. Such apprehensions proved unfounded because nothing ever did. Release your fears and greet your friend. All will be well between you. You'll see that I am right."

With that, he opened the door to the drawing room and escorted me up to Johnny, who was sitting on the couch with his mother and father on either side. He rose as I approached. We embraced, and he whispered in my ear, "Thank you, Percy. We must talk soon—but not now." He squeezed my arm as he sat back down. I almost burst into tears, but Stanley handed me a whiskey, and Bruni slipped up beside me.

She held me around the waist and whispered, "He's really back. Well done."

Grounded once again, I took a sip and looked about. There were tears in the eyes of almost everyone. I was not alone in this.

The doctor cleared his throat and announced, "He lives and breathes, as you can see, and now I must examine my patient more thoroughly. Percy, may I use the library with no interruptions for that purpose? Bonnie, do you have my bag?"

Bonnie reached behind the couch and handed it to Angus. He continued, "Johnny, if it's all right with you, I'd like Bonnie to attend me. She knows her business and will be of assistance, but only if you agree."

Johnny rose. "By all means, Angus. You're the doctor, and I'm the patient, but hopefully not for long. Now, I'd like to take this moment to thank everyone for welcoming me with such enthusiasm. It's good to be back in the world again, and I intend to speak with each of you individually this evening, provided the doctor allows me. On that note, Doctor, I'm ready when you are."

The sea parted, and the three moved to the library. I whispered to Bruni that I needed to speak with Raymond.

Bruni said, "Please do and see me right after."

I gave her a kiss and nodded to Raymond, who was standing discreetly by the door. He followed me through the foyer and out the front. We stood leaning against the hood of the limousine, which ticked as the engine cooled. I passed him a smoke.

We lit up, and I asked him, "So, what's the news?"

"Here's what I got, and then we'll compare notes. The person who made the call to the limo service was a woman. She said she was Mrs. Cushman's secretary, but there is no such person. The mother uses Mr. Cushman's, who's a guy, and the younger one does the same. Likely, it was Casey Cushman, but I don't know that for sure. I do know that the driver who was killed had driven Casey Cushman several times before the accident. They were familiar with each other. The limo scheduled for Johnny that night noted the destination as Long Island, so crashing at the Triborough Exit would make some sense if that was where they were headed. How the accident happened exactly, I don't know. The dispatcher told me that the driver who was supposed to drive Johnny was conveniently unavailable for questioning. It turns out he retired to Sicily with his family and gave notice the day after the accident— no forwarding address. Based on the records, he drove James Cushman a lot and picked up James Cushman instead of Johnny earlier that evening with no destination noted. I saw the dispatch schedule myself. I'm sure there's a connection."

"Likely, you're correct. Somebody wanted him out of the way for sure."

"I got more. On a hunch, I stopped by Le Cirque and asked Antoine, the maître'd, about that night. We know each other. He checked the reservations for that date and said that Johnny and the Cushman woman had dinner there that night and that he remembered that the two had something going on between them.

Johnny's known as a tipper, so the waiters are always extra attentive when he's in the house, but this time, the woman asked that they be given minimal attention like they had something to discuss. The two finished dinner and left in separate cars. The high-end ride picked up Casey Cushman with, get this, James Cushman in the car, but only after Johnny went off with the new guy. Johnny was in bad shape by then and had to be helped out the door by the staff while Antoine supervised. Johnny was placed in the back seat by both the driver and Casey Cushman. Antoine was a little rattled by my questions and told me that he'd heard about the accident sometime later and was relieved that Johnny survived—nobody likes to lose a high-paying customer—but hadn't connected the dates until we talked. I asked him if there was anything else he could remember. He said that Casey Cushman was wearing an unusual perfume. He's French and notices that kind of thing. He said it was intoxicating—his words. That's it."

"Thank you for that. Do you need to be reimbursed?"

"Nah. At the limo depot, I just made sure you got your money's worth. There was no extra charge. I slipped Antoine a hundred, but that's on me as part of an earlier arrangement between me and Mr. Dodge. I make sure that the people at the places he regularly visits are always well taken care of. It's a business expense that Mr. Dodge covers, so that's on him, not you. Make sense?"

"It does. How was Johnny on the drive here? Does he seem fully recovered or only partially?"

"He's in pretty good shape, I think. I briefed him on what's been going on since the accident. I think that kind of shook him. He was quiet after that and slept off and on. Maybe it's what I told him, but he had something on his mind. I'd catch him staring out the window. The nurses insisted he use a wheelchair while he was being discharged, but that was for show. He can walk, no problem. He tires easily, so watch that. I'll tell you one thing: the hospital went crazy when he woke up. I arrived right after, and there were a lot of happy people running around. It took a while to extract him because of all the commotion. Everyone wanted to talk to him. One thing I learned was that the doctor lookin' at Johnny right now is a really big wheel. Mention his name, and doors open. His reputation is just as sky-high in less conspicuous places. In that world, he's known as 'Cobb' or simply 'The Doctor.' Thought you'd like to know."

"Thanks for that. From what you told me just now, the two younger Cushmans likely worked together to arrange the accident. My thought is that they didn't want to kill Johnny, only sideline him, but the driver died at the scene, and that changed the game. So far, the crash is viewed as accidental, but with Johnny's return and his telling what he knows, they're in real trouble. Who knows what they'll do to cover themselves? I'll be speaking to Johnny about that soon. One piece of good news is that Jim Cushman and John Dodge have settled their dispute."

Raymond raised his eyebrows. "No shit? Their fight has had me worried for a long time. Glad to hear it's ended. I'll be interested in what Johnny has to say. That has security implications, and I'll want to know all of it. What about the crazy broad?"

"Still crazy, and that's another worry. Between us, Johnny and Casey had a child."

"*En serio?*" Raymond looked shocked.

"Really. It blew my socks off as well and added to the mess here. The husband doesn't know. Likely, he'll explode when he finds out, which I suspect will happen at dinner tonight."

"Yeah, that younger Cushman's definitely the jealous type and likely to do something stupid. Looks to me like this whole thing's gonna get messy, and with all those knives and forks on the table, very messy. Here's a thought: I've been a waiter before and not in some hole either. In Puerto Rico, I worked at a big hotel in their top restaurant. I know my spoons and forks. Maybe I could stay close, just in case?"

"Good idea. Talk to Stanley. You can say you're Johnny's minder and there to make sure he doesn't overexert himself. I'm sure between you and Stanley, you'll think of something. That will make me feel a whole lot better because I'm pretty sure your services will be needed—just a hunch. I'll be speaking to Johnny and finding out what he remembers. Perhaps things will become clearer."

"Do that. The only bad hunch is the one you don't follow. This is shaping up to be quite a day. *Qué bien.* I love crazy shit like this. I'll talk to Stanley after I put away the car. *Adios.*"

I left him to it and went in search of Bruni. Having Raymond present at dinner tonight was a welcome relief.

B runi was waiting for me in our sitting room. There was a book on her lap, but I doubted that she was engrossed in reading it.

She rose from the couch when I entered and asked, "What's the latest?"

"I'll tell you."

We sat down, and I told her all that had happened since we had last spoken, including the details that Malcolm had provided. I went over the conversation with Casey, the appearance of the huntress at the welcome, and all that Raymond had said. I also mentioned my plan to have him standing by at dinner.

When I'd finished, Bruni looked thoughtful.

"That's a lot to take in. Summaries help me see the big picture. Care to listen for a few minutes while I put some thoughts together?"

"Absolutely."

"Okay. This is how I see it. The Cushmans needed a substantial cash infusion to avoid bankruptcy. There were additional underlying issues, like the longstanding feud between John Dodge and Jim Cushman, as well as the rivalry between their sons, but the unexpected credit event and subsequent insolvency were the catalysts that precipitated everything that happened here. The Cushman solution was to avoid a conventional lender and use a less rigorous private lender. Dodge Capital was their best option, and using them accomplished two objectives. The first was to obtain the needed cash. The second was the possibility of scoring a major victory against John Dodge. To proceed, the Cushmans needed information to put together a sufficiently attractive proposal and a way to make the pitch. Casey Cushman was used for both. She got close to Johnny, gathered the needed intelligence, and convinced him to sit down with her husband to structure a proposal that Johnny could present to his father. With Johnny on board, John Dodge would sign off, the funding would be secured, and a likely fatal blow would be delivered to Dodge Capital through toxic provisions hidden in the footnotes. That was the plan, but it didn't go that way. Clear so far?"

"Yes, that's how I see it."

"The first problem was that Casey got much closer to Johnny than anticipated, creating friction with her husband. My speculation is that Casey decided to hedge her position in case the Cushman plan failed and she was left abandoned. She convinced Johnny to ask her to marry him, only to discover that Johnny didn't have the financial resources she thought he had. Casey strung Johnny along after getting back on board with James and the Cushman plan. Shortly after that, Johnny grew suspicious—either because of the change in Casey's attitude or because something wasn't right with the proposal. Likely, he reexamined it, saw what the Cushmans were up to, and refused to go any further. So far so good?"

"So far so good."

"This next part is much more speculative but incorporates Raymond's information. By now, time was running out, and the Cushmans had a problem. They either had to get Johnny back on board or silence him before he could make his objections known. Since it's likely that they had a draft proposal with Johnny's signature, Johnny was no longer vital to the plan. Casey got to work, but it became obvious that sidelining Johnny was their only option—a severe car accident was the easiest and most expedient way to remove him until after the deal closed. Who arranged that and under whose authority, we don't know. James Cushman is the most plausible candidate. Johnny's affair with Casey likely made that decision not only easy but attractive. I think his father must have been made aware of the situation at some point, and likely Peggy, too. She seems remarkably well-informed for someone excluded from business matters. On top of that, there were substantial costs involved, such as retiring the driver and his family to Sicily. I'm sure she keeps a finger on the financial pulse and would have had to approve such a large expenditure. Likely, Jim Cushman went no further than arranging the money, but he must have tacitly given his son the go-ahead, provided he was spared the details and Johnny wasn't deliberately killed. That last is a guess."

"Plausible deniability?"

"I should think so. At this point, Casey told her husband that she held a secret ace up her sleeve but wouldn't tell James any more than that. I think her intention was to coerce Johnny, using their child, to continue with the plan in spite of the damage it would cause Dodge Capital. Casey scheduled a dinner with Johnny at Le Cirque to make the play. Does that make sense?"

I considered Bruni's scenario. "I think it does. If Casey convinced Johnny, then both would join James in the car with the experienced driver before driving up to Rhinebeck to get John Dodge's signature. If it didn't, Casey would drug Johnny, put him in the car with the inexperienced driver, and the accident would follow."

"That's how I see it, too. Chances are the inexperienced driver was already intoxicated, perhaps with Casey's help. Once she realized that her coercion wouldn't work, she slipped Johnny something at the table and put him in the car with the inexperienced driver. Maybe she gave the driver a little something extra at that point to make sure he was flying high. I'm sure she insisted that he drive Johnny up the East River Drive and out to Locust Valley by way of the Whitestone Bridge. As he drove off with Johnny in the back, Casey got in the other car with James. They followed Johnny's limo up the East River Drive, came alongside, and at the Triborough exit, the driver ran Johnny's limo into the exit barrier.

After that, everyone drove home, and the driver disappeared, having already been paid off. So far so good?"

I thought about that. "That makes a great deal of sense. All the pieces fit. My concern right now is that with Johnny's return, everything Casey wants, everything James wants, and everything his parents want is once again in jeopardy. If I were them, I'd be hoping and praying that Johnny has a relapse."

Bruni nodded. "I thought of that, too. Johnny will need protection. At least that case with the bottles is with Stanley and out of reach, but Casey may have other methods available. Lastly, you mentioned the huntress. Her presence has an ominous feel. We don't know the intended target other than that there was one, and those entities rarely miss. I would take her appearance as a warning to take every precaution to protect our people. As for the Cushmans, they'll just have to take their chances. I intend to add to their woes in any case. Come Monday, I will be writing to everyone in authority I can think of to reexamine the accident and reclassify it as a homicide. Somebody must speak for the dead driver. I may not be legally obligated to do that, but there is something reprehensible and inexcusable about collateral damage. Speaking for myself, anything less would not only be unjust but morally repugnant."

"You're right. I keep forgetting about him. He wasn't just injured; he was killed, and someone must answer. I'll help, but right now, we have more immediate concerns. I must speak with Johnny, brief Stanley, and arrange to have Raymond near him at all times. Johnny is key, and if I've figured that out, others have already come to that conclusion long ago. I think Raymond is about to become Johnny's new best friend."

Bruni smiled. "Speaking of best friends, you might want to ask Mrs. Leland if you can borrow Robert for the next twenty-four hours. He won't let Johnny out of his sight and will happily guard his door."

I laughed. "I'll ask Maw, but first, I must speak with Johnny. It's time I do that."

"It is."

We kissed, and I walked down the hallway to the library. The door was closed, so I knocked.

———⋆———

90

B onnie opened the library door and said, "Just in time. We're finished here."

"Excellent. Thank you, Bonnie. Doctor, how is he?"

Angus was packing up his bag, which was open on the desk. Johnny was sitting on a chair in front of it, rolling down his left sleeve.

"That's up to the patient. Johnny, should I tell him?"

Johnny smiled. "By all means."

Angus turned back to me. "Very well, Johnny's in better shape than anyone has any right to expect, given the circumstances. He's had several surgeries to repair damage to his internal organs and to set numerous bone fractures and breaks. Luckily, his comatose condition and his subsequent immobilization over an extended period were the best possible aids to his recovery. The results speak for themselves. In most cases, obtaining full mobility takes time and can be painful. Massage and physical therapy are required, but in his case, moderate exercise and a gradient diet are all he really needs at this point. He's lost muscle mass, and that will require time to remedy, but given his age, that won't take long, provided he can avoid overexertion. I will allow him to attend tonight's dinner, with the proviso that I sit beside him and monitor everything he consumes or doesn't, as will mostly be the case. It's either that or he's put to bed."

The doctor looked at his patient severely.

Johnny grinned. "Doctor, I'm yours to command. Frankly, just being here and seeing everyone is therapy enough for me. Bonnie, thank you for being in attendance, and thank you, Angus, for all your help, including the shot. I feel much better already. What was in it, by the way?"

Angus snapped the case shut. "B vitamins and a little something to get you through this evening. You're a very lucky man, so keep that in mind. Now, I'm sure the two of you have things to discuss. I will leave you to it. Bonnie?"

He and Bonnie were at the door when Angus turned and said, "By the way, Percy, you and I will be having a conversation, and I'm sure you know the reason. Do I need to make an appointment?"

I thought about that. "How about after dinner, Angus? But then again, should events overtake us? How's immediately after breakfast?"

"Do you expect events to overtake us?"

"In this house, Angus, the unexpected is expected, so yes."

"Then I look forward to this evening, and we'll talk after breakfast. If the last Saturday night I spent in this house is any indication, I would rather have no commitments. Bonnie, what do you say we go upstairs?"

Bonnie gave me a wink before she took his arm. "You read my mind. By the way, I just love to watch you work."

The door closed before I could hear Angus's reply.

Johnny rose from his chair. "Percy, it's so good to see you."

I stood in front of him. "It is the same for me. You gave me quite the scare."

"Given the trunk incident, I think we might call it even at this point, although my recent hiatus was a little more prolonged. Now, I won't discuss a thing with you until you help me up the stairs to the common room. I hate these clothes, and I need to recover and relax in familiar surroundings. We'll use the back stairs. My progress may be a little slower than usual, but if you give me a hug for at least ten seconds, I will be restored enough to make the attempt. Come over here. It's been forever, and I've missed you."

We embraced. In spite of Johnny's travails, he wasn't weak.

370

Johnny put me at arm's length at last and said, "Better?"

I shook my head. "I think I need some more."

We embraced again, and I rocked him in my arms.

At last, I pulled away and said, "Better. Don't you even think about checking out anytime soon. I couldn't bear it. I'm serious. You turned me inside out. I couldn't possibly go through that again."

Johnny smiled. "You and me both, brother, but if that is your wish, then we'd best get busy upstairs. A yellow pad and a number two pencil await. There is so much to discuss, and I hate feeling like a turkey just before Thanksgiving. I love to eat them, of course, but being one … I shudder just thinking about it. Besides, it's Saturday. Saturdays always require meticulous planning to survive them, and this affair is far from over, as you shall hear. Shall we? After you."

91

W e had made it up the back stairs successfully, albeit slowly. Johnny went into his room and closed the door. He opened it for a moment to dump all he had been wearing, including the shoes, into a pile. He came out again with a towel around his waist and made for the bathroom. He looked undernourished and scowled at my expression as he passed. In the bathroom, the shower started and stopped. Johnny came out. He went into his room and closed the door again. The door opened shortly after. He had changed into jeans and a dark blue polo shirt. He carried two packs of cigarettes, a yellow pad, a pencil, two bathroom glasses—unwashed, and a flask. I was content to watch him do the mundane things he always did. He was actually there in front of me, and until that moment, I wasn't fully convinced. Watching him plop himself on the couch made his presence real to me at last.

After a few moments, he said quietly, "If you could burn everything in that pile, I would appreciate it, even the shoes."

"Of course."

I waited. Like we had done countless times before, it was now time to argue about who should go first.

Johnny said, "Since I need to refamiliarize myself with speaking, I think that I should be the one to begin."

He looked at me to confirm. I smiled. It really was like old times.

"By all means."

"You disagree?"

"No, not at all."

Johnny continued. "Very well. Raymond briefed me to some extent on what's been happening here, but with notable blanks. Just the same, I'm certainly glad he did. Thanks to him, I was prepared for the shock of seeing the four Cushmans when I arrived—as treacherous a bunch of thieves as ever lived and breathed, but where to begin exactly? Suggestions?"

I shrugged. "I have none. In truth, Johnny, all I want to do is look at you. Just doing that settles me, and I need to settle right now. You have no idea what it's been like without you—although that may not be completely true. Likely, the coma was worse, although you seem the same as the morning Bruni and I flew off to London on the Concorde. Are you the same?"

"Hardly. What do you think I did all day while I was in that state? Sleep?"

"Well … I don't really know. Sleeping seemed a fairly safe assumption to me. What did you do?"

"I … it's hard to explain. I doubt I slept at all, at least in the usual sense. I was disconnected from everyone and everything, and that prevented me from experiencing any rest—or peace, for that matter. Occasionally, I could sense movements, sounds, feelings, emotions, and the odd murmurings. I'd hear voices, sometimes loud, sometimes soft, but I didn't know who was speaking or what they were saying. At other times, I felt utterly overwhelmed. I'd find myself near water and would hear it flowing and bubbling along. Moment would follow moment like the incessant dripping of a faucet. I was aware of each drop as it fell, but my experience was distorted and strangely variable. Time would slow and then move faster, only to slow again. Such changes precipitated a peculiar, almost visceral, sensation that kept me constantly on edge. I had no control over anything, and all I seemed able to do was endlessly hover."

Johnny sighed and smoked. "It wasn't pleasant. Looking back, I was never certain what was truly real and what was my imagination. Perhaps none of it was real, and I was only dreaming, stuck between life and death, uncertain of which was which. For instance, I would find myself sitting by a quiet pool, gazing at my reflection. I'd feel sad knowing I was lost and weep in abject self-pity. Other times, I'd see stars behind me reflected on the surface or a crescent moon looking over my shoulder. Once, a black cat with pale yellow, almond-shaped eyes sat down beside me. I even saw Robert on occasion. I also saw Alice once, or so I thought, but I don't really know."

"Really? Did she say anything?"

"I'll get to that, but before I do, I should give you a clearer idea of what it was like so you can gauge the veracity and reliability of what I'm telling you. If I can hardly believe what happened, then I can barely imagine what you must think."

"Go right ahead if that seems best. I'm open to whatever you wish to tell me. Just listening to you is therapy for me."

Johnny smiled. "Talking while I watch you listen is the same for me. It's really quite odd. In this world, I can feel objects like this couch and confirm my perceptions. You can do that too. In that other place, I could only sense things. I could never confirm them. Such impressions that I received had no substance, like a thought, and of course, one wonders if thoughts are actually real? Try to touch one, and you can't, but they exist, nonetheless. We know they do, but who can trust a thought? All we can really do with them is choose to believe them or not. In a universe of only thoughts—where nothing else exists, there is never the possibility of confirmation. One must believe, or there is nothing, and as for nothing—nothing is death. I realized that when I was there. It was a moment I can assure you, and so I dreamed. I had to. It was that or die."

"That actually sounds rather scary."

"It was, which is why I never rested and why I feel good just watching you listen to me. In that simple action, I can confirm my existence and conclude rather happily that I'm very much alive."

"You are, and that, to me, is what I hoped for. You are alive. You are here."

"I am, and I'm glad you agree because that, too, is a form of confirmation, but there is more. Most of the time, I wasn't lounging about hopelessly self-absorbed in sorrow and self-pity. Instead, I found myself lying on a bed in a room with a white ceiling and three gray walls. To my left, instead of a gray wall, lay that other world, but I could visit there only occasionally and for no reason that made sense. The room with the bed was my private hell—my special place of torment. Whoever made the mattress must have packed it with prickly burrs specifically selected for their sharpness. They poked into my skin. The pricking sensation never stopped, and the pain was excruciating. I itched all over. I wanted to scratch, but I lay immobilized and helpless, like a mummy wrapped in gauze. I would scream, or so I thought, but after what seemed like days, I stopped.

"My cries didn't seem to help. No one heard me, and I realized then that I could do nothing but put up with the excruciating pain and dream, so dreaming—if that is what I did—and experiencing the pain became my focus. Lest I give the wrong impression, that was all I *could* do—nothing else. I had no choice. After a long while, I made a breakthrough. I realized that an itch, or physical sensation, no matter how painful or prolonged, will always cease eventually. Of course, I've no idea of the scientific merit of that observation, but at the time, I thought it rather impressive. It actually helped. That was the only thing that did until you showed up—or seemed to. Did you?"

"I did, actually. Initially, it was Dagmar's idea. She asked me what was happening with you, and I said that you were lost. She answered that I should find you. So, I tried to, but that didn't go as planned. I was disemboweled, ripped apart, and eaten by the monster that always chased me in that other place."

Johnny sat up straighter. "It finally got you?"

375

"It did if you can believe it. I went to the hut of the person who called me a demon. He said, 'What can't be outrun must be embraced,' and so I did as he suggested. I watched this hideous creature with jagged, crystal-like teeth come racing up the meadow intent on having me for dinner—a meal which I willingly provided by embracing the damn thing. It then proceeded to rip me to pieces and eat me. According to Stanley, it was a form of shamanic initiation. In spite of that setback, I returned the next night. Robert was there. He guided me to where you were and told me how to lure you back. That dog has a wicked sense of humor, I might add. He was most instrumental in returning you to this world. I made you follow me by promising to make you emperor. I recalled that you liked a Roman triumph with that little fellow whispering in your ear that all victory is fleeting."

Johnny smiled. "How could I forget? I remember that, or seem to. Please continue."

"At some point, you told me that you couldn't return with me because you'd done bad things. You said that Casey was evil and then refused to take another step. That's when I begged you to come with me and promised to make you emperor. The truth is, I couldn't let you remain in that place. I was determined to say and do whatever it took to convince you to follow me, and I did. As it was, we barely made it back, but in the end, we did, thanks to the miscreant Robert and the advice of that person in the hut. When I returned to this world, I felt utterly gutted and spent. Bruni was beside me, and without her, I might have died. At least, it seemed that way to me. The next morning, I insisted Angus call the hospital, which is why he wants me to tell him more about that. More recently, I'd sit beside you and tell you stories of our growing up together. You twitched once, and that gave me hope. Anyway, I could go on and on."

Johnny said softly, "If it's not too much trouble, I wouldn't mind."

"Then I will, but all I have is a mishmash of feelings and a patchwork of impressions right now. The truth is you're here because I couldn't let you go. One other thing: When you got out of the car today, I saw a huntress standing beside me. She released an arrow as I looked in her direction. I was so startled by her presence that I missed seeing her target. I may have been dreaming, but I think it was a warning. Something is going to happen soon, and that will require our full attention. Lastly, I'm sorry if I acted like such an idiot when you arrived. I should have swarmed all over you, but I couldn't. Anyway, I'm done for now. It's your turn. Tell me whatever you want, and I'll listen. Eventually, we'll get to a point where we can start putting things in some kind of order and onto your yellow pad. Is that all right?"

"It's more than all right. We're here, Percy ... not there, and from what I've seen, I do believe you've changed."

"I hope in a good way."

"You seem more vulnerable to me now. I don't say that as a disparagement. You feel, Percy, and can express those feelings when you never could before. To me, it's unbelievably disarming. You also seem whole—when I am not. You can let others love you, and so you are loved. I can't seem to do that."

I considered his observation. "I think you and your dad are similar. He has never felt worthy of love or admiration other than by your mom, Hugo, and maybe Raymond. There is a great deal I've learned while you've been away, which I'll tell you, but likely in bits and pieces. The several stories I told both you and your parents about our growing up together have helped me see how truly instrumental you've been in keeping me sane. You are worthy, Johnny. So much so that I can never repay you."

"That may be true, and lest you forget, you still owe me two million dollars. Casey never put that together. She thought I was a pauper, but first, you are correct; there is so much you have to say that it will take days. I, too, have many things to tell you, not all of them pleasant. I may have your affection and admiration now, but will I after?"

"Don't be an idiot. Some feelings can't be altered. Besides, we've had too many adventures together. How about I give you a house credit of two million, and we can weigh your misdeeds and adjust accordingly?"

Johnny looked a little terrified at that idea.

I added quickly, "Not to worry. Your savings invested in this house are safe with me, so relax. How about I give you a hypothetical two million credit? I doubt you'll spend it all."

"I wouldn't be so sure."

"Look, as you once told me, we're stuck with each other. I'll always be your friend. So? Where do you want to start? I want to hear everything that happened to you. But first, what did Alice have to say?"

Johnny lit another cigarette and said at last, "She never spoke, but she did tell me something. One night, a full moon had barely risen when I saw a woman dressed in a loose, thinly woven linen dress that left little to my imagination. She was standing on the other side of the pool. The light from the moon on the water and her image shimmered together. She also wore a diadem that looked very much like the Eye of Ra. She beckoned me to follow. I knew it was Alice. Not only from the Egyptian headpiece but also from the way she held herself. I walked around the pool, and she led me along a forest path and to a ramp that led down into a chamber. In the middle was a solid block of stone, like a large table with writing etched on the surface. She hopped on top of it and sat. She motioned for me to sit on it as well, and I did. Moonlight lit the surface from an opening high up the wall. She put a finger to her lips as if to tell me to keep silent and then turned so that her right knee rested on the table while her other leg stretched down to the floor. It was such a girl-like pose. She was so beautiful. She smiled and nodded as if to acknowledge what I thought.

"She pointed to a series of hieroglyphs and figures. There was the figure of a man. She pointed to me. Further along in the sequence was a woman. Later, a wedding feast. The woman and the man were present, but they were not the ones getting married. They were guests. She put both her hands apart and then together over her heart. She looked at me for a long moment. After that, she hopped off the table and led me back to the pool. I sat back down and watched the moon's reflection in the water. Her image merged with it, and she was gone."

Johnny sighed. "Of all the moments in that other place, it was the brightest and most luminous. I think the thought of it kept me alive, at least until you showed up. It kindled something deep within me, like a dream within the dream of a dreamer. It was quite odd."

"What do you suppose it meant?"

"Marry Bruni and we'll find out."

I laughed.

Johnny smiled. "Why is that so funny?"

"Hugo, Maw, and now Alice have been sending me emphatic messages about getting married. Given what you've said, I think I finally have a solution. I'm placing my wedding arrangements completely in your hands. You have a vested interest in seeing to it at last, but first, we have some matters in the here and now to attend to."

"That is more than likely. How can I help?"

"Can you tell me what happened?"

Johnny sighed and lit another smoke.

"I will, but telling you won't be easy. I would love to spin you a tale of adventure, fierce odds, and ultimate success, but the reality is not so romantic. My story is one of everyday routines punctuated by tumultuous moments of my own creation that never seem to end. The problem, I suppose, is that I've had no driving purpose—unlike those who want to be sports stars, actors, or doctors and are consumed with achieving that from an early age. I've never had such aspirations. After all, why have discipline, purpose, and persistence when brilliance works just as well, if not better?"

"You've always been gifted."

"So I've been told, but brilliance is only brilliant if it's focused. Nonetheless, I've always had a pretty good grasp of how the world works, and I did until Casey. When you wrap your arms around a goddess and feel her naked body quiver in anticipation, then tell me what you think you know. I knew nothing after that. Our coupling burned the heavens and knocked me from my orbit. No wonder the cops came. That was the night I called you to come rescue us. Do you remember?"

"How could I forget? I even read you that story while you were lying in the hospital. You twitched when I mentioned Casey."

"I do recall you telling me, only I never heard you. I dreamed what you said as if the words were alive. Versions of that dream repeated for what seemed like days after that. In one, Casey and I were arrested. In another, we ran away together. Other times, it happened as it did. Each time, I would try to wake up, but I never managed it. Instead, I felt that I had to be somewhere else most urgently, and in my distracted panic, I would forget. That night changed my life in ways I never knew."

"The child?"

Johnny looked at me carefully and then sighed. "Did you put that together, or did someone tell you?"

"Malcolm told me. My mother told him."

"That makes some sense. The words are certainly easy to say— the child ... My child. Maybe I knew all along. In the strictest form of epistemology, ignorance does not exist. In looser versions, we have hints of something hidden that presses on our lives. We know there's something going on, but not what it is. Lord B., being your father, was like that. The child revelation was another. Such impossibilities are inconceivable, but once revealed, the patterns that are our lives fall into place, and everything makes some sense. Of course, we're getting ahead of ourselves by gravitating to the end of my story, but with so much to say, it's little wonder. How do I begin?"

"I think it's me who must start rather than you. I can tell you what I know, and then you can fill in anything I've missed and correct any errors so that together, we can come up with a plan. How does that sound?"

"That would be most helpful. It would be like old times."

"It would, because once again, we're in the thick of it."

I sat back and told Johnny rapidly and succinctly what had happened since the accident up until his arrival. Johnny made notes on his yellow pad.

When I was done, Johnny lit another cigarette and said, "Thank you for that. I've made some notes and have a thought or two, but before we go there, I must apologize for all the anguish that I've caused. The world creaked and groaned. I would never have expected that. Please accept my apology, Percy. There are, of course, several others I must apologize to as well. I don't know what to do about any of that right now."

"It can wait. You weren't completely to blame, anyway."

"So you say, but let's leave that alone for now and get back to the matter at hand. My analysis is fairly simple. The arrangements made so far are only temporary, in spite of the hopes that they are permanent. The Cushmans think that they will leave on Sunday, having gathered the necessary funding to survive. Casey feels secure with James, and James feels the same about Casey, having gathered the means to keep her if he's clever. In addition, my father has successfully ended the feud with Jim Cushman. It is a peace of sorts, no question about that, but peace is just a temporary configuration, like the sanctuary we experience here. Sooner or later, outside events intervene, and we must venture forth and face what we must face. I suppose it's much like waking up from a coma or even getting up in the morning. Once we are awake—the world we left behind is back again, and with it—all that's left unfinished. There is one piece of good news, however. Since what has been agreed upon so far is temporary, it will come undone, and whether we choose to give it a nudge won't particularly matter. Given that, we are free to act in any way we wish. Is there something you have in mind for us to do?"

I considered Johnny's analysis. His higher mental functions had certainly not diminished.

I smiled. "You're still as sharp as ever, and what you've said is true, but before we continue, I need us to go back a step. You mentioned that you feel responsible for all that's happened here, but you are not the only one who feels that way. I, too, am responsible, but in a different sense. Rhinebeck's been a kind of holy place for us—our sanctuary—but I invited the Cushmans here, and with them came their blackness. That in itself was suspect, but I compounded the issue by being so naïve as to think that I could discover what the Cushmans did and dispense a suitable justice. I may have accomplished the first part, but by seeking justice for what they did to you, to me, and to all of us, I've managed to lose that sense of sanctuary in the process. It's disappeared for me. The outside world is inside now. I see it everywhere. It's as if the magic was replaced, and darkness took its place. It's like a cancer that I invited, and that wrong is gnawing away at me."

Johnny considered that. "In other words, you feel overwhelmed and have no idea how to dispense the justice you feel necessary."

"Well put. I don't know what to do at all."

Johnny nodded with a smile. "I did something similar, so in this, we're even—but not to worry. I'm here now, and I've learned a few things. Between us, we can manage it, and maybe that's the point. It takes both of us to do that. For a start, the magic is still about, but I'm not sure making the Cushmans pay for what they did is the best way to use it. Once again, we're getting ahead of ourselves by taking up the end when we're only in the middle. Second, I doubt we can defeat the Cushmans using their tactics. It's simply not our way. Using their methods only reduces us to their level and their standards. We need to come at them from a higher plane. Do you remember Mrs. Spence?"

"Of course. Coincidentally, I even told that story to your parents the other night. Your mom was shocked."

"I bet she was. I would be, too, on hearing it as a parent. The fact is, Mother let the devil in, not unlike you and the Cushmans, but Mrs. Spence was cast out and not necessarily by us or by her. We simply observed that her motives were dark and hidden, and we made the decision that she had to go. What we did at the time was ask the magic to support us in that decision. We used the Ouija for that purpose. I think the same principle applies in this case. I suggest we decide right now to return the Cushmans to the world from whence they came and call upon that which resides here to help us. Everything else will follow. You'll see. Would you agree to do that?"

I thought about it. "Your idea actually makes some sense, although I don't see how we should go about it."

"Rather than a Ouija, we require something more direct—a straight request for deliverance sealed as we did with Stanley. We need an invocation, so repeat after me."

I held up my hand. "Hold up, Johnny. You need to pour us some of Stanley's reserve."

Johnny picked up the flask and shook it. "I have it here. I will pour out equal measures for you, me, and one for those who will grant our request. We need another glass. I'll be back in a moment."

Johnny got up, went into the bathroom, and returned with one. He set it down on the coffee table next to the other two and poured out three equal measures. "See? All is fair. We aren't supplicants in this but allies, united in a common purpose. Are you ready?"

"Ready."

383

"Then let's stand and do it properly."

We stood and raised our glasses to the skylight as Johnny called out loudly, "All who reside here, hear me, awake now, and listen! To those who live among the shadows and the light that wander at the edges of the day and of the night, join us in our task! Let us together cast out the Cushmans forever from our sight! Let them know a night as dark as their souls. Drink once and listen further, for there is more."

Johnny whispered to me, "Pour a few drops on the table from their glass, Percy, and then drink a sip, but not all."

I did as he said.

"Now you say something, Percy. This kind of thing takes both of us."

I found myself saying, "We who call upon you are blessed and in strange ways. Know that we support you as you do us, thank you as you thank us, and keep you in our hearts and minds as you keep us in yours. With this drink, let all of us pledge to undertake this task to its inevitable completion."

I poured some more drops on the table and drank the rest. Johnny drank his.

I sat down and put down my glass. "Do you think that may have been a little strong?"

Johnny rubbed his hands together. "Strong enough is what matters. It had a certain ring."

"That it did. Do you think it'll work?"

"Ye of little faith. Of course it will work. There is magic in this place—always has been and always will be. Consider this. You're here. I'm here. We're at the top floor of Rhinebeck, drinking spirits and invoking them once again. Who could have predicted that even last week, let alone yesterday? Now, shall we continue?"

"We should, but first a moment. I have to catch my breath."

"Fair enough. What's next?"

I thought about it and decided now was the time. "It's time to tell me what you know about this child, Johnny. We've both managed to avoid the subject long enough. I don't quite believe it myself. It makes little sense to me."

"I understand, but know that you had something to do with it."

"Me?"

"Yes, you—albeit indirectly."

"This I'd like to hear."

"You will. You've told me many times how important I was in keeping you sane and pointed in the right direction. Let's turn that around for a moment. Have you ever considered that you did the same for me?"

I thought about that. "No. I suppose I haven't."

"Precisely. You thought you needed me far more than I needed you, and in this, you were mistaken. Without you around, I very quickly went off the rails. Remember when you went off to Germany to study the methods of the Austrian school of economics?"

"How could I forget?"

"Well, I was at Columbia at the time, and who should I run into one sunny afternoon on the northeast corner of Fifth and Fifty-seventh but Casey Duke? It was as if an ill wind blew whenever you were gone."

"Really? I never knew that."

"At the time, I had far too much pride to ever mention that I needed you as much as you needed me, but that was then. I am different now. I can admit it."

"A new beginning then?"

"Most certainly. I see myself more clearly. I suppose a near-death experience tends to do that. At any rate, there was a restaurant nearby in the GM building. I got a table. Now, I know I was warned to stay away from her, but if you'd seen her on that balmy afternoon in spring, you would have forgotten that prohibition just as quickly.

She took my breath away. Over tea, the heat between us grew with the intensity of some human form of nuclear fusion, and there was nothing to be done. What happened next, I'll leave to your imagination, other than to say that she got pregnant shortly after. Once confirmed, neither of us wanted the burden of a baby. Besides, we weren't even married. In one of those odd coincidences, your mother's name came up when we were discussing our options, and this was long before we knew your mother's history. My mom had told me how yours had always felt obliged to help unwed mothers in perilous circumstances. My bringing that up may have been relevant at the time, but I had no idea of its significance to Casey.

"At any rate, we had a situation to contend with, and I made inquiries as to available doctors. She did, too. She found one who was acceptable to her and would do the procedure quickly and well, but she had one condition: that I be present before and after. I thought that entirely reasonable and promised that I would be there for her no matter what. She wrote down the address, the time, the date and gave it to me. We even spoke the night before. Everything was arranged, but providence has a funny way of making a point. Casey is dyslexic. Did I know this? No, I did not. The address she gave me said 58th Street, in her own hand, only the doctor's office was on 85th. The name of the doctor was also misspelled. It was a disaster.

"I ran around the city all that afternoon but to no avail. I called and called her number, but she never answered. Instead, she simply disappeared. I didn't know what to think other than that she must have thought I'd abandoned her after swearing that I wouldn't. It was certainly not my fault, but I knew that Casey would never see it that way. After several weeks of not being able to reach her, I figured she was deliberately avoiding me and decided to move on. Little did I know how consequential that series of small mistakes would be for both of us."

I said, "So, let me get this straight. You knew Casey had gotten pregnant, but not that she carried through with having the baby.

How come you never told me any of this back then?"

"I had my reasons. I didn't think it was relevant for a start. When you returned from Germany, our partnership was just forming. We both had to work every minute of the day and night. Why distract you with my personal life when our future success would require all of our attention? Later, when the business imploded thanks to Maw, it didn't matter anymore. You were gone, having retreated to Los Angeles, and as if on cue, an ill wind blew once again.

"Casey and I ran into each other. We merely said hello. At the time, she wanted nothing to do with me. I understood that all too well and kept my distance—only fate, it seemed, had other ideas. We were tossed together over and over until we finally relented and went out for dinner. Our passion for each other burst into flame once more, and in bed shortly after, she told me that this encounter between us would be our last. She'd finally met someone who promised to take care of her. I wasn't pleased, but I wasn't displeased either. In bed, she was a delight, but afterward, I noted that her attitude toward me was very different. Where before she'd been warm and affectionate, now she seemed cold and indifferent. The more we talked, the happier I was that she'd found someone else—that is, until she told me who it was. She told me his name was James Cushman, the third. I didn't know what to say after that."

I looked at Johnny. "I understand. I couldn't believe it when your father told me. James Cushman is a far cry from your prediction of her marrying someone plain and unassuming."

Johnny smiled. "I wasn't wrong about that. I merely forgot to add bad and nasty. As for the doctor incident, which I eventually brought up, she told me that despite my absence, the whole thing had gone off without a hitch. Of course, I tried to tell her my end of the story. I even showed her the original instructions that I'd kept safely in my wallet in the hope of proving my case, but true to form, she asked me why I hadn't bothered to verify what she'd written down. I had no answer to that and knew then that it was over between us. I let her go out of my life, and I met Laura Hutton shortly thereafter."

"Ah yes, Laura Hutton, the one who loved Hermes scarves and risqué evening wear?"

"That's the one."

Johnny lit a cigarette. "After she married, I saw Casey only at parties. I'd say hello, but she acted cold and aloof. She also didn't appreciate my cutting in on James at the occasional formal dance either. As we danced, I'd smile at James as he stood by watching us, consumed with jealousy, so of course, I made it a point. It's probably just as well such gatherings were few and far between. At any rate, I settled down and started working for my father, as you know. That wasn't easy. I liked being my own boss, and being supervised all the time was not my preference. Nonetheless, I did my best until one day, I heard that you'd made a reservation at the St. Regis. After your visit here, you came back into my life, and I was happy once again—something I hadn't really been since the day you bolted to California.

"You and Bruni hit it off, and even that was pleasing. Later, we renewed our partnership, albeit briefly, since shortly after, Father turned the firm over to us to run. After that, you and Bruni jetted off to Europe to meet the family. As if on cue, the next day, Casey called the office to say she wanted to open an account. I couldn't believe it. I put her off, but she was persistent. Like before, I ran into her almost everywhere until I finally asked her to stop bothering me. She said it was our fate and turned on the charm."

I interrupted. "Weren't you suspicious of her advances?'

"Of course I was, but she told me in a flood of tears that James had turned abusive after they were married. He'd hurt her badly, both physically and mentally. She hated him. She wept at my feet and confessed that I was the only one she'd ever loved."

"Ah, the clincher."

"That it was. It was a brilliant performance. Had she simply told me that James was an abusive husband, nothing would have happened, but she added that she had only ever loved me. There was nothing I could say after that. She seemed sincere, and so I believed her. I succumbed once again, but this time, she let me know that if our sex was great before, it could be positively wicked with a little bit of this and a little bit of that."

"She gave you drugs?"

"She did. At the beginning, she said they were exotic herbal powders and oils that generated extraordinary sexual experiences. She said that with James, she needed them, but with me, our shared experience would be pure pleasure. I must admit, I agreed rather quickly—not the best idea, but what else was I to do? I was already smitten."

"In other words, she hooked you."

"She did, and her tactics really worked. I found myself in her thrall—a veritable puppet. Our sex was beyond anything I ever imagined. Frankly, I've never been so electrified in my life, and so little by little, she had me tell her everything about myself, and I mean everything. Some secrets I should never have mentioned, but I was filled with a desire to be honest and completely open. It may have been the drugs, but I don't know for sure. I told her about the vault, about you, everything I could remember, and in hindsight, that was inexcusable. My only justification is that I really thought she loved me. I even asked her to marry me."

"I know about that and more besides, but what's done is done. Let's move on. When did you suspect she was up to something?"

"Although I had my suspicions from the beginning, I never suspected the depth of her manipulation or her real purpose until the end. One night, she whispered in my ear as we lay together that she had one last thing to do to be free of James and be with me forever; only she needed my help to pull it off. She said I had to work with her husband on a deal that involved Dodge Capital.

Doing so would not only make up for my abandoning her years ago but, if handled well, could make Dodge Capital a fortune. Of course, working with James Cushman was the last thing I wanted to do, but she kept on about it, and I thought that making even a small fortune for Dodge Capital was certainly in my interest. Besides, it also happened to be my job. I agreed and met James at his office. He sketched out the basics, and the idea actually sounded good. I was surprised, but James was always as clever as he was deceitful. Together, we worked out a package to present to my father. I signed the draft proposal, but as I glanced back through it one last time, I noticed that a few of the footnotes and one or two of the figures had been changed. I pointed this out to James. He dismissed it and said they weren't material. I thought they were and became suspicious. As I looked over what I'd signed in more detail, I saw that much had been altered, and I realized that everything, including Casey's advances, had been a skillfully executed setup. I'd been maneuvered and manipulated for the sole purpose of drafting and signing the proposal to my father, and having done so, Dodge Capital was now in grave danger."

"Why didn't you pick up the draft with your signature and walk out?"

"My head was reeling at the time. Besides, it was only a draft, not a formal submission, and I could always call Father later and tell him of the scheme. At that point, I stood up from the table in the Cushman conference room, told James to go fuck himself, and walked out the door.

"Casey phoned me at the office shortly after. She apologized profusely and said she had no idea that James would do that. She pleaded with me to meet with her and see if all could be put right. She said the deal didn't matter; only the two of us together did, and so she begged me to listen to her one last time. I refused. That's when she hit me with the story about our daughter, Sylvia—Sylvia Dodge. I hung up the phone. Her having a baby by me was preposterous, but the more I thought about it, the more it made a kind of sense. Of course, she'd either lied to me about the doctor or lied to me about the child. Either way, she lied, and that made me wonder if anything she'd told me had ever been the truth."

"That's when you knew. Why didn't you see it earlier?"

Johnny sighed. "I think love blinds us to the faults and machinations of the ones we think we love until it's too late. After she told me about my supposed daughter, I stood at my office window for a long time gazing out at the city, thinking about Casey and the changes I'd observed in her. I recalled her contempt for me in sporadic looks and words that raked my heart. On those occasions, I had wondered if she secretly loathed me. Of course, such moments passed, and the woman I thought I loved would reappear, but on one occasion, she let me see her true self. She let me look into her eyes, and I saw something predatory looking back at me. It was as if she wanted me to know that the only criteria for deciding between my living and my dying was not how much she loved me but how much contempt she felt for me at the time. I remember being so shocked that I asked her what she was thinking about. She laughed in a delightful way and said she was thinking about James, but that, too, was a lie. She was looking and thinking about me. I believed her at the time that it was about James because I was blind. Standing by the window in my office, I realized how blind I'd really been and how completely I'd been taken in."

Johnny sighed and said nothing for several moments.

He continued. "My world crumbled at that moment. Everything fell apart. I understood at last how completely I'd been a fool and that I was a patsy in the worst possible way. Everything I utterly despised and never wanted to be—I was. My brilliance? What brilliance. Everything good I believed about myself—I wasn't. I don't know what would have happened had the phone not rung again at that moment. I'm quite sure I would have fled the office and thrown myself in front of a subway train. Looking back, I can't believe how close I came to doing that. The phone rang again, and I picked it up. It was Casey trying to convince me to go ahead. I heard the anxiety in her voice and felt the presence of James as he listened in. That shifted something inside me. I heard myself agree to meet her—just the two of us."

92

I looked at Johnny for a long moment. "I don't know what to say. You were betrayed and in the worst possible way."

"I was, but who's to blame for that? No one but myself. That conclusion took me a while to accept, but life always finds a way to show us what is true by shattering our illusions and our misconceptions. It happened in my case. That night, we met at Le Cirque. I said I wanted proof, and Casey replied that if she gave me what I wanted, I would either use it to take the child away from her or blackmail her to James. I said I wanted one piece of physical evidence—just one, and that was all. She paused and asked me if I'd suddenly grown stupid. This was another Casey speaking— someone I'd seen in glimpses—a Casey who didn't need to lie or hide behind a façade of feigned affection.

"I didn't reply, and she told me that keeping any physical evidence was impossible. James was insanely possessive. He had her followed everywhere and went through her possessions regularly to see if she was hiding anything. He knew everything about her, including what we did together moment by moment and had from the very beginning. He was incredibly smart—smarter than me. She said she always told him everything because if she didn't, he'd hurt her. The only reason she was still alive, having screwed my brains out day after day, was because he needed her to close the deal with Dodge Capital. That was absolutely necessary for him, for her, and for his parents. She thought that both of us were in serious danger. Nonetheless, she had a plan and a proposition for me in plain and simple language: a completed deal in exchange for information about my child. She'd tell me everything, but only if I agreed.

"I said I'd consider her proposal over dinner. She commented that our last meal together should at least be decent and asked to see the menu.

"Over coffee, she was sitting close beside me and wanted my answer. I told her to go to hell. Having received it, she leaned in, closed off one of her nostrils with a finger, and snorted in the direction of my face. I remember thinking what an odd thing to do. It was the last thought I remember from that night. What happened afterward, I have no idea, and that's the end of my story."

I paused for a moment to consider what he'd said. "Well, thank you for telling me all you have. I'm glad you told her to get stuffed in the end. What happened after, I think we know. Casey used the Devil's Breath, by the way."

"Really. That is rather ominous. Where'd you learn that?"

"From Angus, of course."

"I'll be sure to ask him all about it then. Do you have some thoughts?"

"I do. Our invocation could work, but we need something more to be effective."

Johnny smile. "I know. I thought about that extensively on the drive here. It may sound odd, but I don't wish for revenge or anything like that. I'll leave that to others. So much has changed in me that I have no idea whether I'd be too harsh or too lenient. I think my father has the better idea. Evil people trap us in the fears they induce in us. We end up playing their game by using their tactics in our efforts to defend ourselves. We see their evil everywhere and with good reason. They sully our hopes and dreams and turn the world into a dark place, much darker than it is. I thought about killing all of them, of course."

"Really?"

"I did, and I could, you know. It wouldn't be that difficult, but what then? There would be repercussions, and I'd merely be substituting one travail for another. Of course, if I were attacked, I would have sufficient justification, and I suppose I'm clever enough to arrange that, but again, to what end exactly? I'm back to dealing with the fallout. The best I can do, I think, is to disengage from them, like Fabius Maximus did with Hannibal. He outmaneuvered Hannibal time and time again by refusing to engage. Eventually, Hannibal ran out of time and was forced to abandon Italy. It took a while, but Hannibal's end was far from pleasant. Likely, the Cushmans will have a similar one, and so I think it best I let them find their own. Of course, it's always possible that they will prosper. Prosperity and evil are not mutually exclusive, but I'll be damned if I'll let the Cushmans dictate my life any more than they already have. I refuse to give them that power— not now and certainly not anymore. What I want most is for the truth about what they did to be known to everyone here. After that, I want the Cushmans gone, and in a way that they'll always remember. That is what I want. It's what we've asked for, only I doubt they'll go quietly. They'll resist somehow, which is why what I must do will require some thought."

"Well said, Johnny. Do you want this to occur before, during, or after dinner?"

"During would be best. Perhaps you could stand up whenever it seems appropriate and announce that I have some words to say? I'll do the rest."

I nodded. "Very well. I'll make the necessary arrangements. I'll also be sending Raymond up to help you change and guard you. He'll be beside you at all times until the Cushmans leave."

"You fear for my safety?"

"You can unhinge everything they want, so yes, that did occur to me and likely to them as well."

"I agree. In the meantime, I'll bar the door."

"Excellent. Do you have any idea what you're going to say?"

"I've been thinking about that extensively. Perhaps I'll surprise you."

"That's what I'm afraid of, but this is your show. All of us here will support you, no matter what you come up with. Just remember you're swimming among sharks."

"Let's not insult the sharks. See you downstairs, and thank you for listening, for agreeing to our invocation, and for your willingness to let me speak. After this weekend, I'll begin taking charge of your wedding. I mean, how hard could it be?"

I laughed. "Difficult enough to inspire an entire industry."

"Child's play compared to what we have going on here."

93

I met Stanley in the foyer as he stepped out of the door to the cellar with a brace of ancient bottles under his arms and asked if he had a moment. We moved to his office.

Once he'd placed the bottles carefully on a side table and we were seated, I said, "I'm sure you're pressed for time, but I just finished speaking with Johnny."

Stanley assured me he had the time. I told him rapidly about all that had happened since we spoke last. I included Malcolm's news of the child, the conversation with Casey, and Johnny's story. My report took longer than I expected.

When I finished, Stanley said, "Well, I'm thrilled in many ways. Johnny is certainly back and in good shape. The news of the child is another matter. I don't quite know what to make of it. Dinner will certainly be bumpy. It's also possible that the agreement between Jim Cushman and John Dodge will collapse, and I'm in the dark as to what will follow. Given that, I'll find Raymond, brief him, and send him up to help Johnny change and guard him, lest an attempt be made to silence him before dinner—not that I expect one, but Johnny will feel secure, and Raymond will feel useful. I'll also be extra vigilant."

"Thank you, Stan. That would be wise. Anything else?"

Stanley paused. "Your invocation was a nice touch. As Johnny said, it sets what's happening here on a higher plane—one we sometimes forget exists. Just the same, I have my own concerns in that regard. I was the one who suggested we gather the Cushmans in one place. I feel responsible to a large degree, and so I wonder if we might be on our own in this in spite of any other appeals."

I leaned back in my chair. "I understand your concern, but let's not forget that in spite of it being your suggestion, the decision to invite them was mine to make, and I made it. Am I right in thinking that you feel we must rely more exclusively on our own resources than those of a higher power at this point?"

"I do."

"I see. I will try to orchestrate events as best I can tonight with that in mind. That being said, I doubt we would have discovered all we have so quickly had we not invited them. I also think the Cushmans would have shown up at our door eventually, given the time constraint they have and Mr. Dodge's decision to ensconce himself at Rhinebeck. Likely, that was deliberate. He's quite clever in that way—Johnny, too. Johnny's suggestion that we disengage and allow others to handle their demise is sound. Doing that at least prevents us from descending to their level—always a temptation, and especially so in this case."

"You are correct. It also touches on an important point. As custodians of Rhinebeck, we are bound to a higher standard of personal conduct, not only as reflected in our behavior and performance but through our insistence that our guests do the same or be sent off. Perhaps it's our adherence and demonstration of those standards that allow us to partake in the power and the transcendence that permeates this house. What surprised me was that I needed to be reminded of that. Perhaps we all must be from time to time. For now, let's end our talk on a higher note by suggesting that once we get through this evening and rid ourselves of the Cushmans, we get this wedding of yours sorted out. It's time that takes center stage. What do you say?"

I smiled. "I'm all for it, Stan, but to round off what you said, we're all to some degree responsible for the Cushmans being here. Maybe we should have acted better. I suggest we resolve to do so and move on. By the way, I'm also putting Johnny in charge of the wedding, at least on my end, since he now has a vested interest."

"I like the idea."

"Me, too." I stood. "Now, I must get ready for dinner, and speaking of which, there will likely be some pauses in the normal flow of courses given Johnny's announcement. Angus also asked me to tell Dagmar that he wanted a word with her about what Johnny could eat and how much. I doubt that's possible right now."

"It isn't, but I'll speak with him and convey his message."

"Thank you, Stan. Let me know if you need anything further, and I'll do the same."

At the door, I turned and said, "That huntress thing still bothers me."

"I, too, have concerns, but I don't know what to make of it other than to say all omens are good, yes?"

I smiled. "Of course. I keep forgetting. I'm off."

As I walked down the hall, I realized that I was looking forward to this evening, and that was a marked improvement, given my usual thinking. I just hoped I was justified in embracing a more hopeful outlook.

94

B runi was sitting at her dressing table with her back to me, wearing very little. She was making faces in the mirror and doing things with tiny brushes, pencils, and little jars.

She looked up at my reflection. "I've laid out your dinner clothes for tonight in case you were delayed talking to Johnny. I very much want to hear everything he said."

I plopped onto the bed. "Thank you for doing that. I also spoke with Stanley. With all my reporting, I feel like a combination newscaster and quick-change artist."

"It comes with the territory, I'm afraid. How is Johnny, really?"

"Better than I hoped and changed in ways I can hardly express. He has a mystical side now that is intriguing."

"I hope I sit next to him at dinner then."

"Whatever Anne decides. I don't envy her having to figure out the best configuration of guests for tonight. At least, that's out of my hands. Now … ready for the latest news?"

"Always. By the way, be prepared to seriously help me into my dress. That will take some effort since it's likely to be tight. I might even need a new bra size."

"Really? I like that."

Bruni smiled. "I'm sure you do. Perhaps you'd better begin. Telling me will distract you."

I laughed. "Good idea."

I repeated everything Johnny had told me and noted that Bruni stopped what she was doing shortly after I began and listened with all of her attention.

When I finished, she said, "I see what you mean. How extraordinary. What do you think he has in mind for tonight?"

"I'm not altogether sure, but I think he wants to say what needs to be said. Given also that he's pretty much risen from the dead and is straddling both worlds at the moment, it's likely to be unexpected."

"Then I can't imagine what will happen. Since it's getting late, and I need to dress, it's time for you to help spoon me into my gown, and then you'll need to change."

"Good idea but kiss me first."

We both managed to make ourselves presentable, but it took some time, since Bruni was beginning to show her pregnancy in every possible way and reconciling that with what she had available to wear required as much thinking as it did undulation. Progress was measured in millimeters rather than inches but was ultimately successful.

Bruni looked at herself in the mirror and said, "Well, I look all right for the moment, but what do I do when I have to eat something?"

"Take small bites and eat tiny portions."

"At a Dagmar feast? Not likely. Halfway through dinner, I'll need a knife to make some slits. I can barely move even now."

She turned this way and that as she looked at herself in the mirror with a critical eye and said, "Well … you may have to cut this off me when you take me to bed."

"I can do that."

She smiled. "I bet you can. Oscar de la Renta will have a fit, but I may not have a choice. I'm ready. Are you?"

"I am. You look sensational."

And she did. She glowed like a beacon in deep green satin. She wore an emerald and diamond necklace I'd never seen before. It alone was dazzling. I lifted it off her throat for a moment to examine it more closely.

"Really outstanding, Bruni."

"I rarely wear it. It's almost too much."

"With gems like these, the entire concept of what's too much doesn't exist."

Bruni looked pleased.

We made our way slowly to the drawing room. I had no idea whether we were early or late, but since she and I were host and hostess, I figured it didn't really matter.

———•———

95

Everyone had made it down before us, even Malcolm. Conversation paused as we entered. All attention shifted to Bruni, which was understandable, given her radiance. Her mother came up beside her. Elsa was decked out in even larger diamonds and wore an off-the-shoulder, black satin gown with a provocative white slash up the side. Elsa took Bruni's arm and led her off to speak with her father, but not before Bruni was handed a flute of Crystal. I took one as well. I looked around the room, dazzled by the colors and the flashes of sparkling gems. To my right, Johnny was sitting in the middle of the couch with Angus on one side and Bonnnie on the other. Angus looked comfortable in white tie and tails while Bonnie sported a brilliantly colored gown of red and black. Raymond was within reach in a surprisingly elegant dark business suit, white shirt, and tie of plain black silk. He stood close to the wall—his presence more imposing by the difference in his dress. His face showed no expression, but his eyes were moving, observing everyone and everything, hands kept loosely at his side, weight balanced on his feet like a tiger relaxed but ready. Johnny looked to be enjoying every minute. I noted that his champagne glass was a quarter filled, and a single triangle of smoked salmon on toast lay before him on a small plate with a napkin beside it. As servers would offer him more, Angus would *shoo* them away. Johnny raised his glass to me, and I moved in his direction.

Casey, in dark blue silk configured to accent every available curve, watched me over her flute beside her husband, whose attention seemed to flick toward her every few seconds. He looked to be talking to Malcolm out of the side of his mouth, but his attention was on Johnny. Malcolm seemed amused. John, Anne, Maw, and the senior Cushmans were in a circle to my left. Maw wore her usual black satin gown with her necklace of eye-popping emeralds. Jim Cushman could barely keep his eyes off them. His wife noticed. She looked annoyed—not that she didn't have a designer dress of her own or jewels in insufficient numbers, but there really was no comparison in terms of size and brilliance with those of Maw, Bruni, or Elsa. Hugo was beaming at the sight of his daughter talking to her mother. He raised his glass to me as I passed, just as Stanley gave me a sign. I altered course once more to stand by the dining room doors.

Stanley leaned in toward me and said, "Dagmar would like Johnny to make his announcement after the first two courses of pâté and lobster bisque have been served. She thought that would be not only strategically advantageous but would also allow him to make his announcement with sufficient energy, and well before he has a chance to tire himself."

"Very good, Stanley. I'll deliver the message. How soon before you start serving?"

"I'll be opening the doors in five minutes."

"Good. See you later tonight … depending."

"Yes, sir, depending."

"And that's what worries me. I'll speak with Johnny now."

I moved toward Johnny, who rose to greet me, followed by Angus and Bonnie. I commented on how well they all looked and said, "Sensational dress, Bonnie."

"Like it? Gianni made it for me. It's one of a kind."

"Just like you. Now, Johnny, Dagmar says you're up after the second course. All set?"

"I am. You know, after the complete lack of physical sensation for so long, being here is like wandering in paradise. I look around, and I'm dazzled to be alive at all. The doctor was just telling me all about the Devil's Breath. Absolutely fascinating. What an extraordinary thing."

"It is. I meant to ask you earlier—where did Casey come up with such a fascination with poisons and intoxicants? Do you know?"

Johnny looked in her direction. She was watching us and quickly looked away. James frowned, and Raymond grew still. The triple exchange was over in less than a second. Johnny smiled at the reactions and said, "From what she told me, toxins and poisons were a point of fascination for her from a very young age. When she visited Florence, she said that she became enchanted by the life and death of Pico della Mirandolla, likely by poisoning arranged by Piero de' Medici. She broadened this to include other assassinations and intrigues of the period. She traveled to many places after that, even to Colombia. We were just talking about poisoners in general. Weren't we, Doctor?"

Angus took a sip of champagne and nodded enthusiastically. "Indeed, we were—particularly about what drives them. Those who develop such a taste are both fascinating and deadly. I've come across their work often enough. I read somewhere that some originally suffered from toxicophobia, a fear of poisons, and in an effort to identify them, they investigated the subject so thoroughly that they often discovered their preference for experimentation. Of course, the first doesn't necessarily lead to the second, but the control of fear can be a powerful motivating force, and when successful, particularly in this domain, their proficiency not only protects them but allows a taking back of control of their lives, and those of others as well. Perhaps, it's really all about domination."

I smiled. "Good heavens! Bonnie, do you find this fascinating as well?"

"Of course. Who doesn't?"

"Then I hope we all sit together tonight. We should be going in shortly."

They sat back down while I continued to stand and look about the room. Everyone appeared so bright and shiny, staff and guests alike. Stanley turned the lights off and on once before he turned them off altogether and threw open the doors to the dining room. Tonight, the theme of the feast blazed before us in gold, red, and black.

96

The tablecloth was blinding white; the plates had white wells with wide jet-black lips and thin gold rims. The many knives, forks, and spoons at each setting were as golden as the spreading candelabra whose candles lit the scene. The glassware of many sizes and shapes were clusters of deep ruby-red. The table had the opulence of a prince's table when entertaining kings. There were soft cries of admiration.

I walked Bruni to her end. She sat down carefully. She whispered, "One point of Beluga—just one—and I'm already stuffed."

I whispered in her ear, "Only two courses, and then Johnny will speak. That will likely be followed by a pause to digest."

"Oh, I like that. Best of luck at your end."

"And at yours. Interesting configuration."

Bruni looked down the table and said, "The Cushmans looked to be corralled. Well done, Anne. The enemy's surrounded. Just the way I like it."

I walked back to my end. Bruni was correct. Bonnie was on my left, followed by Jim Cushman, Casey Cushman, her husband, James, Peggy Cushman, and then Malcolm to Bruni's right. Six were facing seven, with the four Cushmans in the middle. Johnny was to my right, followed by Angus and Anne Dodge. At the center of the opposing seven was Maw, followed by John Dodge and then Elsa. Hugo was next to Bruni. Raymond was by the wall behind the Cushmans, out of direct view and free to engage however he wished. Stanley stood by the Chinese screen.

The home team was seated and arrayed with Maw in command at the center of what appeared to be a developing pincer movement.

As I sat down and nodded to those at my end, I noted that whether by accident or design, the table arrangement maximized the differences rather than the two sides' similarities. I supposed that was just as well. It seemed to me that some form of conflict was about to begin, and I imagined standards flapping in the breeze, heard the squeak of leather, and felt the jostle of nervous hooves beneath me. I almost reached out to pat the table to settle it. All that was needed now was the call of a trumpet to set the lines in motion, and the carnage would begin.

As if on command, a file of uniformed staff wearing white gloves marched in, each holding a single plate of duck pâté with slices of what looked like baby pears and orange-colored compote. Each plate was placed smartly before each guest. A Montrachet Chardonnay of brilliant clarity was poured as Bruni picked up her fork, and we began.

97

The first course of pâté was a surprise in both its refinement and its texture. Combined with the mango compote, I had never tasted better. All those at the table were lost in silent savoring. If ever there was magic in our senses, I was experiencing it now. I finished faster than I wished and looked about. My guests were doing the same. Bruni, at the other end, was looking at her plate in awe. Whether it was the taste or that she'd eaten all of it, I wasn't sure.

Johnny only nibbled at his food, much to Angus's satisfaction. I wondered if the doctor was about to ask him if he might finish what was left, but Angus turned to me instead and said, "Well, I'm determined to meet this Dagmar of yours, Percy. That was exquisite. Johnny, how are you doing?"

Johnny took a sip of wine and said, "I'm still in heaven, although I can't eat much right now. I suppose I'm a tiny bit nervous, but the taste of the pâté is so refined and the wine so smooth it has settled me. All is well, Doctor."

Angus nodded and said, "Excellent. Keep to small portions, and you'll continue to feel that way."

I turned to Johnny. "Do you know what you're going to say?"

"I do. I've made some adjustments and shortened things quite a bit."

"Probably a good idea."

"I thought so. Bonnie, how goes with you?"

"Doing peachy, Champ. God, I love this place. I just hope there's lobster."

I smiled. "Your wish is my command. Lobster bisque is coming."

"That'll work!"

The bisque came next, and once again, there was no conversation. The soup was consumed as quickly as the duck pâté, and Stanley ghosted up to Johnny and informed him softly that he would make the introduction.

Stanley stood to my right and announced to all in a clear, commanding voice that there would be a pause at this time for Johnny to speak. The Cushmans looked at each other in surprise. Wine glasses were filled as Stanley made his way back to his station, and Johnny stood. He looked at each of us in turn.

Johnny smiled and said, "Good evening. I have some words to say. I won't be long. To begin, I wish to make an apology. As you know, I've been in a coma, but I awoke, and since then, I've had some time to reflect on how and why I came to be in that condition. What struck me most was how rarely we perceive how our *being* in the world affects others. Much rarer still is our awareness of what our *not being* brings about … unless we die, of course, but few of us have been resurrected from that state to see the holes we created when we are no longer there to fill them. Speaking for myself, I had no inkling of the pain my absence brought about. It was as if I broke the hearts of those who knew me when that was never my intention. I was insensible to that possibility because deep down, I'd never felt worthy of what was given to me so freely. I won't take that gift for granted again. In keeping with that, Mother, Father, Maw, Percy, Bruni, Bonnie, Angus, Malcolm, Elsa, Hugo, Stanley, Raymond, and Dagmar, in absentia, please accept my most humble and sincere apology for that unintended hurt."

There were soft murmurs as we nodded. The Cushmans remained stoic and drank their wine.

Johnny continued. "Thank you for that. Now, I think we can agree that I may have been the cause of that pain but not necessarily the reason. If that is true, then what was? I think mortality is the answer. To be mortal is to be subject to death. Speaking for myself, that definition is hopelessly inadequate since it omits the contradictory and distressing nature of our existence. To be mortal is to live with the awareness of having an unknown yet finite time limit while having to consume other mortal creatures—to have any time at all. Speaking for myself, that's hardly a recipe for tranquility and harmony. It means we all must scramble for existence, and that means occasionally running roughshod over fellow human beings. It is that which concerns me. Shortly after I awoke, I remembered the specifics of my accident."

Johnny picked up his glass and took a sip of wine before he continued. "I asked myself at that point: How should we live, given the wrongs done to us by others in their own desperate struggles with mortality? Do we forgive them or punish them? How about the wrongs we do them? What should happen to us? How *should* any of us live, given these cruel constraints that we all have in common? I realized at that moment that there were as many answers to those questions as there were people on this Earth because that's what everyone here is doing: dealing as best they can with their own mortality. Given that, if God is splashed across the universe in broad strokes, then our lives are rendered in the details, and the nitty gritty that results and it is only in the specific that we can know the personal answer to the question: How should we respond to provocations and attacks when we find ourselves on the receiving end?"

Johnny paused and looked at the Cushmans.

"As I was driven here, newly resurrected and recently released from the hospital, I wondered what to do. What should be my role? Should I be a saint and forgive our trespassers? That is an available path to me. Perhaps I'd simply gotten in the way of someone else's struggle and been trampled underfoot, all being fair in love, war, and life. Could I not forgive and forget? Maybe I could. On the other hand, I could make up a story instead and lie boldly. I could spin a tale of betrayal, manslaughter, assault, drugs, poison, money, lies, tainted schemes, and the best of intentions that didn't work out well. I could portray myself as a victim—cruelly treated. That could be a story, too. It might even be the truth, but then again, I might be exaggerating.

"I realized after some thought that if I told you *any* story at all, I would be placing the burden of deciding what is true and what is false upon you, the listener, and that would not be right, let alone appropriate, at a feast like this one. Besides, I'm running out of time, and we must eat. ... That was a joke, in case you wondered, but I see that nobody's laughing. To solve my dilemma, I decided to use an indirect approach, and so about an hour ago, I called your mother in Florence, Percy. I hope that was all right?"

I shrugged. "Fine by me. How was she?"

"Quite well. She sends her love and asked about the wedding. She also wished that she was here in person to tell us about Sylvia, Sylvia Dodge—the child of Casey and myself, a child I never met. Unfortunately, she's dead now, having passed away at the age of two quite some time ago from poisoning of the blood, I'm told. She rests in a quiet churchyard beneath a small slab of pale marble, unknown to all who pass by during the day, but tonight, she is publicly acknowledged—a forgotten child in a foreign land. I'm done speaking for now. All I ask is that at some point this evening, you reflect on what I've told you and carefully consider what it might mean—all of it: the beginning, the middle, and the end."

Johnny remained standing as this news was digested. Everyone other than Malcolm, Bruni, and I had their mouths open in shock. Johnny stared at Casey and James, and so did I. We all did. Casey was white. James looked wild. Noticing our attention, he sprang to his feet and cried out, "Liar! There was no child!" Raymond moved within an arm's length.

Johnny looked at James for a long moment. "I only wish I was, James. You obviously had no idea. Would that have made a difference when you asked Casey for her hand? I don't know your answer to that question, but what I do know is that we've *both* been fools. But if we've been fools, then what is Casey? She'll deny and deny and lie and lie. It's what she does. I'll tell you who she really is. She's poison, plain and simple, so be warned. That's all I wish to say. Thank you for your attention, everyone. I will sit down at last."

It was skillfully done on Johnny's part. He said only what could be proved, but it was costly. Johnny looked pale and tired.

Casey was trembling and breathing heavily. Her chest heaved as she tried to catch her breath. Suddenly, she seemed to choke and then blew her nose violently into her napkin. Shaking, she reached up to grab onto her husband's coattail. He turned and looked down at her, his expression oscillating between rage and fear. Casey spoke hoarsely, "The case, James ... Something's happened. Get the case, James ... For me ... Please ... The case."

James turned and said to me in a surprisingly even voice, "I need the case, Percy. The small one. It's vital."

Stanley was looking at me. I nodded. Stanley disappeared and returned almost immediately. He passed the case to James, who laid it down on the floor behind Casey's chair. James fiddled with the combination, got it wrong, and then got it right. We all looked on in silence as Casey looked about, terrified.

Bonnie whispered across to Angus, "Should I get your bag, Angus?"

Angus stood, watching what was going on intently. He shook his head, "No, my dear. She is not my patient. I have no obligation to treat. I much prefer to observe right now. You might do the same."

Bonnie turned and put her attention on James as he opened the case, took out a syringe, counted the many vials across, one at a time, and then counted down before he took one out and looked at it. He stuck the needle in and filled it halfway. He went over to Casey, sat down beside her, and discreetly injected the contents into a vein on Casey's forearm. From the ease with which that was performed, he must have had a lot of practice. Both of them seemed to relax. James put the syringe and vial back in the case, snapped it shut, and gave it to Stanley, who took it away.

When Stanley returned, he announced, "Dinner will resume shortly."

During the pause before the next course, Peggy said loudly so that all could hear, "Anne, I do hope there'll be no more interruptions tonight and that dinner will continue uneventfully from this point forward. Obviously, from what was said, there have been happenings of which we've had no inkling and no knowledge. To me, what I've heard about the child, even if shocking and unexpected, must be accorded the status of a private matter, one that was sadly closed some time ago or should have been. Whatever its ramifications, it is for my son and his wife to work through and should not be open to public discussion. Would you do me the favor, and I ask everyone at this table to do the same, to please refrain from speaking about it? To me, it would not only be impolite but highly inappropriate."

Anne looked at Peggy for some moments. "I understand. As a mother, and a grandmother, I suppose, I hardly know what to think. The fact that it has remained hidden for so long points to something even deeper—a pervasive dishonesty and deception of which we've seen too much of lately. Given what I've heard, I can't help but wonder about the accident itself and the fate of the two drivers. One died at the scene. I want to know about the other one. Perhaps we should follow your suggestion, and you tell me about him instead?"

Peggy shook her head. "I can't. I know nothing about it, and I can't see why you would expect me to. The accident had nothing to do with me. I wasn't even there."

"You weren't, but I was talking to Bruni before dinner and heard that the other driver retired to Sicily the next day, and that seems to me as convenient as it is unsettling."

Peggy looked at Anne coldly. "Did he? You're remarkably well informed, Anne, much more than I, but I understand your interest,

414

considering that your son was involved. Thankfully, and I would be supremely thankful if I were in your shoes, Johnny appears to have survived unharmed, and considering the arrangements that have been made between our husbands, perhaps it's best we move forward rather than look back. Wouldn't that be wiser at this point?"

Anne looked equally frosty. "I'm inclined in that direction; however, I've heard it said that the wheel of fortune turns inevitably of its own accord, and balance is often restored unexpectedly. I wonder how that will happen in your case. The night is far from over, but for now, it is right that we enjoy what is delightful while we can. Would you agree with that?"

"I would. The future is bright from where I sit."

"It is from where I sit as well. I just hope for both our sakes they're not mutually exclusive."

Their exchange was interrupted by the entrance of the next course of plain green salad, sprinkled with lemon croutons and drizzled with a balsamic vinaigrette.

I turned to Johnny and said, "I thought that was an interesting and unusual approach, Johnny. Did you say all you wished?"

Plates were set in front of us, and Johnny picked up his fork with a questioning look at the doctor, who nodded his agreement. "I think so. One of the most potent weapons in the battle of wills is doubt. It can be more effective than an arrow because once it finds its target, questions and misgivings multiply, leading to possible reassessments. Of course, such things take time."

The doctor said, "Quite true, Johnny. Do you consider the Cushmans an enemy?"

"I have no doubt of that, but they are formidable and not to be underestimated. I did that once and barely survived. I won't do it again. Directly accusing them would have only led to arguments that I could never win. The indirect approach seemed better, and I had confirmation from your mother, Percy. *That*, they couldn't dispute."

415

I nodded. "That was clever."

Angus nodded also and leaned in closer to the three of us. He said almost in a whisper, "I'm also curious as to what James injected Casey with and why. It seemed that something happened when she inhaled a bit too forcefully after your speech. I couldn't help but be reminded of the risks involved in using the Devil's Breath. Of course, I have a somewhat jaundiced view of the world and wonder if perhaps the mention of an unknown child might have generated sufficient questions so as to provoke a more immediate reassessment by her husband."

Bonnie whispered, "A reassessment, Angus?"

Angus leaned in closer. "In the criminal world, of which I'm unfortunately familiar, trust is always an issue, and when that is withdrawn, I have often had to autopsy the results. There were many vials in that case, and with the need to act quickly, mistakes are possible. It's the pressure to act that does it. It's like a form of panic, and for that reason, I'm such a stickler for procedure. There are also those occasions when what appears to be a horrible mistake was no mistake at all. I've seen that, too."

Angus leaned back. "I apologize if I'm being overly macabre, but it's how my mind works."

There was silence from our end after that. I suppose I wasn't the only one whose mind moved along such paths. I just hoped we made it past the fish before things went south, but which direction events would ultimately take, I wasn't altogether sure. Johnny gave me a long look but said nothing. I knew what he was thinking.

Bonnie said, "I see. I had a similar thought. I suppose I'm just as bad."

Our end lapsed back into silence as we contemplated what Angus had said.

The salad was replaced by a delicate cube of grilled salmon drenched in lemon butter and placed in a creamy green pool of watercress sauce, with a sweet fruit coulis surrounding it, but it was scarcely touched before a shivering and sweaty Casey rose from her chair and said, "There's something wrong, James. What have you done? What did you give me?"

James looked around the table, not sure how to respond.

Casey clutched his arm. "James? James?"

James, first at her and then at all of us, cried out, "The usual, of course. What's wrong? What do I do?"

Angus answered loudly, "I suggest you run her to a hospital as soon as you can. Don't just sit there. You have little time."

"I will."

He leaped to his feet, yelling as he left the table, "I must get my keys. Someone take her outside while I get my car."

Pandemonium reigned. Everyone was on their feet. Raymond scooped up a convulsing Casey as Stanley held the door to take her outside. I heard James running just before the door shut, and all was quiet.

Jim Cushman pointed at Angus. "You're a doctor. Why don't you do something?"

"She's not my patient, but your son's. Besides, what would you suggest I do?"

"I don't know. That's your area of expertise, not mine."

Angus rose and said, "That may be, but I've no idea what your idiot son shot her up with or why. I doubt he knows himself. I can't imagine what he gave her. There were many vials in that valise, all of them unmarked, in case you hadn't noticed. I suppose he does this type of thing regularly, and you consider such actions normal. Well, they're not. They're dangerous and risky. I will give you some advice, however."

Jim Cushman was shaking with emotion but said icily, "And what is that?"

"Pray! Pray your son drives fast. Pray the girl survives. Pray that her chances are better than those I believe them to be."

"And what do you think those are?"

417

"Very remote. She'll likely be dead before she arrives. Care to make a wager?"

"You are callous, sir."

"And you people are unconscionable. The only question I have is whether it was deliberate or accidental, and given what I heard tonight, I suspect the former, so sit back down. We wait. We'll hear soon enough. Too soon, if I am not mistaken. I'd drink more wine if I were you. I think you're going to need a great deal of it."

Jim Cushman sat. Likely, he didn't know what to say. None of us did.

Maw's cackle broke the silence. She laughed again and said loudly, "I told you both to flee while you had the chance, did I not, Mr. and Mrs. Cushman?"

Jim Cushman squirmed, and Peggy looked like she was ready to hit someone. Maw continued anyway. "And how did you respond, Mr. Cushman?"

He cleared his throat and answered, "I said that I had nothing to fear from anyone or anything here and that I preferred to stay."

"You did, and I said, 'Oh, but you do. You do, indeed.' Long ago, you and my son caused Senator Fowler's daughter's horse to be put down. You broke one of its legs. That horse was foaled, raised, and trained in my stable. Together, that girl and that horse were a rare match. They would have become champions, maybe even Olympic champions, but you callously ended that future before it had even begun or had a chance to bloom. I haven't forgotten what you and my son did—not for a moment. To add to that despicable crime, you played a part in my grandson's accident. You may deny it, but I know you, Mr. Cushman. I've kept a close eye on you and your activities over the years. I know all about you. I even made both of you a prediction. Do you recall that, Mr. and Mrs. Cushman?"

The Cushmans said nothing. Maw paused and looked at them for a long moment. "I told you both that you would rue the day my grandson returned to this house and that if you were still here when that happened, nothing in Heaven or on Earth, could save you. Do you recall me saying that, Mrs. Cushman?"

Peggy was a picture of restrained fury and could contain herself no longer. "I heard you well enough, and I answered that I respected your age and your reputation, but your threats were merely words and meant nothing to me—not then and certainly not now."

"You did, and you added that the horse incident was ancient history and to move on. Of course, telling me that took some spunk, I grant you, but such bravado won't help you now. I would go while the choice is still yours, but you won't. In which case, I will watch with no small amount of satisfaction and enjoyment as your world breaks in pieces and your hearts with it."

Mr. Cushman looked uncomfortable. "I can't leave. My son will call. I must know what happened."

Maw didn't answer but merely looked at both of them like they were some wriggling, tweezered specimens that had no inkling, no thought, and no conception of what was to follow.

Conversation ceased, and since everyone had returned to their seats and were now sitting down, I asked the table, "Perhaps we should continue with the feast while we wait. You may not feel like eating right now, but I'm quite certain you will be tempted to have a bite or two. There is magic in this food, and maybe that is what's needed now."

Everyone nodded, even the Cushmans. After all, what else was there to do?

98

I t was not long after that Jim Cushman was called to the telephone. He returned after several minutes and announced that he and his wife would be leaving for the hospital. The doctors there wanted them to bring the case. Given the puzzling nature of Casey's symptoms and the extremely remote chance that she would survive the night, they had notified the police. Apparently, they, too, had questions. I thanked Jim for the information and suggested he and his family find a hotel near the hospital. Both protested, but I held firm. I told Stanley to see that every one of their belongings be packed up immediately, and I ordered Raymond to drop them and their baggage wherever they wished, provided it wasn't back here.

That last order didn't go over well, but enough was enough, in my opinion. I needed some peace, and so did everyone else. I didn't bother to see them leave. None of us did. Stanley announced the fact that they had finally departed and that Raymond would see they were dropped off as efficiently and as quickly as possible.

Stanley then said, "Given the circumstances and unless anyone has an objection, I think it would be best if we move directly to dessert. Dagmar has made a cake in honor of Johnny's return, and since the night has been trying for him, it might be best if that happened sooner rather than later."

Johnny had not fully recovered since his speech and looked worn out. There were no objections to this change in plan.

Shortly after, the lights were dimmed and a large white cake with a single candle on top was wheeled out, but not before the Cushman place settings had been removed and a redistribution of guests was completed to balance the table. Dishes of homemade vanilla ice cream soon followed as the cake was sliced and served, and we picked up our forks.

Bonnie was the first to respond by announcing that this cake was the best she had ever tasted and that Dagmar should receive a standing ovation at the very least.

Dagmar was duly summoned and applauded, and I stood to make an announcement of my own.

I said, "Before we conclude tonight, I would like to express to all of you my thanks for being here this weekend. Johnny has returned, and I cannot say how much that is appreciated not only by me but by all of us. I think it's time he has some rest. Johnny, anything you care to say?"

Johnny remained seated and said, "See you all in the morning. I haven't been able to say that in so long; it almost seems unnatural, and yet, to me, it is so comforting and hopeful. I will speak with each of you individually tomorrow and answer any questions you may have. I do, however, have one of my own right now: How am I going to make it up the stairs to my bed with Raymond gone, Percy?"

At that moment, Raymond entered from behind the Chinese screen and said, "Settle down. I'll help you up the stairs and tuck you in before you know it.' Raymond looked at me and said, "By the way, sir, I drove the Cushmans to the hospital after dropping all their bags at the Beekman Arms. They weren't a happy bunch."

"Thank you, Raymond. Wonderful news. You did splendidly."

Johnny rose, and Raymond helped him through and out the dining room doors. I turned to Bruni at the far end and said, "Bruni, would you like to do the honors?"

Bruni rose carefully from her seat. "I would. Tonight, it would be best if all of us, men and women alike, adjourn to the library rather than the drawing room. Not only are the chairs more comfortable, and I'll be able to spread out a little, but the liquor is better and more immediately available. Would everyone agree?"

Maw stood up and laughed. She clapped her hands loudly in acknowledgment. "Nicely put, Bruni. I've always thought the library a better place to congregate than the drawing room, and if I may, I'll take the big chair next to yours. We'll spread out together, smoke, and make rude comments. This night has ended with the enemy in full flight. I'm thoroughly pleased and content, and that, for me, is a rare occasion. Percy, I hope you have something suitably ancient for me to drink. I intend to celebrate and be carried up to bed by that very handsome Raymond, but right now, Bruni, will you take my arm? John, please take the other one. Let us head to the library!"

As they went by, I heard Maw whisper to John, "I trust Raymond handled that other matter?" But they had passed me before I could catch John's answer.

99

B efore the party in the library started, I grabbed some cigars and slipped away to see Stanley, who was waiting for me in his office. Dagmar was with him, which surprised me, but when Stanley pulled out the bottle of Hamish's brew, I knew why she was there. I offered them each a cigar. Dagmar took one and lit hers like she knew what she was doing.

She commented, "There's nothing like a nice Havana to accompany Hamish's brew. It doesn't come any better."

Once our cigars were smoking well, we stood and toasted Hamish and the absence of any Cushmans with a rowdy cheer, a single shot of the brew, followed by a cloud of cigar smoke. We sat back down and smoked for a time before Stanley said, "By the way, I managed to crack the combination with Dagmar's help."

I looked at him in surprise. "Really? However, did you manage that?"

Stanley said, "The combination for both was 31415 only in reverse. I must admit that whenever I had some time, I'd fiddle with the smaller case and try out various numbers. Eventually, I asked Dagmar for help. She suggested the constant *e* since James Cushman was into finance and exponential growth … ."

Dagmar interrupted, "I did suggest that at first, but thinking about the wife, it would have to be more well-known. *Pi* is fairly easy to remember, so I thought the first five digits might work. It didn't, but then I thought they might reverse them to be safe, and sure enough, it opened. I must say that I was shocked by what I found inside. I examined many of the vials but with great caution. I recognized belladonna, strychnine, some ketamine compounds, various alkaloids, several different cyanide salts, mercury salts, organic acids, and several powders, including some very pure heroin and cocaine. She had enough toxins to poison a city. I heard that the police have it now, and well they should. There's a world of questions and legal trouble in those vials, make no mistake. What's troubled me is that I may have inadvertently played a part in what happened tonight. The bottles had no labels. I realized belatedly that the order was important, but only after a dozen or more had been removed. Whether they all went back in the exact same sequence, I'm not altogether sure, to be honest. I thought to make a clean breast of it by telling you, but it doesn't make me feel much better."

I thought about that. "Well, clever of you to open the thing, but I doubt you were the cause of what happened with Casey. The doctor thinks that Casey planned to use the Devil's Breath again. Are you familiar with it?"

Dagmar answered, "Oh, yes."

"I don't know if she had a target. Maybe it was purely defensive. After James found out about the child from Johnny, Casey freaked out about what her husband might do and began to hyperventilate. I think she inhaled a little too forcefully and informed James. He responded by injecting his wife with half a syringe of what he termed *the usual*. Likely, it wasn't that at all. From what I know of him, James would have quickly taken what he had just learned about Casey and added it to the thought that if she was removed, any alleged wrongdoing could be blamed on her. With that, the solution became obvious, and he decided to get rid of her, hence his choice and the amount."

Dagmar considered that and smiled broadly. "You are correct. That amount of anything from that case would have been enough to kill her several times over. By giving her more than was necessary, he showed his true intentions. You're right. I'm not to blame. You have no idea how relieved I am to know that. In fact, I feel so relieved that I must insist on another toast to Hamish. What do you say to that, Stan?"

Stan agreed immediately. We toasted Dagmar's innocence and gave Hamish our thanks once again. I said good night and went back to the library to collect Bruni. When I arrived, everyone was singing together as a chorus. Angus was leading them in the gospel song, "Have You Got Good Religion." When I entered, my guests started singing in earnest, after which everyone drank a toast. Before they could begin again, Bruni and I escaped.

100

Breakfast the next morning was a subdued affair. Other than Johnny, who looked bright and cheerful, we all kept our heads down. Stanley announced, after sufficient coffee had been consumed, that Casey Cushman had passed during the night from an as yet unidentified substance and that James Cushman was so distraught at the news that he fled to his car and drove away from the hospital like a madman. Shortly after, his car struck a tree at high speed. Since he hadn't been wearing a seatbelt, he was ejected from the vehicle for such a considerable distance that it was initially thought he had fled the scene on foot. A search was organized, but it was only much later, when an officer chanced to look up, that his body was discovered among the branches of a tree.

This news was met with nods and very little else. What was there to say? As I got up, Maw asked Johnny and me to take Robert for a walk. Johnny protested that he was in no condition to run madly after Robert anytime soon. Maw gave him a long look and countered that I had taken Robert for walks quite successfully this weekend and to get on with it.

Since there was nothing more to be said, we did just that. I let Robert onto the south lawn so that he might explore the morning that spread gloriously before us in greens and golds beneath a sky of the most exquisite blue.

Johnny and I walked slowly, following Robert, who disappeared into the underbrush beneath the woods to the south.

I said, "Strange times, Johnny."

"They are, and death came nosing about rather closely, I might add."

"True, but you survived while they died sooner than perhaps they should have."

"They did. I don't know the rightness or the wrongness of that other than to say it's just as well. Their evil deeds and their many legal entanglements will be buried with them."

"They will be, and hopefully with a robust combination lock. It is a kind of justice. One I could never have arranged. I've given up any aspirations in that direction. I don't have the necessary harshness. I'm sure I'd be an awful judge. I'd be far too lenient."

"That is actually one of your better qualities, but you're right, Percy. Justice is best left to its own devices. I also wonder whether Jim Cushman will have the nerve to call Father on Monday with the amount he needs. Bonnie told me in detail about their lunch conversation."

"Your father wanted to end their feud by letting go of his end, but in answer to your question, business is business. Jim either makes the call or files for bankruptcy. He'll make the call."

"That will be an awkward moment. Do you think Father will carry through on his promise?"

"That is difficult to predict. He might just let them go under. The Cushmans killed the driver and almost murdered you. Once that was confirmed, which you did rather brilliantly in your speech, your father made his response. Letting them drown would follow from that."

"I'm missing something. Tell me."

"It happened after Raymond took you upstairs. When Maw was leaving the dining room, she was arm-in-arm with your father and Bruni. She asked him if Raymond had handled that other matter. I didn't hear his answer and asked Bruni about it. She said she was unaware of the exchange."

Johnny considered that as we strolled. "What I think you're saying is that Raymond did a little fiddle on James's vehicle prior to his accident. Am I correct?"

427

"Yes. It's what I think."

"Likely, you are correct then. If Maw took his arm, Father has now become worthy in her eyes. He lived up to her expectations at last. Besides, Maw doesn't just do an eye for an eye. She expects value for her efforts and will go for both eyes, an arm, and a head if possible. Given that, I'd say you are correct. That is exactly what happened."

"So much for our high-mindedness and civilized values."

"Those are for us to cherish and hold dear, but have you noticed, Percy, that some people really are above such things? Maw is. She's elemental, like the sun. The only physical constraints she has are time and space. She knows she won't be around forever and likely didn't want any loose ends dangling about, like James, who could potentially upset her plans for the future. She was merely weeding the garden. I know that isn't exactly nice, but *she* isn't exactly nice. She simply *is*, and that seems to be enough, unlike the rest of us."

I sighed. "She is elemental."

"And speaking of elemental, Bruni is getting bigger."

"You noticed."

"I did. Of course, I won't be mentioning that to her, but it does bring our next project, your wedding, front and center. I mean, really, Percy, you two should have handled that far earlier than now."

I stopped short. "Johnny! I can't believe you're saying that."

Johnny chuckled. "That pays you back for trying to reduce the amount I sank into this estate."

"I did no such thing. It was all hypothetical. You just want me to do something. I know your tricks. So, what is it you want me to do?"

Johnny laughed. "You're becoming sharper in your old age, so here it is. Go to Austria with Bruni this week. Have Hugo and Elsa personally show you how they live. I think that might be enlightening."

"A message from beyond?"

"No, just a good idea since you will have to convince your in-laws to have the wedding here at Rhinebeck rather than at the castle."

"Here? Why not there? I thought the bride's parents handled all that, including the location."

"They do, but you put me in charge, and those are my terms. You will be married here, not there. You'll thank me in the end, but arranging for that to happen may take no small amount of effort and persuasion, hence my suggestion."

"I see. You seem to be taking this wedding seriously all of a sudden."

"You bet I am. According to my vision of Alice when I was in my coma, I will meet my future bride, or at least my heart's desire, at your wedding. I want to know what she looks like and intend to carefully control who comes and goes. Now, having said that and giving you once again my sincere thanks for all you did for me, it's time I head back while you retrieve Robert."

I chuckled. "You're recovering. You're getting pushy and assertive again but know that you won't be able to avoid that dog forever. He's out there, biding his time until you're fully well, and then watch out. He'll have you bounding over hill and dale like an overgrown puppet."

"He will, but not today, thank God. So good luck with that, Percy. I'm off to the house. Shall I see you in an hour, or will it be two?"

"Minutes, Johnny. Watch and learn."

I yelled, "Robert!"

As if by magic, Robert streaked toward us and then sat in front of me, panting.

Johnny looked shocked. "I can't believe it's that easy. I'm sure I can do that. Perhaps I should give it a try? Wait a second—he almost had me."

Johnny looked at Robert again more carefully and leaned down. "Soon, you beast, but not today. Remember, Robert the Bruce, I now have the power to make you a ring bearer. They'll force you to take a bath. Think about that for a minute and be very afraid of my awful majesty." Johnny straightened up and said, to me, "Now, I really am off to the house."

We watched Johnny head back. I turned to Robert. "What do you say we visit the crows? They can tell you the latest news, and then you can tell me. Deal?"

Robert looked up at me and gave a soft yip. With that, I knew I really was blessed, and in strange ways.

THE END

Last Note

Dear Reader,

There are limited avenues to spread the word about my stories, and reviews are a significant way to connect with potential readers. Please consider posting a review with your favorite store, library, social media, or even my website. Writing a review makes a difference. I read every one of them, and appreciate the time spent sharing your thoughts and opinions, whatever your experience. I welcome it.

In addition, please sign up for my monthly newsletter to keep updated on my projects. You can also reach out to me by replying to it, and I do answer.

Lastly, thank you for purchasing this Special Edition. This book has been published exclusively for extended distribution channels such as libraries, bookstores, book clubs, educators, and more. Please read on for a selection from the Feathered Quill Interview I did with Kathy Stickles about *Dark of the Earth*.

Wishing you the best,

Ivan Obolensky

Feathered Quill's Interview with Ivan Obolensky for *Dark of the Earth*

FQ: As always, I really adored this new book and I am so grateful to have the opportunity to read it and keep up with what is happening in the characters' lives. You are simply a master at this type of storytelling I must say. Do you go through a lot of questioning yourself (and your characters) and rewriting things in the books or is this just a knack you have and it comes out on paper easily the first time?

IO: Thank you so much for the compliment. Having a reader really enjoy something one has written, after having put in so much time and effort, is the best reward for having written it.

Nothing is ever easy, and writing novels requires a special kind of skill. In the beginning, one has unlimited possibilities as to what to write and which direction to take. As the story is put down, the pathways available become fewer and fewer, like context. Context provides definition to what one is trying to communicate. The more context there is, the more defined and precise a fact or a situation becomes. It is the same with stories. At the beginning anything is possible. At the end, the choices are few, and the plot gathers its own inevitability from all that went before like a slow-moving avalanche.

Because I wish to convey a sense of realism, the stories I write are built moment by moment into scenes (chapters). I rarely have any idea where a story is going when I start. The only rule I follow is that there must be consistency and continuity once I begin. All the actions, every dialogue, and each description must contribute to forwarding the story and must be rooted in what went on before, so the plot develops organically and is continuous rather than discontinuous. For me, writing is like running a marathon on a road one has never seen. One plugs away step by step and word by word into a distance that is uncertain and undefined.

To begin, I require an interesting situation that has consequences. The middle needs brilliant language and clarity because middles can be confusing, but endings are where the writer really has to shine. A good ending is vital because it makes whatever the reader had to go through to get to it worth the effort they put in. Fail there, and all is lost. For me, a good ending must be surprising, suitably outrageous yet believable, and satisfying—all at the same time. If it is brilliantly executed, then so much the better. I worry a lot about endings. I wonder constantly how I will make what is inevitable a surprise. It's what I think about most when I'm in the middle.

To answer your question, writing is relatively easy if one's thoughts are clear. It is the thinking to gain that clarity (before, during, and after) that requires so much energy and effort. In addition, the writing is rarely right the first time. I will read what I have written hundreds of times to make it smoother, better, clearer, and, most of all, memorable.

FQ: *Dark of the Earth*, even though it includes all of the characters we have come to adore, really pushes Percy to the forefront and we see him transform into a very strong and determined man who is willing to do just about anything to help Johnny and to protect the entire family and business from those who might be trying to cause harm. Was it fun to show us this new "Percy" or was it extremely challenging to make him different and more of the real main character given Johnny's not being around so much in the beginning of the story?

IO: To me, novels are long stories that ask and answer deep questions. How to prove oneself worthy in one's own estimation is one of many grand themes that are woven through *Dark of the Earth* and the earlier books of the series. Accomplishing that task in the real world is difficult for everyone. One can fool others, and even oneself for a time, but in the end, it is one question we all must answer.

In ancient India, a man had to have produced a son who produced a son to be released from the obligations of family. He was then free to go off into the forest by himself in search of wisdom. Having garnered special knowledge, he could return and teach others what he had discovered. He became a *guru*.

In the West, we have the "hero's journey", where an individual leaves all that is known and ventures into the unknown to experience the world and discover who he really is. The hero then returns with that understanding and perhaps some treasure. This hero's journey is handed down in different ways across a great many cultures, in the form of myths, legends, and ancient tales. It is almost universal as a theme. In modern culture, this yearning for the journey is still present, but given our modernity, how is that to be done?

In Percy, we see him discover who he really is in *Eye of the Moon* as he confronts and quiets the darkness and terrors that lie hidden within himself. In *Shadow of the Son*, Percy steps out from beneath the shadow of his father and his heritage to cast his own shadow. In *Dark of the Earth*, the circle expands, and he must confront the desperation of those who value wealth and winning above all else (the world of the modern corporate economy). Saddled with our natures, how does one live well and in harmony, given the incessant economic pressure, society's demands for compliance and acquiescence, and the sociopathic tendencies of a few? Percy develops because he is without Johnny to rely on and has no choice. He must step up or be trodden under.

What was challenging about showing this new Percy was portraying his development (the hero's journey) in a modern context and in a story that does not devolve into the all-too-familiar dystopian drama, where evil is met with greater evil and victory goes to the stronger, the most expedient, and the more mercenary. There are no dragons to slay, or so it seems, but that is hardly true, even today. They have simply assumed different guises, and down deep, we all thirst for adventure, even if we must create it ourselves.

How to illustrate the hero's journey using a single location was certainly a challenge. Percy surprised me nonetheless, and as in real life and in my novels, surprise is always just around the corner and never to be underestimated. It was Lenin, of all people, who said, "There are decades when nothing happens; and there are weeks where decades happen." I prefer to have those decades happen in days. My novels would be too long otherwise.

FQ: I liked seeing more of Johnny and Percy's past through the flashbacks and stories that Percy told to Johnny and to the family. Will we see more of that in the next book or was it more of a tool used just because of the situation in this story?

IO: Oddly, the book I started was originally supposed to be a collection of short stories as a stopgap before I wrote the next in the series. I had written several stories about Johnny's and Percy's earlier adventures and thought to myself, "What could be easier?" That didn't go as planned. I was rereading Boccaccio at the time and thought of using an overarching story—the accident in this case—as a literary device to showcase them. I patted myself on the back and merrily began, only to have that self-satisfied feeling rapidly disappear.

I began to wonder if Johnny's accident had really been an accident. Suppose it had been deliberate? By the time I had gotten to the middle, I still wasn't sure. The Cushmans had a plan and were up to something, but what? It was a puzzle. Added to that was the conundrum of how Johnny was to recover? It took a great deal of thought and a lot of writing to solve.

In truth, the stories were an idea that spun completely out of control, and there was nothing I could do but follow along. I am certainly glad I did. What I find amusing is that the stories are microcosms of what happens in the big story and add nuances that could not have existed without them.

FQ: I know that you are thinking four books will be it for this series so can you tell us about the final installment? Will we see a baby and a wedding? Is Johnny going to get an "end" to the story like Percy or is there the possibility of more books in the series in the future?

IO: I never say never, but the idea was four—like the acts of a play. At some point, one must draw the curtain and let the audience go home to consider the experience and perhaps revisit it. Len Deighton wrote nine in his spy series, so anything is possible. I suppose if I get lonely for their company, I might add another because I've lived with the characters for years, and they are never completely silent. For sure, there is the wedding, and what if Bruni has twins in the middle of the ceremony among the pews and kneelers? One question I have is: How will Percy convince the baron to acquiesce to Johnny's demand that the wedding take place at Rhinebeck? Dagmar's cooking may be the deciding factor, but then there is the von Hofmanstal castle, where nannies have dropped like flies, and the dungeon waits underneath. Surely, that will enter in at some point. It's all a giant swirl. To entangle it starts with a single word—but only when I sit down to write it, and I'm not there yet …. There is also a nonfiction project that I plan to complete called "Challenges" likely before number four is complete. It is about success, failure, and their similarities—other than the endings—and has its roots in the many previous articles I wrote between 2011 and 2018. I want to use the skills I developed writing novels to create a nonfiction book that readers will find useful, thought-provoking, as well as entertaining.

FQ: I simply adore the way you give readers little bits and pieces of the secondary characters in each book so that we learn more about them as the stories move forward. I loved seeing Angus … and Raymond … will they both be returning the next book?

IO: I'm sure they will. When I write, I feel like one of those jugglers who spin plates on top of canes and other pointy objects. They get twenty going and have to run back to the first one to spin it again before it falls and breaks. Depending on how the plot develops and how each character can forward it determines how much we get to know about them, but each is a story in its own right and worthy of exposition. Both Angus and Raymond have dark histories but then so do all the other characters. Only the elegant environment of Rhinebeck and the civilizing influence of tradition keep them in check and playing nice with everyone else.

FQ: I am guessing that deciding to write novels takes a whole lot of time and very hard work so you must have an excellent support system behind you. How much does your family support you and how does that help in your writing?

IO: I do. It is one of the hallmarks of those who are successful. Successful people, who last, have one thing in common: an emotional infrastructure that supports them when they wobble, dusts them off, and puts them back in play. The number of sports figures who went south after a parent died and were no longer there to fulfill that need is worth noting. Behind most successful men (or women) are partners of extraordinary worth who are blessed with mental and financial acuity. You don't see them, but they are there if one looks closely.

My wife, Mary Jo, is one, and she is also my first reader. That task and responsibility is not as easy as it might appear. There is the constant waiting between chapters and should the chapter end on the edge of a cliff, I suggest you proceed immediately to the next, and then deliver both. A first reader is important and must be treasured and cared for. I note every expression. I listen to the cadence and the rhythm when she reads a chapter aloud, and that helps me make refinements. She also lets me know when she's enchanted, and her encouragement helps me continue.

There is also Joanna, my stepdaughter, a stickler for details once the work is done. I may dismiss four out of five things that she suggests, but it is that fifth that makes all the difference. Disagreement is always as important as agreement when building anything.

I have also come to writing late in life. I never had to write to live. I can't conceive how hard that must be.

I think it is also hard for many to appreciate how strongly our infrastructure (personal, economic, familial, and global) supports us as much as restrains us in our efforts to succeed. Life doesn't happen in a vacuum, even though we might wish it was up to us to either win or lose. Alone, the chances of success are minimal. Supported, the odds of succeeding are better.

In the end, it is also up to the writer to take advantage of the years of literature that has been written in the past, to be conversant with it all, and to know how the greats succeeded and why. Commercial success is often dependent on embracing social issues, and that has been the case for the last two hundred years. I don't particularly subscribe to that line, but I know it works. The research says so. I prefer to do something altogether different, and that is a lonely road to travel, but the one I have chosen. I thank the stars for having those in my life who believe in me. If I didn't, I would be alone, and nothing would come of all my efforts—absolutely nothing.

FQ: What authors and/or types of stories have had a huge influence on you and your writing? Any authors that you are really partial to?

IO: I read everything and anything. I read escapism to escape, textbooks for knowledge, and writers of all types to discover what they did to move me either negatively or positively. I want to know why I felt the way I felt. I want to know how they managed to enchant me or do the opposite. I read because I enjoy reading. I read as often as I can. When I find myself staying up late, I note the reason. What did the author do? Can I do that? Should I do a Faulkner in my next book and put the last chapter first? Not likely, but I could because I've seen it done. Could I start in the middle? Absolutely. I also use film and play direction and directing techniques. I try to get into a scene late and get out early à la David Mamet. His insights on directing are gold. I also try to appeal to the reader's imagination and intelligence to stay with me. I study plays. I study history. I study mathematics. All of it is useful and comes out in my writing.

Jane Austen, Raymond Chandler, Frank Herbert, Edith Wharton, P. G. Wodehouse, Booth Tarkington, O. Henry, Homer, Euripides, Ovid, Roald Dahl, and a thousand others have made their contributions, and I have gladly accepted their examples and been inspired by their brilliance. To me, a really good book is a rare and glorious treasure to be savored, marveled at, and revered. To write one of those is what I strive for.

—◆—

For more of Ivan's interviews, visit ivanobolensky.com.

Acknowledgments

Writing is a lonely business and cannot be done alone. A writer must have support, feedback, and the necessary infrastructure before, during, and after the writing takes place. Without that assistance, the result will fall short of expectations, and the work, no matter how brilliant, will remain unknown and unread.

Knowing that is the case, I would like to acknowledge the many who helped me along the way—particularly my wife, Mary Jo. She has supported me through thick and thin. It is not easy to read a chapter and be left hanging in the middle of a novel, wondering what will happen next, knowing full well that the author has no idea either. But that is how I write. I put one thought down, and then the next, and the story forms as if by magic. Climbing such a mountain to stand above the clouds, where all is clear, takes fortitude and faith. And not just mine—hers, too. For all her sacrifice and encouragement, I have no words.

There are others who have had a material impact on the result, in particular, Tom Hyman, my editor. We have had a long, constructive, and encouraging relationship that I value and give thanks for. Nick Thacker, too, has come up with award-winning cover designs that are superb. Joanna Cook has been instrumental in many of the behind-the-scenes details that would normally be overlooked. There are also Michael Smith and his audiovisual help, as well as Fred and Jen of Grid Graphics for their website and technical support. There are also many advanced readers who donated their time to read and comment on the pre-release versions prior to publication. I thank you all.

www.ingramcontent.com/pod-product-compliance
Lightning Source LLC
Chambersburg PA
CBHW020923020726
47495CB00002B/314